THE BLANK PAG

Balzic lit a cigarette, not because he wanted to smoke, but because he wanted to throw a match at the ashes in the ashtray on the desk. He had just flicked off the first ash when the door opened and a short, compactly built man in his mid-thirties came in, closing the door quietly but firmly behind him. He stepped briskly toward Balzic with his hand extended, saying, "Dr. Beverley. And you're?"

"Balzic. I'm chief of police here," he said, shaking hands and watching Beverley's eyes to see if he glanced at the ashtray.

Beverley didn't look at the ashtray but said, "There's an ashtray on the desk."

It amounted to the same thing, Balzic thought, suppressing a smile.

"Sorry to keep you waiting," Beverley said. "My wife neglected to tell me that you'd called earlier. I, uh, assume it's important."

"It is. One of your students is dead."

A FIX LIKE THIS

"So now tell me what you said to Muscotti."

"Huh? Oh. Nothing much. I just told him that if anything happens because of Manny getting chopped up, I was going to guarantee him his whole operation was going to the slammer, that's all. Just the god-damnedest threat I ever made in my life. And then I sat there with all the face in the world and tried to make out like it's no threat. Like it's a sure pop. Christ, I must be watching too much television or something. But you know the real capper?"

Stramsky shook his head.

"I think he bought it, how's that grab you?" Balzic shook his head and snorted softly. "Now you can feature me walking into the U.S. Attorney's office in Pittsburgh, bigger than shit, and I'm trying to convince those guys that I let the second biggest banker and lay-offer in the county—I let him run for sixteen years, and not only did I never bust him or anybody connected with him, but I never took a penny from him. Now just what do you think they're going to say? They're not going to be able to say anything. They'll all be laughing so hard they'll have hernias."

About the author

K. C. Constantine has been described as 'one of the four best American crime writers now active'.

THE DOUBLE DETECTIVE:
The Blank Page
and
A Fix Like This

K. C. Constantine

CORONET BOOKS
Hodder and Stoughton

British Library C.I.P.

Constantine, K. C.
  The double detective
  I. Title
  813'. 54 [F]

ISBN 0 340 50823 X

Printed and bound in Great Britain
for Hodder and Stoughton Paper-
backs, a division of Hodder and
Stoughton Ltd., Mill Road, Dunton
Green, Sevenoaks, Kent TN13 2YA.
(Editorial Office: 47 Bedford Square,
London WC1B 3DP) by Cox & Wyman
Ltd., Reading, Berks.

The Blank Page

If there was one part of his work that Rocksburg Chief of Police Mario Balzic loathed doing, it was preparing the budget for submission to the city council. If he needed another reason to procrastinate further on it, it was hot. The temperature on Memorial Day had tied a record set in 1910. In the five days since, the forecasts were notable only for their sameness: the temperature was far above the average. There was nothing in the upper air flow, nothing in the ground level patterns out of Canada, no highs to collide with lows coming out of the Gulf of Mexico or South Atlantic to bring rain.

Balzic's mind reeled from the heat and the numbers. He forced himself to check all his calculations twice over, morosely certain that he was making mistakes correcting earlier mistakes. All he could hope was that the council would listen to him for once and allow him to hire an accountant for a couple of weeks the next time a budget was due.

Balzic heard an odd humming about the same time he smelled something burning. He glanced around his tiny office twice before he saw that the oscillating fan atop his file cabinets had quit and was giving off a lazy rope of smoke.

"That caps it," he grumbled, jumping up to shut off the fan. He stood glowering at the fan for nearly a minute, lamenting silently that on this of all nights, when the temperature was locked in the eighties, his fan had to break. He leaned back across his desk and made a note of it, adding that one to a pile of other notes jumbled in a basket on the corner of his desk marked "Essential." He straightened up with a sigh, took one last glance at the heap of papers on his desk, and went out into the squad room where he saw Desk Sergeant Vic Stramsky nodding off at the radio console.

The hair above Stramsky's ears was slick with perspiration, and Balzic observed with some small malice that the fan near Stramsky's head was still working, though all it seemed to do when its breeze passed over Stramsky was cause his collar points to flutter.

"Vic. Hey Vic!"

Stramsky roused himself. "What's up?"

"I'm going to Muscotti's to get a couple beers. You want me to bring you back one?"

"Nah. It'd just make me sleepier than I am."

The dull chatter of the switchboard sounded, and Stramsky rolled his chair over to plug in the line. He listened for a long moment and then motioned for Balzic to pick up an extension phone.

Balzic heard Stramsky saying, "Yes, ma'am. Would you mind repeating that so I can write it down?"

"All right," the voice said, a voice full of years. "My name is Miss Cynthia Summer. I live at 226 North Hagen Avenue."

"And what's the trouble again, Miss Summer?"

"Well, I hope there isn't any, but something's very odd. You see, I rent rooms to students, ones who attend the community college, don't you see."

2

"Yes, ma'am."

"And there is one I haven't seen for about two days."

"Maybe he went home for the summer."

"No. That couldn't be. In the first place, it's a she. Janet— oh my, I have to look it up. I have to write everything down. I had a stroke, don't you see, and I just can't remember things the way I used to." There was a pause. "Here it is. Janet Pisula. And she didn't go home for the summer because her classes weren't over until Friday, the twenty-eighth of May. That's today. And then she has final examinations to take, don't you see. All next week."

"Uh, Miss Summer," Stramsky said, "today is the fourth of June."

"It is? Oh my."

"That would mean her classes were over a week ago today, ma'am."

"Well, that makes it even worse, don't you see."

"No, ma'am, I don't."

"Well, young man, if her classes were over last Friday, then she would have had her examinations by now and she would be preparing to move out for the summer, don't you see."

"Uh, Miss Summer, are you sure she didn't leave already?"

"Young man, I do not want to seem impertinent, but I know when my students come and when they go. She didn't leave her key. If she had moved out and I'd forgotten it or didn't notice it, her key would still be here, don't you see. I keep all the keys on a board, right here by the telephone."

"How many students do you have there, Miss Summer?"

"Seven. But I only let six rooms. Two boys are sharing."

"And how many keys do you have there?"

"I have all the keys here."

"What I mean, ma'am, is are we talking about duplicate keys or are we talking about the keys the students themselves had?"

"Why, I have only duplicate keys here, don't you see."

"Then that would mean that none of your students left for the summer."

"Oh my, I'm afraid I don't understand that. But—but that

3

couldn't be, don't you see? Because I have seen all the others."

"Well, ma'am, if you have only the duplicate keys there on your board—"

Balzic interrupted. "Miss Summer, this is Mario Balzic. I'm chief of police here. I've been listening on another phone. Let's just forget about the keys for a minute. Why do you think something's wrong?"

"How do you do," she said. "I've heard a good deal about you."

"Yes, ma'am. Now about this student of yours?"

"Oh. Yes. Well, I haven't seen that girl for, oh my, I thought it was just two days, but if this is the fourth of June, then I haven't seen her for more than a week. And that's just not like her. What I mean to say is that I used to see her every day. We used to chat often. She was a very nice young person. Very lonely, don't you see. But she made a point to stop and chat every day."

"Miss Summer, is it possible you could have seen her and, uh, not remembered? I mean, you said yourself you were having a little trouble remembering things."

The old woman took a moment to reply. When she did, her voice was quivering. "Young man, I did indeed have a stroke, and I do indeed have difficulty remembering things, but I'm not a complete fool."

"Yes, ma'am. I didn't mean for a second you were. But I just thought—never mind. I'll be up to your place in a couple minutes and we'll get this thing straightened out, how's that?"

"Do you think it's necessary for you to come?"

"Well, Miss Summer, we won't know whether it's necessary until we check, now will we?"

"All right. I'll leave the porch light on for you. Oh, what am I saying—I always leave the porch light on. You'll have to excuse me."

Balzic said good-bye and hung up, looking questioningly at Stramsky.

"Why don't you send somebody else up there?" Stramsky said. "What are you going for?"

4

"If you think a minute, you'll remember who that old lady is."

"Oh yeah. From the coal family. Summer coal. Yeah, how could I forget that? She gave all that land for the community college."

"That's her. I think she rates a chief. Besides, if I don't go there, I go to Muscotti's, get half drunked up, and then I come back here and make like a bookkeeper—and I can't do that sober."

Balzic headed for the door and went out, letting the screen door bounce against its spring.

Lightning flashed vaguely on the horizon as Balzic got into his cruiser. The lightning was a long way off, and he doubted that a storm would reach Rocksburg—if it ever did—before morning. He turned the cruiser around in the lot and then headed north on Main, thinking it was going to be another miserable night for sleeping.

At the last intersection on Main Street serviced by traffic lights, Balzic turned onto North Hagen Avenue, recollecting the gossip and local lore about the Summer family.

As Rocksburg went, the Summers were as near to aristocracy as the town had ever known. Anybody else who had made money in town, either from the mills or from coal or natural gas, had moved out at the first opportunity. The Summers, for reasons no one bothered to speculate about anymore, had chosen to live where they'd made their fortune.

Clarence Summer had risen from timekeeper through college and law school at night to become attorney for a half-dozen small mines working north of town. Sometime during the three decades from 1890 to 1920, when the steel and coal strikes were at their bloodiest, the mines Summer represented went out of production and into receivership, and when they reopened, by some paper shuffling perhaps only Summer himself understood, they were owned by Clarence Summer.

Sometime in that same period, Summer married. The rumors had been various: he married a Jewess, a Welsh chargirl, a

5

Canadian prostitute. Whatever she had been, she became an alcoholic hermit. Her tastes were odd—gin and beer—and her consumption legendary. The empty bottles that were carted away by garbage collectors were the subject of bets. No one in Rocksburg could say with certainty he had ever heard her first name.

Summer and his wife produced four daughters, and the general opinion was that if Summer was trying to build a dynasty he couldn't have made a worse start. The daughters couldn't wait to escape. Whether they fled from him or from their alcoholic mother or from Rocksburg itself, no one knew. The only one who stayed was the one everyone—including herself—called Miss Cynthia, the first born, the only one who never married.

For years, well into the late 1950s, Miss Cynthia sustained her wealth and her remoteness. Then, bit by piece, things began to slip away. The mines veined out. Where once there had been four main shafts, each bearing the name of a daughter and the number of the order of her birth—Cynthia Number One, Edna Number Two, Elaine Number Three, and Roseann Number Four —each employing nearly a hundred miners, by 1960 all four shafts had been sealed on orders of the state bureau of mines to prevent the possibility of surface air feeding a fire that had begun in a shaft owned by another company but which came very near Elaine Number Three.

Clarence's wife died in the last great diphtheria epidemic in the thirties. Clarence himself lost to cancer in the early forties. The other daughters, Edna, Elaine, and Roseann, appeared only as names and faces on the society pages of the Pittsburgh newspapers and then, one by one, on the obituary pages. Miss Cynthia clung to the house and life.

The chauffeur went first. Then the gardener, the maids, and the cook. The Lincoln Continental went soon after the chauffeur. The rock gardens, the rose gardens, the hedge gardens with the fountains and the sundials began to look like parodies of themselves.

Miss Cynthia shopped for herself; she could not even command a taxi to wait until she finished. When she entered the supermarkets, she clutched a sheaf of coupons cut from *The Rocksburg Gazette* offering discounts on certain products, and when she left and waited for another taxi to pick her up, she tried not to lean on a shopping cart in which a solitary bag was filled mostly with frozen dinners.

Sometime in the mid-sixties, she made an arrangement with the Conemaugh County commissioners for the land behind the house. The commissioners had been planning for some time to begin a community college, but were stymied by the price of land at a time when they'd been advised the bond market was unfavorable. Miss Cynthia, it was said around city hall and in the county court house, offered the forty acres behind her house in return for an exemption from real estate and school taxes on the house in which she insisted she was going to live until she died. It was also said that the house would at her death automatically become county property with the provision that it become part of the community college and be named Clarence Summer Hall.

In 1968, when the first college building was completed on her land—a combination of classrooms, library, and student union—Miss Cynthia's financial desperation became clear: she placed an ad in *The Rocksburg Gazette* welcoming students to lease rooms from her at the incredible rate of twelve dollars a month; this, when a single room with bath in Rocksburg was going for a minimum of fifty dollars a month.

Balzic approached the house now, once an imposing and impeccable two-story red brick structure said to have six bathrooms, over a pitted asphalt drive leading to the front portico. Two faded white columns supported a weather roof over the drive. As Miss Cynthia had said, the portico light was on, but only one light of the two still burned. When Balzic knocked, he saw that the other lamp no longer had a bulb in it.

Miss Cynthia answered the door herself. Her left eye was half closed and her left cheek sagged, drawing down the corner of her mouth. She was disconcertingly thin, and her left arm dangled lifelessly.

"Miss Summer," Balzic said, holding out his ID case. "I'm Mario Balzic."

"Please come in, Chief Balzic." She tried to smile. "I can't tell you how sorry I am to have to meet you like this." It was an effort for her to close the door. "You'll want the key, won't you?"

"Yes, ma'am," Balzic said, following her across the foyer, noticing with a vague remorse the difficulty with which she walked, her left shoe never leaving the floor but sliding along. She led him to a telephone under a stairway. Balzic was not surprised to see that it was a pay phone.

Miss Cynthia took a key off a square board by the phone and handed it to Balzic. "Her room is the last one on the right upstairs. I'm sorry I can't take you up. Those stairs are just impossible for me these days. I really hope . . ."

"We'll see, Miss Summer. But first we have to look."

He took the stairs slowly, observing the house as he went. It was more generally deteriorated than he'd expected, and he had the feeling of being in a house just a signature away from a sheriff's sale.

At the top of the stairs he oriented himself. There were two halls: one led straight ahead of the stairs, the other began about ten feet back from the stairs and led to the left. Balzic went straight ahead to the last door on the right.

He could hear voices in the room opposite, young male voices involved in what sounded like a mild argument over a problem in mathematics.

Balzic had trouble with the lock. It seemed a fairly new lock and the edges of the key were still sharp. It took Balzic a moment to realize that rather than opening the door he had done the opposite. He repeated his motions with the key and was certain when he finally pushed open the door that it had been unlocked when he first inserted the key.

Inside the room, a gooseneck lamp was burning on a tiny desk against the far wall. Balzic noticed that first. Then the smell hit him and he saw the rest and nearly gagged.

She was on her back on the floor beside the bed and naked except for her panties. Twisted around her neck was another undergarment, a slip or a brassiere perhaps, but Balzic did not want to get close enough to look. Her features were horribly distorted from the swelling, and her flesh from her neck to her hairline was the color of a week-old bruise. On her stomach was a plain white sheet of paper. As far as Balzic could tell there was nothing written on it, but he couldn't bring himself to reach down and pick it up.

Something kept wanting to come up in Balzic's throat. He had to force himself to look at her. Her body was slender, boyish almost, with small breasts, and she did not appear to Balzic to be much taller than his eldest daughter. He swept his gaze around the room long enough to notice that there was no particular disarray, then he backed out, locked the door, and hurried down the stairs to the phone.

As he was dialing, he heard Miss Cynthia ask him if everything was all right.

"No, ma'am, it isn't."

"Oh my," she said.

"Rocksburg Police, Sergeant Stramsky speaking."

"Vic. Mario. Get the D.A., the coroner, and the state boys. We got a homocide at 226 North Hagen Avenue. I'll be waiting out front for them."

"Got it," Stramsky replied, and the phone went dead. Balzic hung up and saw Miss Cynthia. He reached out and touched her on the shoulder.

"Oh my," she said. "Oh my . . ."

The state police Criminal Investigation Division squad, under the temporary command of Lt. Walker Johnson, arrived first. Much to Balzic's spiteful pleasure Johnson had been transferred from Erie to replace Lt. Harry Minyon while Minyon rode out a bout with his ulcers in Conemaugh General Hospital. Any replacement for Minyon would have pleased Balzic, but Johnson was especially welcome to him as their friendship went back to days when Balzic had first made chief and Johnson was a sergeant on the narcotics squad. Two nights ago, on Johnson's first night back in Rocksburg, the two of them had gotten pleasantly drunk on Balzic's back porch, regaling each other with decade-old anecdotes. . . .

Johnson came downstairs after he'd put his squad to work and waited for Balzic to introduce Miss Cynthia. A moment after the introduction, Johnson nodded to Balzic and led the way out to the foyer near the front door.

"This is a hell of a way to start," Johnson said.

"Well, at least it won't be dull."

"Yeah. It won't be that. So, old buddy, what do you have?"

"Next to nothing. The lady had a stroke—which you noticed —and I don't know what we're going to get out of her. She thought today was the twenty-eighth of May."

"How about the two kids in the room across the hall—you talk to them yet?"

"I'll tell you what, Walk. I damn near got sick up there. That girl's not much bigger than my Marie. Older, I'm sure, but not any bigger. It just got to me, so I just locked up and came down and called you."

"Say nothing. I couldn't stand it myself. By now every one of those poor bastards up there'll have a handky in his mouth." Johnson thought for a moment. "Is Grimes still coroner here?"

"Yeah. He should've been here by now. The D.A., too."

Johnson shrugged. "You want to stay with the lady? Or you want the two kids upstairs?"

"I better stick with her. She's supposed to have four or five more roomers in here, you know."

"Wonder where they are. They live here, they can't be locals. This is a hell of a time. School year's damn near over. They're all students, aren't they?"

Balzic nodded.

"I hope to hell they haven't left for home," Johnson said. "If they have, we'll be chasing all over hell." He shrugged again and went back upstairs.

Balzic went back into what had once been the living room where he found Miss Cynthia sitting listlessly on the corner of a worn and faded maroon velvet couch.

He sat beside her. "Miss Summer, I'm going to have to ask you some questions, so is there anything I can get you before we get started?"

"No, thank you. You're kind to think of it, but no. I'm just worried that I won't be able to help, and . . ."

"And what?"

"Well, all these police. Is it really, I mean—"

"I'm afraid so, Miss Summer. The girl—well, didn't you hear me when I was talking on the phone?"

"Yes," Miss Cynthia said slowly. "Yes, I heard you. I suppose I didn't want to believe it." Her mottled hand went to her papery lips. "She was such a lovely person. But so lonely."

"How so?"

"She was an orphan. She was raised by an aunt and uncle. That much I remember, but for the life of me, I can't think where. I have it written down. I can get the address for you."

"Not right now. Later on you'll have to give me the names and addresses of all your roomers. But for now, let's just talk about what you remember about her."

"What I remember—oh my. I don't even remember very clearly when I last talked to her. I thought it was three days ago. Now, I'm just not sure."

"Well tell me what you are sure of."

"I'm sure that she had no parents or brothers or sisters. I'm sure she was kind. Practically the first thing she said after she said hello was to ask if there was anything she could get me. Why, that first week I was home from the hospital after my stroke, she stayed down here with me all night, don't you see. I never asked her to, but when I'd wake during the night, she'd be asleep in a chair near my bed. We had even discussed the possibility of her

11

living down here with me next year as a sort of, oh you know, a sort of companion to me."

"She must have had friends," Balzic said.

"I really can't say. I don't know how she got along with my other students. She never discussed them with me—or if she did I just don't remember."

"Do you remember anyone visiting her?"

"No. I can't say for certain. She may have. The students are always coming and going. I can't say if anyone was coming to see her. I just have this impression that no one did. I can't say why."

"Did she have dates?"

"I don't think so. We talked about that occasionally. I used to tell her that youth was not to be squandered, things like that. Things old people try to tell young people. But it struck me that she really wasn't aware that she was a woman. She could have been very attractive, but she seemed not to know how to make herself attractive. She had a rather plain face, and it seemed she didn't know anything about cosmetics. She had a lovely, slim figure, but she didn't think about clothes at all."

Balzic nodded. "Do you remember hearing anything unusual?"

"No. I'm sorry. I just missed seeing her. That's why I called you. But I don't recall any noises, anything out of the ordinary. But you must understand, chief, this stroke has also left me deaf in my left ear. You have a very powerful voice. Very resonant. It's easy enough to hear you. But much goes on that I don't hear. I suppose for that reason I make a very accommodating landlady for my students. Their music—well, all I hear is a rhythmic thumping. I would dearly like to hear it, but . . ."

"Did she ever speak to you about any trouble?"

"No. She wasn't rich, heaven knows. But she had been cared for, some sort of trust fund. She told me about it once, but I don't remember any details. I don't think she was having any difficulty with the relatives who raised her. At least I don't recall her speaking about anything like that."

"Didn't she ever talk about anything that was bothering her? There must have been something."

"The only thing I remember like that was something about a course she was having problems with. A composition course I believe it was. For a time she was bewildered by it all. I recall her saying once that she didn't know what that man wants, something like that. But that was some time ago. In the winter. December or January, I think. Of course, you must consider my sense of time these days."

"That was the only thing?"

"I'm sorry, chief. You must understand. That's all I can remember."

Balzic stood. "Miss Summer, I'll have to see your records now. The students' names, home addresses, how they stood with the rent."

"I'll get that for you. I keep it all locked in my desk in the kitchen. I can tell you now that all of my students were very prompt about the rent."

Balzic helped her up and then followed her into the kitchen. He had just finished copying the names and addresses from her ledger when Dr. Wallace Grimes, the county coroner, appeared in the foyer. He was still wearing his suit coat and his tie was knotted tightly. He wiped his forehead with a folded handky and replaced it carefully in his breast pocket, nodding to Balzic and saying, "Mario," by way of greeting and asking at the same time where he was to find his work.

"Upstairs, doc," Balzic said.

Grimes went up without a word, and a moment or two later Johnson came down. Balzic met him at the foot of the stairs.

"What did you get, Mario?"

"Not much. Names and addresses of the other students. Nobody owed. The lady's hearing is bad and her memory's about the same. The only thing she could say for sure was that the girl was an orphan. No brothers, no sisters. Raised by an aunt and uncle. The only thing she thought might have been bothering the girl was some trouble in her classwork. A composition course. But she thought that was around last December or January. She couldn't remember hearing anything more about it since. What did you get?"

"The two kids are a blank," Johnson said. "All they remember is seeing her once in a while. They didn't even miss her. One of them thought he heard something funny about a week ago, but he didn't think anything more about it. The other one thought he saw a guy standing in front of her door a couple of weeks ago, but then when he thought about it he couldn't say whether the guy was standing in front of her door or was just standing in the hall. He says he never saw the guy before or since. Couldn't give me the vaguest make. Had no idea whether the guy was old or young, tall, short, nothing. All he said for sure was the guy was white. And then he started to think about that."

"Your people come up with anything?"

"Well, who knows what was there? But there's plenty of money still around. For a college kid, I mean. Twenty-five-something in bills and change in her desk drawer, another couple bucks in bills and change in her wallet. Nothing was knocked over. The rest of her clothes were on the foot of the bed, laid out neat, like she was just undressing and hadn't thought to hang anything on hangers.

"Just as a first guess," Johnson went on, "I'd say somebody either talked her into getting undressed and when she got that far he just slipped the brassiere around her neck and strangled her with it. Either that or else he walked in on her when she had got down to just those two pieces of clothing. Either she knew him or else he caught her completely by surprise because the two across the hall definitely did not hear anything resembling a scream or a yell for help. And they also claim they've both been in their room every day and night for the past two weeks except to go to classes and to eat. They both say they're too broke to do anything else."

"You don't think them?"

"Who knows? But right now, they just look too goddamn goggle-eyed. You know the look. Couple of squares. They got all this information to volunteer, they want to say all this stuff to help, but it all comes out a lot of words."

"What do you make of the paper?"

Johnson gave a barely audible snort. "That's the goddamndest thing I've ever seen. The guy that did it had to put it there, but why?"

"Nothing on it?"

"Not a damn thing. Unless you count the smudge of a print. Just a piece of white typing paper."

"More like it in the room?" Balzic said.

"Yeah. About half a ream by the typewriter on the desk. Same stuff."

"Anything else?"

"I looked at her fingernails. I got a man scraping them, but I have the feeling he's not going to find a thing. I couldn't see anything myself. Not even a crack in one of them. Like she didn't put up any resistance at all."

"Maybe she was surprised."

"Sure, there's that possibility. But you'd think she'd have made some attempt to save her life. I mean, what the hell, Mario? Even if she was grabbed from behind, caught completely unaware, you'd think she would've dug her nails into something. Her own throat, something, just trying to get that thing off her neck. Nobody loses consciousness that fast. But nothing—unless it's something that has to go under a scope. But that paper. Wow . . ."

Dr. Grimes came down the steps then, buttoning his collar and running up his tie.

"What's the word, doc?" Balzic said.

"That should have been obvious," Grimes said evenly. "Suffocation caused by strangulation. Six, seven, maybe eight days ago. Give me some time and I'll get it down to the day.

What's keeping the ambulance people—or did somebody not think to call?"

"They should have been here long ago," Balzic said. "I'll get on them."

"Tell them to go right to the hospital morgue," Grimes said, going for the door. "I'll be waiting for them. Good night."

Balzic called Stramsky to hurry the ambulance and learned that every available one was on a call. "Couple heart attacks and a four-car pile-up coming out of Conemaugh Shopping Center. Nothing serious, but every car had a family in it," Stramsky said. Balzic grunted and then hung up. He went back to tell Johnson and saw him talking to a plump, barefoot girl who kept peeking around Johnson's shoulders, darting glances at the officers coming and going on the stairs.

Johnson introduced the girl—Evelyn Embry—to Balzic. She had a pleasant enough face, softened by its roundness, but her reticence in answering Johnson's questions had an edge of arrogance about it that Balzic found immediately disagreeable. In spite of himself, Balzic kept glancing at the girl's feet and the dirt caked between her toes.

". . . so you didn't know her very well," Johnson was saying.

"Yeah, uh, I mean I talked to her, you know, but that's all."

"Do you recall the last time you saw her?"

"Uh-uh. Couple days ago, I guess."

"She's been dead longer than that."

"Oh. Well—I don't know. Maybe a week ago."

"Did you ever see anybody with her?"

"No. But like I said, I really didn't know. I mean, I didn't see her that much. I only talked to her a couple times." She thought for a moment. "Does this, uh, mean I have to stay around? I mean, I am getting ready to leave. I'm all packed and everything."

"Stay around for what?" Johnson asked.

"Oh, you know—I don't know," she said, giggling nervously. "Don't you guys always make the witnesses stay around or something?"

Johnson shot a wearied glance at Balzic who, again in spite of himself, was looking at the girl's filthy feet. "No, Miss Embry. We have your home address if you want to leave. If we need to talk to you again, we'll get in touch with your parents."

"Oh, I'm not going home."

"Well, your family will know where you'll be, won't they?"

"I hope not."

"Uh, Miss Embry, it's not likely that we'll need to talk to you again, but just in case, you better let your family know where you're going to be. You can go now. Just please stay out of the way upstairs, okay?"

Johnson shook his head at Balzic as the girl went up the steps.

"You know," Balzic said, "I was talking to a chemist a couple weeks ago. If these barefoot kids only knew how much crap they walked through in a day. . . ."

The ambulance came and left, the attendants soaked with perspiration by the time they got the stretcher to the bottom of the stairs.

District Attorney Milt Weigh stopped on his way home from a county Democrat meeting, staying only long enough to make general inquiries and to offer the services of his squad of detectives.

"He looked like the Democrats are serving better booze than they used to," Johnson said after Weigh had gone.

Balzic smiled weakly, feeling too hot to make a rejoinder. "Think your boys came up with anything yet?"

"About time I checked," Johnson said, going slowly up the steps.

Balzic walked through the foyer to the front door, catching sight of Miss Summer sitting on the worn velvet couch, fanning herself with an envelope. He stepped out onto the portico and scanned the horizon looking for lightning. When it flashed, it seemed even duller and more distant than it had earlier.

He smoked and thought about that single sheet of paper on the girl's stomach and then about the girl and then about his own daughter, Marie. His thoughts were a jumble. Nothing made sense. He felt the way he felt when he read a newspaper account of some seemingly isolated act of violence, when the reporter called the act "senseless." The word annoyed and angered him because he believed that no violence was truly senseless. It always made sense if you took the time to analyze it. He believed that was as true about the violence done upstairs as about any other violence he had known, except that everything about this violence did indeed appear senseless. There had been no robbery, no sound, no struggle, and he was willing to bet that there had been no sex. He would have to wait for the coroner's report to be certain of that, but, without being able to explain or justify his feeling to himself, he was sure sex had had no part in what had happened to this orphan, this Janet Pisula. He was as sure of that as he was unsure what the piece of paper on her stomach meant. There was a message there, but one without words and one that therefore said everything at the same time it said nothing.

Balzic flipped his cigarette butt into the night and went back inside just as Johnson was coming down the stairs.

"Anything?" Balzic said.

"About a thousand prints up there. Naturally, the ones we'd like to have—off that paper—we're not going to get. Whoever it was probably licked his index finger and just got enough of his index finger and thumb to lift it and put it on her. We'll have to send it to the FBI lab anyway to make sure. They're the only ones with the equipment to get a print off paper, but my man says they're not going to be able to do anything with what's there." Johnson scratched his chin. "Mario, tell me again how the room was when you went in."

"The door was unlocked, I'm certain of that. The desk lamp was on, nothing was knocked around. That's about all I really noticed. The smell got to me and I had to get the hell out."

"How do you figure that?" Johnson said. "In this heat—God. You'd've thought somebody would've smelled it before this. They all had to come down these steps. Her door's not fifteen feet away from the top."

"I didn't get it until I opened the door, if that's any help. Do you remember when it first hit you?"

"Now that you mention it, no," Johnson said. "But it doesn't make sense. It goes against all the laws of the nose." He looked thoughtfully at the floor. "Where the hell are the rest of them? How many are there again, total?"

"Seven. We've seen four. That leaves three."

"Male or female?"

"Two females, one male."

"And they're all still here? None left for the summer?"

"According to Miss Summer and to the keys on her board, they should all be here."

"Did you try to get the next of kin?"

"Not yet. But I hate like hell to tell anybody that over the phone. And that's a long drive down there. Thirty-five, forty miles. Why don't you see if you've got some people in the vicinity?"

"I suppose I better," Johnson said.

Balzic handed him the address of Mr. and Mrs. Michael Pisula, and Johnson went outside to his cruiser to make the call to the barracks to have the detail assigned. He returned in a few minutes and said, "We got some people in the area. They'll handle it."

"A piece of paper," Balzic said, shaking his head. "One piece of blank typing paper . . ."

They were standing there, smiling absurdly at one another when the front door opened and two girls came timidly into the foyer. The first was very tall, very slim, dressed in faded jeans, a sleeveless cotton jersey, and sandals. The other, shorter but equally slim, also wore jeans and sandals with a man's tee-shirt which had been dyed a myriad of pastel colors. Both carried books and notebooks and had similar shoulder bags made of fringed suede.

Johnson introduced himself and Balzic to the girls.

"Which one of you is Kimberly Marsinsky?" Balzic asked.

"I am," the taller one said, flushing.

"And you're Patricia Kein?" Balzic said to the other.

"Keim," she corrected him.

"What's the matter?" Kimberly asked. "What happened—I mean, what's going on?"

"One of your fellow tenants is dead," Johnson said. "Janet Pisula."

"Janet who?" Patricia asked.

"I never heard of her," Kimberly said. The girls looked at each other quizzically.

"She lived in the room at the top of the stairs. On the right."

"Oh. Her," Patricia said.

"Why do you say it like that?" Johnson said.

"Well, I didn't mean it to sound like it sounded—I guess. It's just, well, I don't know. But if you're here, then . . ."

"I'll save the speculation," Johnson said. "She was murdered."

Both girls sucked in their breath. "Oh my God," Kimberly said. "When—how—you mean right here?"

"Right here. In her room. We know how, but we don't know when exactly. We were hoping you could help us with that."

"I didn't even know her," Kimberly said. "I never even talked to her. I didn't—I'll bet I didn't see her four or five times. And every time I saw her, she was in there talking with the old lady."

"You knew her, Patricia," Johnson said.

"I didn't *know* her. I talked to her twice. Once for about fifteen minutes over in the Union. She wanted to know about an assignment we had in comp. The other time was outside the library about, oh, three or four weeks ago. We talked for about a half-hour or so."

"Why did you say, 'Oh, her,' the way you said it? Before, I mean, when we told you who it was."

"I don't know. I guess because she impressed me as being a very unaware person."

"Unaware in what way?"

"I don't know. It's hard to say why you think somebody is

aware and why somebody else isn't. Awareness is a difficult thing to define."

"Well try," Balzic said. "We have to have some idea what you're talking about."

"She was just out of it, that's all."

Johnson scratched his neck and glared at the wall beyond Balzic's shoulder. Balzic let out a heavy sigh and said, "Look, Patricia—"

"Please don't call me that. Just Pat, okay? I hate Patricia."

"Okay, Pat. But look. I've got two daughters, and I know what it is to try and understand them when they start using their slang, and I'm aware—huh?—aware that slang changes pretty fast. The point I'm trying to make is you got to put your impressions and feelings about this girl into something specific, something solid that a couple foggy bottoms like the lieutenant here and me can understand. Saying she was a 'very unaware person' or 'out of it'—that tells us nothing. Because I'll tell you something she was and is for a plain fact. She was a victim. She is now a corpse. And whoever victimized her and turned her into a corpse—no matter how out of it you thought she was—that somebody did it right here. Where *you* live. And there is nothing we know now to guarantee us or you that he doesn't have it in his head to turn some other young girl into a corpse. Is that plain enough for you?"

"Oh wow," Kimberly said.

"That's plain enough," Pat said. "I'm sorry. I'll try."

"Good," Balzic said. "Now let's start with the first time you talked to her. What was that about?"

"Well, that's funny—I mean, obviously it isn't funny. It's ironic though, because the first time I talked to her was last semester. About the second week. We were in the same comp class, and the assignment was to define an abstraction as concretely as we could. And I remember telling her almost exactly what you just told me, I mean, I told her she had to be as specific as she could. I tried to tell her to take as simple an abstraction as she could think of, something very elemental like a season of

21

the year and just make a list of all the things she could think of when that word came into her head. But she didn't even have the awareness that a season of the year was an abstraction."

"And that's all you talked about? Nothing else?"

The Keim girl nodded.

"What about the second time, by the library I think you said."

She nodded. "Well, that time she stopped me and said she had to talk to somebody about something very important but she didn't know who to talk to. And then she said something—I couldn't help it—when she said it, I just started laughing at her. Oh, wow, what a bummer for her."

"What did she say?"

"Oh wow, she said she'd always admired me. It was the way she said admired. So worshippy, God, it was like she should have been lighting a candle or something."

"Go on," Johnson said.

"Well, she got so embarrassed, she just turned crimson. I've never seen anybody blush like that in my life. And then she started talking real fast and it was all about comp again, but I could see right away that wasn't what she really wanted to talk about and that she was just making that up as she went because she didn't know how to get out of talking to me."

"So," Balzic said, running his tongue over a molar, "you got the impression—well, let me ask you. Did she talk about anything else?"

"No. And after a couple more minutes, she started blushing again and said she had to go someplace, and then she practically ran away from me."

"Let me get something else straight," Balzic said. "You were both in the same composition class the first semester. Were you still in the same class this semester?"

"No. She couldn't get along with Keenan at all. She used to catch a lot of flak from him. So did everybody, really. But everybody gave it back to him. Except her. And I really gave it back to him. I guess maybe that's why she said she admired me. I couldn't think of any other reason. I never saw her anyplace else. Just class and here. But I never talked to her here. Just to say hello."

"Keenan was the teacher?"

"He's also chairman of the department. And the only one with a doctorate. The others, Winoski and Farrell, they just have their master's."

"Don't forget Snavely," Kimberly said.

"That toad," Pat said.

"I don't think he even has a bachelor's," Kimberly said.

"Who did Janet have for composition this semester?" Balzic asked.

"Farrell, I think," Pat said. "I'm not sure. She told me that time outside the library, but I forgot."

"Do you know, Kimberly?"

"No, I don't."

"Okay, let's forget about teachers for a while. What about the last couple weeks? When was the last time either of you saw this girl? And please think carefully."

"The last time I saw her was a couple weeks ago," Kimberly said. "She was in there talking to the old lady."

"Pat?"

"A week, maybe ten days ago. She was just going into her room and I was coming up the steps. I didn't talk to her though."

"Ever see anybody going into her room or standing outside her door or knocking on her door or coming out of her room?"

Both girls shook their heads.

"Did you hear anything or see anything out of the ordinary in the last week or so—anything at all?"

Again, the same negative response.

"What the hell," Balzic said under his breath, half turning away from the girls and speaking softly to Johnson. "A girl lives here since when—last September? Six other people pass fifteen feet from her door every time they go out or come in and nobody knows a goddamn thing about her. You tell me, Walk."

Johnson shrugged and scratched his neck. "Listen, girls,

thank you very much for your cooperation. There's just one more thing. Let whoever you live with know where you're going to be. If we want to ask you anything else, we'll get in touch with you. We have your home addresses. You can go now. And thanks again."

The girls apologized for not being able to help much, then went up the stairs to their rooms, leaving Balzic and Johnson once again to stare at each other and shake their heads foolishly.

"Who's left?" Johnson asked.

"Uh, one Nicholas Cerovich," Balzic said, reading from the list he had copied from Miss Summer's ledger.

"What do you bet he knows as much as the rest of them?"

"No bet," Balzic said, going into the living room to ask Miss Summer if she knew anything about him.

"Cerovich," she said slowly. "Oh, yes. Nicholas. He's working. He won't be here until after midnight."

"Do you know where he works?"

"You'll have to give me a moment, chief. It's here in Rocksburg, that much I know. I'll think of the place." She frowned and closed her eyes as though trying to visualize the name of the place.

"Is it one of the mills?"

"It's a mill, but give me another word for a mill and I might be able to think of it."

"Uh, factory, fabricating plant, foundry, forge—."

"That's it. Forge. He works at a forge."

"Fort Pitt Chain and Forge?"

"Yes. That's it."

"Thank you, Miss Summer," Balzic said, going to the phone and rooting through his pockets for a dime. "I located him," he said to Johnson. "You got any dimes?" he said, flipping through the pages of the directory. Johnson handed him some dimes just as Balzic found the number. He dialed, identifying himself when he got an answer, and asked for someone familiar with the names of employees. "Just a routine verification that a man is employed there, that's all."

"I'm only a security guard, chief," the voice replied. "There's nobody here in any of the offices."

"What's working now?"

"Just the forge crew. Plus some guys on the loading dock."

"The name Cerovich mean anything to you—Nicholas Cerovich?"

"Oh yeah, sure. The college kid. Yeah, he's here. He's down with the labor gang in the forge. You want to talk to him?"

"No. I'll tell you what. Let me talk to his boss."

"Sure, sure. Hold on." There was a click, a buzz, then a ringing.

"Forge. Sokolosky," a voice shouted over the roar of the furnaces and the thunderous slamming of forge hammers.

"This is Chief of Police Balzic," he said, holding the phone away from his ear. "I'm just trying to verify that you have a Nicholas Cerovich working for you. Is he there now?"

"Yeah. You wanna talk to him?"

"No. Just tell me what shift he works and whether he misses work."

"He works steady second trick. He don't miss any work. Hasn't missed a day since he started. He's a good kid. Helluva worker."

"When did he start?"

"Four o'clock like everybody else."

"No, no. I mean, when'd he start working there?"

"Oh. Last summer. June I think. Been about a year now."

"Have you been his boss all this time?"

"I been everybody's boss on second trick for eleven years."

"And he hasn't missed any work at all? Especially in the last couple weeks?"

"Hey, look. Maybe you ought to talk to him. I don't like this talking about somebody that works for me with a cop. If he did something wrong, you come talk to him."

"I don't need to talk to him. All I want from you is your word that he hasn't missed work, that's all."

"Well you got it, brother. Not only don't he miss work, the

25

sonuvabrick is always yapping can he get some overtime. Is 'at what you wanna hear?"

"That's good enough," Balzic said. "And thanks for your help."

"Yeah, sure. Anytime. Just remember me the next time my old lady gets a ticket. Joe Sokolosky. See you around, chief." The phone clicked, and Balzic was laughing as he hung up.

"So?" Johnson said.

"So, Nicholas Cerovich works steady second trick at Fort Pitt Chain and Forge, he's been working for almost a year, and he hasn't missed a day. Which means he probably knows as little as the rest."

"Oh boy," Johnson said. "You know what that means."

"Yeah," Balzic said. "I wonder how many people there are tied up with this damn college."

"Well, how about you finding out, okay? I'll hang in here until we run everything down or pick everything up. I also want to talk to those two across the hall from her room again. They might've remembered something; I might've forgot to ask them something. See how many names you can get, and then we'll see how we divide the labor. We'll probably have to use the D.A.'s people . . . you got somebody you can call?"

"I can start with the president of the college," Balzic said. "I met him last year at some banquet or other."

"Well, he's all yours," Johnson said, starting up the stairs again and muttering something about the heat while Balzic thumbed through the phone directory looking for the home address of Dr. J. Hale Beverley, president of Conemaugh County Community College.

Dr. J. Hale Beverley lived in the Crestmont Plan, a post-Korean War development known among Rocksburg's blue collars as Pill Hill. As a hill it didn't seem much, a gentle rise of ground on the northeastern edge of Rocksburg, but from its crest on clear days when there was no suggestion of a temperature inversion, all of Rocksburg was visible beneath it. As for the pills, most of the staff of Conemaugh General Hospital lived there, plus the majority of specialists, generalists, and dentists who kept at least one office in Rocksburg or its environs. Lately, some lawyers had moved to its fringes, and here and there an engineer had crept in, but among the thirty-five or forty houses clustered on the slopes there was not one chiropractor, mortician, minister, insurance agent, or automobile dealer. How Dr. J. Hale Beverley had managed to find entrance piqued Balzic's curiosity. Either realtors were becoming more democratic or else they didn't know one doctor from another.

Balzic counted fifteen cars either in or near the driveway to the Beverley's two-car garage, and he knew he was going to have to interrupt a party, most likely the year-end bash a college president was expected to throw for his faculty and staff.

As Balzic pushed the button and listened to the two-toned chimes, he caught the sound of a stereo, and when the door opened, a tall, stiffly erect man with a wispy reddish mustache and beard stood in the door frame. He had a nearly empty tumbler in his hand and a tipsily foolish grin on his face.

"Welcome," he said. "Come and join us. Don't tell the host, of course. I was just on my way to the ice and thought I'd stop and invite you."

"Uh-huh," Balzic said, taking out his ID and holding it up. "I'm here to see Dr. Beverley. I called about five minutes ago and talked to Mrs. Beverley, I think. She said she'd tell her husband I was on the way, but maybe you could tell him I'm here—on your way back from the ice."

"Of course. I'll be more than happy to tell him. But why don't you step in and have a drink while you're waiting?"

"No, thanks. Just give him the message."

"Who is it, Mal?" asked a woman, coming up behind the man.

"The fuzzzzzz," Mal said, holding his finger up to his lips in a hokey gesture to be cautious, spilling in the process the last drops from his glass on the lapel of his corduroy jacket. "Whoopsey," he said. Then he abruptly shifted the glass to his left hand

and thrust out his right at Balzic. "Forgot my manners," he said. "Malcolm Keenan here. I'm a poet who teaches as a public service."

Balzic took the hand and felt the shaking up to his shoulder.

"Your name again, sir?" Keenan said.

"Balzic."

"Ballsy did you say? I remember a limerick which goes, let me see now—ah, yessss. 'There was a man from Boston, who had a little red Austin; there was room for his ass, and a gallon of gas, but his—' "

"Mal, for god's sake, you're not going to start with those awful things again, are you?" the woman said. She put her hands on Keenan's shoulders and gently began to turn him around and away from the door. "To the kitchen with you," she said.

" '—but his balls hung out and he lost 'em,' " Keenan said, grinning over his shoulder as he submitted to her pushing.

"Don't mind him," the woman said. "Now. What can I do for you?"

Balzic held up his ID again and said, "I called a few minutes ago—"

"Oh yes," she said, studying the ID while Balzic studied her. She was young, thirty at most, with a rather ordinary face that was meticulously made up, and her black dress had what struck Balzic as an improbable combination of propriety and allure about it which he imagined she must have spent some time trying to find. It was unadorned, buttoned to the neck, sleeveless, but made of a material which clung to her more than ample figure.

"Well, I must apologize," she said. "I'm the person to whom you spoke on the phone. I'm Mrs. Beverley, but I'm afraid I haven't had a chance to tell him that you want to see him. Why don't you come in while I do that?"

"Fine."

"I imagine you'll want to be alone," Mrs. Beverley said, "so why don't you just go into the den? Right through that door." She pointed to a door down a short hall. "Right next to the john," she said, turning back into the large living room on the right.

Balzic paused in the opening to the living room on his way to the den. He saw at least twenty-five people, the men dressed for the most part informally, the women wearing a variety of styles. One rather blocky woman wore short denim culottes, flat-heeled sandals, and a blue tee-shirt upon which were painted the words "POT POWER" above a crude outline of a toilet. Another wore a long-sleeved white blouse buttoned to the neck and a red satiny skirt that nearly touched the floor but was split halfway up her thighs. Still another wore silver backless pumps, an extremely short silver lamé dress to show off her very good, very long legs, and clutched a silver bag like a shield to her chest.

They all turned to look at Balzic as Mrs. Beverley approached someone just out of Balzic's view and announced, "The chief of police is here, Jay Hale, and he wants to see you."

Balzic waited a moment longer to see their reaction. It was mostly curiosity he observed, except for the blocky woman in the tee-shirt who went immediately to the stereo and turned up the volume on a rock song and began a provocative dance which belied her construction. After she was sure Balzic was watching her, she danced her way to a squatting, bullishly built young man who looked familiar to Balzic, pulled him to his feet, and continued her dance with him, looking then straight into Balzic's eyes.

Balzic couldn't resist. Before he stepped out of the doorway, he blew the blocky dancer a kiss. It stopped her cold, and then she threw back her head and shook with laughter.

Balzic found the john and was about to open the next door when Keenan reappeared, his glass a deep amber color with only one ice cube in it. "Say," Keenan said, "have you heard the one that goes, 'There was a young lady named Alice, who peed in a Catholic chalice; 'twas done out of need, the bishop agreed, and not out of Protestant malice'—have you heard that one?"

"I just did," Balzic said, smiling.

"Oh," Keenan said. "Too bad. It's one of my favorites." He weaved around Balzic and headed back toward the living room, stumbling once on a deep-pile throw rug.

"Oh boy," Balzic said, going into the den and switching on a desk lamp. "So that's Keenan."

He recalled what Patricia Keim had said about Keenan: chairman of the English department and the only Ph.D. And how had he described himself? "A poet who teaches as a public service"—was that what he'd said? Of course, he was in the bag, Balzic thought. Then again, *in vino veritas*. In boozo, trutho. . . .

He looked around the den, stepping over to the shelves of books behind the walnut and stainless steel desk. He ran his fingers over the shelves and then over the tops of three or four books. The Beverleys had an efficient and dedicated cleaning woman.

He took note of the desk. Everything was in order, making Balzic wonder whether Beverley did any work here. The room seemed more a refuge than a shop. The few pencils in the leather-covered oval container had been recently sharpened, or perhaps they had been sharpened some time ago and never used.

Balzic lit a cigarette, not because he wanted to smoke, but because he wanted to throw a match and the ashes in the ashtray on the desk. He had just flicked off the first ash when the door opened and a short, compactly built man in his mid-thirties came in, closing the door quietly but firmly behind him. He stepped briskly toward Balzic with his hand extended, saying, "I'm Dr. Beverley. And you're?"

"Balzic. I'm chief of police here," he said, shaking hands and watching Beverley's eyes to see if he glanced at the ashtray.

Beverley didn't look at the ashtray but said, "There's an ashtray on the desk."

It amounted to the same thing, Balzic thought, suppressing a smile.

"Sorry to keep you waiting," Beverley said. "My wife neglected to tell me that you'd called earlier. I, uh, assume it's important."

"It is. One of your students is dead."

30

Beverley's face drained of color and for a second it appeared he was going to lose his balance. He recovered quickly and said, "I presume from the way you said that, uh, that it was not—that it was unnatural."

"You presume right. She was murdered—"

Beverley wavered and had to support himself on the desk. "Oh, good Lord."

"We don't know when exactly, but our first guess is that it happened at least a week ago. We won't know for sure until we get the coroner's report."

"My God, that's awful. Terrible."

"In more ways than one," Balzic said. "The semester's over, right?"

"Huh? Oh yes. The last exams were given today. Who was it?"

"Name was Janet Pisula. She lived with Miss Summer. Rented there, I mean. We've talked to all the people there except one and we'll get to him as soon as he gets off work, but we're going to need all the help we can get from you."

"Certainly. Of course. Anything I can do, just say it . . . my God, this is awful."

"Yeah, well, I get the drift of what you're thinking, Dr. Beverley, but it, uh, was a hell of a lot worse for her than it's going to be for you or the school."

Beverley flushed. "I'm sorry. I—"

Balzic held up his hand. "Say nothing. What I want to know right now is if there is any way you can notify the students here to stay around. They get away from us now, we're going to be chasing all over the county trying to run down whatever information they might have, and it would make things a lot simpler if you keep as many of them around as you could."

"I don't see how," Beverley said. "Most of them have left already. Some finished with their exams yesterday. There were a number who finished Wednesday. There would be no reason for them to remain here unless they were planning to attend the

31

summer sessions. Even so, they would more than likely have left because the summer session, the first one, the six-week session, doesn't begin for three weeks."

"Well how about the ones who took exams today and tonight? Is there any way you could get word out to them to stay put?"

"That's going to be rather difficult."

"Uh, Dr. Beverley, there isn't any of this going to be easy, I'll tell you straight. We don't have diddly-damn to go on so far, and the people we've talked to already haven't given us a damn thing except that the girl kept pretty much to herself. We also know she wasn't robbed, and we've got pretty fair odds she wasn't raped, and that's about it. Which means, in short, that we've got a lot of talking to do to a hell of a lot of people. Which means, furthermore, that all the people you can keep close for a while is going to make it just a little bit easier. Not much, but a little. So if you can get the word out, I'd appreciate it."

"Yes, of course, I understand what you're saying, chief, but I don't even know where to begin. We don't have dormitories. All our students live wherever they can. A great number of them commute."

"Well you must have a list of students. Somebody has to have a roster with addresses, right?"

"Right. Of course."

"Well would you mind picking up that phone and calling whoever that might be and asking him to get over here with that roster?"

Beverley flushed again. "Certainly." He reached for the phone and then rubbed his temples. "What am I thinking about?" he said to himself more than to Balzic. "He's here now. In the living room."

"Oh sweet Jesus," Balzic said to himself, turning his back as Beverley wheeled about and went out. A minute later he returned with two men, both in their mid-to-late thirties, both dressed casually, and both looking as concerned as the amount they'd obviously had to drink would allow.

32

"Chief Balzic," Beverley said, "this is Roy Weintraub, our treasurer, and this is Dr. Larry Ellis, our academic dean."

"Gentlemen," Balzic said, shaking hands.

"I haven't told them what this is about, chief," Beverley said. "I just told them that it was extremely important."

Balzic nodded. "I'll keep it brief, gentlemen. A student of yours, one Janet Pisula, was murdered approximately a week ago and—"

Weintraub's hand shot to his mouth. Ellis's lips parted and he sucked in a breath with an audible hiss.

"—as I was saying, so far we have practically nothing to go on. All the people we've talked to either didn't know the girl or, if they did, they hardly spoke to her. The only person who did speak with her often was her landlady, Miss Cynthia Summer, and if you know Miss Cynthia, you probably also know she had a stroke not too long ago, which means she can't remember very much about the girl except that she was kind and pretty lonely.

"I've already learned from Dr. Beverley," Balzic went on, "that most of the students have gone home for the summer and that a lot of others are commuters. What I want from you gentlemen is a roster of students—with addresses."

"Are you assuming it was another student?" Ellis asked.

"We're not assuming much of anything right now. What we want the roster for is to try and find somebody who knew this girl, knew something about her, knew who she was with, maybe knew somebody who wanted to be with her. And when I say I want a roster with addresses, naturally I mean both addresses. Home addresses and addresses of the places where they lived in town."

"Well, home addresses are easy to obtain," Weintraub said. "They'll be on permanent record cards. But residences here are another matter."

"Why's that?"

"Because we just don't have one. We don't keep track of who rents rooms to students," Weintraub said. "Our experience has been that students move around a lot anyway. They're always looking for ways to save money—moving in and out with one another. And that's perfectly understandable."

"Then how do you go about finding a student in an emergency? What do you do—wait until they show up in class or what?"

Weintraub, Ellis, and Beverley looked sheepishly at one another.

Balzic cleared his throat and waited. When he got no response he said, "Well, gentlemen, I'm not about to start telling you how to run your college. That's out of my line. But right now, I've got a problem, and I'd like to hear some suggestions."

"About what?" Weintraub asked.

"Hey, goddammit," Balzic snapped, "maybe you didn't hear me right. One of your students is dead. Murdered. That was five, six, maybe eight days ago. We won't know for sure until we get the coroner's report tomorrow. In the meantime, whoever killed her is still walking around, and nobody gave us any guarantee he won't get it in his head to do it again. So you people better get organized. I want some names and addresses. Everybody connected with this college—faculty, students, custodial people—everybody. And I want them now. What do I have to do—drive you all over to Conemaugh General so you can watch the autopsy?"

"Uh, Chief Balzic," Beverley said, "if you'll give us a moment to discuss this, I'm sure we can provide you with what you need, and I give you my word, you'll have our full cooperation on this."

"All right," Balzic said, going to the door. "I need to use your bathroom anyway." He shut the door to the den and knocked on the door to the bathroom. When he heard nothing, he opened it.

Inside, the short blocky woman with the blue tee-shirt and the bullish man who had looked familiar to Balzic reluctantly broke apart from what had obviously been a strenuous kiss. Rather, the bullish man tried to break away. He dropped his arms and backed up, but the woman clung to him and only the sink against his backside prevented him from losing his balance entirely.

"Excuse me," Balzic said, looking away. "I didn't hear anybody say anything when I knocked."

"That's all right," the woman said. "We don't mind."

"Uh, I'm sure you don't, but I'd like to use the facility."

"The what?"

"The toilet. You know. You got one painted on your shirt."

"Oh well. You can't use this one. I mean, it's already in use."

"I can see that. But I really do have to use the one on the floor. The one behind you?"

"Be our guest," the woman said.

"You're not going to leave?"

"Leave? Whatever for?" she said. "I mean, my God, man, it's just a simple biological function. You don't have to have a doctorate or anything."

Balzic nodded several times, muttering, "Yeah," each time. "Well," he said, slipping past the woman and unzipping his fly, "when in Rome and all that . . . teachers, huh." He shook his head and caught a glimpse of the woman grinning at him.

"What's so funny?"

"Oh, I was just making a bet with myself. I bet you were the kind who got down on one knee so you wouldn't sound like a shower. I guess I lost."

"You made a study of that, huh?"

"I know Rocco does it that way, and you two look like you've got other things in common."

The bullish man groaned and rolled his eyes.

Balzic zipped his fly and pushed the toilet lever. "Rocco," he said, "your last name wouldn't be Cimoli, would it? The reason I'm asking is when I saw you two dancing out in the living room, I had the feeling I knew you from someplace. Am I right?"

"Yeah. Yeah, you're right," Rocco said, putting his thick hands on the sink to support himself as the woman continued to lean into him. He looked suddenly apprehensive.

"Uh, young lady," Balzic said, "if you don't mind, I'd—"

"I do mind. I am not a lady. I am a woman."

"Okay. Uh, woman, would you mind very much excusing us? I got something I want to talk to Rocco about."

"I most certainly do mind. I have things I want to *do* with Rocco, and I'm not about to go sit with the ladies while you boys talk about football."

"Have it your way, woman," Balzic said, facing Rocco. "Rocco, you correct me if I'm wrong, but the last time I saw you, you were crawling in the back of the sheriff's wagon on your way to Southern Regional. That was about, oh, four, maybe five years ago—am I right?"

"Six years ago," Rocco said, closing his eyes and pursing his lips.

"Rocco!" the woman nearly shouted. "You were in prison?"

He opened his eyes and nodded slowly.

"That's great!" she said, throwing her arms around his neck and trying to kiss him on the mouth, but missing because he turned his face away and began to pull her arms from around his neck.

"Come on, willya. I mean, Jesus . . ."

"Rocco, what's wrong? That's terrific that you were in prison. You never told me. Why didn't you tell me? Oh, we have lots of things to talk about now. And do. And doooo. Do we ever!"

Rocco took the woman by one arm and moved her toward the door. For a second she looked as though she was going to resist, but Rocco's strength surprised her. She even began to look a little frightened.

"Rocco, you're hurting me."

"That's right, I am. 'Cause I want you to leave and I don't want to hear anything about the National Organization for Women or anything like it. I have some things I got to say to the chief, and they're not about football. And one more thing," he said, pushing the door shut again after he'd started to open it, "you get out there in that living room, you just forget what you

36

heard in here, you hear me? I mean, I know you like to tell the people what you think the people ought to know and all that jazz, but you just put a lock on your mouth, honey, 'cause if you don't, I *will* hurt you."

"Rocco . . ."

"Go, baby. Now." Rocco pushed her out the door, shut it, and locked it.

"Okay, Rocco, let's have it."

"Okay. Straight. And I know you'll check the papers."

Balzic nodded. "I will."

"I got eleven and a half to twenty-three. I did thirteen months and out. I finished high school in there, and when I got out I went to West Chester State. I got a bachelor of science in physical education, and I did it in three years. I worked my ass off. I pumped gas, washed dishes, swept locker rooms, worked in a laundry. I never cheated on a test, and I came out of there with better than a B average. And believe it or not, twelve more credit hours and I get my master's degree. And what you just saw is the first time I put my hands on anybody outside of a gym since you know when—for any reason. I even got into karate to learn how to control myself, and if I keep going the way I'm going, I'm going to have a black belt in about two years. In other words, man, I'm straight. I'm so straight that broad was right. I do go down on one knee so I won't make noise when I piss."

Balzic nodded. "Who knows?"

"One person too goddamn many right now."

"Rocco, you kidding yourself, or what? That even made the Pittsburgh papers."

"Hey, man. That was six years ago. Do you know there's not one person from this town on this faculty? They're all from out of town. Hell, most of them aren't even from Pennsylvania. And this place has only been in operation for three years."

"What about students? There have to be a lot of them who remember, right?"

"Well, all I can tell you is they never let on if they know. In fact, sometimes I get the impression the ones who do know, sort

37

of, I don't know, look up to me, like I'm some sort of a guy who got trapped into something and then got himself untrapped—on his own. I don't know. Maybe that's just what I like to think." Rocco paused. "What about you? What are you going to do?"

"Me? I'm not going to do a damn thing. Why should I? Be happy for you. Ask how your mother is, that's all."

"She's okay. I'm making enough now so that she doesn't have to do that shit anymore."

"You see her often?"

"Once a week, maybe twice. I make sure she's all right."

"Well, next time you see her, tell her I said hello."

"I'll do that," Rocco said, sighing and looking at his shoes.

"Let's forget about it, okay? Tell me about something else. You ever hear of a student here named Janet Pisula?"

"I don't know anything about the female students. You should ask Toni."

"She the one just in here?"

"Yeah. She's the girls' phys-ed teacher. She talks a lot of garbage, but she's all right. At least I hope she's all right. I don't know whether I wanted her to hear that."

"You think it would do some good for me to talk to her?"

"I doubt it. As far as she's concerned, you're an oink-oink. I'm surprised she let you off as easy as she did. Man, she can really put some bad mouth on people. Wow. Course, you broke her up when you blew her that kiss. I never saw her laugh that hard at anything any man ever did. I mean, except when she's laughing at them. But when she was laughing at you, that was real. She really enjoyed that."

There was a knock, and then Dr. Beverley's voice asked for Balzic. "Are you in there?"

"Maybe I'll talk to you later, Rocco," Balzic said, opening the door and confronting Beverley.

"I think we can get you what you want," Beverley said.

Balzic nodded and followed Beverley back into the den. He found Ellis and Weintraub staring blankly at one another, caught in that limbo between where the alcohol they'd drunk was start-

38

ing to wear off and the reality of the situation was beginning to crowd in.

"You can get the rosters?" Balzic asked.

Ellis nodded. "Yes, but I wonder if it would be possible for someone to drive me to my office. I'm afraid I've had more than my share of party."

"No problem," Balzic said, going to the phone. He called his station and asked Stramsky to send a mobile unit. After he hung up, he told Ellis to take the rosters to the Summer house and turn them over to Johnson.

Ellis nodded and said, "I think I better have some coffee while I'm waiting."

"Wouldn't be a bad idea," Balzic said. Turning to Beverley, he asked, "How many people from your English department are here?"

"All of them, I think."

"How about getting them in here, will you please?"

Beverley followed Ellis and Weintraub to the door, but stopped. "You mean one at a time or—"

"No, no. All of them."

Beverley left and returned a minute later leading Malcolm Keenan and three other men. All had had too much party and were trying, with the exception of Keenan, to look properly somber. Beverley excused himself without making introductions, saying that he had to explain to his wife what was going on, and Keenan took command, or tried to, at once. He made the introductions, mispronouncing Balzic's name each time as he presented Joseph Winoski, James Farrell, and Edward Snavely.

Snavely gave the appearance of a man who worked at trying to disgust others. He had one button missing from his shirt, another missing from the front of his suit coat, and still another missing from his sleeve. He seemed unable or unwilling to open his mouth fully when speaking so that saliva bubbled at the corners of his mouth, and he kept inhaling the mucous in his nose with a sound that must have set his students' skin crawling. He weighed easily two hundred seventy pounds and was adding to

39

his girth with a beer and a salami and cheese sandwich plastered with yellow mustard. When he shook Balzic's hand, mustard dripped on the rug. A man, Balzic thought, who did everything he could to make certain no one got close to him, probably bemoaning the fact all the while.

Joseph Winoski was as neat as Snavely was sloppy: his ankle-high boots seemed spit-polished, his double-knit suit, though a conservative blue-gray check, was up to the minute in cut, and his build was of a man who spent his lunch hours in the YMCA gym. Balzic could smell Winoski's after-shave lotion as they shook hands, a brand advertised on television by seamen and adventurers, and could feel the hours at the gym in the handshake. He couldn't help wondering how Winoski would react if he were told that he was just a step away from Snavely in motive, that his neatness probably had the same fear behind it as Snavely's sloppiness. Somebody who told Winoski that would more than likely have to learn what sort of physical shape he was in, Balzic thought, resisting his urge to smile.

James Farrell was the only one of the four who seemed at ease with himself. He dressed, moved, and spoke like a thousand other men who would have been lost in crowds. His only distinction seemed to be that he had no distinction, except for his name, which, when Balzic said the same sounded familiar, he said was the result of his father's love of author James T. Farrell. "He used to call me Studs when I was a kid."

"I don't get the connection," Balzic said.

"My namesake wrote a book, well, three books actually, called *Studs Lonigan,* and my father loved them so much, he took it out on me." He smiled when he said it, without the slightest trace of resentment.

"You never heard of *Studs Lonigan?*" Snavely asked, his mouth full of sandwich.

"Sorry," Balzic said. "I just thought the name sounded familiar."

"Well, chief," Keenan said, "don't you think you ought to tell us what this is about?"

"Sure. But first I'd like you to get my name straight. It's not Ballsy. It's Balzic."

"Sorry about that," Keenan said, laughing much too hard and then putting his hand on Balzic's shoulder and saying, "No offense intended—or no intense offended, whichever the case may be."

Balzic nodded. "Yeah, sure. Okay, gentlemen, here's the problem. One of your students was murdered. Her name was Janet Pisula." He watched their faces as he spoke. Their reaction seemed genuine enough: Snavely and Winoski looked astonished at first and then baffled; Keenan and Farrell looked plainly shocked.

"Did you say Janet Pisula?" Keenan asked.

"Yes. And I understand she was in your composition class last semester. What I want to know, among other things, is whose class she was in this semester?"

"She was in my section," Farrell said, shaking his head. "Little Miss Nobody."

"All right," Balzic said. "Mr. Snavely, Mr. Winoski, unless you know something about this girl, you can leave."

"I never heard of her," Winoski said.

"Neither did I," Snavely said, chewing his sandwich as though he had forgotten how to swallow.

"You know nothing about her—never heard anything about her?"

Snavely and Winoski both shrugged and shook their heads, waiting a moment longer until Balzic nodded toward the door, and then left.

"All right, Mr. Keenan, Mr. Farrell, whatever you know."

"I think I should begin," Keenan said, "but since, uh, I mean, I had no idea—I think I better get some coffee. I've really had a lot—no more than my usual, understand, but . . ."

"Go ahead," Balzic said. "Why don't you see if you can bring back the pot? If it won't be too much trouble for the host."

"Of course. I'll do that," Keenan said, leaving the room.

"Mr. Farrell," Balzic said, "a minute ago when you said the

41

girl was in your section, I think I heard you say something about 'little Miss Nobody,' am I right?"

Farrell nodded. "Yes, I did. That's the way she struck me."

"How did she strike you? What did she do? What didn't she do?"

"That's just it. She didn't do much of anything. I can't recall ever hearing her say anything at all in class. She just sat there, looking pretty much bewildered. Sometimes when I'd call on her, ask her opinion about something we were discussing, she wouldn't answer. She'd start to say something, and then she'd— she'd just go mute. Literally dumb. As though some circuitry between her brain and her voice box had been shorted. She looked as though she would have given anything to be able to say something, not necessarily something intelligent or brilliant or even charming—but she apparently couldn't say anything."

"Did you ever talk to her privately about it?"

"Yes, I tried to. Twice, as a matter of fact. Privately, it was even worse. She was petrified. She couldn't speak at all. All she could do was nod her head and blush. I never had a student like her before—of course, this is only my third year of teaching. The second time, I tried to suggest to her that she might do well to get some kind of counseling. I must've approached it completely wrong because she practically ran out of my office. It was embarrassing."

"Embarrassing?"

"Well, the fact is, I like to think of myself as knowing something about communication. After all, that is supposed to be my profession, and there she was, a person with whom I couldn't communicate at all. She brought me face to face with my limits. That's what I meant by embarrassing."

"How did you suggest it to her, about getting counseling?"

"I don't recall what I said exactly. I think I told her that she had to have some kind of blockage, that it didn't seem logical or even sensible that she should be able to write the way she did and then on the other hand, have so much trouble talking."

"Was she a very good writer?"

"Oh yes. One of the best. She had a very good eye for detail. Her papers were always filled with solid examples of the abstractions she used. That's something you generally have trouble with in freshman comp. Freshmen are generally in love with abstractions. I keep trying to tell them that the further removed one is from fact the more difficult it is for one person to understand another."

"I take your meaning," Balzic said, "but that's damn strange. Because I'll tell you, the one person who seemed to know anything about her—I mean the one person I've talked to so far—another student, a girl named Patricia Keim—do you know her?"

Farrell shook his head.

"Well, the Keim girl said just the opposite of what you said. She said that was the one thing the Pisula girl couldn't do. She said one of their assignments the first semester was to take an abstraction and break it down, and the Keim girl said she tried to explain to the Pisula girl how to go about it. I think she said she told her to take a season of the year and write everything solid she could think of when she thought of that season. But the Keim girl said that the Pisula girl wasn't even aware that a season of the year was an abstraction. Now how do you figure that?"

Farrell shrugged. "I can't figure it. I don't understand it at all. Unless . . ."

"Unless what?"

"Well, unless she took a great jump in understanding. Sometimes a student may not be able to comprehend what you're saying for a long time, and then suddenly, for no reason that anyone can explain, the insight comes to them. It's not uncommon. In fact, it's the thing you hope for, the thing you hope will happen in a classroom, or at least that's what I hope for. That's what bothered me so much about her. She wrote so well, yet she wasn't able to talk. Usually, it's just the reverse. They all talk well enough to be understood, given, of course, that they know what they're talking about, but when they sit down in front of that blank page, they just come unhinged."

"What did you say?"

"I said they come unhinged. Lose their confidence—"

"No, no. Before that. You said something about a blank page."

"Yeah. I said that some people talk well enough, but when they sit down in front of that blank page, they—"

"That's it."

"What's it?" Farrell said.

"Blank page."

"I don't understand. What's that have to do with this?"

Before Balzic could answer, though he was not saved from answering as much as he was saved from making up some reason for being concerned about a specific blank page, he saw the door being pushed open. Keenan came in with a large silver tray, balancing a pot of coffee, some mugs, and a creamer and sugar bowl.

Keenan poured, acting a perfect host, giving Balzic the impression that much of what Keenan did was an act. Balzic couldn't put his finger on why exactly, except that Keenan's smile and gestures while pouring were laced with an exhuberance that seemed contrived, an exhuberance Keenan immediately turned off the moment Balzic asked him what he knew about Janet Pisula. Then Keenan switched faces at once, going from perfect host to concerned head of department, from smiling waiter to frowning, fretful witness to tragedy.

"I can't tell you very much about her at all," Keenan said. "I can only, in all candor, give you some impressions. I found her to be as inarticulate as any student I've ever had—and I don't mean to say for a moment that I had her."

Balzic had to turn his back to Keenan to keep from telling him to shut off the nonsense.

"That was not meant as a pun, I assure you," Keenan said quickly when Balzic turned back to him. "I wanted that to be clear. The reason I want that clear is that, well, I have somewhat of a reputation as a, well, uh, a seeker of pleasure."

"You fuck around with your students," Balzic said evenly.

"Yes. You could put it that way. Well, not exactly that way—"

"And you don't want me to get the idea that there might be some connection between you and Janet Pisula in that way."

"Yes. Right. Absolutely. Because there wasn't. She was, in a word, incommunicado. And I cannot make it with females who are incommunicado."

"Well, Mr. Keenan, now that we've eliminated that possibility, would you mind giving me some impressions that I could use?"

"Of course. Though I don't know what you mean when you say you need impressions you can use."

"Oh Jesus Christ, man, tell me what you know about her."

Keenan flushed. "Yes. Uh, well, as I said, she was incommunicado."

"Which means exactly what?"

"Which means she wouldn't respond verbally. Anywhere. In class or out."

"I see. What was your reaction to her?"

"Well, to be perfectly candid, I thought she was rather doltish. Not someone on whom I should waste my energy. She was one of the thousands too many young people who don't belong in any college classroom taking up the space. In my opinion she would have been much better off touring the country on a bicycle or waiting tables at some resort near the ocean."

"Uh-huh," Balzic said, "and what did you think of her writing?"

"Incredibly bad. Worse. Atrocious." Keenan reflected for a moment. "Except for near the end of the semester. Then, as I recall, she turned in a couple of papers that were very good. So good, in fact, they made me suspicious. And then when she took the final, I was sure of my suspicions. I had to get drunk to give her a D."

Farrell, who had been listening calmly, suddenly couldn't keep his hands still. "You had to do what?"

45

"Get flat out stoned," Keenan said. "Sober, I couldn't have given her a Z."

"I don't believe that," Farrell said. "She was one of the best writers in my section."

Keenan shook his head. "Jim, just as a friend and absolutely not as department chairman, I'd have to say she may have *known* the best writer in your section, but there's no way she could have *been* the best writer in anybody's section. I'm making no judgments about her as a person, you understand, but, well, no one with her limited ability should be in college. I'm sorry."

"I can't believe you said that," Farrell said, jamming his hands into his pockets and hunching his shoulders.

"Well," Keenan said, "there it is."

"Uh, let's get off this," Balzic said. "Let's get on to something solid. Mr. Keenan, who was she with, who did you see her with, who did you see trying to be with her?"

"Nobody. I can't recall ever seeing her with anybody. I don't recall ever seeing her talking to anyone. She'd come into class, sit in the seat nearest the door, keep her head buried in her notebook most of the class, and she'd leave as soon as I dismissed the class."

"Mr. Farrell, how about you?"

"She did exactly the same thing in my class. Even to the point of sitting in the seat closest to the door."

"You never saw her talking to anyone?"

Farrell shook his head. "And I've already told you about the times I tried to talk to her out of class."

"Hmm," Balzic said. "Anything else? Anything at all?"

"Nothing," Keenan said. Farrell just shook his head and jammed his hands deeper into his pockets.

"Then I guess that's all, gentlemen," Balzic said. "Just do me a favor. When you go back out there, tell anybody who had her in class to come in here, will you?"

"Certainly," Keenan said. "Would you, uh, like more coffee, or would you like me to take the tray out?"

"Suit yourself. I don't want any more coffee. You can take

the tray." Balzic watched them go, fuming to himself about what he'd just heard. It made no sense. A girl who never talked to anyone. That was impossible. There had to be someone. Someone who knew her well enough to know she lived alone, someone who knew her well enough to know she probably wouldn't make a sound if she got in trouble. Then again, whoever killed her didn't have to know any such thing. Whoever killed her didn't have to know a damned thing about her—except that he wanted her dead.

Moments after Keenan and Farrell left, Balzic went to the phone and dialed the Summer house.

"Summer residence, Lieutenant Johnson speaking."

"Walk? Mario. My man get there with the dean?"

"About two minutes ago. He's still here."

"Well, I busted into a party at the president's house. Most of the faculty is here. There might be a couple missing, I don't know. But right now, from the ones I've talked to so far, I'm getting nothing. The only thing anybody's agreed on is that the girl wasn't one for talking. What d'you come up with?"

"About the same," Johnson said. "Our print man won't know for sure until tomorrow, but as of right now, his best guess is that all the prints in the room belonged to the girl. Except for a couple on the door which probably belong to you."

"Yeah. Did you talk to those two across the hall again?"

"Yep. They say the same things. Didn't hear anything, didn't see anything—except for that guy one of them thinks he saw, but he still can't say anything definite about that guy. Now he thinks the guy was young and white, but he shakes his head everytime I ask him if he thinks he could identify the guy. And they swear they weren't out of their room except to go to class, take tests, and eat."

"How about the Cerovich kid—he come back from work yet?"

"Yeah. He's a zero, too. He never even saw her. Her name didn't mean a thing. And we know where he's been every night for the last year. Course, what we don't know is time of death. So he's still a remote possibility. But from talking to him, I'd say no. He's too goddamn solid. He wasn't here five minutes and he had two phone calls from broads. Good-looking kid. Probably getting more ass than a toilet seat. Guys like that just don't kill broads. You didn't get anything at all from her teachers?"

"I haven't talked to all of them yet. I just talked to her compositon teachers so far. One of them thinks she was the best writer in his section. The other one, the chairman of the department, thinks she was the worst. He suspected her of cheating, still thinks she was, and told the other one, the one who thinks she was the best—he told him he'd been suckered. But both of them agree, the girl talked not at all. Big fucking deal."

"Yeah."

"Hey. Did her guardians, her aunt and uncle, did they show yet?"

"No, but I got a confirmation they were notified, so they should be pulling in soon. If they don't need a doctor."

"Oh boy. Well, I'm going to hang in here a while. There are a couple more teachers I want to talk to. You going to stay there?"

"I'll have to until the relatives show. Christ, that's going to be fun. How 'bout you taking them up to identify the body?"

"Up yours, buddy. That's one party I don't need." Balzic was going to hang up, but then said quickly, "Hey, Walk, when the dean showed with the rosters, did he have one for local addresses for the students?"

"No. He apologized all over the place for that. But what could I say? He didn't have it, he didn't have it."

"If that isn't bad enough, when I asked the president if there was any way he could keep the students here, he just shook his head. That's when I found out they didn't have local addresses. Christ almighty . . ."

"How much longer you think you'll be there?"

Balzic looked over his shoulder as the door opened and a man and a woman walked in. "Not long," he said to Johnson. "I

48

think the last of her teachers are coming in right now. Soon as I finish with them I'll be down." He hung up and introduced himself to the two who had come in.

The woman, short, roundish, in her late thirties, with no make-up and her hair cut severely short, introduced herself as Miss Ulishney. "Janet was in my advanced shorthand course," she said somberly.

The man, shorter than the woman, a collar of jet black hair flowing downward around his ears but shiny bald on top, shook Balzic's hand and introduced himself as Phil Castro. "The girl was in my American history course, but I'll tell you right now and save us both a lot of time. I know practically nothing about her except that she never missed class and that she was just an average student. A low C student, and her grades were more a matter of my generosity than her effort."

"Mr. Castro, did you ever see her talking to anybody? Ever see anybody talking to her?"

"I never paid attention to that sort of thing."

"Uh-huh. Where did she sit in your class?"

"Sit? What does that have to do with anything?"

"Just tell me, if you can remember."

"I remember that clearly. Last seat, last row. Right next to the door."

Balzic nodded. "Well, unless you can tell me something more than that, you can go."

"All I can tell you is that the last time I saw her was last Wednesday, the next to the last class, and the only class she missed was the last class."

"That next to last class, that would've been, uh, the twenty-sixth of May, right?"

"That's right. Last class was the twenty-eighth of May. Last Friday."

"Well, thanks for your help. But if you think of anything, call me at City Hall or call Lieutenant Johnson at Troop A, Rocksburg Barracks."

"I'm sorry I can't be of more help," Castro said. "I'm sorry that it happened. How did it happen, by the way? Nobody out there seems to know."

"Let's just say she was murdered and let it go at that, okay?"

Castro shrugged and left.

"Miss Ulishney, I hope you can tell me more than that."

"I wish I could," she said. "I just feel very bad for her. But I really don't know much about her."

"She was quiet, she didn't talk to anybody, she didn't say much in class—are those your impressions of her? I'm asking, not to put words in your mouth, but because those are the impressions everyone else seems to have."

"I'm afraid I have to go along with the rest. I really can't recall saying anything to the girl."

"Your class was probably all girls, right?"

"Yes. All my classes are. I also teach business math and office machines."

"How was she in your class, as a student, I mean."

"Not very good, I'm afraid. Oh, she mastered the shorthand characters well enough, but she wasn't nearly as fast as she should have been. I think her top speed was no more than eighty-five words a minute. Not nearly fast enough for an advanced class. She should have been able to take at least a hundred words a minute."

"Good but slow."

"Well, not really good either, because when I played my practice tapes at a hundred words a minute, she would naturally miss a lot. She was really competent only when I played the slower tapes."

"I see. Uh, one more thing. Well, two more. When did you see her last, one, and two, where did she sit in your class?"

"I saw her last Wednesday. Yes, I'm sure of that because I remember that she didn't come to last Friday's class and I remembered thinking how unusual that was. She hadn't missed a class for two semesters."

"And where did she sit?"

"Like Phil—Mr. Castro, I mean—I don't understand that

question, but I'll answer it. She sat in the middle of the front row. Right in front of my desk. Why do you ask that?"

"I'm not sure. It's just that her two English teachers, Keenan and Farrell, happened to mention it as though it was important, and then when I asked Mr. Castro—well, you heard what he said. Seems the only thing you people are sure of about this girl was where she sat. That, plus she wasn't a very good student, plus the other thing everybody's agreed on, which is, she didn't say anything, or as little as she could and still get by." Balzic scratched his chin. "Is there anybody else out there who had her in class? So far, I count three courses she was taking. Yours, Mr. Castro's, and Mr. Farrell's. Would that be a full schedule?"

"No. A full schedule is generally twelve to fourteen hours, but I doubt that half our students take a full schedule. Most can't afford it. A great many of them work part-time, and most are from lower-middle-income families."

Balzic thanked her for her help and then went to the door and opened it for her. "Just one more thing, Miss Ulishney. Take a quick survey for me out there, will you please? Ask if there's anybody else who knew her."

"Certainly," she said, going past him.

Balzic left the door open and stood rocking on his heels and toes. It was only then that he noticed he'd stopped perspiring and that he knew the reason: J. Hale Beverley's house was more than adequately air-conditioned. He was thinking about the broken fan back in his office when the blocky woman, the one Rocco Cimoli called Toni, came striding through the doorway and had to stop short to keep from bumping into him.

He backed up and pursed his lips. Apparently she'd responded affirmatively to Miss Ulishney's survey, but Balzic wasn't sure he wanted to ask this Toni, whatever her information, much of anything. He had the feeling that whatever she was going to say about Janet Pisula was going to be starched with feminist propaganda.

"Uh, we didn't meet before, in the bathroom, I mean. Rocco told me your first name was Toni. Your last name?"

51

"Rosario."

"Uh, Miss Rosario—"

"Pronounce that miz, if you don't mind."

Balzic shook his head and started to laugh.

"What's so funny?"

"Oh, I was just wondering what you say to guys with speech problems. You know, the guys who talk like thith? Or hasn't that come up in your meetings yet?"

For the briefest moment, Toni Rosario looked almost ready to laugh at herself, but she instantly put her fences back up and said, "Well, so we haven't got around to that, but I'll tell you what. If that girl had listened to me, she might've grown up to be a woman."

"She was a student of yours then. In your gym class?"

"She was. And I told her just like I told all the others, just like I *tried* to tell all the others, that they would have to learn how to protect themselves."

"The beasties are all around, right?"

"That's right, they are."

"And if she'd just listened to you and learned karate or judo or something, she'd still be alive today, right?"

"Exactly right. No man would've been able to rape her, never mind kill her."

"Well, Miz Rosario, I hate to spoil all your fun, but as far as we know—though we won't know for sure until we hear from the coroner—but right now we're pretty sure she wasn't raped, and, uh, there's nothing really to tell us that it was a man who killed her."

"Well out there," she said, pointing testily in the direction of the living room, "everybody's saying she was raped."

"I have no idea what they're saying out there. A couple minutes ago a guy walked in, Castro his name was, and he gave me the impression nobody knew what happened. Now you come in saying everybody's got the information."

"Well? How did it happen?"

"All I'm going to tell you is what I told the others. The girl was murdered, and she's been dead at least a week, maybe longer. And whoever did it did it very quietly 'cause she didn't make a sound—or else everybody where she lived is deaf."

"Well, that sounds like her, not making a peep. A regular house-mouse. She couldn't do this, she couldn't do that—"

"You mean in gym class?"

"Well of course. Where else would I come in contact with her?"

"I don't know. You tell me."

"Well I didn't. She was in my gym class for two semesters and half the time she'd just stand around looking like something out of a Victorian novel. Like if somebody touched her, she'd just crumble into a heap of sugar and spice and everything nice. Gawd."

"What did she say about standing around? I mean, what reason did she give? Did she have a doctor's excuse for not doing anything?"

"Well, if she'd had a doctor's excuse, she wouldn't have even been there. There wasn't anything wrong with her. Nothing but a stupid, simpering idea that a woman was supposed to be delicate and fragile and weak."

"Did she say that or is that your conclusion?"

"It's my conclusion."

"Ever think you might've been wrong?"

"I'm not wrong about her. One day, gawd, I had them playing field hockey and one of the girls got a bloody nose. It was an accident. She got hit in the nose with the ball and it bled a little. It was nothing. I got it stopped in about two seconds, but the next thing I knew somebody was tapping me on the shoulder and telling me we had other problems. And there she was. Janet Pisula. Stretched out on the ground. Fainted. It was disgusting."

"Didn't you ask her about it? Didn't you check around about her? I mean, there might have been some reason why she was like that. I don't know what happened to her parents, but I do know she doesn't have any. She was raised by an aunt and uncle."

"So? Lots of people don't have parents. That's why there are orphanages."

"So you're telling me that because a lot of people are able to accept being orphans, uh, everybody should, is that it?"

"Everybody has things happen to them. You adapt. What's the big production?"

"And those people who can't adapt?"

"Oh bullshit," she said.

Balzic chewed the inside of his cheek. "Well, let's get back to Janet Pisula."

"I thought that's who we were talking about."

"More or less. But mostly what you've told me is what you thought of her. You haven't really told me what you know about her."

"Well then, I guess I don't know anything about her."

"Boy, I'll tell you something. I never met a bunch of people who know as little about a person as you people do. The girl was one of your students. Do you all know that little about all your students?"

"Do you have any idea how many students I come in contact with each semester?"

"Don't give me that, Miz Rosario. Do you know how many people there are in this town?"

"Are you going to tell me you know them all? Gawd."

"No. But I know the ones in trouble, and if I don't know them myself, then I go find somebody who does."

"Still—"

"Still nothing," Balzic said. "There are a lot more people with some kind of trouble in this town than there are students in this college—ah, forget it. That's all. You can go—oh, one more thing." Balzic stepped around her and closed the door. "What you heard in the bathroom, you didn't hear."

"About Rocco?"

"That's right. Do him and yourself a big favor, and forget you heard it. And don't get your head full of those goofy ideas

I see wheeling around in your eyes. Because I'm going to tell you what he did—for one reason and one reason only. I don't like people walking around with bad information. And I'm really going out on a limb telling you this. You better not make me think I made a mistake."

She shifted her weight to one foot and crossed her arms. "It can't be all that bad."

"With some of the ideas you have, it could be dynamite."

"I'm not a complete ass."

"I hope not. Because what he did was kill a guy. He beat him to death with a baseball bat. And he did it because the guy called his mother a whore. The thing was, she was a whore, and Rocco knew it, and the reason he knew it was because she told him she was.

"I didn't know the family at that time," Balzic went on, "and the only reason I found out about it was because she'd gone to a priest and asked him whether she should tell Rocco or not. This was a couple years before this thing happened, and the priest advised her to tell him. I didn't agree with the priest's reasons for telling her to tell him, but it was over by the time I found out about it. I didn't find out until the priest came to me, which was after Rocco killed the guy.

"I was out of town when it happened. Rocco went into a bar to pick up a pizza, and while he was waiting for it, he overheard two guys talking, and one of them was really putting his mother down for doing what she was doing. He took the pizza home and went back with the bat. The owner of the bar was a friend of mine and he knew I was out of town, so he called the state police. I didn't have a chance to do anything about it until right before the trial when the priest came to me and gave me the background. I'm not trying to make myself out a big man, but if it wasn't for me going to the judge Rocco would've got life. He would've done thirteen years instead of thirteen months. And tonight's the second time in my life I've seen him. The other time was when I said, when I saw him crawling in the back of the sheriff's wagon."

"Oh wow."

"Oh wow is right, sister. Rocco's mother is still alive, and she loves her son more than she loves life itself. When she heard from the priest that I'd talked to the judge, she came to me, and if you think a minute, you'll know what she wanted to give me."

Toni canted her head. "Oh, now wait. Are you going to try and tell me that you didn't take it?"

"No. I took it," Balzic said. "Because if I hadn't, I would've shamed her. Also," Balzic said, breaking into a wide smile, "she was a fine-looking woman."

"If that isn't the most typical male bullshit I ever heard—"

"Listen. You think what you want, but that—what I just told you about Rocco's mother and me—that is exactly why you aren't going to say anything to him or about him. 'Cause like I said, I don't like people going around with bad information, and I just gave you good information. All there is. So take it in and then forget it." Balzic studied her face. "Think about it this way. Rocco didn't kill that guy because his mother was a whore. He knew that. He killed the guy because the guy put her down for being what she was. And I did what I did for him and I took what I took from her because that's the way it should have been. I told you because I didn't want you saying, in a party or someplace, something stupid like, 'Tell us what prison was like, Rocco,' or 'Hey, everybody, you want to hear from a real victim of a sexist society?'"

"And what would happen if I did?"

"You just might get to be questioned about who did what to your face, if you know what I mean. Rocco's not the kind of guy you fool around with. Now, unless there's something else you can tell me about Janet Pisula?"

She shook her head and then stood a moment, shifting her weight from one foot to the other, looking confused, then aggressive, then regretful. She started to say something, but then shook her head and stepped past Balzic and opened the door and went out, leaving Balzic hoping weakly that he had not made a mistake in telling her. He knew he had to hope that he'd done right, otherwise he had left himself wide open for a problem. What he'd said about Rocco Cimoli not being the kind of guy you fool with

56

was as true for him as it was for Toni Rosario. "Be right, you big man," he said to himself as he left the den and went into the kitchen.

He found Dr. and Mrs. Beverley facing each other but both staring at the floor, sharing a tense silence.

"Uh, Dr. Beverley," he said, "I think I've learned all I can here. For now anyway. If anybody thinks of anything, tell them to call me down at City Hall or Lieutenant Walker Johnson at Troop A Barracks, okay?"

"Yes. Of course." Beverley moved as though to show Balzic out.

"Don't bother," Balzic said. "I can find my way. Goodnight, and, uh, I'm sorry I had to spoil your party."

Mrs. Beverley did not look up, and Dr. Beverley said nothing, leaning backward to put his rump against the sink. He'd moved farther away from it than he'd thought and hit it with a thump that caused him to throw out his hands to catch his balance, looking as though much more than his balance was at stake.

Johnson was leaning on a pillar on the portico with his thumbs hooked in his pockets when Balzic drove up to the Summer house.

"Whatta you know, Walk?"

"I know it's hot."

"You ought to try walking out of an air-conditioned house into this."

"I'd like to try walking into one."

"All your people gone?"

"There's one guy up there putting a lock on the door. I sent all the rest back with all the girl's notebooks, letters, anything she'd written in. I got three men going through that. Shouldn't take them too long. There wasn't too much."

"Grimes call?"

"Oh yeah. Small surprise there. Not only was she not raped, her hymen was still intact. A very inactive virgin." Johnson stretched and yawned. "You know, I didn't think a girl could get

57

through eighteen years and still have one. You'd think she'd have broken it doing something. Riding a bike, running around in a gym class, something.''

"Well, from what her gym teacher told me, she wasn't much for running around."

"What else did you get up there?"

"Not a hell of a lot. I told you most of it when I called you."

"You didn't get any more than that?"

"Just a couple of goofy little things. One—which isn't all that goofy—she passed out when another girl in her gym class got a bloody nose. Two, she was taking four courses: English, history, shorthand, and gym. Except for English, she had the same teachers this semester as she did last, so that makes three men and two women. Never mind the gym class, in the other classes where the men taught, she always sat in the seat next to the door. In the shorthand class with the woman, she sat right up front. First row, right in front of the teacher's desk. Three, the English teacher she had this semester, guy named Farrell, said something about certain people just coming unhinged when they sit down in front of a blank page. I looked at the guy real good when he said it, but it looked to me like something he was just used to saying.''

"What was he talking about?"

"He was talking about how some people can talk pretty good, but when they have to write they just can't do it. From the way he said it, I gathered it's a pretty common thing. And Christ knows, whenever I have to write something I go through a shit fit—"

"Yeah. Me too."

"—it was just that he happened to use those words. 'Blank page,' or 'Blank paper'—no, it was page, and they jumped at me."

"Was he talking about her specifically?"

"Yes and no. Yes, if you believe the other teacher she had, this Keenan guy, the department chairman, 'cause he thought the girl couldn't write worth a damn. I told you that on the phone."

Johnson nodded.

"And no, if you believe this Farrell, 'cause he thought the girl was the best writer in his class. Those two had a real difference of opinion over that. I mean, if I hadn't been there, I got the feeling those two would've had a pretty fair go-round over it. But that Keenan—what a ballbuster he is. He lets me in and he introduces himself, you know, with the handshake that dislocates your shoulder, and he says, 'Malcolm Keenan here. I'm a poet who teaches as a public service.' Then he started telling me these raunchy limericks, oh boy . . ."

"What do you make of her sitting close to the door with the men teachers—scared of men?"

"That's what it sounds like to me, but all I know is, that was the one thing all those men were certain of. Hey, you hear anything from her aunt and uncle?"

"Yeah. The woman collapsed. Had to get her to a hospital. And the uncle was shaking too bad to drive, so he's coming down in one of our units. He didn't want to come at all. Which is normal enough."

"How long ago you hear that?"

"Twenty minutes. Should be here in fifteen, twenty minutes."

"You got the rosters, right?"

"Hey, pal. You know how many people there are connected with this college? Close to seven hundred, that's all. Six hundred and twenty-one students. A hundred and four of them full-time. The rest taking two or one course. Then there's the faculty, the deans, assorted other bureaucrats, buildings and grounds people, janitors, charwomen, manager of the student union—oh, shit, from all over the county."

"Well, we start with the ones from in her classes. That cuts it down. That should get us under a hundred."

Johnson yawned again. "You know, Mario, we're starting close to home, but what do we do if it's a goddamn transient?"

"The first thing we do, Walk, is we don't even think like that."

59

"I always like to think the worst. Just to make myself comfortable. Like those two little girls, remember? In that town just north of Edinboro?"

"I remember reading about it."

"Yeah. Well, you know how many people we talked to with that? Over five hundred. More than a hundred grade school kids. And you know what we come up with? Nothing . . . that's what bothers me about this one. Those two little girls were strangled with their own clothes." Johnson stared off into the night. "Sure wish the hell it would rain."

The front door opened and a state trooper came out carrying a small tool chest. "Here's the keys, lieutenant," he said, handing Johnson two padlock keys.

Johnson thanked him and told him he could leave.

"So now we wait for the uncle," Johnson said, stepping off the porch and walking slowly toward his cruiser. "You coming?" he called over his shoulder.

"Yeah. I'll see you up at the barracks."

Michael Pisula came into Troop A's duty room on the arm of the state trooper who'd driven him. He was a short man, slender, with a slight paunch below his belt. His white shirt was sweat-stained and his trousers rumpled. He had a handky wadded in his right hand and kept putting it to his mouth as he was directed to a chair. His eyes were raw and he had difficulty clearing his throat.

Balzic brought him a paper cup of water, but Pisula waved it away. Then he broke down, weeping uncontrollably for what seemed to Balzic an hour, though it was not more than a minute.

"Who would do this to her?" he said after he'd got control. He had not asked Balzic or Johnson; he seemed to be asking as though praying.

"Mr. Pisula," Johnson said, "I know how difficult this is—"

"Difficult! My God, man, you don't have any idea what this girl's been through in her life. And then to, to—like this . . ."

Johnson and Balzic looked at each other, loathing to begin

60

to ask the questions they knew had to be asked.

"Do you know," Pisula said suddenly, "she was just eighteen two weeks ago? The Sunday before last. She came home and we had a party for her. Ann made a beautiful cake. We had turkey. It was like Christmas. We were so happy for her she was finally getting out, getting to meet people. And she said she was doing so well and having such a good time. She kept saying how much she liked the people in her rooming house, how nice they were to her . . . now, my God—is there a God? Tell me. I'd like to know if there's a God. Would he do this to her, would he allow what's happened to her to happen to anyone? I hope I'm forgiven if there is a God because—because for the first time in my life I don't believe there is."

"Did she tell you which people were nice to her, Mr. Pisula?" Balzic asked.

"Yes. There was a girl, a Pat something. Patricia—"

"Keim?"

"Yes. She said she was very nice to her. Very friendly."

Balzic and Johnson exchanged frowns, remembering too clearly Patricia Keim's indifference to Janet Pisula.

"Mr. Pisula," Johnson said, "were you told what happened?"

Pisula nodded and then started to cry again. In a moment he stopped and blew his nose. "Do you know, she was so beautiful when she was a child. She was my brother's. So beautiful . . ."

"What happened?"

"To my brother?"

Balzic nodded.

"An accident. She was seven. She was in the back seat. They were out for a drive. He'd just bought a new Ford. My God, was he proud. Their first time in that car. The next thing I know, a state police standing at the door. Just like tonight . . . she was brilliant, you know that? They had her tested when she was four. When she was four, she could add three-figure numbers in her head. She could read—and nobody taught her! They put her in kindergarten when she was four, and when she was five, they put her in second grade. The nuns did that. My brother and his wife, they were against it. They wanted her to stay with her own age, but the nuns insisted. And the nuns were right to do that. She was brilliant . . . and then they went for a drive. Some son of a—that idiot, passing a truck on a hill . . . my brother hit a utility pole. They were both dead. My sister-in-law instantly, they said. My brother, that night. . . ."

"Janet?"

"My wife and I, we—we couldn't have children . . . you're not supposed to want what your brother has, I know, but we wanted that little girl. The only envy I had for my brother . . . and then we got her. But how we got her, my God. In a coma for two months, brain surgery, and then, never again the same. How could it? But wasn't that enough? How much torture does God allow in one life?"

Johnson went for a cup of water. Balzic lit a cigarette and looked at the floor.

"And then he came to see her. The day after she regained consciousness. He'd been calling every day. The nurses told us. And then he walked in, just like that, and you know what he said to her? He looked at her for a long time, just looked at her, and then he said, 'You should've died.' Just like that. And then he turned around and walked out . . . it was eight months before Janet said a word, two more months in the hospital, six months at home, and we were sitting down to eat, and she said—the first words in ten months—she said, 'Why did he say that to me?' Then she just played with her food. And what could we say to her, why that—that idiot, why he would even want to say anything at all?"

"Who was he, Mr. Pisula?"

"The driver of the other car, the one that passed that truck. A punk! The only time in my life I ever felt as though I could actually kill somebody myself. All wasted thoughts . . ."

"Why wasted?"

"Because he did it for me. Drove his car off a bridge—that same night. I didn't know until the next day even who he was. The police told us. I guess they thought they were doing us a favor."

"When you say that same night, you mean the night he came to the hospital?"

"Yes, yes."

"And Janet never got over that?"

"Never. It wasn't only the brain damage, it was that, you see? What possessed him to say that? Couldn't he realize what that would do to her? . . . I guess not."

"Did Janet know about the other driver?" Balzic asked. "I mean, did she know he'd killed himself?"

Pisula shook his head. "She never heard it from Ann or me. If she heard it from somebody else, I can't say. I know she never talked about any of it again—not with us anyway."

"Uh, Mr. Pisula, didn't she ever talk to anybody about it?" Balzic asked. "I mean, didn't you think it was a good idea for her to talk to somebody about it?"

"A psychiatrist you mean? Sure. A couple of them. Oh, I don't know what they talked about with her. Not very much, I know that. Because they all said the same thing. All they wanted to do was talk about the brain damage. They talked about percentages. They said we'd have to learn to accept things as they were, that she would never be any better. I thought I would go crazy talking to them when they talked like that. I didn't under-stand—I still don't—how knowing a figure could make a differ-ence. They talked like her mind was an adding machine, like a couple keys were broke and everybody would just have to go on adding, but without those keys. It didn't make sense to me . . . she was scared to death of them anyway . . . but I never thought the injury was as bad as what that punk said to her. She didn't have trouble taking care of herself. It was only in school that it showed up. She became average, a little below. From brilliant to average, from skipping grades to just keeping up. And she worked very hard. We never pressured her—Ann or me. We just wanted her to have some happiness—wasn't she entitled?"

"But she had trouble getting along with people?"

"With people? My God, yes. She was terrified of strangers. For a long time she wouldn't even go shopping with us. Only to school and then home. Then, little by little, she'd go out at night with us, but she wouldn't sit in the back seat. She'd sit right between us, and we could feel how tense she was all the while the car was moving. Then, when we were in the stores, she'd stay so close to Ann and me that sometimes we'd trip over each other's feet. She was in high school before she'd go anywhere without us. Even then it was only with Francey—my God, what'll this do to her?"

"Who's Francey?"

"Her friend. Oh my God, I can't tell her . . . I have to."

"Who is she, Mr. Pisula?"

"Francey—Frances Milocky. Our neighbor's daughter. She goes to Penn State. More than anyone, she's responsible for Janet coming out of herself. My God!"

"What's the matter?"

Pisula's body quivered as a chill racked him. "She's the one, she persuaded Janet to come here. Janet wouldn't have done it if Francey hadn't convinced her she could do it. Oh, God, what will this do to her . . ."

"She's in school now? At Penn State you said?" Balzic took out his notebook and wrote the name and address as Pisula gave it to him.

"Are you going to tell her?" Pisula asked.

"If you'd rather we did."

"Please. I don't think . . ."

"Did they keep in touch with one another?"

"Oh yes. They wrote all the time. They were very close."

"Did Janet say anything to you or your wife about anybody bothering her? Did she say anything about any trouble she was having? With anybody, about anything."

"No. Only with the work in class."

"Anything in particular? Or was it just generally hard for her?"

"No. The thing I'm talking about happened last semester. In her English."

"Was her teacher's name Keenan?"

"Yes. Dr. Keenan. She didn't like him at all. She was very afraid of him. He talked loud. And she said he was very rude."

"She had trouble doing work for him, didn't she?" Balzic said. "I mean, I know that she barely got a passing grade from him."

"Yes. She got a D. She didn't know what he expected. She didn't know what she was supposed to do."

"Did she talk to you about that? I mean, did you suggest anything to her?"

"I told her to take the course from another teacher. But that wasn't my idea. I didn't know you could do that. I never went to college. Francey told me to tell her that. And Francey told her too. And so she did. This semester she was in a Mr., a Mr., my God, I can't even think of his name."

"Farrell?"

"That's him. She liked him. She said she got along very well with him. She said he was very understanding. Nothing like the other one, that Keenan."

"And she never talked about having problems like that again?"

"No. Oh well, she had problems. But we knew what those were. Like her shorthand course. She used to worry that she couldn't keep up with the others, but I told her, my God, don't worry about that. Do the best you can. We have girls in our office making four hundred dollars a month, and they can't take shorthand at all. And their typing is terrible. And she could type very well. I said that's all you need. Don't worry. But she worried . . ."

"You said you knew what her other problems were," Johnson said. "What were they, aside from the one you just mentioned."

"Well, mostly the big problem. Coming out of herself, getting over that mess with the accident. . . . I remember she called us one night, and she said she was sick. And when I asked her how, she said it was because another girl got hit in the nose in her gym class, and the girl's nose started to bleed, and Janet said she passed out. And I said there was nothing wrong with that if she felt okay then. She said she did, so I wanted to know what was wrong, and all she could say was, 'Mommy, mommy.' She sounded awful. Just like a little girl. And it took me a couple minutes to figure it out, that she must've seen her mother like that in the car. . . . I asked her if she wanted me to come to be with her, but she said she was all right. She just had to tell somebody. And that was the only time she ever said anything about the accident . . ."

Balzic blew out a heavy sigh and wished that Toni Rosario was there to hear this.

"See," Pisula said, suddenly very animated, "I was convinced then that she had never been as badly injured as those doctors had said. Because if she had been hurt that bad, that would've meant to me that the coma she was in began in the car, that she had been knocked unconscious in the collision. But if she has a memory of seeing her mother's face with blood on it, maybe coming out of her nose, then . . ." His voice faded and he became still.

"Are the doctors who worked on her still around?" Balzic said.

"No. The one who did the surgery, Henderson, he's dead. He died years ago. The others, I'd have to look up their names in my records. But they were all old men then."

"Anything else, Mr. Pisula? Anything at all, anything she said about anybody?"

Pisula shook his head and closed his eyes. "My God," he cried out, "if there was anything, don't you think I'd tell you!"

"Easy, Mr. Pisula, easy," Johnson said. "That's enough questions. There's just one more thing, and God knows I hate to do it to you, but it has to be done." Johnson turned to Balzic, but Balzic shook his head and stepped quickly to the water cooler, still shaking his head as he filled a paper cup and drank. Nothing in the world could have made him go along with that man to watch as he identified the body. The sound of hell was the voices of the next of kin in a morgue—Balzic knew that in his bones. And he did not need to be reminded of it again tonight. . . .

Balzic hunched himself into a corner of Johnson's office, the letters of Frances Milocky to Janet Pisula in his lap, smoking and sipping coffee, trying to piece together the picture he was getting of Janet Pisula. All the pieces said "victim," but Balzic was uncomfortable with the pieces. Yet the more he read Frances Milocky's letters—there were thirty-one of them—the more sure he was that the pieces would form the pattern of a victim than that they would not.

What contributed most to the pattern of a victim he was getting about Janet Pisula was that of the first ten letters to her from the Milocky girl every one closed with the same words: "A lively understandable spirit once entertained you. It will come again. Be still. Wait." The words were always the same, always in quotation marks, and always the last words above Frances Milocky's signature.

Balzic went through those ten letters again before he got any clear thought why those words should not only add to the pieces making a picture of a victim but should actually become the frame for it. It was the advice of a doctor to a patient. "Be still. Wait." Be patient. A patient, Balzic had heard from a doctor once while he waited to visit someone in a hospital, was called a patient because he was waiting for someone else to heal him. "That's why doctors make such lousy patients," the doctor had said. "They have no patience—not that kind anyway." The doctor had not smiled when he said it. Balzic tried to think of that doctor's name, but knew that he had never known it. His recollection was part of a conversation between strangers. . . .

In the eleventh letter, the same words in quotation appeared, but were followed by more, these set down in the form of poetry:

> *The world is for the living. Who are they?*
> *We dared the dark to reach the white and warm.*

She was the wind when wind was in my way;
Alive at noon, I perished in her form.
Who rise from flesh to spirit know the fall;
The word outleaps the world, and light is all.

"Jesus Christ," Balzic said, and the three men from Johnson's squad who were going through the rest of Janet Pisula's papers and notebooks looked up expectantly.

"Find something?" one of them asked.

"Nah," Balzic replied. "Just some stuff my daughters would call real heavy."

Of the letters Balzic had read, most contained the usual exchange of information he expected to find: descriptions of Frances Milocky's room, her roommates, complaints about her roommates' bathroom habits, harangues about studying to be done, books to be read, assignments to do, grades anticipated and received—everything except even the most casual reference to a boy. Frances Milocky seemed scrupulous about avoiding it.

It wasn't until the twelfth letter that a man was even mentioned, and that was a brief paragraph about how considerate Janet's uncle ". . . had been to think of it." Whatever "it" is, Balzic thought.

In the thirteenth letter, dated December 1, near the end Frances Milocky wrote: "I hope you'll take my advice. Just don't even think about the worm. Any man who has to use that tactic to motivate anybody has got to be warped. Do what we talked about over Thanksgiving. Do it please, Janet. For your sake. I give you my word, he'll never know the difference." Then came the line about the "lively understandable spirit," followed by some of the poetry from the earlier letter.

In the fourteenth letter, dated December 9: "Quit feeling guilty about doing that, Jan. There's no need to. Really. People do that here all the time. They pay lots more than you're paying, believe me. There are people here who make a living from it. It's as much a part of this place as pot. Nobody even wonders about whether it's done; all they wonder about is whether they should

68

do it, though of course they also wonder if they can afford it. But for God's sake, quit feeling guilty about it. Next semester you'll be all right, as soon as you're out of Keenan's class. Just be sure to get to registration early enough so you won't have to take him again. Registration here is pure chaos. It can't possibly be as bad where you are."

In the fifteenth, dated December 14: "See, dummy, what did I tell you? I told you he wouldn't know the difference. What counts is you still got the grade. And what do you care anyway? Besides, if he had suspected something, don't you think he would've called you in and said something about it? He probably thinks he made some kind of giant progress. From the way you talked about him Thanksgiving, I'd say he has to have the biggest ego in the western world. He's probably telling all his colleagues (don't you just hate it when they call each other that?) that he's really Super Teacher. Can't you just see him? He goes into the faculty-lounge john, rips off his corduroy jacket, and comes flying out in a cap and gown with a big red S on his chest—Super Prof! I'll bet he wears bikini shorts."

I wouldn't take twenty to one against that, Balzic thought.

The sixteenth, dated December 18: "Just a note, Jan. I have to hurry. Going to Scranton with Diane. See you on the 20th." It was the first letter in which the line about the "lively understandable spirit" and the poetry did not appear.

In the seventeenth, dated January 8: "Jan, why do you do that to yourself? I mean, really, there's no point. It's such a waste. If you hadn't done it, you would've flunked for certain. And what difference does it make to Uncle Mike? How can he be hurt by something he doesn't know? And who's going to tell him? You? Do you think I would? Jan, only three people know, and two of us don't want to hurt anyone, especially not Uncle Mike, and why would the third person have any reason? Everything he does depends on maintaining your confidence, otherwise he's out of business. Sometimes you make me so crazy I could scream. Just please put those dumb ideas out of your head because, Jan, please believe me, they are dumb. You've been paranoid long enough. We both know that, and we both know you had every right to feel paranoid. But not about this. There just isn't any reason. How many times have we talked about how your paranoia slips over? We've talked about it too many times to count, and I really thought you were getting over that part of it. Maybe you'll never get over all of it, but at least tell yourself that the original reason for it was valid but that all the others aren't. I know. It sounds so easy for me to say, but I can't help it. It is easy for me to say because for me it is easy. Please don't take this wrong, okay? Remember? 'Who rise from flesh to spirit know the fall'? Think about it some more, okay?"

The eighteenth through the twenty-fifth letters contained nothing out of the ordinary. Everything in them was usual, cordial gossip. In the twenty-sixth, dated April 11, Balzic found this postscript: "As for what we talked about last week, all I can do is repeat what I said. Just keep thinking that you only have to put up with him a couple more weeks."

In the twenty-seventh, dated April 17, again in a postscript: "As for you know who, you have to learn to deal with people like that, Jan, that's all there is to it. I know it can get icky, and I'm not half as hung up about this sort of thing as you are. But you have to get tough. Otherwise, people will be stepping on your mind forever. You've been stepped on enough. Come on, Jan, toughen up!"

The twenty-eighth through the thirtieth letters were gossipy, girlish, drifting occasionally into something about schoolwork that was bothering one or the other but with no sense of urgency. All ended with some poetry. The thirty-first, and last, letter wasn't that much different. There was just one short passage referring to ". . . you know who." Frances Milocky wrote: "Some people give you things and if you aren't careful you'll give everything you have to them. But you owe him nothing!!!! Don't forget that, okay?"

Balzic put aside the stack of letters, took out his notebook, and copied from one of them all of the poetry. Then he put the letters in a manila envelope, marked them, and handed the envelope to one of the three troopers still going through the rest of the papers. He stretched, stifled a yawn, and looked at his watch. Two A.M. He felt suddenly very tired, and he thought the best thing he could do was go home and go to bed. He started out of the office but heard footsteps coming down the hall and waited, leaning against the doorframe.

Johnson came in, looking drained, shaking his head.

"How'd it go, Walk?"

"Shit, Grimes lifted the sheet and that poor bastard went down like somebody hit him in the head with a brick."

"Is he okay?"

"Hell, I thought he had a heart attack, but they got him into intensive care and wired him up to one of those EKGs. The head nurse said it looked normal, but they're still going to keep him until tomorrow anyway . . . man, those nurses in that outfit are really something. You know how old the head nurse was? Twenty-six, and she looked like seventeen."

"Yeah, I know. That's some group they got there. All of them are young. Did, uh, Grimes say anything else?"

"He pegged it down to last Wednesday night. That's as close as he can get."

"You get anything else out of Pisula?"

"Enough. 'Course I didn't want to pressure him. He did tell me how much money he gave the girl. Twenty-five a week, which I thought was a hell of a lot until he said she had to eat out every meal. He also said she went home every weekend—"

"Couldn't have been."

"What do you mean?"

"She couldn't have gone home every weekend, otherwise why didn't they say something last weekend—when she didn't show?"

"You didn't let me finish," Johnson said.

"Oh. So go ahead."

"The reason she didn't go home last weekend was because she told him she wanted to study for her finals. As a matter of fact, she called home last Wednesday afternoon and told him she'd

71

decided to stay the weekend, which would have been her first, and he said he was happy about it. He said he had it measured how well she was getting along by how often she called home. The first month he said she called every day, sometimes twice. Then, he said, little by little, she got to the point where she was only calling once a week. He also said he and his wife made it a point never to call her. And that's about all I got out of him."

"Well," Balzic said, "there's some letters in that envelope on your desk you ought to read. From that Milocky girl who's supposed to be her best friend. There's a guy in it, that's for sure. But no names. Just Keenan's a couple times, and unless I read them all wrong, he's not the guy." That said, he started for the door. He suddenly had to get out of the room. He couldn't say why, and he didn't want to stand around explaining.

"Where you going?" Johnson said.

"I think I'll hit Muscotti's for a couple cold ones, and then I'm going home. My ass is draggin'."

"Don't you want to go through the rest of her stuff?"

"What for? Christ, you got three guys doing that. What do you want me around for?"

"I just thought you might want to stick around. What's the matter? You look edgy as hell."

"I don't know. Maybe all this efficiency scares me. It's hot. I'm tired. You don't do any good when you're beat. I'll call you in the morning." He left before Johnson could say anything else.

He wasn't sure at first what had driven him out of Johnson's office. All he knew was that he had to get out. He sat in his cruiser for a couple of minutes before turning the ignition, telling himself that he probably shouldn't look too carefully at the cause of his leaving the way he did, but he knew that something drove him out and that that something ought to be looked at.

He was halfway to Muscotti's when he got down to it, and he had to laugh out loud at himself. He knew he'd have to be careful who he told about it, otherwise he might have to turn in his shield and resign from the Fraternal Order of Police. There was only one way for him to say it honestly: he really could not stand being around Pennsylvania State Police.

He knew it didn't have anything to do with any one of them or with anything that any one of them had ever done to him. He took them as they came. It had to do with the gray color of their uniforms and the words that came to mind when he tried to describe that color. Anybody else might simply have said their shirts were light gray and their trousers dark gray. But Balzic thought of their shirts as being the color of shale and their trousers the color of slate. Shale and slate—the words a coal miner would use to describe them. No wonder he could not be around them for long. . . .

Inside Muscotti's, Albert Margiotti, Dom Muscotti's son-in-law, was tending the bar and drawing a beer for Father Marrazo who sat in his poker clothes massaging his temples.

"S'matter, Father," Balzic said, "little early for you to be out of the game. It's not even quarter after two."

"I have a headache, Mario. I think it's my sinus. How are you?"

"Okay, I guess. That beer's not going to help your head."

"Naturally not," the priest said.

"Then you—"

The priest swiveled around on his stool and held up his hands. "Mario, please. A homily from you—as much as I like you and you know I do—but please, no homiletics. I'm drinking this beer out of spite for my head. Every man is entitled to spite himself once in a while, ridiculous as it may seem, if for no other reason than just to remind himself at times that he is ridiculous."

"Wow," Balzic said, shaking his hand limply from the wrist with the fingers together. "Give me a beer, Albert. And I got the Father's."

Albert put his hands on the bar and looked at his shoes. "Hey, Mario, uh, Dom asked me to ask you about your tab."

"Ask me about my what?"

"Uh, your tab, Mario—and hey, Mario, please don't come down on me, okay? You know I don't even like this job. I'm just helping the old man out, and if he tells me to ask somebody something, I ask, that's all. I don't want no grief over it. I got enough just being here."

"Hey," Balzic said, leaning on the bar, "you tell that old friggin' Tuscan to ask that skin-head Calabrez who works day-light what he did with the thirty-seven-fifty I handed him Memorial Day morning? You got it?"

"I got it, Mario. Okay? Just remember, I'm just asking, that's all."

"And you remember I'm just telling."

"Mario, not so loud," Father Marrazo said. "My head, remember?"

"Hey, Father, I don't mean to be loud, but goddammit I been drinking in this saloon since 1946, and since 1946 I been running a tab and I never walked him yet. I don't mind Vinnie ragging me about it. That's a standing joke between him and me, but this ain't the first time Vinnie took my tab and played it six bucks around on a number. And Dom knows that. You get what I mean, Father? And I don't like Dom asking Albert to ask me. Dom wants to know, he knows who to ask. This go-through-your-relatives is strictly bullshit, Father."

"Mario. Please," the priest said, rubbing his nose with his index fingers.

"Okay, Father, okay. I'm done." He looked at Albert. "So what're you gonna do, Albert? Do I get a beer or not?"

Albert drew the beer and set it in front of Balzic and then went to a cigar box under the cash register and wrote some figures on a piece of paper taken from the box.

"Thank you, Albert. How's your wife?"

"She's okay. Feeling a lot better."

"Good. Glad to hear that. Tell her I said hello."

Albert nodded. "Mario, you know—"

Balzic held up his hand. "Say no more. You're out of it."

Albert backed away and busied himself filling the beer coolers.

Balzic drank his beer without pause and motioned to Albert to draw another. He sipped the second and said, "I guess I should apologize, Father, for being loud, but to say it straight, I don't feel like it. I'm in a pretty foul mood—"

"I'll drink to that," the priest said.

"—from being around those state cops. Driving over here I was thinking about why I can't stay around them for very long. Yeah. Me. Who'd believe it? I have to work with them all the time. But I can only put up with being around them so long. And I know why, too. Which makes it even goofier."

"You are in a foul mood."

"The thing is, I'm not really. Most of the time I don't show anybody, that's all. I manage to keep it covered—usually. But sometimes things haunt you, and you can't keep them covered anymore. I mean, you can still cover them from other people, but you can't cover them from yourself. Like tonight, I was around all these state guys and I was looking at their uniforms, the color, and the words that kept coming into my head were shale and slate. Coal miners' words. And—ah, this is a load. You don't want to hear this."

"Go ahead and say it. Get it out."

"It's not important. Doesn't matter a damn to anybody."

"All right," the priest said. "I won't coax you."

Balzic stared at his beer, running his finger up and down the side of the glass. "We found a girl tonight, Father. Up in the Summer house. Been dead since last Wednesday. Strangled. And I'm really involved with that since maybe ten, ten-thirty, and all of a sudden, I can't stand to be in the same room with state guys. And one of them is a very good friend of mine. And you know why?"

The priest shook his head.

"My father is buried in Edna Number Two. Summer's mine."

75

"Your father?" the priest said. "You never said anything about that before. I don't know why that surprises me, but it does."

"I was three years old. I have no memory of him at all. None. I mean, except what my mother told me. And tonight, just being there, it's funny how I managed to put that out of my head until three or four hours later when I find myself in a room with four state guys . . . you know, my mother had a real fit when I told her I was going to be a cop. She wouldn't talk to me for two or three days. And I couldn't understand it. I kept asking her what was so bad about being a cop, and she wouldn't say a word. And when she finally did decide to talk to me again, the first thing she said —I'll never forget it—she said, 'If your father was here, he'd spit in your face and throw you out.' The look on her face, God . . ."

"Did he hate cops that much?"

"He was a miner, Father, and all he knew when he was in the mines was the Iron and Coal Police, the Pinkertons, and the Pennsylvania Constabulary. The Pennsylvania Constabulary became the state police. You know what the miners used to call them? The Black Cossacks. I thought my mother was exaggerating, but I did a lot of reading about it in the big Carnegie Library in Pittsburgh. There's another joke for you. I had to read about it in a library set up by one of the most heartless bastards who ever lived. But I found it, pictures and all. You ought to read about that time in this part of the state, Father. It's unbelievable.

"But anyway," Balzic went on, "it all came back to me tonight, and I thought I was going to choke in that room with those state guys. How's that? I felt like I was going to choke. That's what happened to the girl. What do the psychologists call that?"

"Identification? Is that what you mean?"

"Yeah. Something like that. The mind's a hell of a thing. Always surprises me the way it jumps around on you—course, I just might not be too bright."

"Oh, Mario, I doubt whether most people would have the

76

honesty to question themselves about the way they were feeling. Now I understand."

"Understand what?"

"Why you reacted the way you did over your tab, over being asked to do something you'd already done."

"I'm not sure I want to know," Balzic said, motioning to Albert to draw two more beers. "Let's forget me for a while, Father. You read a lot, right?"

"That depends what you mean by a lot."

"Skip the modesty, Father. We both know you read a lot of books, especially psychology. Most of what I know about it, I got it first from you."

The priest shrugged.

"That girl we found tonight—another thing just came to me."

"What's that?"

"Why I made that identification with her."

"Why?"

"The more people I asked about her—except for her uncle —the less anybody could say about her. It's almost the same way with my old man and me. Lots of people knew him, but damn few can tell me anything that gives me a real feel of him, you know what I mean? It's the same with the girl . . . anyway, the thing I wanted to ask you about is this: she had a blank sheet of paper on her stomach. She's naked except for her panties, she's strangled with her brassiere, and according to the coroner, she was still a virgin. But what about that piece of paper, Father? What do you make of that?"

"I don't know. There's nothing on it? It's blank?"

"Nothing at all. And it was her paper. She also wasn't robbed. I'll tell you, it is the goddamndest thing I've ever come across."

"What do you make of it?"

Balzic shook his head. "I don't have the first idea. Neither does Johnson."

"Who? I don't know him."

"He's an old buddy of mine. He's a lieutenant in charge of CID until that asshole Minyon gets out of the hospital."

"What's wrong with him?"

"Ulcers or something. I wouldn't cry if he died."

The back door opened slowly, and, hat and tie askew, eyelids drooping, the left sleeve of his blue blazer ripped at the shoulder, Mo Valcanas shuffled in, singing in a way that only every third or fourth word could be heard.

"Holy hell," Balzic said. "What war'd you lose?"

"None of your goddamn business," Valcanas said. "Just direct me to the head. I have to speak to the ship's captain. Ship's company needs liberty."

"The head's the same place it's always been," Balzic said. "If you don't know where it is now, as many times as you've been in it."

"I'll be a sonuvabitch," Valcanas said. "Muscotti's. Didn't recognize the place. Now hell the how'd—how the hell'd I get here?"

"I hope you didn't drive."

"Who are you? Lou Harris? What do you care how I got here? Oh, it's you, Mario. Should've known. Well, pardon me while I relieve myself. In the meantime, before you arrest me for drunken walking, be advised to go pound sand. . . ."

Valcanas tottered toward the steps leading to the downstairs lavatory. The seat of his trousers and down to his knees was stained with blood.

"Hey, Mo," Balzic called out, "you got blood all over you."

"Wrong," Valcanas called up. "Usual for a cop. The blood is not *all* over me. It's restricted to the area immediate to and directly below my anus. My hemorrhoids cut loose. . . ."

Balzic looked at the priest and they shook their heads.

"What do you suppose happened to him?" Father Marrazo asked.

"Six'll get you five, Father, he smarted off at somebody a lot younger and a lot bigger. That's his style."

"With his intelligence—why?"

"My mother says some people have too much brains for their own good. That's Valcanas. He sees too good, hears too good, and he doesn't like what he sees or hears. That's about as near as I can figure him. Course, I don't try to figure him too much. I just take him the way he is and hope he stays out of trouble."

"It strikes me as a terrible waste."

"Oh, I don't know if I'd say that. I think he just doesn't like being sober—hell, what do I know? You want to know, ask him when he comes up. If he feels like it, he'll tell you. But if he doesn't, don't be offended if he tells you to take a flying trip to the moon."

"I won't be offended. I'll just feel sorry."

"Ouu, you better mean you'll be sorry for you. That's one thing I know he'll take your head off for, you give him a reason to think you feel sorry for him."

". . . oh say can you see, the Coast Guard at sea, through the fog, through the smog," Valcanas sang to the melody of the National Anthem as he weaved up the stairs and to a stool beside the priest.

"Don't stop now," Balzic said. "Let's hear the rest of it."

"I would," Valcanas said, grinning, "only I can't remember it. Innkeeper! A large whiskey and water. Canadian Club, if you please."

"Think you had enough, Mo," Albert said.

"I never met a bartender yet who could think. All they can do is add fast and everybody knows that doesn't take anything approaching thought. Pour the goddamn drink. I'll tell you when I've had enough."

Albert looked questioningly at Balzic.

"Go ahead," Balzic said. "Give it to him. He'll just go to sleep."

"Sleep, sleep. Valcanas hath murdered sleep . . . Valcanas doth murder sleep. Fuck you, sleep. You're dead. Bang. . . ."

"You, uh, read Shakespeare?" Father Marrazo said.

"Past tense. Read. I'm possibly the only person alive who

79

ever finished *Timon of Athens* to the last hideous line. I thought I was going to learn something about Greeks. What a crock. And if that isn't masochism for you, give me a better example." Valcanas took out his billfold and, licking his thumb, stripped out a five. "That's the purest form of masochism I know—reading *Timon of Athens* to the last goddamn line. Hey, aren't you Father Marrazo?"

The priest said he was.

"Well, good, 'cause I have a question for you. And be honest. Don't quote me some goddamn papal bull."

The priest smiled and shook his head.

"What's so funny about that?"

"Nothing."

"Then what the hell are you laughing for?"

"I was thinking of something."

"There, Mario. See? An honest priest. He admits to thinking. Better be careful, Father. You'll get drummed out of the corps for doing that. Oh, you can do it. You just gotta be careful who you tell."

"So what is your question?"

"Oh. And remember. An honest answer. Did Jesus ever fool around with Mary Magdalene?"

"Aw come on, Mo," Balzic said.

"Stay out of it. You'd've been there, you'd've busted her for assignation, solicitation, and you'd've probably tried to trump up an attempt to commit sodomy. Shut up a minute. I want to hear what the priest has to say."

"You really expect me to answer you?" Father Marrazo said.

"I don't ask questions unless I expect an answer. Did he or didn't he?"

"Well, going on the evidence of the scripture, I would say no."

"Okay, then tell me this: do you think he wanted to?"

"That I can't say," the priest said, smiling.

"Well in that holy trinity he was supposed to be, one-third of him was man, right?"

"Yes."

"And men have desires, don't they?"

"Yes. I suppose most men do."

"All men, Father. All men. You guys are just experts in conning yourselves that you don't."

"Okay, okay," the priest said, laughing.

"Then answer me. Did he desire ol' Mary Mag or not?"

"I can't say."

"Well shit, man, what do you think? I mean, I just got the hell kicked out of me by some wop football player who didn't like my saying that Jesus had to have some eyes for Mary Mag, otherwise he wouldn't have been so damn quick to forgive her. Now, did I get the hell beat out of me for nothing?"

"I'm afraid you did."

"Why?"

"Because any answer would be conjectural. There's nothing written about it one way or the other."

"Then the only other explanation for his forgiving her was nothing but goddamn arrogance. Who the hell was he to forgive any woman for trying to earn her living?"

"Boy, you really are cranked up," Balzic said.

"A hell of a lot of satisfaction I'm getting out of you two," Valcanas said.

"Let's change the subject, okay?" Balzic said. "I got something I want to ask you, Mo. You read a lot—"

"I haven't read four books since Christmas."

"You read enough. I know that. So tell me. Why does somebody kill somebody and leave a blank piece of paper on her stomach? What's the message?"

"Do what?"

"Why would somebody strangle a girl, not rape her, not rob her, and then leave a blank piece of paper on her stomach?"

"Where the hell did you hear that? Did this actually happen or is this supposed to be hypothetical?"

"I wish it was hypothetical. We found her tonight. She's been

81

dead at least nine days. Two people right across the hall from her and they didn't hear a peep."

"A piece of paper. With nothing on it?"

"Plain, ordinary typing paper. It belonged to the victim. And nothing on it."

Valcanas drained his glass and motioned to Albert to bring another drink. "That's the goddamndest thing I ever heard—oh, wait. Wait a minute. Right before Hemingway killed himself—the poor sonuvabitch—one of the last things he said to anybody, he was talking to his doctor. And he said something like, 'Doc, I can't make a sentence any more.' Something like that."

"So go ahead and make the connection," Balzic said.

"Well, he couldn't make a sentence. He couldn't write. He couldn't get it out of him. He couldn't get it on the page. And everytime you start, the page is always blank, right?"

"Right," Balzic said. "But he killed himself."

"Aw, come on, Mario. What the hell's suicide? It's self-murder. And murder's murder. It all depends which way the gun's pointed."

"Okay. So what you're saying is, it was a writer who couldn't write."

"Well, hell, that's just a guess. I mean, there were lots of other reasons Hemingway killed himself. He was sick, his liver was shot. He'd just had a couple trips to the Mayo brothers' hotel. Shock treatments, that bit. But I'm just telling you the last thing he said to anybody before he did it. The connection to that and what you're talking about seems pretty obvious, that's all I'm saying."

"Uh-huh," Balzic said, taking out his notebook. "Well, here. Listen to this. I want to hear what you two think of this. 'The world is for the living. Who are they? We dared the dark to reach the white and warm. She was the wind when wind was in my way; alive at noon, I perished in her form. Who rise from flesh to spirit know the fall; the word outleaps the world, and light is all.'"

"What the hell is this," Valcanas grumbled. "I feel like I'm on some goddamn quiz show for crissake."

"Just tell me what you think of it," Balzic said.

"Are you asking me what I think of it, or you asking me what I think it means?"

"Both, I guess."

"Well I'll tell you what I think of it. I think it was written by somebody who's a bigger goddamn manic-depressive than I am —and that's going some," Valcanas said.

"Doesn't mean anything else to you?"

"What the fuck you want? I come in here all chopped up and you start reading things at me. Christ, I didn't even know I was here when I got here. Still don't."

"What about you, Father? What do you think?"

"I'd have to agree with Mo, at least partly. It certainly sounds like somebody had a very bad time of it and then pulled himself together a little too euphorically."

"I'll drink to that," Valcanas said. "What was that one part again—who rise from what to what?"

" 'Who rise from flesh to spirit know the fall,' " Balzic read.

"Christ, that's a roller-coaster ride if I ever heard one. Even got the rhythm for it. Down up, down up, down up, Jesus. Where the hell'd you get that anyway?"

"I found it in a bunch of letters to the dead girl."

"Well, if somebody was trying to cheer her up, they sure picked some heavy artillery to do it with. Christ, I hear any more of that I'll have a relapse right here—what the hell are you doing making me think about crap like that anyway? All I wanted to do was stay fogged in. I didn't want to think about anything."

"You drink to avoid thinking?" Father Marrazo asked.

"Now you got it, padre. If you think, don't drink. If you drink, don't think. Christ, I should've been an ad man . . . have a Canadian Club adventure, go everywhere and never move off a bar stool. Walter Mitty was really a lush . . ."

"That reminds me of something," the priest said. "I remember reading about a study done by some psychiatrist that of all America's Nobel prize winners in literature, only one, Pearl Buck, wasn't a heavy drinker or an alcoholic. O'Neill, Sinclair Lewis,

Hemingway, Steinbeck, and, oh, who was the other one?"

"Faulkner," Valcanas said. "Champion of them all. He made his own when he couldn't afford it. And that, padre, is true dedication to the pursuit of oblivion. Life, liberty, and the pursuit of oblivion. Liberty, equality, oblivion . . . up everybody's." That said, Valcanas drained his glass and tottered toward the door.

"Hey, Mo, " Balzic called after him, "you're not going to drive, are you?"

"Hell, no. I'm going to my office. I have a cot in the cellar. Maybe there'll be an earthquake."

"Well throw your keys here then."

"Then how do I get into my office? Break a window? Then one of your clowns busts me for breaking and entering."

"Just your car keys."

"Oh, will you quit acting like somebody's goddamn mother. I told you I'm not driving for crissake. It's only two blocks from here. Since when do I have to listen to this horseshit—concern for my safety, Jesus . . ."

"I'm not concerned about your goddamn safety," Balzic said, but before he could say more, Valcanas had bounced off both door and frame and shuffled out.

Father Marrazo shook his head. "I still say it's a waste."

"If it's a waste, Father, I don't know what it's a waste of. I've seen him in court just slightly less juiced, making jerks out of assistant D.A.'s. Why don't you talk to one of them about it?"

Balzic left the priest sometime between three thirty and four, he didn't know exactly when. At home, he prowled back and forth between the living room and the kitchen, drinking cans of beer and eating a sandwich he'd made from crusty provolone, eating the sandwich to satisfy his hunger though it tasted flat as old provolone always does. He threw the last bit away, telling himself that it was a sin to waste food but a bigger sin to insult the stomach. By five thirty he was standing in the kitchen, looking out the window at the birds and squirrels waking, the birds bursting by his window like black darts and the squirrels rushing up and down the maples and diving from the sturdy, stiffer branches of the maples to the whippy, pencil-thin branches of the Chinese elm hedges Balzic used to plan to trim but never did. The hedges and the lilacs he'd planted in front of them formed a nearly opaque wall for most of the year, and what pleased Balzic most about that was that now the neighbors could only guess at how much he loafed. It had taken years for the hedges to grow as thick as they had, but it had only been in the last few years that Balzic felt he could loaf in peace without hearing later on from God knew who about how he stood around with his hands in his pockets when he should have been out rounding up the beasties and nasties and things that went bump.

The neighbors, Balzic snorted thoughtfully. He had to ask himself what their names were. He couldn't think of it. Yurkowski, Yurhoska, something like that. Good solid squares, scared shitless of niggers, dope heads, commies, rabid dogs, girls who went without brassieres, and people who made love with the lights on. His mother told him that about them. They were always complaining to his mother, and every once in a while, when she couldn't think up something new to put them off, she came to him and complained about them. The last time, a couple of months ago, he'd told his mother, "Ma, if I lock up everybody they're scared of, who's left? I'd have to lock up the world." To which his mother had replied impishly, "You big man, you no can do that?"

He turned away from the window and was startled to see his mother standing in the doorway of the kitchen. She was in her flannel gown, barefoot, her swollen ankles showing under the hem, her fingers over her mouth. She looked like she'd been standing there for some moments.

"Hey, kiddo, you still up. You sick?" Her voice was husky with sleep.

"I'm okay," he said. "What're you doing up?"

"I ask you first."

"I said I'm okay. Just didn't feel like sleeping. What about you?"

"Ahh, same thing. Ankles hurt like crazy. Back, too. I think I sleep on floor from now on. You want light?"

"Yeah. Go ahead, turn it on."

She flipped the switch by her shoulder and the overhead fluorescent hummed and then slowly filled the room with its bluish light. His mother sat at the kitchen table and rubbed one ankle with the other. "Hey, Mario," she said, squinting up at him, "what you decide?"

"About what?"

"Oh boy, you forget already?"

Balzic frowned. "I guess I did. What was I supposed to remember?"

"The cottage. You and Ruth and the girls and me. Next week. Tony's cottage. You forget to decide?"

"Oh that." Balzic sighed and rubbed his eyes. "Ma, I was thinking about it. I really was. But something came up and I quit thinking about it. It doesn't look like I'll be able to go anyway even if I wanted to."

"But you don't want. You still no like Tony. What for? What's he do for you? How come? Ruth very disappoint. Her only brother, Mario. All she got left. And you don't like."

"I know, Ma, I know. I can't help it. I just don't like the guy. I never did. I'm sorry he's all she got left out of her family. I wish she didn't have . . ." He let it hang there, wishing he hadn't said even the start of it.

"Oh, Mario. Not nice. Not nice what you was thinking."

Balzic looked away from her and yawned and rubbed his cheeks briskly. "I know it's not nice to think like that, Ma, but I can't help it."

"Mario, no kid around. What's he really do for you, you no like?"

"Ma, don't ask me, okay? It's embarrassing to talk about."

"So he really do something for you. Why you no tell Ruth? Why you never tell me before? Save lotsa trouble, kiddo."

"Ma, believe me, it would cause more trouble than it saves. I know what I'm talking about. Besides, I think it would probably be better if just you and Ruth and the kids went. The river doesn't really do all that much for me anyway."

"Oh, Mario, think how much cooler goin' to be there."

"All right, listen. I'll think about it some more, okay?"

"Hokay, I don't say nothing no more, but you got to say something to Ruth. She wants to know you goin' or not. Kids too. They looking forward, Mario. You know they goin' be swim all summer with that team. They no have more chance after next week." She stood, then winced and felt her lower back and had to hold the edge of the table to steady herself.

Balzic reached out to help her, but she shook her head.

"It's hokay," she said. "Just stiff. I think I go sleep on floor in living room. Don't step on me, hokay, kiddo? Good night."

He said good night and watched her go, still tilted forward from the waist, her feet flat on each step. He scratched his shoulders and wondered why he could not bring himself to tell her why he didn't want to spend a weekend at his brother-in-law's cottage on the Allegheny River. If she kept pressing him about it, he was going to have to tell her and Ruth something. They deserved some explanation, but he knew that when he finally got the nerve to give them one he was going to have to make it good. He arched his back and stared up at the ceiling. Shit, he thought. They'll see through anything I come up with. I'm going to have to lay it out, and is Ruth going to love that. Is she ever . . .

He tip-toed into the bedroom and started to undress. He was down to his socks and underwear when he thought to set the alarm. He set it for nine, hoping he'd hear it but knowing that he wouldn't, and then hoping that Ruth would know he'd set it for a reason and get him up.

He edged into bed beside her and stretched out. The last thing he remembered seeing on the insides of his eyelids was a blank piece of paper on the middle seat of an empty rowboat floating in slow circles past his brother-in-law's cottage. His mother and Ruth and Emily were standing in front of the cottage. Their faces were all confusion, the beginnings of panic. His brother-in-law was on the opposite shore, laughing obscenely

87

and pointing at the skiff with his middle finger. Nobody seemed to know where Marie was; worse, nobody seemed to be doing anything about finding out where she was. Then he saw himself, standing on a sandbar in his underwear and socks. He had a pencil in his hand and he looked like he was trying to find something to write on. . . .

Balzic never heard the alarm. What he thought was the alarm was the phone ringing, and when he rolled over to shut the alarm and saw that it was a quarter after one, he bolted out of bed and hustled out to the kitchen phone, rubbing his eyes, scratching his belly, and swearing.

He picked up the phone and saw the note on the kitchen table in the same instant. He said, "Wait a minute," into the phone and picked up the note and read it. "Mario, I've taken Ma and the girls shopping. Didn't wake you when the alarm went off because you were really snoring and looked like you needed the sleep. Hope I didn't mess you up. Be back around three. Love, Ruth."

"I didn't get you up, did I?" Lieutenant Johnson said. "I mean, the last thing I want to do is fuck up your rest."

"Okay, okay. I'm up. So now what?"

"Well, listen, if you can tear yourself away from that bed, I'd appreciate your help. I'm getting a blister from dialing the phone."

"What, you don't have people there?"

"Hell yes, I have people. Four of my people and three county guys. But they're all getting blisters too. We've only made about a hundred and three phone calls."

"About a hundred and three, huh," Balzic said. He sighed, coughed, brought up some phlegm, and leaned over and spit it into the kitchen sink, turning on the water in the same motion. "Listen. Give me twenty minutes. Just let me get cleaned up and get some coffee."

"Don't get too pretty. It's not your face I need. It's your finger. And we have all the coffee you want right here."

"You got my finger, friend," he said. "The middle one." He hung up before Johnson could retort, and twenty minutes later, with a patch of toilet paper congealed to a cut on his chin, he walked into the duty room of Troop A Barracks.

The air was heavy with cigar and cigarette smoke and the smell of both hot and cold coffee. Balzic nodded to the state men he knew by sight and to the three county detectives, Frank Rusa, John Dillman, and Tony Funari. Johnson appeared out of another office with both hands full of papers and started passing them around.

"Well," he said, "let's see if we can get the other twenty-seven." Seeing Balzic, he said, "Morning, sunshine. I thought you said you were going to get cleaned up."

"Save the smart mouth till somebody makes a movie about you," Balzic said. "Just tell me where's the coffee."

Johnson nodded to a table in the corner, and Balzic went to it and poured himself a cup from the large urn. "Well," he said, "what do you got?"

"I don't know whether you're ready for this," Johnson said. "The thing is, I don't know if I'm ready for it. But here it is. There are one hundred and three people who were in one of four classes with the girl. So far, we've called all of them but we contacted, uh, seventy-six. Of the seventy-six—you hear this?—only fifteen remember ever even hearing her name. And of those fifteen, six were fairly sure they could put a name with a face. And of those six, only two ever remember talking to her, and those were the two who sat on either side of her in her shorthand class."

"And naturally," Balzic said, "all they remember talking about is what they had to do for the next class."

"Oh, one of them had a hell of a conversation with her one day. She asked her if she had an extra pen, and the Pisula girl said, and I quote, 'Yes.' "

"How the hell's that possible?" Balzic said, sipping his coffee.

"Well don't forget what her uncle said about her being scared stiff of strangers."

"Well shit, somebody had to say something to her. I mean, goddamn . . ."

"The newspaper still only come out six days here?" Johnson asked.

"Yeah. No Sundays. What'd you give them?"

"Everything I had, plus a plea for cooperation from anybody who might've seen anything. That was about ten this morning."

"That means it won't be in until Monday. Shit." Balzic sloshed his coffee around. "I been meaning to ask you. What's the word on the Milocky girl?"

"I got her mother around nine this morning. She expects her home sometime today, but she doesn't know when 'cause she's riding with somebody. The mother wasn't even sure when the girl's supposed to leave."

"You tell her mother?"

"I couldn't very well not tell her. People hear from a cop, they want to know something."

"Shit."

"What's the matter? Why the 'shit'?"

"Well, you read those letters. You heard what Pisula said. Those two were close. More than close. I hope she doesn't get the scrupulosities when she hears what happened and do something dumb."

"The what?"

"The scrupulosities. The guilties. That's what the priests call them when they get the people who run to confession after they crossed against a traffic light or got a parking ticket. Some people run to a priest, some run to a friend, some run to a psychiatrist, some of them just run."

"I thought you were the one who said not to think about all the things that could go wrong."

"Hey, Walk, she's it as far as I can see. If she can't tell us, nobody can. And when you get a situation like that, when you get two people and one of them doesn't have any trouble making it and the other one does, and the one who does breaks away from the one who doesn't—especially in this situation. The Milocky girl tells the other one to enroll here and then enrolls someplace else and then this happens—Christ, that's a dynamite situation. It might be that for the first time in their lives the situations are reversed."

"I'm not sure I follow," Johnson said.

"Well, all along, it's the Milocky girl who's the prop. She's holding up the Pisula girl. Now the Milocky girl needs a prop, and maybe the real jolt is going to be for her to find out she needs one. And then, what if there's nobody around? I mean, just for the simple reason she never thought she might need one, so she never looked for one—how about that?"

"Yeah, I see what you're getting at, but I don't necessarily think she's it for us. We still have a lot of lab reports to come in. We really don't know what we have."

"Which means you also don't know what you don't have either." Balzic chewed the inside of his lower lip and reached for a phone book.

"Who you looking up?"

"That Keenan. The one who's chairman of the English department."

"Why? I thought you said he was a real ballbuster."

"I'm not sure. I'd like to talk to him when he isn't half-juiced. Besides, I'm not cut out to sit around dialing phones. I hate fuckin' telephones. All you get is the voice. I want to see the face." Balzic found Malcolm Keenan's home address and made a note of it. He started for the door with a wave to Johnson.

"Well. Let me know," Johnson said.

"Yeah, sure," Balzic said, and went out to his cruiser and headed east to the Rocksburg city line and the beginning of Westfield Township.

Keenan's house, two-storied, covered with white aluminum, was situated on a sloping lot at the corner of Route 286 and Westfield Avenue. Though the township had recently annexed the land, the house and lot still had the complexion of the city, with sidewalks on two sides, an alley in the rear, a mailbox on a utility pole at the corner, and a fire hydrant in the middle of the block.

The house was old and boxy. Fifty years earlier it might have been built by one of Rocksburg's more prosperous businessmen; now, the white aluminum siding made it appear prim at the same time the taped window in the storm door made it appear as though the owners were indifferent to property. Balzic was reminded immediately of Keenan spilling the last drops of a drink on his corduroy jacket.

Balzic knocked on the storm door and was greeted by a large, collie-like mongrel which had been sleeping on the other side of the door and could not make up its mind whether to bark an alarm or wag its tail. It did both.

The door let into the kitchen, and from around a corner appeared a woman Balzic recalled seeing at the party at Dr. Beverley's house, the woman in the very short silver lamé dress.

She spoke through the screened upper third of the door. "Yes?" Before Balzic could reply she said, "Oh, it's you."

"Yes, it's me. Your husband here? I'd like to talk to him."

She hesitated, then said, "Won't you come in." The voice was Southern, possibly from North or South Carolina. She held the door open for Balzic and reached for the dog's collar to pull it back. "She'll jump all over you," she said, smiling nervously first at the dog and then at Balzic.

"As long as she jumps friendly, I don't mind."

"Oh my Lord, yes. She's spoiled rotten and thinks everybody who comes, comes just to see her. Won't you sit down? May I get you something cool to drink before I tell Mal you're here?"

Balzic sat and let the dog sniff at his shoes and legs. "A glass of water would be fine."

Balzic watched Mrs. Keenan moving from cupboard to refrigerator to sink. She was taller than Balzic had remembered, and like many tall women she tended to slouch. She seemed to be moving quickly, but for some reason Balzic couldn't figure she also seemed to be taking a long time to get him the glass of water.

When Malcolm Keenan appeared around the corner, Balzic thought he understood. Keenan was nearly as drunk as he'd been when Balzic met him at the door of the Beverley's house, and Mrs. Keenan was doing her best to avoid looking at him. When she set the glass of water in front of Balzic, she didn't look at Balzic either.

"Yesss?" Keenan said, scowling as though he'd been interrupted in the middle of something extremely important.

"Sorry to bother you," Balzic said and was cut short.

"You have already bothered me," Keenan said.

"Mal!" Mrs. Keenan said.

"Is he a friend of yours, or am I not permitted to know that?" Keenan said, breathing deeply twice and trying not to weave.

"It's the chief of police, Mal. You talked to him last night. At some length. About a very serious thing—or don't you remember that either?"

Keenan focused on Balzic and seemed to make the association and then broke into a loud, staccato laugh, throwing back his head. "Surely," he said. "I was just rehearsing."

"Rehearsing?" Balzic said, watching their faces. Mrs. Keenan looked on the edge of tears, though whether it was from anger or humiliation Balzic couldn't guess. Probably both. Keenan tried to look sincere but could not bring it off. He excused himself, disappeared around the corner, and returned, rattling ice cubes in a tumbler. He opened a cabinet under the sink, took out a bottle of Scotch, and poured himself a couple of inches. Mrs. Keenan winced at the amount and then said quickly, "I think I'll leave you two alone."

"It isn't necessary," Balzic said.

"Oh but it is," she said. She patted her thigh twice and said, "Come on, Keenie." The mongrel lurched away from Balzic's feet and trotted after her. Before she went around the corner, she fired a look of reproach at her husband which seemed to amuse him.

"Women," Keenan said, drawing up another stool and settling uneasily onto it. He shrugged and said, "You are aware of

93

course of what Freud said near the end of his life."

"No. Afraid not."

"He said that after forty years of working with women, he still had no idea what they wanted."

"I didn't know that."

"Neither did he," Keenan said, bursting into that staccato laugh.

Balzic let that go and said, "Uh, a little while ago you said you were rehearsing, and I asked you about it but you didn't answer."

"That's a very bad joke my wife doesn't appreciate. I use it whenever I think she is about to reprove me. I tell her that I am rehearsing for my life which is going to begin its run next week." Keenan smiled wistfully. "It infuriates her."

Balzic had to laugh in spite of himself.

"What is it that brings you here, sir?"

"The same thing we talked about last night."

"Well, sir, I have told you all I know about that girl. It was little enough, but I know no more."

"I didn't come here thinking you knew any more. I just came to have some things cleared up."

"Such as?"

"For one thing, last night you seemed pretty sure she wasn't doing her own work, and I'd like to know the reason you're so sure of that."

"Sir, I have been teaching for eleven years. Four at the University of Pittsburgh as a teaching assistant while I did my graduate work, four at Slippery Rock, and the last three here. One just gets a feel for such things."

"Yeah, well, I can understand that, but, uh, exactly how does one get this feel?"

"Aha! A man in search of cement."

"Cement?"

"Surely. Concrete, cement, the hard. As opposed to the abstract, the nebulous, the soft. You want water, not merely rain. You want the it, as in it is raining."

94

"Okay," Balzic said. "As long as it's about the Pisula girl, you can call it whatever you want."

Keenan made a humming sound and closed his eyes. "Let me think how to put this," he said, opening his eyes. "In a sentence, sir, the girl's prose took a quantum jump that was simply extraordinary."

"You lost me with that jump, what was it?"

"Quantum. A mathematical premise. The promise of arithmetic. Her words took the leap of a dwarf who suddenly realized his dream of becoming the Jolly Green Giant. It was impossible for me not to notice."

"So did you ask her about it?"

"No. As a matter of form, I complimented her on her jump."

"Even though you were pretty sure it was faked?"

"Even though. Surely. I mean, something must be said for the initiative to cheat, if for no other reason than for the imagination it requires. No. Demands."

Balzic shook his head. "Somehow I get the feeling you could, uh, make cancer sound like a good deal."

"Ah, well, words are the call, and mind outleaps pen, all in all."

"What was that?"

Keenan gulped more Scotch. "What was what?"

"You said something about mind outleaps the pen."

"What I said was, 'Words are the call, and mind outleaps pen, all in all.' "

"Did somebody write that by any chance?"

"I did. But purely as an exercise in form. Purely exercise."

"Sounds familiar."

"It does?"

Balzic took out his notebook and thumbed through it until he found the poetry he'd copied from Frances Milocky's letters to Janet Pisula. "Yeah, here it is. 'The word outleaps the world, and light is all.' "

"Theodore Roethke."

"Who?"

"Theodore Roethke. The sanest lunatic of the last forty years."

"What you're telling me is he's the guy who wrote that."

"Indeed, sir, he did. Between vacations to the mind sanctuaries. Or maybe during. But tell me, sir, what is a chief of police doing with the words of a poet in his notebook? Does that mean I can still hope for the age of the philosopher king to come upon us?"

"I don't know about that. I just know that what you said sounded familiar, that's all."

"Aaaaah, we're to cat and mouse, dog and cat, man and woman—is that it? You're to get me to confess that I'm familiar with Roethke. I'm dismayed, sir."

Balzic waited for Keenan to continue, but Keenan stood and poured himself another dose of Scotch. He returned to his stool, eased himself onto it, and took another long drink. Three full swallows.

"If it be treason, sir, to love poets," Keenan said, "then I am a traitor. Do with it what you will."

"Well, treason's a little out of my line. I'm just a cop here in Rocksburg. I don't work for the FBI."

"Your point, sir—" Keenan laughed uproariously. "Forgive me. What is your point?"

"I'm not really sure right now. Just tell me something. Is this, uh, this—"

"It's pronounced Ret-Key."

"Yeah, well, is he popular among college kids?"

"Popular? No, not popular. But his voice reaches those with certain ears."

"Uh-huh. Do you talk about him much in your classes?"

"I do. But that's because I have a singular affection for him. He has got me through more than one long night." Keenan closed his eyes and said, chanting in a voice like an aging priest's: " 'This shaking keeps me steady. I should know. What falls away is always. And is near. I wake to sleep, and take my waking slow.

96

I learn by going where I have to go.' That quatrain, sir, has got me through more than once."

Balzic studied Keenan's face for a moment. Keenan's eyes were still closed and his face was lifted slightly. Balzic turned to another page in his notebook and read, " 'A lively understandable spirit once entertained you. It will come again. Be still. Wait.' Did the same guy write that, what I just read?"

Keenan nodded ponderously and opened his eyes slowly. "He did. It's from 'The Lost Son.' " Keenan closed one eye and opened the other very wide. "Again I must say, sir, I find this extraordinary. A chief of police with poetry in his notebook. Extraordinary."

"Not as extraordinary as you think," Balzic said. "But that's neither here nor there. Last night you said the Pisula girl shouldn't have even been in college, right?"

Keenan nodded slowly.

"You didn't think she was smart enough. She would've been better off waitin' tables someplace."

"Everybody would have been better off."

"Well a little while ago you said this Roethke wasn't popular, and I think you said something about him reaching those with certain ears—I think that's the way you put it."

"I did."

"So, uh, it sort of sounds like you think the people who hear him, the ones with those certain ears, it sounds like you think those people are pretty smart."

"Let me say this. I would not generally equate those with ears sufficient unto Roethke with undue intelligence, but I would say that they have made a wondrous beginning toward an awareness of the limits of their intelligence—yes, I would say that much."

"Okay, then tell me. How can you say what you just said on the one hand and then say on the other that the Pisula girl was dumb, how can you make that add up when I found all this poetry in her room?"

"You found those lines of Roethke's in her room?"

"That's right." Balzic was not about to say exactly where in her room he had found them.

"I'm truly perplexed," Keenan said. "Truly . . ." His chest came forward, his shoulders squared, he took several deep breaths, and he squinted unpleasantly. He started to speak, but before he could say anything, his wife appeared at the corner and said, "Mal, I would like to speak with you." Her teeth were clenched.

Keenan excused himself and followed his wife around the corner. For a minute their words were a jumble of harsh sounds, but then her voice rose and her words came clear.

". . . the third time this week, and I'll be damned if I am going to clean it up this time!"

"Patience, woman, patience—"

"Patience my behind! If the boy is sick he should be under a doctor's care. This is not a hospital. This is my home!"

"Control yourself. I will clean it up."

"I not only want it cleaned up. I want him out of here."

"I will ask him to leave."

"Ask him! Who does he think we are? Who do *you* think we are? Answer me, Mal. It is very important to me to know that at this moment."

"Lower your voice, woman, before you start to sound like a flaming hysteric."

"Do not tell me to lower my voice. And stop calling me woman. I do have a name. Or have you forgotten?"

"No, I have not."

"What is it, Mal? Tell me my name. Say it. I'd just like to hear you say it."

There was a long pause. Then Keenan said, "If you'll be good enough to get the mop and a bucket and some rags, I will go and clean the bathroom."

Mrs. Keenan strode heavily into the kitchen, her eyes brimming with tears, and she went from cabinet to broom closet to sink, gathering rags and sponge mop and filling a bucket with

98

soapy water, taking everything around the corner. In a moment she was back, trying hard to compose herself.

"You'll have to excuse me," she said, taking a paper towel off a roll above the sink and wiping her eyes. "Last night he called me Keenie." A sob caught in her throat. "That's our dog," she said and bolted out of the kitchen.

Balzic chewed his lower lip, then stood and got more water. He was going to drink it and leave, but something told him to stay. He had an impulse to see who it was the Keenans were quarreling about.

He didn't have long to wait. He still had a third of a glass of water left when around the corner slouched a young man—he could have been anywhere from seventeen to twenty-five—wooly-haired, slender but unusually muscular, who was trying with hands and arms that would have fit a body forty or fifty pounds heavier and several inches taller to get a sleeveless denim jacket over a wrinkled and soiled tee-shirt.

His skin was pale, his eyes rheumy, and his nostrils wet. He looked as though he either suffered some allergy or had a cold or had recently been crying or vomiting. Because of the argument the Keenans had had, Balzic surmised the last.

"Afternoon," Balzic said.

"Is that a greeting, a declamation, or a policy position?" the boy-man said, staring, open-mouthed, at Balzic.

"Greeting."

"Then consider yourself greeted." The boy-man turned away from Balzic and looked thoughtfully at the cabinets. "Where the fuck're the glasses?" he asked, going from one cabinet to another.

"I think they're in this one," Balzic said, moving aside and pointing to the cabinet where he'd seen Mrs. Keenan get his.

"Hope you don't expect gratitude for that information," the boy-man said flatly, getting a glass and filling it.

"No."

"Good. Terrific. 'Cause I am philosophically opposed to that. I don't want anybody to get anything they don't expect." He drank the water, emptying the glass without pause, then filled it again.

Balzic couldn't avoid wondering about the disproportionate size of the boy-man's hands and arms. They were so large and obviously powerful that, taken with the boy-man's narrow body, they were grotesque.

The boy-man leaned against the sink and sipped more water. "So you're wondering about my hands, right?"

Balzic thought he had been more subtle. He nodded.

"To save your brain the sweat, my old man almost made the '36 Olympic gymnastics team. Almost, but not quite. So I was supposed to make the '60 or the '64 or the '68 or the '72 Olympic gymnastics team. That's what my old lady kept telling me my old man would've wanted. The thing was, I was never sure what my old man wanted 'cause he got himself killed saving the world from the Communist hordes in Korea. But that didn't matter to the old lady. She had me on the rings and parallel bars before I could walk." The boy-man finished his water and set the glass in the sink. "Satisfied?"

Balzic shrugged. "Are you?"

"Sat-is-fied. I like the first two syllables. Sat is. That's me. I's sat."

"I take it you don't do it anymore."

"You take that right, dad. You take it rickety-rackety right."

"What do you do?"

"You ask a lot of questions, man. You know that?"

"Yeah. I guess I do."

"Don't tell me. You're a cop."

"That's right."

"How about that. First test I've passed in a year."

"You a student?"

"No more I'm not." The boy-man canted his head. "And I'll tell you why, since I see you're gonna ask me. For the same reason I ain't going to the '72 Olympics. I got tired. I got tired doing giant swings, tired practicing dismounts, most of all I got tired trying to keep those fucking rings still."

"You'll have to explain that. I don't know very much about gymnastics."

"You never saw rings?"

"On television a couple of times I think."

"Well, they're just what they sound like. Two metal rings on the ends of a couple of straps. Somebody lifts you up to them and you start out with the rings as still as you can get them. Then you do your routine, man, whatever you do, but the important thing is you have to keep those rings still. Which ain't easy, man. I mean, they're on straps, you know? The more they move, the more points the judges knock off. And that's the way I felt about being little Stevie Student. Every time I took a test, every time I gave a paper in a seminar, I felt like I was just trying to keep those fucking rings still. And I just got tired, man. Sick and fucking tired. I got an ulcer as big as a silver dollar, man. That's how sick I got. And that's how sick I get."

"That why you throw up?"

"That's exactly why I throw up."

"And you don't bother to clean it up."

"You must've heard that little go-round between Keenan and his old lady."

"I couldn't help but hear it."

"So now you want to know why I don't clean it up, right? I mean, you throw up in somebody's house and make a mess, you're supposed to save the people the trouble and clean up after yourself, right?"

Balzic nodded.

"Man, nobody is going to save them their troubles. He wants to be a fucking bohemian and a college professor, chairman of the goddamn department no less—and he don't know how. And her, she wants to be married to the chairman of the department and a bohemian, in that order, plus she wants to be a liberated woman, and she don't know how to be that either. Meantime, they're both something straight out of a Romantic novel—no, Romantic Gothic. No. Romantic American Gothic. Percy and Mary Shelley moved to Rocksburg. . . . I figure I'm doing them a favor throwing up in their bathroom. They both need to look at a little puke with blood in it every once in a while. Just to let them know."

"Let them know what?"

"That it's there, man. That it smells. That it looks like nothing else. I go to my old lady's house every once in a while, and I barf in her bathroom, too."

"Just to let her know what it looks like?"

"Nah. She knows what it looks like. Just to remind her. She gave me the fucking ulcer. And him," the boy-man pointed at the ceiling, "the one mopping up up there, he just made it bigger. He took it from a quarter and turned it into a dollar."

"So you miss the toilet on purpose."

"Oh no, man. I make sure I hit part of the seat. To make it look like I tried. I mean, Christ, I could hit the toilet. I know when I got to heave, man. But every time I bend over, it looks like one of those goddamn rings, and I figure fuck it. I know it's not going to move, but I know I'm not going to stay fucking still."

"What's your name by the way?"

"Segalovich. Anthony George Segalovich, the third. How do you like that—the third, no less. You can bet your hat, ass, and elbow there ain't goin' to be a fourth."

"Why not?"

"Are you kidding me? This line ends with me, dad. The old lady couldn't even come up with an original name for me. Who the fuck ever heard of a hunky with 'the third' after his name. Jesus . . ."

"How'd you meet Keenan?"

"I met him at Slippery Rock State College. Old Slimey Pebble. Yeah. And when I met him, I actually still thought I was happy. Shit, phys-ed major, two-time all-around gymnastics champ of Pennsylvania state colleges, third place NCAA College Division my freshman year, second place my sophomore year. Man, I was getting ready for the university division, the AAU, for those guys from Penn State and Southern Illinois . . . then I had to take an elective course. So I shut my eyes and put my finger in the catalogue and the next thing I know I'm in his poetry class. And the next thing I know, I'm not a phys-ed major anymore. Nah. I'm an English major. All because of Doc-tor Keenan."

"Now you come and throw up in his house and miss the can on purpose," Balzic said. "That's some switch."

"Right, man, right. And his old lady goes crazy, and he walks around, juiced out of his skull and making pronouncements which he thinks are going to move the world right off its axis, you know, except the trees just keep right on growing."

"A lot must've happened."

"I wised up is what happened. He wants me to keep the rings as still as my old lady did. He walks around saying, 'Thisss shaking keepssss me steady,' and all that shit, but he don't have the first idea how much you can shake trying to keep those rings steady, man. He's never been on those rings. Not once in his life. That's why I miss his toilet, man. And that's why I don't even think about cleaning it up. Fuck him. And fuck his old lady, too."

"Doesn't it ever get a little boring?" Balzic said after a moment.

"What?"

"Getting even."

Segalovich snorted and turned toward the door. "Doesn't it ever get a little boring for you, always playing question man? Doesn't that ever bore you?"

"Not as long as the answers are interesting," Balzic said, smiling.

"Then, question man, all you have to do is find answer man, and your life will be endlessly interesting. Stimulating even. See you around." Segalovich stepped out onto the porch and let the storm door bounce against its spring.

Okay, smart guy, Balzic said to himself, figure that monkey out. Figure Keenan out. Figure his wife out. Hell, Balzic thought with a grunt, how can you figure them when their dog doesn't even know what it's supposed to be.

He put his glass in the sink, ran hot water in it, and was starting for the door when Mrs. Keenan came into the kitchen.

"I'm sorry," she said.

"For what?"

"For losing control. I don't usually lose control like that. Usually I am very much in control."

"Well, we all slip once in a while."

She sat on the stool farthest away from Balzic and rested her forehead on her hand. "I presume you met the source of our— my irritation."

"Segalovich you mean. Yeah. Met him and listened to his story."

"Oh, he will do that. He will tell you his story."

"Listen, uh, I'd like to ask you something that isn't very pretty."

"If it's about him, not much is."

"Yeah. Well, uh, does your husband know Segalovich can't stand him?"

"Oh Lordy. My husband—" Mrs. Keenan laughed bitterly. "My husband not only knows. My husband actually thinks it's healthy. There is something affirmative, something positive, even in loathing, that is what my husband says. After all, if you cannot loathe properly, then you cannot admire properly either. And poets must know the depths of their loathing, else they will never know the heights of their admiring—that's what my husband says. Do you want to hear more?"

"That's enough. I get the drift. But what about you?"

"I thought that was fairly obvious."

"Well, your feelings are pretty obvious, but I'd like to know more than that."

"What can I tell you then? We met him—"

"He told me that."

"What do you want to know then?"

"A minute ago you said something about your husband thinking that a poet ought to know his depths, and so forth. Am I right in thinking that because your husband puts up with Segalovich, that he, Segalovich, is also a poet?"

"Absolutely. Mal wouldn't have it any other way."

"Okay. So then how does he make his bread—his living?"

"That would take some telling."

"Well, you know, just briefly."

"I can't be brief about him. I know this isn't going to make any sense, but the reason I can't be brief is because I don't really know. I only have intimations of what he does. He used to go to school. He was working on his master's at Pitt, the main campus in Oakland. Then, he was doing all sorts of things: stealing, shoplifting, selling marijuana, selling practically anything anybody wanted to buy, writing papers for other students. Ostensibly, he had a job as a stock boy in one of the department stores in downtown Pittsburgh."

"What was that one thing you said—writing papers for other students? What's that mean?"

"Oh, that's a flourishing racket these days."

"Well I figured it was some kind of hustle, but exactly what kind of hustle is it?"

"Well, not having participated in such things when I was a student, I can only surmise."

"Go ahead."

"I imagine it's quite simple. A student's workload piles up, or he lets it pile up either because he can't or won't keep up, term papers come due, and when there is demand there is generally supply. I'm told it's a sellers' market."

"You mean one student pays another student to write his paper for him? Do his work for him, is that it?"

"That's what it comes down to. And from what I hear, it's gotten so far out of hand that it has even come up in the state legislature. Some university teachers are demanding that a law be passed making it some kind of crime."

"Yeah," Balzic said, "I remember hearing something about that, but since I didn't have anything to do with it, I didn't pay any attention to it. Well, let's get back to Segalovich. You know for a fact he did these things, or are you sure he wasn't maybe just bragging a little bit?"

"No, I don't know anything for a fact. And he most certainly does have a tendency to distort the truth in his favor—and that is being as polite as I can be."

"So you heard him talking about shoplifting and so on, but you're not sure he actually did these things."

"Well, I would have no way of being sure. All I know is that he hints at lots of things. And he always makes gross statements about himself. I've heard him say things like, oh, 'I have a bottom-less well of evil,' or, 'I have an endless capacity for the corrupt.' They weren't about particular things he had done—or claims to have done. They were just general comments like that, which, I suppose because he disgusts me so much, I chose to believe that he is as capable of those things as he tries to make himself out to be."

"But you really don't think he's just bragging."

"He may be. It may be his way of playing the poet. On the other hand . . ."

"On the other hand what?"

"Well, he certainly has no qualms about freeloading here. He'll take anything he can get from Mal. Money, food, anything. And things that are not Mal's to give."

"You?"

"Yes. He tried that once. Mal went out somewhere, probably to get another bottle of Scotch. And he even tried to take that."

"Without the details—was he clumsy?"

She canted her head, looking half-surprised, half-pleased. "You were very sure of that, weren't you?"

"Just a guess," Balzic said.

"Well, boorish is a better word than clumsy. He disgusted me."

"Did he get a little rough?"

"For a moment I thought he was going to, but then Mal drove up. We both could hear the car. He just backed away and sat down."

"How long ago was this?"

"That was when we were at Slippery Rock. Five years ago at least. Now, he never comes near me."

"How long's he been here? I take it he's been living here, am I right?"

"This time he's been here only a little more than a week. I try not to think how long. Maybe it hasn't been quite that long. Maybe I just think it has. It seems a month."

"Where's he from?"

"Someplace near Pittsburgh. I really don't know. He claims he stays on the road—that's how he puts it."

"Do you know where he was before he came here?"

"Oh, he's back and forth. I don't really care to know so I never ask. I just sit and hope he's not planning to stay when he shows up."

"Okay, Mrs. Keenan, thank you very much. I might be talking to you again. Hope you don't mind."

"Mind? Lordy, nobody's—what I mean to say is, I'll be glad to assist in any way I can." She smiled and then blushed. "I presume all this has to do with last night."

"More or less. Anyway, I might have to talk to you or your husband again. Thanks again. And thanks for the water."

Balzic stepped off the porch into the brilliant sunlight. Coming from the subdued light of the Keenans' kitchen, he felt for a second as though someone had thrown sand in his eyes.

His cruiser was scorching—handles, seat, steering wheel—and opening the vents wide relieved little. He stopped at the first gas station he came to as much to get out of the car as to get gas. As an afterthought, he asked the attendant if there was a phone. The attendant motioned toward the inside, and Balzic went in, mopping his face and neck, and called his station.

"Rocksburg Police, Sergeant Stramsky speaking."

"Vic? Balzic. Where's Clemente? It's not four o'clock yet, is it?"

"It's five till three. Angelo's sick. His old lady called me this morning to take his shift for him."

"What's wrong with him?"

"She didn't say. All she said was they were getting ready to

107

go to the doctor's. Said he didn't sleep last night."

"What, that's the second time this month. You know what I think? I think Angelo's starting to wonder whether he ought to retire."

"Hell, that ain't for six months yet."

"Ah, Angelo worries. He wonders and he worries. So. What's happening?"

"You really want to know?"

"On second thought, unless the Japs bombed the Rocksburg Boat Club I don't want to know nothing. Did my wife call?"

"No. Johnson did though. He said for you to go on up to Troop A."

"Okay, Vic. And listen, don't spend all that overtime on kolbassi. Buy a little cabbage too, you know."

"Funny man."

"Vic, don't hang up. There's about six or seven mobile homes coming through. Should be around quarter to four. See if Angelo set up escorts for them, and if he didn't, you take care of it."

"Front and rear?"

"You got it," Balzic said and hung up. He went back to his cruiser, paid the attendant, and drove to Troop A Barracks.

The county detectives had gone, and the duty room was empty except for the radio operator and a typist. The typist told Balzic that Johnson was in his office, and Balzic found him leaning back in his chair, toying thoughtfully with a pencil.

"So what's the good news?" Balzic said, straddling a chair.

"You're going to love this," Johnson said, closing his eyes and rolling his head from side to side to loosen a kink in his neck.

Balzic lit a cigarette and waited.

"The Milocky girl got the word and took off."

"Took off? For where?"

"Who knows. She came home about an hour ago, her mother told her what happened, she stewed around for a while, and then, according to her mother, she picked up a couple bags and just walked out. The old man was visiting Mrs. Pisula in the hospital and it took Mrs. Milocky a while to reach him."

"And?"

"They drove around looking for her and finally got around to the bus station. The nearest thing anybody could figure was that she caught a bus to Pittsburgh. Christ only knows where she'll go after that."

"You called the Pittsburgh police."

"Yeah, sure. Right before I called your station. About forty minutes ago. I don't know what the fuck they're doing. How long's it take to check the bus stations?"

"Beautiful," Balzic said. "I take it you decided she's it. The lab came up zilch, right?"

"Double zilch. Nothing from her fingernails, nothing from the floor, all the prints in the room were hers—except for the ones on the door which are yours—plus that one lousy smudge on the paper. Man, I read through all those letters and I have to agree with you. If anybody's going to tell us anything, it's going to be Miss Milocky."

"How about the rest of the people who were in her classes?"

"Nothing. I'll tell you, Mario, I never saw anybody as cut off from people as this girl was. She may as well have been in solitary for the last nine months. Nobody knows anything about her." Johnson shook his head wearily. "I got two men nosing around at the campus, but they just keep reporting back goose eggs. They've talked to the manager of the student union, the manager of the bookstore, librarians, janitors, everybody. Nobody can remember talking to her. It's fucking unbelievable. I was just sitting here thinking about it. Never mind that she got murdered. Imagine what her life was like, being that separated, that isolated. I'm really starting to feel for her uncle."

"Yeah, and the poor bastard thought she was coming out of it. Well, goddammit, Walk, she talked to somebody."

"Sure. But who? How about you, you get anything from that Keenan?"

"I got more out of his wife than I did out of him. All he wants to do is make jokes and drink."

"What did the wife say?"

"First of all, Keenan is certain the girl wasn't writing her own papers, then the wife tells me that's a pretty big hustle these days. She told me something I forgot, which was that it's getting so bad some professors are lobbying in Harrisburg to make it illegal."

"What is? What's the hustle?"

"Just what I said. There are people who are making money writing papers for other students."

"Oh, yeah, yeah. I remember hearing that in Harrisburg the last time I was there. But, shit, I always thought that was a hustle."

"It may have been, but apparently it's never been this widespread before. Anyway, you put that with the information in those letters and it's twenty to one that's what we're dealing with. What the hell else would she've been talking about? She kept on urging her to do it—where are those letters?"

Johnson nodded to the corner of his desk, and Balzic leaned over and picked up the manila envelope. He rooted through the letters until he found what he was looking for. "Here, listen to this one: 'Do what we talked about over Thanksgiving. Do it, please, Jan.' And this one. 'Quit feeling guilty about doing that, Jan. They pay lots more than you're paying for it, believe me. There are people here who make a living from it. It's as much a part of the place as pot. Nobody even wonders about whether it's done; all they wonder about is whether they should do it, though, of course, they also wonder if they can afford it.' See what I mean? I mean, what—"

"Hey, Mario, friend, buddy, compadre, I've read it," Johnson said, standing and stretching. "I've read them twice. The fact is, the only name mentioned in any of them is Keenan's, and nobody's going to tell me that the guy teaches a class and then writes papers for his students for money. Christ, that doesn't make any sense at all. Why do the work? If he wants money, why not a straight bribe for a good grade?"

"Agreed."

"Okay, so then where does that leave us?"

"Maybe they advertise."

"I'm ahead of you. One of the things I told my people down on the campus was to check all the bulletin boards, see if there was anything that looked even remotely like a pitch."

"And?"

"Everything posted on the boards was ordered off on a memo from the president's office. The boards had to be cleared by the time the last exam was given yesterday. Seems they don't have too much space and they needed all they could get for information for the summer school."

"So it's in the garbage, right?"

"Right. And I already talked to the sanitation department—"

"Oh shit," Balzic said.

"Right. City ordinance number-who-knows says that all garbage must be buried in a landfill the same day it's collected. All of a sudden the whole fucking world gets efficient."

"Christ," Balzic said, "I'll lay a hundred against one if I wanted to go to summer school, if I wanted to do that today, I'd have to go to some dean's house to get the information. It wouldn't be on any goddamn bulletin board if I was looking to find out how to go about it. And if I don't put my garbage cans in exactly the right place, I can start a rat farm waiting for somebody to tell me why they didn't pick it up."

"Well, what the hell, suppose the guy we're looking for is in the business of writing papers. He couldn't make a living off a school as small as this one. He'd have to be working everywhere he can, right? I mean, there are a hell of a lot of colleges around here."

"Three big ones in Pittsburgh," Balzic said, "plus all the small ones. There gotta be twenty, twenty-five within fifty miles."

"So? We run them down. We don't have any choice. I'll—"

The phone rang then and Johnson picked it up.

"Speaking," he said and then said to Balzic, "It's Pittsburgh. Yeah, go ahead . . . Greyhound eastbound . . . Ocean City . . .

yeah, certainly we'll get a mugshot . . . yeah, I'll put it out on our wire . . . hey, man, thank you. I'll take it from here." Johnson hung up. "That guy was something else. He tells me to make sure I get a mugshot and put it out. He must've just got promoted."

"They got her?"

"Yeppie. Ticket seller remembered her because she was very nervous and he asked her if she was all right, and she said no, because a very good friend of hers just died. She's on her way to Ocean City—well, you heard that. So, all I do is get the route and have her picked up. Christ, what could be easier?" Johnson smiled. "How's that for luck?"

"The last time I thought about it, I figured there were at least two kinds of luck."

"Hey, pessimist, look at it this way. If we miss her all the way to Philly, we just wake up the Jersey state people."

"As long as she goes where the ticket says."

"Why wouldn't she? You called her right before. You said it would be a dynamite situation if she found out she needed a prop as much as she thought the Pisula girl did. So? She just found out she needed one. And it looks like there's none around. So she's running where there is one. If she's half that predictable, she's going where the ticket says. I don't think there's any sweat."

"Your confidence in my ideas, lieutenant," Balzic said, "is enough to make a man think he still has a right to go to swimming pools."

"Do what?"

"You know, when you hit a certain age, the legs get a little whiter and the gut hangs and you get a little nervous being around all the young snappers. The ones with the flat bellies and the tight asses. You wonder how they see you."

"Mario, I didn't think you thought about those things anymore."

"Hey, are you kidding? The only time I go to the pool is to watch my daughters swim for the rec board team."

There was nothing to do now but wait. If Frances Milocky was on a Greyhound going to Ocean City, New Jersey, it was simple. A state cruiser would be waiting at one of the stops, if not one, then the next. Balzic knew Johnson knew how to coordinate things like this. It was what Johnson did best.

Still, Balzic fretted about it. Frances Milocky went to the largest university in the state. Unlike Janet Pisula, she had to have made many acquaintances. Balzic remembered the letter in which she wrote about going to Scranton with somebody for a weekend. Scranton was east. Suppose she changed her mind about going to Ocean City. Suppose she—ah, suppose, suppose, suppose, Balzic groused. I could sit here supposing until my ass turns to plaster and winds up on somebody's ceiling. Best thing for me to do is relieve Stramsky so he can eat. . . .

He drove to his own station, told Stramsky to take an hour off, and settled himself at the radio console. He found a deck of cards and started to lay out a game of solitaire, then snapped his fingers and went to a phone and dialed his home.

His wife answered. "Mario, where the hell are you?"

"Some hello I get. Where you think I am? At the station."

"Well, I wish you'd come home. I want to talk to you."

"You can't talk to me now? I could swear you were talking to me."

"Mario, don't get smart. This is important and I can't tell what you look like over the phone. I want to see you when I talk to you."

"Awww, you just want to look at my face. I like you, too."

"Mario—will you stop. This is serious. Your mother told me something, and I want to know what it's about. You been holding out on me."

"Holding out on you? About what?"

"About my brother, that's what. And don't play dumb. I know you."

"Listen, Ruth, I don't know what Ma told you," Balzic lied, knowing too well that she knew him. She didn't need to see his face to know when he was trying to con her.

"Listen, you," she said, "ever since I started talking about going to Tony's cottage, I can see something's wrong. And don't try to tell me you didn't say anything to your mother. 'Cause she told me something and I want to know the rest of it. If you have something against Tony I want to hear it. 'Cause I'm not going to spend a weekend with the two of you in that little place and not know there's a war going on behind my back."

"Ruth, listen. Maybe you're right. Maybe we ought to talk about this when we're looking at each other. You started out okay, but your tone's getting a little sharp, and if I told you over the phone, I think you're going to get madder than you should."

"Mario, is it that bad? Is he doing something illegal?"

"No, nothing like that. Look. Give me some time to think how I want to say it, okay? And I promise, I won't hold out. I'll give you the whole story, okay?"

"Promise?"

"I promise. It may take me a couple days to figure how I want to say it, but you'll hear it."

"Okay," she said, her tone softer now. "But don't take too long, okay? If we're going, I'd like to have a couple days to get ready."

"You'll have time," he said. "So how's everybody?"

"The girls are all right. Ma's having one of her bad days. Her back's bothering her. But she doesn't want me fussing over her so it can't be too bad. Listen, when are you coming home?"

"I don't know. Something happened. I'll probably be here for a while. Maybe most of the night. Tomorrow, too."

"So when are we going to have this talk?"

"Will you quit worrying? I told you I'll tell you and I will. I just can't do it right now, okay?"

"Okay, Mario. I'll see you when you get here."

She hung up and Balzic let out a long sigh and cleared his throat. Whatever he told her would have to be said softly, with the right words. This was touchy. He was trying to think of his first words to Ruth when he finally got around to explaining to her what was really bothering him about her brother, talking to himself at first, and then whispering to hear how the words sounded. He thought for a moment he had the perfect way to approach it but lost the thought when he swiveled around and saw A. J. Scumaci standing on the other side of the counter. Balzic had not heard him come in.

Angelo Joseph Scumaci—A.J. to those who indulged him, Johnny Scum to those who didn't—his eyes wildly confessional, swayed from foot to foot, his battered black fedora going in eccentric circles in his arthritic hands.

"A.J., what the hell do you want? If you want to borrow some bread, say so, but save the stories. I don't want to hear anything."

"Mario Chief, I didn't mean to do it, honest to God, I didn't. I don't know what makes me do these things. I'm not right. Everybody knows that. I'm dangerous—"

"A.J., the only time you were ever dangerous was when you used to cook in Romeo's place." Balzic hung his head and laced his fingers and stretched his hands in front of him.

"I mean it," A.J. said. "I should be put away. I shouldn't be allowed to walk the streets. I murdered a girl and I should be put away for the rest of my natural life."

Balzic went through the lifting door in the counter and took A.J. by the arm and led him toward the door. "A.J., you never had a natural life and you're never going to have a natural life. Now get outta here. You want a free ride on the state, do what I told you a hundred times already. Go sign up for welfare. Now go. Out."

"Mario Chief, on my mother's soul I murdered a girl—"

"If you murdered all the girls you said you did, A.J., there wouldn't be a woman alive in Pennsylvania. Now please get outta here. Don't make me lose patience with you."

A.J. shuffled out, but turned around on the porch and stared glumly through the screen. "Mario Chief, could you please—"

"How much?"

"Two—a dollar would be plenty."

Balzic reached in his pocket, brought out some bills, and

held up two dollars. A.J. opened the door far enough to get his arm through. He snatched the bills, jammed them into his hat, and pulled it down to his ears. "God bless you, Mario Chief. I won't forget this. You know me. A.J. never forgets nothing. A.J. remembers all the details."

"Yeah, sure. Go on now. Go someplace." Balzic went back to the radio console, shaking his head, sighing, swearing, asking himself what he'd done to deserve A.J. for a penance. Why A.J., he asked himself. Why not go to Rome and go across St. Peter's Square on my elbows and toes? . . .

He picked up the cards and dealt out another game of solitaire, then another, and another, losing thirty-some times before he quit counting. A few hands later, he stacked the deck, put it back in its box, and tried to tell himself he had been concentrating, which he knew was a ridiculous lie.

All the while he'd been playing, he had been worried by the idea that Frances Milocky wouldn't be able to tell them any more than they already knew. He was sure Keenan was right: Janet Pisula had not been doing her own work. He was just as sure that she had made a deal with somebody to do her work at Frances Milocky's insistence. He was equally sure that, unless they were dealing with a transient as Johnson had first worried about, unless Frances Milocky had a name for them, they'd be no further ahead than they were now. They'd have to run down every piddling, puzzling little note on every college bulletin board in three counties, all on the long chance that those notes were still available, all on the guess that the somebody who had written Janet Pisula's papers was the person who'd killed her, and all that on the even longer chance that that somebody advertised that way. Then there was the reason . . .

Suppose it had been that someone who had written her papers. Why would he kill her? Surely not because she owed him money. If it had been that, then why was there all that money in her desk and in her wallet?

And rape? Forget it. The girl still had her hymen. Sodomy? Nothing doing there either. Grimes's report made a point of noting the absence of sperm or semen anywhere in or on the body.

Which left the blank sheet of paper. And left Balzic with the idea he'd heard from Mo Valcanas: Hemingway blowing his head off because he couldn't make a sentence anymore. Was it that simple? Was that why a man killed himself? If that was so, would a man kill someone else because he couldn't make a sentence anymore? Balzic chewed his teeth. The whole idea, as simple as it had seemed when Valcanas explained it, now seemed as porous and fragile and mysterious as cobwebs.

Yet there had to be a parallel, something Balzic could understand, something he could reconcile himself to, and he fumed about the duty room, telling himself that if only he thought about it enough, he would find it. A half-hour later, he still had not got anywhere closer to the substance of the idea than he'd been when he put the cards away. He'd never felt more inadequate in his life.

The screen door jerked open, and Stramsky, swearing and scowling, came in and stood on the other side of the counter. He put his head in his hands and nearly shouted at Balzic. "Sometimes, Mario, my old lady makes me so fucking mad. She is so goddamn dumb sometimes. Most of the time she's okay, understand, but there are times, Jesus H. Kee-rist . . ."

Balzic started to smile and then to laugh.

"Hey, it's not funny, Mario."

"Vic, you're beautiful."

"What the hell are you talking about? Beautiful, Christ. My old lady just went out and made a deal to sell toys. So she can have Christmas money, she says. The only thing is she don't read the fine print in the contract she signs, and now she gives me the good news she got to come up with five hundred for her inventory. I say where the hell we gonna get five bills, and she says she already borrowed it from a finance company. I say how can you do that without my signing, and she tells me she forged my name. She does all this last week and just now she tells me about it, and you, you goddamn half-breed, you stand there laughing and telling me I'm beautiful. Jesus fuck!"

Balzic went through the lifting door and put his arm around Stramsky's shoulders. "Vic, Vic, I don't mean to laugh, honest to God I don't. And I can appreciate your situation—"

"You can, huh? You know what that fucking loan is going to cost us? That five bills is going to cost seven hundred and thirty-something by the time we get through paying it off. And you can *appreciate* my situation! I said, Jesus Christ, woman, there went all the profits you think you're going to make from those toys—that's if you sell them—and she says, oh no, I'll make a terrific profit. She thinks she's going to make so much money she's going to pay off that loan in twelve months. That's what she actually says to me. And you, you bastard, you *appreciate* my situation."

"I do, Vic, honest to Christ I do. It's just that I was sitting in here breaking my head trying to figure something out, and I couldn't, and you just walked in and laid it out for me. Believe me, I'm not laughing at you. I'm grateful. No shit, I am. And I'll tell you what. I'll call Mo Valcanas for you and ask him to get you out of it, how's that?"

"She signed, Mario! How's anybody going to get me out of it? She signed. The toy contract may be a hustle, but that don't cut nothing with the finance company. They don't care how you spent the money. You signed, you pay."

"Yes, but fraudulently, Vic. Fraudulently. She forged your name, right? Listen, if anybody knows how to get you out of this, it's Valcanas—that is, if you want out."

Stramsky hung his head. "Oh, Mario. You should've seen her face. She wants to do it so bad. How can I make her get out of it? She was so excited she was going to make some money by herself. This is the first time since we been married, you know? She never worked, you know that. And she really wants to do it. I almost got to admire her guts."

"Well, you do what you want, then let me know. You want out, I'll get Valcanas for you. If not, just say so, okay? Just believe me, I wasn't laughing at you."

"I believe you," Stramsky said. "I just hope it works out. You want to play some gin?"

118

"Not now. I'm going up to Troop A. I want to talk to Johnson and wait it out with him. They're picking up a girl I want to talk to. I'll give you a call later unless something comes up. Take it easy, Vic. It'll be all right," Balzic said, going out to his cruiser.

"We got her," Johnson said as Balzic walked into Troop A's duty room. "Picked her up in Blairsville. She should be here in thirty, thirty-five minutes."

"That's the second best news I heard today," Balzic said.

"Second best? Christ, what do you want? What was first?"

"Ah, I'll tell you after we hear what she has to say."

"Okay with me. You eat yet?"

Balzic shook his head.

"Let's go get one of those good antipastos Funari makes. He's still in business, isn't he?"

"Oh yeah."

"Still making those antipastos? It's too hot for anything else."

"They deliver now. We don't have to go."

"Nah, I want a couple beers too. Besides, I got to get out of this place for a while."

"Let's go then."

In Johnson's cruiser on the way, Johnson asked, "So what's this first best news you heard today?"

"One of my people's old lady got sucked into a toy-selling thing."

"That's good?"

"Good, bad, who knows. It really doesn't matter. What mattered was the way he looked and the way he was talking when he told me about it."

"He couldn't have looked too good."

"As a matter of fact, he looked mad enough to strangle her."

"You serious?"

"Yeah I'm serious. He wouldn't do it, but he looked like he wanted to. And that was the thing that's been bothering me about this Pisula girl. Why'd the guy do it, you know? That was really

119

bugging me. He didn't rape her, he didn't rob her, so what's with him?"

"I figure he's a psycho, especially because of that paper."

"Yeah, but, Walk, nobody's just psycho. They're psycho for a reason. Lots of reasons. So he left a message, the paper. But why? I mean, I'm not saying I know, but at least now I think I got a start."

"Which is?"

"She was dumb."

Johnson mulled that over as he pulled into the parking lot of Funari's Bar and Restaurant. He looked at Balzic a few times but didn't say anything until they were inside at a table and taking sips of their first beers. Then, after the waitress had taken their food order, Johnson leaned over and said incredulously, "She was dumb?"

"Yeah, yeah, I know. It sounds ridiculous, but that's it. I mean, she was. Remember what her uncle told us? She went from skipping grades to barely keeping up. I got more or less the same story from all her teachers. Dumb—literally. Practically a mute. Which wasn't her fault, but that's the way she was. You can't get around that."

"And a guy kills her because she's dumb?"

"Yeah. He loses patience with her. He gets frustrated about something. I don't know what. But I'll bet it was something she wouldn't tell him. Wouldn't or couldn't, I don't know which."

"Then, just for the sake of argument, Mario, then what the hell was she doing with just her pants on? Why don't you think he killed her 'cause she wouldn't come across?"

"I don't know why I'm not thinking that way, but I'm not. Maybe it's because of the paper."

"You're thinking if he killed her because she wouldn't screw him, he would've just left, is that it?"

"I'm not sure," Balzic said. "But I think that's the way I'm thinking. I mean, that piece of paper took some thought. It isn't something a guy in a panic does. If he's panicked, all he wants to do is get the hell out of there."

"Okay, then tie it up with her being dumb," Johnson said, screwing up his face.

"I don't know. Maybe he's telling the world she couldn't write. Maybe he thought that was something really terrible. If he's in the kind of business we think he's in, maybe he thought all his customers were extra stupid. Maybe they pissed him off. Christ, I've known more than one bartender who couldn't stand drunks. I even met a doctor once who really couldn't stand sick people. He said they were sick because they were all stupid and didn't take care of themselves. I'm not sure where I'm going with all this. All I'm saying is this is a start for a motive. Christ knows we got the body. But without a motive?" Balzic spread his arms wide.

"I don't know, Mario. You always were one for the psychology bit. Me, I just get them off the streets. Let the head-benders figure them out."

"Well, listen, Walk, look at it this way. How many times have you wanted to cream somebody for doing something stupid? One of your own people—how many times? How many times have I? How many times has anybody? Why do teachers paddle kids? Why do parents? What the hell business are we in, you and me?"

"Oh, come on, Mario. There's a hell of a difference between what's dumb and what's illegal."

The waitress brought the antipastos then and asked if they wanted more beer.

Johnson nodded to her, but Balzic just handed over his glass to her and demanded of Johnson: "Well? What's the difference?"

"To answer the thing about teachers and parents paddling kids, most teachers and parents I know don't really paddle kids for not being able to learn. They do it because the kids misbehave."

Balzic nodded vigorously. "Sure. That's what they say. But most misbehavior is nothing but kids doing what grownups think are dumb things."

"Not only dumb, Mario. Sometimes dangerous. To themselves as well as to other people."

"Yeah, but dangerous things are usually dumb things. Things that aren't good or sensible or reasonable or prudent. How many court decisions go with that one, that prudent?"

"A lot. No argument there."

"Well what's prudent mean? When a judge says a guy did not act in a prudent manner, what's he talking about? I mean, hey, when you get right down to it, if the guy was really prudent, how'd he get grabbed in the first place? What the hell, man, prisons are for screwups. People too dumb to not get caught."

"I think you're oversimplifying it."

"Tell me how."

"Right now I just want to eat. But don't let me stop you. Keep talking," Johnson said, biting into a ripe olive and chewing around the pit.

"Look," Balzic said, gesturing with a piece of Genoa salami, "right now there's a second-story guy I know, and I know he is. Christ, I've had him in so many line-ups in front of people who just caught a glimpse of him that he gives me the rag that I ought to put him on the force. His whole story is burglary, beginning to end. You know how many convictions? One. When he was eighteen. That's like ten years ago. He did six months in the workhouse in Allegheny County. Since then, nothing. The bastard's a pro. He works alone, he never looks the same way twice any two times I've had him picked up, he lives quiet—that fuckin' guy must've knocked over three hundred houses in the last ten years and nobody can come up with even circumstantial on him. You know what he says? He says three things whenever I pick him up. He says, 'Hi, Chief,' 'When's the line-up?' and 'Can I go now?' The last time was the first time he ever said anything else. He said, 'Geez, I been in here so much, maybe you oughta give me a job.'

"Right now," Balzic went on, "there's a lot of noise in Harrisburg about no-fault car insurance, no-fault divorce, and what's the word they're kicking around about drugs? Decriminalizing, that's it. There's a lot of noise. Maybe these things will happen, maybe not. But as it stands now, practically everything is the adversary system. Somebody's at fault, and somebody got hurt, and whoever's at fault has got to give up some time or some money. At least in the civil system, whoever gets burned has a shot at compensation. In the criminal system, whoever gets hurt is supposed to be satisfied his taxes are keeping the criminal off the streets, which is supposed to deter others." Balzic snorted. "Deterring others, Christ. Some satisfaction that must be. I can see me running a gas station or a grocery and some junkie comes in, cleans out my register, and then blows it all on three fixes before he gets grabbed. Then I go give my testimony against him and watch him get one to three and five years pro. I keep on paying taxes to support the whole goddamn system, meantime I don't get my money back, the money the junkie copped in the first place. There's no provison for it."

"What's all this have to do with killing a girl because she was dumb?" Johnson said, smiling ironically at Balzic.

"Not a goddamn thing. You just said to keep talking. You wanted to eat."

"Well, it was a hell of a speech while it lasted. You sounded for a while there like you wanted to be a lawyer for the Chicago Seven."

"Oh boy," Balzic said, laughing, "you should've heard me last winter when I talked to the Lions Club. Three or four guys walked out. You could've heard a flower hit the floor when I sat down, and the president of the club, Christ, he looked like he wished he'd shown a travelogue or something."

"What did you talk about?"

"More of the same I just gave you. You'd be surprised how little the squares want to hear how the criminal justice system really works. What they really want to know is what a good job I'm doing keeping the dopers and long-hairs out of their neighborhood."

"What kind of job are you doing?"

"Aw, shut up and eat, willya? Jesus."

Frances Milocky, disheveled from hours of riding, was waiting in the duty room when they got back to Troop A Barracks. She sat on the front edge of the chair, her face vacant, her left leg crossed over her right, her foot swinging, her fingers turning a pack of cigarettes end over end on her knee.

Johnson introduced himself and Balzic and then asked, "Do your parents know where you are?"

She nodded, her long, straight hair falling over her cheek. "I just called them," she said.

"Would you like some coffee? A Coke maybe?"

"Nothing, thank you."

"I think it would be better if we talked back in my office," Johnson said, leading the way back to it. "We won't have to put up with the radio."

The girl lifted herself out of the chair with great effort and followed Johnson with labored steps, her sandals sliding along the floor. Once inside Johnson's office, she slumped into the chair Balzic held for her.

"Miss Milocky," Johnson began, "I'm sure this isn't going to be pleasant for you, so if there's anything we can do to make it easier, just say the word, okay?"

She chewed her lower lip and nodded, turning the cigarette pack end over end against her knee as she'd been doing in the duty room.

"You ought to know, Miss Milocky," Johnson said, "that we've read the letters you wrote to Janet Pisula."

"I guessed that you did, otherwise you wouldn't want to talk to me. Of course, you could've heard about me from Uncle Mike. Janet's uncle I mean. He's not mine. I've just called him that for so long I sort of think of him as my uncle. Anyway, he would've told you about me."

"He did. But what we're really interested in is some of the things you wrote to Janet. You mention what seems to us—the chief here and myself—at least two men. One of them you named, and we know he was Janet's English teacher last year. Keenan."

"Yes," Frances said, nodding slowly. "Janet was terrified of him."

"Was there any particular reason?"

"You have to understand, lieutenant. Janet was afraid of all men. It didn't have anything to do with sex. Don't get that idea. It was because of the accident."

"Her uncle told us about that."

"Well, then you know. Then he must've told you about the man who caused the accident, the one who came to see her in the hospital."

"Yes, we know about him. The one who told her she should've died."

Frances nodded and pressed her fingers against her forehead. "Well, you must have figured out what that did to her."

"We have a pretty rough idea, yes. But we'd like to hear anything you can tell us."

She shook her head impatiently. "What can I tell you? It was traumatic, that's all. Not the kind of dopey little things people are always calling traumatic. That was a real trauma. It was a real wound. And it never healed. Someday maybe it might have. I mean, coming here to school, getting out of her house and on her own. Nobody will ever know what kind of courage that took. She went into a kind of frenzy whenever we'd be someplace and some young guys would want to talk to us. I could feel her shaking beside me. It was real hell for her to meet strangers. And if they were young guys, it was all she could do to keep from passing out, and I mean literally passing out."

"We gathered as much, but what in particular was there about Keenan? Or was there anything about him?"

"No. I don't think there was anything special about him except that he used to harp about the open admission policy the college had, and if there was anything particular, it had to be that. I mean, Janet had enough reason for feeling that she didn't belong. Anywhere. Not just in college."

"What's an open admission policy?" Balzic said.

"Anybody gets in who wants to. There aren't any prerequisites. As long as you have the tuition, you have to be admitted."

"And you advised her to transfer out of Keenan's class, is that it?" Johnson asked.

"Yes. She didn't have to listen to him. She'd been told once that she didn't belong. That once was enough for anybody, more than enough."

"You also advised her about something else," Balzic said.

"I was always advising Janet. I may be the world's greatest non-stop adviser. I know everything. Except it turns out I didn't know very much at all." Tears started to roll down her cheeks. She blinked a few times but didn't wipe them away.

"What didn't you know?" Balzic said.

"Oh God, what didn't I know! Everything. I didn't know how really terrible it must have been for her. And it was so easy for me to do cartwheels on the sidelines. A regular pom-pom girl of the mind, that's what I was. Bouncing up and down and yelling Janet locomotives."

"I'm sorry," Johnson said. "You just lost me."

"Oh, you must've seen football games. The cheerleaders spell out the name of their team. They yell a letter, the crowd yells the letter back."

"That's what you were for Janet?"

"That's what it turns out I was. Without intending it, but I must've really thought I knew what I was doing, I must've actually believed that all I had to do was cheer long enough and loud enough and Janet would just go out and beat her problem, as though it was a game or something. The really stupid thing is that I didn't realize it until I was on the bus."

"Where were you going?"

"I don't know. I really don't. All I could think of was I had to go somewhere. I just couldn't stay around and face Uncle Mike, even though I knew he wouldn't think I was responsible. But I felt I was. And I felt so stupid. The worst was that my major is psychology. And I went to Penn State actually thinking I was already a clinical psychologist because of the miracle I'd performed on Janet. All I had to do was get the degrees. What did anybody really have to teach me? My God, I'd guided a practically autistic girl into emotional stability just by cheering . . ." She broke down completely then, sobbing into her hands and swaying on the edge of the chair.

Minutes passed before she got control of herself and when she did, she said, "I never thought how cruel and mean good intentions can be. The best intentions. I've heard that platitude about history being bloody with good intentions, or however it goes. I can't even think of it now. But I never thought for a minute I could ever be stupid enough to be one of those people, those super sentimental creeps who think they have all the answers and really believe they know what's best for other people. But, well, here I am." She tried to smile but had to bite her lower lip to keep it from trembling.

"Uh, Frances," Balzic said, "did you advise Janet to get somebody to do her work for her, to write her papers—"

"Yes," she interrupted him. "You have to understand. All Janet wanted to be was a secretary. She didn't want to be a reporter or a novelist or a poet or any other kind of writer. Janet wasn't stupid. She was slow—what other people would call slow—because she had a hard time articulating her thoughts because for a long time everything she thought was so terrible, she just refused to talk about what she was thinking. Then, when she finally did start to talk, she went through a period when she questioned everything, when unless she had a completely satisfactory answer for why she was doing something, she just wouldn't do it. Then, when she started to talk with me pretty easily about what she was thinking I persuaded her to write everything down so we could talk about it—oh, God, she was my project. I had all these methods, these asinine therapeutic methods. . . ."

"I know this is tough for you, Frances," Balzic said, "but you're thinking about yourself now and, uh, you're feeling a little too sorry for you now and you're not doing us much good."

"I know, but I have to give you some background, otherwise

you won't understand why I told Janet to pay somebody to write her papers for her."

"Okay," Balzic said, "tell it the way you want."

She took a deep breath. "Okay. Well, Janet started to write everything down and then we'd talk about it. Her dreams, her questions, her reactions to things that happened to her. They were really amazing things. She had a really terrific insight into herself. That's why I never believed she was badly injured in the accident, or if she was injured, brain damaged, then all it did was bring her down to my level. Not in school. In school she just barely got passing grades, but that wasn't because she couldn't do the work. She'd get sidetracked. She was always questioning why she was doing something. She never took anything for granted. Not the simplest things.

"Like once," she went on, "she was supposed to write a term paper, a research paper with at least ten references in the bibliography, an outline, footnotes, the whole bit. But she never did any research at all—not in the library. She wrote the whole paper on the act of writing. The whole paper was a description of her hand and a pen and the movements and thought which directed the movements. Her teacher didn't know how to react to it—or to Janet. She gave Janet a D because she said Janet just didn't do the assignment. And that's why she had trouble in school. She did exceptional work, only it was never what she'd been assigned to do, and then when the teachers called her in to talk about it, Janet wouldn't say anything to defend what she'd done."

"Is that what happened in Keenan's class?" Balzic said.

"That's exactly what happened."

"So you told her to get somebody to do the papers for her."

"I had to. Because if she went on the way she was, she was going to flunk and I knew she'd just get the guilties over spending her uncle's money and disappointing him—which he wouldn't have been—but that didn't matter to her. It was a choice I really forced on her. I mean, I knew if she paid somebody to do the papers, she'd pass, and then she could get on with what she really wanted to be good at: typing, shorthand, bookkeeping. That was really all she wanted to be. A secretary. And it isn't any great mystery why. She understood it very well."

"Not that there's anything wrong with that, but why did she?" Johnson asked.

"She wanted to get a strange man's approval. She was absolutely honest about it. She used to say that just once in her life she wanted to have the confidence in a few skills so she could ask a strange man for a job and he would give it to her and then he would have to give her raises because of her competence. She never wanted anything to be given to her that she didn't deserve, but she desperately wanted approval from a man she didn't know."

"I don't get that," Balzic said. "Didn't she see Keenan as a strange man? I mean, why wouldn't she try to get his approval? Why didn't she try to write papers that would suit him?"

"In Janet's mind, getting a grade from a teacher wasn't approval. That was just a grade. Approval to her meant getting money to live on. Earning her way was the same in her mind as life itself, especially if the money came from a stranger. Do you see what I mean? I mean, being a good secretary, getting a job from a stranger, being competent, gaining the stranger's approval, all that would have wiped out what that other man said. The one who killed her mother and father and told her she should've died. It may not sound logical to you, but it is psychologically sound, and it was how Janet interpreted her life."

"She had this all figured out?" Balzic asked.

"Oh, yes. She was completely honest about it."

"Then why did you put her in a position where she'd have to be dishonest?" Johnson asked. "I mean, that's what it looks like you did to me."

Frances hung her head. "I know it sounds like that, but what else could I tell her to do? If she kept up the way she was going, she'd get hung up on something that was very important to her but didn't have anything to do with the assignment. And then she wouldn't have been able to become what she wanted. That's why she had the most trouble in English classes. All through school.

As long as it was grammar, she was fine. But when she had to write something, when she saw that blank sheet of paper in front of her, she was just overwhelmed by the possibilities of what she could put on it."

Balzic and Johnson exchanged surprised frowns.

"Would you say that again?" Johnson said.

"What?"

"What you said about the blank sheet of paper and the possibilities."

"Well, I don't know how to say it any differently. She'd look at the paper and she'd say something like, 'I can put anything here I want.' And then she'd say, 'Now what do I want here? There are thousands of words I could use. Which ones do I really want here?' That's the way she used to talk about it."

"So you told her to get somebody who was all business, is that it? Somebody who'd get the assignment from her and wouldn't get hung up. He'd just get right to it," Balzic said.

"Yes. Otherwise, she'd spend hours picking the first word."

"Well," Johnson said, "that leaves only one thing. Do you know who that person was?"

"I don't know him, no. I arranged it through a girl Janet and I knew who went to Pitt in Oakland. I'll have to think a minute to remember his name. It was unusual. I mean I thought it was unusual because his first name was Italian but his last name was Slavic. Serbian or Croatian probably."

"You could be talking about the chief here," Johnson said, smiling vaguely at Balzic. "He's got an Italian first name. Mario. What was your father, Mario? Serbian?"

"Yeah," Balzic said, rubbing his mouth and chin. Then he canted his head and said to Frances, "Wait a minute. That guy's name wasn't Anthony, was it?"

"Yes, that's it. Anthony—oh, it starts with an S."

"Segalovich?"

"Yes, that's it. How did you know?"

"How did I know, huh? How did I know." Balzic was snorting and fumbling for his notebook. "I had him, right in my lap

I had him and was too dumb not to put two with two." He found the Keenans' phone number and address and dialed the phone on Johnson's desk.

"Mario, what're you talking about?"

"I had him. This afternoon at Keenan's house. He was who they were arguing about. Didn't I tell you about him?"

"No," Johnson said.

"I had to tell you. That's how I found out about the paper-writing hustle."

"You told me Keenan's wife told you."

"Yeah, but she told me 'cause I was curious about him. I wanted to know how he made his living. How do you like those potatoes, huh? Right in my mitts I had him. And boy, do things start to fall into place now—hello, Mrs. Keenan? This is Mario Balzic, the chief of—"

"I remember, chief. Can I help you?"

"I hope so, Mrs. Keenan. You remember that guy who was at your house this afternoon?"

"I can't very well not remember him."

"Yeah, well I know you said you weren't sure where he lived, but maybe your husband can, and I'd—"

"That person—for want of a better word—is here right now. Do you wish to speak with him?"

"He's there now?"

"I'm sorry to say he is."

"Terrific. You just keep him there. I'll be right down to take him off your hands."

"Chief, you, uh, sound a little ominous. I might even say a little frightening."

"It's nothing for you to worry about, Mrs. Keenan. I'll be there in a couple minutes." Balzic hung up and headed for the door, tearing the page with the Keenans' address out of his notebook and giving it to Johnson. "Come on, Walk. I'll go sit on him and you go get a warrant. And oh, Frances, you do us a favor and see if you can locate your friend, the one who arranged for Segalovich to write Janet's papers, okay? And when you get her, you tell her to sit tight. We're going to need her, okay?"

Frances nodded slowly, her face slack with remorse, bewilderment, betrayal. . . .

Mrs. Keenan was pacing in the kitchen when Balzic knocked on the screen door. She was startled by the sound and stood very still in the middle of the room. "Is that you, chief?"

"Yeah, it's me. All right if I let myself in?"

"Please do. I'm shaking so much I don't think I could open the door."

Balzic let himself in quietly and said, "Is he still here?"

She nodded once. "Chief, I'm scared to death. I really am."

"You got no problems. There won't be no hassle, believe me."

"You don't understand. I know why you're here, but something happened while I was talking to you on the phone—I mean, I think I can guess why you're here. To arrest Segalovich?" She was talking just above a whisper.

"Yeah, but nothing's going to happen to you—"

"That's not what I mean. While I was talking to you, Mal came out to the kitchen and he—he got some grass, some marijuana. They smoked it in Mal's study and I . . ."

"They're stoned? Both of them?"

"They were having a giggling fit when I last saw them. But I haven't heard anything for a while."

"Well, that'll make things easy."

"Easy?" Mrs. Keenan looked unbelieving.

"Sure. Potheads are the easiest collar—arrest, I mean. They just get nervous in the car. They always complain I'm driving too fast. They see a red light, they start hollering for me to stop a block away from it. I get a kick out of them, to tell the truth. They really make me laugh."

"Yes, but my husband, I mean, isn't possession a felony?"

"Mrs. Keenan, I could care less what your husband's holding. I want Segalovich. If you're worried about your husband, forget it. I should thank him for putting Segalovich in the shape he's in. Hell, now I can sit down and wait until the warrant gets here. If you don't mind."

"Please do."

Balzic settled onto a stool and lit a cigarette. "Mrs. Keenan, when I talked to you this afternoon, I asked you how long Segalovich had been here, and you weren't too sure. Try to think now, will you please? And put your feelings about him aside. I know that part's tough, but try to remember exactly when he showed up."

Before she could answer the sound of heavy, unsteady footsteps came to them, and then Malcolm Keenan appeared from around the corner. His eyes were red and wet, and he was having trouble trying not to giggle.

"Did I hear someone say when was the last time they showed off?"

"No, Mal, you did not. You most certainly did not hear that."

Keenan ignored his wife and tried to focus on Balzic. "You look similar, sir. Are you an original or are you a copy? Have you been . . . where was I?" Keenan started to rumble with giggles. "I remember not, I mean I remember now. Similar, Similac. Baby food. You're a diaper salesman."

Balzic laughed and said to Mrs. Keenan, "See what I mean? They're really funny."

"I am not amused," she said.

"No, no," Keenan said. "It's *we* are not amused. We. Not us. Not I. We are not . . . what aren't we?" He shook with giggles again.

"Amused," his wife said, "and if you could get yourself together you wouldn't be either."

"Wouldn't be what?"

"Oh Mal, for God's sake!"

"God," Keenan said. "Theism, I-ism, you-ism, we-ism, they-ism."

"Will you stop your word games just once! Just this once," Mrs. Keenan said, dropping her head and covering her ears with her hands.

"Women," Keenan said, grinning lopsidedly at Balzic. "Woman is a contraction of woe and man. And you can spell it either way; you can spell it *w, o, e,* or *w, h, o, a.* Sorrow and stop. That's women, or whatever . . ."

"Mal, your fellow free spirit, your poet in my residence, the one you always told to test the depths of his loathing, the one you encouraged to despise you, that same person may very well have found the depths of his loathing—do you understand me? Mal? Answer me."

"I would if I could but I can't seem to want to," Keenan said. "I'm trying to make some other association that is very important. Aha! This man is not a diaper salesman."

"Bravo, Mal. That he is not. He is a policeman. The chief of police, and unless I'm mistaken, another policeman is on his way here with a warrant to arrest your friend."

"Aaaaah, yes. The fuzzz. The fuzz with Roethke in his notebook. The commissar cum dilettante, the better to know me. And one can spell that *k, n, o, w,* or *n, o.* Either way, he is here to know me or no me . . ."

"Not you, Mal. Segalovich. Your friend is suspected of killing that girl."

"Really? I mean, really? That's, oh my . . . I'm afraid my toes are sending me messages. They say the world is spinning very fast and that gravity is very grave . . ."

"Damn you, Mal. Damn you!" Mrs. Keenan wheeled out of the kitchen. Her footsteps could be heard going through the house and then up some stairs. A door slammed overhead.

Keenan shrugged wearily at the sound, then turned to Balzic. "Did I hear her correctly? Or did I miss something?" He giggled. "Do you know what I almost said? I almost said, 'Did I thing some miss,' but I knew that would never do . . . oh, Shazam, Shazam, why don't I ever turn into Captain Marvel?"

"I give up," Balzic said, laughing, "why don't you?"

Keenan took a very deep breath, then another, and said, "I have no idea . . . say, did you say you suspect someone?"

"If I didn't, then your wife did."

"Who? And of what?"

"Anthony Segalovich. Murder."

"Are you serious? Murrr-der. That's impossible. Don't you see, I mean, can't you see—a poet who's in shape is never accused of rape."

"Yeah, well, that might be, but I didn't say anything about rape. I said murder."

"You yes—I mean, yes, but you see, it follows that if he's in shape and he's never accused of rape, why then he would never conceive of murder . . . where was I?"

"You're still right here, Mr. Keenan."

"*Doctor* Keenan. I have not been a mister for some months, or is it years? No matter . . . excuse me, but don't you think it would be wise to discuss this with Tony? I mean, but you should talk with him."

"Okay," Balzic said, standing. "Let's go discuss it with him. Where is he?"

"Follow me," Keenan said, gesturing dramatically, sweeping his arm in a great arc which came to a painful stop when his hand slammed into the refrigerator.

"You sure you can get us there?"

"Certainly," Keenan said, grimacing and opening and closing his hand and wiggling his fingers. He weaved around the corner and led Balzic through a formal, almost Victorian dining room, past a flight of carpeted stairs, and into a cluttered room with a desk, on which sat an old, office-size typewriter, heaps of papers, magazines, and books. Books were stacked haphazardly on a set of shelves which leaned precariously away from one wall, and there were more books stacked on the floor near the desk. There were two chairs, one a Boston rocker, the other a large wooden chair of indistinguishable manufacture, and a short couch.

On the couch, sitting with his shoulders slumped, his large hands hanging between his knees, his head tilted to the left, his eyes wide and red, sat Anthony Segalovich breathing deeply and slowly. His mouth curved up to the right in a half-smile. Without looking at either Keenan or Balzic, he said, "Man, am I skyed. This stuff is wow. Super wow." He made a faint whistle and let his head roll slowly to the right.

"Tony, it's the fuzz," Keenan said, settling uneasily into the Boston rocker.

"You ain't shittin' it's the was," Segalovich said.

"No, no, Tony. Not was. Fuzz."

"Fuzz, was. Was fuzzy. Was fuzzy ever wasy . . ."

Balzic lit a cigarette and looked around for an ashtray. He found one on a small table beside the Boston rocker and balanced it on his knee as he sat in the wooden chair.

"What're you smokin', man?" Segalovich said, focusing momentarily on Balzic.

"Tobacco."

"Ouu, that's bad for you. You can get cancer and every . . . wow, you should've felt that one. That one, that was like, wow, like nuclear . . . hey, man, tobacco's bad. You can get strokes, heart attacks, cancer. You can get cancer of the ass . . . you gotta shit through a hose into a bag and everything . . . hey, Mal, didn't I tell you?"

"Tell me what?"

"What what?"

"What didn't you tell me?"

"I forget," Segalovich said, smiling and rolling his head slowly while staring at something on the braided rug.

"Segalovich," Balzic said, "I guess it's about time I informed you of your constitutional rights."

"Consti-what? Man, I haven't shit in over a week. All I do is throw up."

"No," Balzic said, laughing. "Constitutional rights. Try to read my lips. Con-sti-tu-tion-al rights."

"Oh, them. Yeah, I got them. I got them all over the place. I can pray anywhere I want. I can assemble. I can even reassemble. I can do a whole bunch of stuff, man. I can even speech. Guaranteed."

"Yeah, well that's close but not close enough. So try to pay attention."

"Oh no. Nothin' doin'. I'm not standin' up for nobody. Are you kiddin', man? I'm nailed to this, whatever this is." Segalovich pounded the couch with the flat of his hand.

"Then try listening carefully."

"Oh yeah. I can do that. Go ahead. Listen something at me and see if I do it carefully. I bet I can do it, man."

"Okay," Balzic said, "in a little while, a state police lieutenant will be here with a warrant for your arrest. The charge—"

"I'm with you so far, man. And carefully, too. Don't forget that, man. Carefully."

"Yeah, I've noticed that," Balzic said. "The charge will be murder."

"Murder? Phew, that's a baaaad rap. That's almost badder than gettin' busted for dealin'."

"A little worse, I think."

"Well, 'sa difference of opinion. So go 'head."

"You have the right to remain silent."

"Silent, man. Wow, that's really, you know, like quiet."

"You have the right to legal counsel, and if you don't know any or can't get one, it's the obligation of the Commonwealth to provide you with one."

"Hey, that's pretty nice of them, you know? You know that, Mal? I mean, providin' me with all that."

"Only if you're unable or unwilling to get one by yourself."

"Hey, like right now, I don't feel like gettin' one, you know? I mean, I couldn't even find the phone right now, you know? I mean, my ass is really tacked to this thing here. I mean, stapled, man."

"Yeah," Balzic said, "I know what you mean."

"Well, my arse is not stapled," Keenan said, getting wobbily to his feet. "And I will call one for you, Tony. The best one I know."

137

"Hey, that's really nice of you, Mal. I mean, no shit. It really is."

"*De nada,*" Keenan said, weaving around Balzic and out of the room.

"Okay, so he's going to call a lawyer for you," Balzic said, "but I want you to understand, clearly understand, that anything you say between now and the time the lawyer gets where you are —anything at all—will be used against you in a trial. Do you understand what I just said?"

"Yeah, man, I can understand that. But do you understand that I'm fuckin' skyed? I'm like up there with the seven-forty-sevens, man."

"That doesn't mean a thing. It doesn't make a bit of difference to a court. Booze, grass—a court doesn't care if it's marshmallows. All I got to testify to is that you said you understood me when I told you your rights. So just between you and me, I wouldn't say anything if I were you. I'd just sit there and enjoy that stuff until the lawyer shows."

"Man, you don't understand," Segalovich said, giggling. "I got nothing to hide. My life's an open book. It's a lousy book. Corny characters, stale plot, bad dialogue, no style, no nothing, but it's open. Just like a shithouse in a state park or someplace. I mean, you *know* people been shittin' there before you. You can smell their stories, man, so you don't sit all the way down. You just sort of go into a crouch and let her plop." Segalovich giggled again. "That is, if you ain't constituted, you can go plop. But if you're constituted, well, tough shit." Segalovich rocked with silent laughter, and then doubled over, rolling back and forth on the couch.

Balzic continued to sit and smoke, watching Segalovich as he sat upright finally, his eyes wet and red, his diaphragm heaving, his face slack. He sat like that for a minute or so, smiling vaguely at some sensation from the marijuana, rolling his head ever so slightly from side to side. Occasionally, he would throw his shoulders back, take a deep breath, and expel it audibly.

138

"You know," Segalovich said, looking at the floor, "you can never really control anything . . . you can try. You can really break your ass and your brain trying, but you can never really get anything under the kind of control you think you ought to have . . . you know what the fuck I'm talkin' about?"

"I think so," Balzic said.

"I mean, all the time I spent in the gyms, man, all those hours and weeks and years. All that time, man, on the side horse, on the high bar, the parallel bars, vaulting, working on the free exercise, working the still rings . . . all those hours. All those exercises, all those weights I lifted, all those isometrics I did . . . all that to control my body, man. And for what? All because my old man almost made somebody's Olympic team about a thousand years ago . . .

"Ain't that something? I mean, really. All that to learn control, to learn when to get your hips under, your legs together, your toes pointed, the exact moment when to take off and when to start your shoulder turning . . . all that because a guy I can't even remember used to do it. All that because the broad he married, the one he screwed to pop me out, all that because she thought I should do it because he would've wanted me to do it . . .

"And you know, for a long time, man, I really believed I should be doing it because I really believed in it. I mean to tell you, man, I really ate that crap up, just scarfed it up. I thought, yeah, baby, this is really where it's at, this is really the way to control things, really control things. Get so good at those things, man, you could make your body do damn near anything. And all the while, man, it wasn't my life. I was doing it and really diggin' it and really bein' good at it, and I wasn't in control of nothing. No, man. It was my old lady was in control. All the time. She was in charge of my whole life . . .

"I'd be in a meet, man, and there she'd be. She wouldn't have to tell me she was going to be there, man. I could feel her there. I swear she breathed different, and I could hear her breathing in the stands. And when I'd fuck up, when I'd miss a move, start it too soon or come off it a fraction too late, I could hear her breathing change.

"And then she'd start to shout, man, and carry on. She'd start shouting, encouraging me. A one-woman cheering section. The better I got, the louder she got . . . and then she'd start anticipating me, man. Yelling at me when to start my next move, what to look out for, what mistakes I could make . . . it was fuckin' embarrassin', man . . .

"That last time, what a circus . . . it was an AAU meet, and I was on the rings. There was, like, two events to go, and I'm so far out front in points, I'd have to break a leg to lose, you know? But I got started wrong on those fuckin' rings. Man, those fuckers just started swayin', man, and I couldn't get them stopped. A foot in each direction, and I just could not get those bastards still . . .

"I was going to go from a handstand right into an iron cross, two strength moves in a row. Lots of points . . . but goin' into the handstand I almost went over the top and the goddamn rings were swayin' worse than ever. I mean, I was having a real bitch holding two seconds up there. It was like two minutes . . .

"And I came down too fast. My feet went way out in front. Christ, I arched my back so hard I pulled something in it, just trying to keep my ass under . . . I go into the cross, and the place is quiet, man, the way it always gets when people see somebody goin' wrong. They get quiet, man, 'cause they're really watchin' to see if the guy can pull it off. And there I am, swayin' like I'm on a fuckin' trapeze, countin' the seconds—you got to hold it for three—and my old . . ." Segalovich started to laugh hard so that it became difficult for him to talk. ". . . and my old lady is down out of the stands, man, and she's praying. Praying, man. She's saying, 'God, don't sway. God, please don't sway. Please, God, don't sway.' And you know what?"

"No, what?" Balzic said.

"I felt like I got hit by lightning, man. I mean it. Like fucking lightning. There I was, two seconds into the iron cross, waiting for the third second to pass, gruntin' my ass off, goin' nuts 'cause I can't get those rings still, and there's my old lady, praying. It was the sequence that got me, man. First it was, 'God, don't sway.' Then it was, 'God, please don't sway.' And then the clincher: 'Please, God, don't sway.'

"And there it was, man. In the third second, it hit me. Like lightning, I knew, man. I knew! I mean, it was so fuckin' corny, but it was perfect. You can't write that kind of stuff, man. You can't make a story out of it. You can't make poetry out of it. It's too fuckin' corny. I mean, there I was, man, crucified doin' an iron cross, and there was my old lady down there prayin' for me, prayin' *to* me, man, to satisfy somebody I didn't even know who was God around our house . . . like lightning, man, I was Jesus. I mean, I wasn't, but I was! I actually knew what it felt like to be up on that cross waitin' to die, man, listening to the women prayin' for him to be what nobody can ever be. What nobody can be, man. Nobody."

"What's that?"

"Perfect, man. Nobody can be that. I mean, I know what a perfect performance on the rings might look like. Might. But nobody ever does it. Nobody ever has and nobody ever will . . . but there was my old lady down there, tryin' her ass off to turn me into the son of God . . . 'Please, God, don't sway' . . . and all because that bastard was dead and I was all she had. . . ."

"What did you do?"

"I just started to cry, man. Just bawl. And then I just dropped down out of the cross, man, and I started to swing, back and forth, just like kids do in a park. I was swingin' so hard, I was fuckin' near goin' over the top. And then I started to laugh . . . you should've seen the people, man. They were goin' bananas trying to figure out how to get me down off those rings. The judges, man, the coaches, they were all running around like wild, man. And my old lady, she's screamin' at me. 'Please, God, Anthony, stop it.' Over and over and over. Christ, it was funny. . . ."

"How did they stop you?"

"I don't know. Next thing I knew I was in a hospital some-where. Pittsburgh, I think. I don't even know. They had me so fogged up with Thorazine, man, I didn't know what my name was. . . ."

Keenan came in then and said, "Attorney Louis Margolis will be here within the hour. He advised me to advise you, Tony, to say absolutely nothing until he arrives."

Segalovich listened to Keenan and then shook his head and laughed. "Hey, Mal, no shit. How come everything you say got to sound like the Gettysburg Address? I mean, really, man, all you need's a beard and a top hat."

"What do you mean by that?" Keenan said.

"What do you mean by that?" Segalovich mimicked him. "Now what the shit do you think I mean? Everything you say, man, you say like you're running for Congress. That's the way you sound, man. Like you're giving a position paper or a news conference or some goddamn thing. Like everything you say is going into a briefcase which is gonna get handcuffed to some-body's wrist and wind up in Istanbul or Helsinki or some fucking place."

Keenan took several very deep breaths and squared his shoulders. "In view of the fact that I have taken it upon myself to obtain counsel for you, Tony, and especially in view of the seriousness of the charge against you, I think it's about time you began to take an altogether different attitude—"

"There you go again, man. Another fuckin' speech."

"As I was saying, I think it's about time you began to assume the attitude apropos the situation, which attitude it seems would be one of the most practical realism."

"Oh, I am, man, I am. I have never had a more realistic attitude than I have right now. I mean, I've leveled off, man. Super Jay, the joyous Jamaican, has got me up to twenty-seven thousand feet, and I'm locked into automatic pilot. I got time to look around and survey the crew, see if everybody's in order, and, man, you're as out of order as anybody I've ever seen. And the reason you're so out of order is 'cause you spend your whole life trying to get out of order. Man, you're the only guy I know who's made a career out of being disorderly in an orderly way. You're full of shit, man, precisely because you got diarrhea, if you know what I mean." Segalovich started to laugh, but his face was no longer slack and his eyes no longer vague. Either the marijuana was starting to wear off or else he had reached an interval of lucidity on his way to another of giggling, seemingly disjointed indifference.

Keenan, for his part, was standing as though prepared for military inspection. His chest was out, his heels together, his thumbs resting on the seams of his trousers. "This is not the time for acrimony," he said solemnly. "You are in serious trouble. I am befriending you. This is not, most definitely not, the time for acrimony."

"Aw, for crissake, man, sit down," Segalovich said. "You keep standing there like that, you're gonna rupture yourself or something . . . 'not the time for acrimony,' Jesus. Befriending me, shit. All you ever did was finish the job my old lady started, you know that? Between the two of you, my old lady and you, you two fuckers got me crazy . . . she wants to turn me into a chimpanzee, and you want to turn me into a chimpanzee that can type . . . still rings and sestinas, the horizontal bar and heroic couplets, the side horse and satire, free exercise and free verse . . . is it any fuckin' wonder I'm doing giant swings inside my head? And all the time tryin' to figure out how I'm goin' to dismount? I should've killed you two . . . what the fuck'd I have to kill her for? Come on, Doctor motherfuckin' Keenan, tell me why. You're so goddamn full of announcements, pronouncements, affirmations . . . 'The universe announces yes, who am I to profane the universe by announcing any less,'—ain't that your fuckin' story, Doctor Keenan? What the hell are you a doctor of anyway? Doctor of Philosophy, shit. Doctor of sick ideas, is that what you are? Tell me something, doctor of sick ideas—d'you ever cure one yet?"

"Tony," Keenan said evenly, "I would adivse you to say no

more. I am advising you of this because if you continue to speak as you are, you will only succeed in getting into greater difficulty than you are."

"Greater difficulty than I am?" Segalovich howled with laughter. "Man, how much difficulty could I be in! You don't understand nothing, man. Nothing! I could split your head open with an ax and pour in some real information, only you got so much shit backed up in there, none of it would filter through. The joke is, we're the same, you and me. I'm constipated in my ass, you're constipated in your brain. You haven't had a new idea since Christ was a carpenter. The bigger joke is you know it. You've known it all along. That's why you're a fucking poet, man, instead of a man who writes poetry. Any asshole can be a poet. *Be* one. But write it? Uh-uh, no way. Man, that takes work. You got to sit down at the machine and get the words on the page, man. Anybody can walk around makin' fuckin' announcements he's a poet. But when you sit down at the machine and look at that blank page, man, that's like standing under those goddamn rings, waiting for somebody to lift you up so you can take hold and do it, man. *Do* it!

"All the talk in the world about keeping those rings still won't keep them still. Just like all your bullshit about being a poet don't get any words on the page . . .

"And I believed you! I actually believed you . . . this is all a bad joke, man. One box inside another box. I believed my old lady, my old lady believed in my old man, she believed in me, I believed in you. And you—you told me I could be a poet. I should've known right then from the way you said it. I could *be* a poet, you said. Shit, man, I can't even write a simple goddamn story. First this happened and then that happened. I can't even do that. Now go ahead, ask me how I know I can't. Go ahead. Either one of you. How about you, cop? You probably the only one really wants to know anyway. The doctor of sick ideas here wouldn't understand."

"How do you know?" Balzic said.

"Because I tried, man. Because I tried over and over and

over. And you know whose story I was tryin' to write?"

"Janet Pisula's?" Balzic said.

"See there, Keenan? The cop knows more than you ever will." Tears filled Segalovich's eyes. "The cop knows, and you know what he knows? He knows I couldn't even tell how a girl got so scared of living she wanted to die. You know how many different ways I wrote her story, man? I lost count, that's how many. Because no matter which way I wrote it, it came out wrong. All it was was words. All words, just words . . .

"And you know what finally came to me? There was nothin' but words on those pages about her because there was nothing in me to put on those fuckin' pages. All I knew was she was like me. Something got in her head that somebody else put there. She didn't have a life. She'd been dead for years. All I did was make her stop breathing. . . ."

"Is that why you went there?" Balzic asked.

"Hell no. I went there to get some bread she owed me."

"But we found a lot of money in the room."

"Hey, you just asked me why I went there and I told you. I didn't say anything about taking any money. When it hit me, I mean, when I saw it . . . shit, money was the last thing in the world that made any difference. What good was fifteen bucks going to do me? What good is fifteen thousand going to do me right now? Fifteen million . . . man, you only need money when you got some tomorrows coming. . . ."

"You didn't even ask for the money, did you?"

Segalovich shook his head. "What for? I wanted to see what was inside her—can you understand that? That's what I really went there for. I wanted to find out how come she was dead. So I could write it, man. I mean, when somebody's dead and they're still walking around, it's a goddamn story, you know? But how the fuck do you find out?"

"You might've tried talking," Balzic said.

"Goddammit, man, that broad never talked! She never said one more word than she had to, and half the time you couldn't hear that." Segalovich heaved his shoulders in a deep sigh.

"When I used to go there to do her papers for her, she'd have the assignment written down, and she'd just hand it to me. Then I'd sit down and write it and I'd try to show her what I was doing, you know? So she might learn a little something for herself, you know? But I never knew whether anything I said was getting through."

Balzic thought for a moment. "Is that—that last time—is that what made you try to make love to her?"

"You're too much, man, you know that? Too much," Segalovich said, shaking his head. "How did you think of that?"

"Well, it looked pretty obvious. She didn't have anything on except her panties. There wasn't any struggle. You had to've at least started with that in mind."

Segalovich's shoulders sagged. "Yeah, that's the way it started out. For the dumbest-ass reason in the world. I went in my head from trying to get inside her head to find out why she was dead to getting in her to see if maybe she was still alive and I was too dumb and too blind not to see it. I thought maybe I could feel it. Like, shit, I don't know, like maybe my body could feel something my head couldn't think. I mean, hell, there was a time when I could make my body do damn near anything. Maybe it could even think. . . ."

"But it didn't work," Balzic said.

Segalovich gave a snorting, self-deprecating laugh. "That's got to be the all-time understatement of the world, man. The all-timer to end all-timers. 'Cause that's when I found out I was dead, man. I couldn't feel a thing. All the while she was undressing, man, I couldn't feel a single motherfuckin' thing. All I remember is I started to shake. Just shake all over. And then that fuckin' line of Roethke's Keenan is always quoting jumped at me. 'This shaking keeps me steady. I should know.' That jumped at me and it had a hammer in both hands. It just started pounding on my head . . . I could hear Keenan, just like he was there, reciting it . . . and then my mother was breathing funny in the stands, I could hear her like she was there. And there was this broad right in front of me, this dead broad with her nipples as

146

round as round could be, and all I could think of was those fuckin' rings, and, man, so help me, that brassiere was the same color, the exact same goddamn color as the gloves I used to wear . . .

"The next thing I knew she was saying something about I was him. She just kept saying it, over and over. 'You're him, you're him, you're him,' and I was asking her, who am I? Who am I supposed to be? But all she said was the same thing, over and over. And I knew it was important. I mean, really important. Like if she'd only tell me, then maybe I could go somewhere and write her story and get it right and get it out of me. But I couldn't get it out of her. She wouldn't say who I was or who he was or why I was him . . .

"And then, my head just zipped out on me. Zip-zip, gone. And there she was, man . . . all I did was lay her down real easy, like, as though, like I was trying not to hurt her. Can you imagine that? I just strangled the fuckin' broad and I'm laying her down easy 'cause I don't want to hurt her. . . ."

"What did you do then?" Balzic asked.

Segalovich shook his head. "I don't know. I can't remember a thing. Nothing. All I know is I was here, heaving my guts out in the bathroom upstairs."

"You don't remember how you got here?"

"Nothing. I don't remember how or when or why. I was just there one minute and the next minute I was here, that's all."

"What about the paper?"

"What about the what?"

"The paper. That blank sheet of paper."

"Man, I don't know what you're talking about."

"There was a blank sheet of paper on her stomach. You had to put it there."

"Man, I'm telling you, the last thing I remember doing was laying her down real easy. That paper you're talking about, I don't know anything about any paper. And I'll tell you straight, man, this fuckin' Jamaican, you cops ought to use it. If it gets everybody else the way it gets me, you guys ought to find out

147

about it, 'cause I can't lie when I got this shit in me. I see the lies startin' in the back of my head and runnin' around and gettin' close to my tongue and then I just see them goin' back where they started from.

"Like a minute ago, one started. I was going to tell one about how it's everybody else's fault that I killed that girl, Keenan's, my old lady's, my old man's, everybody's. It was one of those lies some jackoff Ph.D. in sociology or psychology would've come up with. Like I didn't have any choice. Like given the givens, man, somebody like me would just naturally wind up killing somebody . . . statistical determination. Freudian determination. Calvinistic determination, whatever the fuck you want to call it. But that was a bullshit lie, man. I killed that girl all by myself. I killed her 'cause she was me. 'Cause I didn't have the fuckin' guts to kill myself . . .

"And you know what she said, man? Right when I was doing it? She said, 'Please.' Yeah. Not, 'Please don't.' No. She said, 'Please.' . . . poor, dumb fuckin' broad. She couldn't write either. . . ."

Segalovich stood then, momentarily lost his balance, but steadied himself by holding onto the arm of the couch for a few seconds. He straightened slowly and said, "Come on, cop. Take me wherever the fuck you're gonna take me. I stay here any more, I'm going to throw up all over Keenan's typewriter, and he wouldn't appreciate that. I mean, he'd say throwin' up was also part of the affirmation of the universe, but I still think it'd piss him off."

Balzic stood and started to lead Segalovich out of the room, but stopped short of the doorway and said to Keenan, "Listen, when that lawyer gets here, you tell him we'll be at Troop A Barracks and we'll wait for him so he can be at the arraignment, okay?"

Keenan seemed not to hear.

"Uh, Dr. Keenan, d'you hear what I just said?"

"I'm sorry. I was—I was. Yes, I was, that's what I was."

"Yeah, well, did you hear what I said about the lawyer and where we'll be?"

"Yes, I heard. It just took a moment. I was thinking of something."

Segalovich faced Keenan. There were tears in his eyes. "Mal, I hope you do think of something, man. I really do." Then he turned to Balzic and said, "Let's go, okay? Only one thing."

"What's that?"

"No handcuffs, okay? I couldn't stand that. I couldn't stand to have those things on me, you know?"

"I know," Balzic said, leading him through the house and onto the porch where they met Johnson coming up the steps.

"This him?" Johnson asked.

Balzic nodded. "Keenan called a lawyer for him, and I told Keenan to tell the lawyer we'd wait for him up at your place."

"You mean we're not going to have him alone?"

"We don't need to, Walk. Not that way. He'll tell you everything you want to know. Maybe a couple things you don't want to know."

"He confess?"

Balzic nodded. He was going to say something, but was interrupted by Segalovich's laughter.

"What's funny?"

"I was just thinking, man," Segalovich said. "The first thing I want you to know, it's not funny. I'm just laughing 'cause I don't feel like crying. But what I was thinking about was my old lady got a scrapbook about this big." He held his hand about three inches apart. "Filled with pictures and clippings, all about me. I was just wondering if she was gonna cut this out of the paper too, you know? I mean, she was always saying she was saving the last couple pages for when I finally made it, whatever the fuck she thought that would take. But what I was laughing about, man, all of a sudden it just came to me. I mean, now I know why they call them scrapbooks, you know?"

"Yeah," Balzic said, "I see what you mean."

Johnson took hold of Segalovich's elbow and led him down the steps and to his cruiser. Just before he opened the door, he called back to Balzic, "You coming?"

"Nah. I'll catch you in about a half-hour or so. I got to go talk to my wife."

"Something wrong?"

"Not yet," Balzic said, going to his own cruiser, "but there's going to be if I don't go talk to her. I got to tell her her brother's turning into a dirty old man and I don't want him around my daughters. I been putting it off for a couple years, but right now I suddenly got the feeling this is the time to say it."

"Well, if that's what you have to do," Johnson said, shrugging.

"It is," Balzic said, getting into his cruiser and turning the ignition. He watched Johnson drive off, then turned around in the alley behind the Keenans' house and headed for home.

He found Ruth in the kitchen and he told her as gently, as kindly as he could what was bothering him about her brother. Though it settled nothing about their spending a weekend in her brother's cottage, and though much of what he said made Ruth angry, he was glad he had not wasted any more time figuring the right way to say it. In the morning, he was very glad for that.

A Fix Like This

Balzic waited for the woman to be done. She was in her sixties, her white hair grew in tight curls, and she smelled of garlic. Her floral print housedress was ripped under both arms. Though she'd been talking to the admissions clerk for nearly five minutes, she was still shivering from the cold. She'd obviously left her home too quickly to think of wearing a coat or sweater.

The admissions clerk explained twice to the woman how to file for government health insurance for her husband, who had been conscious but torpid when he was wheeled into the Emergency Unit of Conemaugh General Hospital. Except for her shivering now, the woman seemed calm enough, though every time she asked a question, she put her hand to her mouth and her fingers trembled.

When she'd asked every question she could think of, she turned away from the counter and said aloud to herself, "My God, what am I going to do now?" Then she turned back abruptly to the counter, bumping Balzic with her hip. "Can I go be with him? I'm allowed ain't I? My mister, he's all I got."

"Certainly," the clerk said. "Through those doors on your right. Mrs. Havrilak will show you where he is."

The woman bumped Balzic again as she turned away from the counter and hurried, her bosom heaving, through the fire doors leading to the treatment rooms.

"May I help you?" the clerk said.

Balzic held out his ID case because the clerk was new to him. "I got a call about a stabbing a while ago, and I got tied up in something or I would've been here sooner. Who do I talk to about it?"

"Dr. Kamil, I think. He's the very dark-complected one. Just go through those doors—"

"I know where to go," Balzic said. "I just wanted a name."

He pushed through the fire doors and walked past treatment rooms on both sides until he came to the office. Off to his right he could hear a youngster bawling and a woman cooing reassurances. In another of the rooms a man was swearing quietly about a foot, probably his, though he was cursing about it as though it belonged to somebody else, somebody not very smart.

The office was empty. Balzic took a seat at one of the desks and waited. Shortly, a tall, freckle-faced nurse appeared in the doorway. She fumbled through her pockets while staring at the floor, then stepped quickly to one of the other desks and began to pat with both hands on papers jumbled on it. Only then did she notice Balzic, and she smiled brightly.

"Mario! How are you? I haven't seen you in a month of bad Saturday nights."

"Hello, Louise. How's business?"

4

"Listen, go get a lab coat. Some of these people you could take care of. I don't know where they came from today. God." She found what she'd been looking for and held it up for Balzic to see. "Around here, pens are more precious than blood." She started out the door but stopped short. "You waiting to see Kamil about the guy who was stabbed?"

Balzic nodded.

"I'll tell him you're here. He's just finishing up with some sutures. At least I hope he is. God, is he slow. I could put a zipper in a dress in the time it takes him to do ten stitches."

"He the only one on duty?"

"No, but the other one's right out of school. Last week, I think. I gotta go," she said, her crepe soles squishing as she broke into a trot.

Balzic took out his keychain and opened the nail clipper and began to clean his fingernails. He pared them over an ashtray, looking up every time he heard footsteps, but none turned into the office.

He closed the clipper and put his keys away and waited some more, looking around the office, mildly curious for a time about a poison chart under glass on the desk where he was sitting. He had just started to read the antidote for copperhead venom when a slight, short man in a lab coat came in. His brilliantly black hair grew in swirls and came very near to his eyebrows.

"I'm Dr. Kamil," he said. His accent was Middle Eastern, Syrian perhaps or Lebanese. "You are the chief of police?"

Balzic introduced himself and shook hands with the doctor. He could not remember shaking a man's hand so delicate.

"Ah, yes. So. What do you want to know?" The doctor clipped his words and spoke rapidly in a thin, tenor voice.

"Whatever you can tell me."

"I have the record here. Yes. So. Here it is. The patient is male, Caucasian, forty years of age, and very, very obese. If his brother had not been here to assist us, I do not think we are able to place him on the cart. His brother is also very obese. I have never seen such obesity as you have here in America. But these two brothers are beyond even my belief. Still in all—is that how you say that? Still in all? You have so many idioms here too—"

"Was the guy's name Manditti?" Balzic interrupted.

"Say again please?"

"Manditti. His name."

Dr. Kamil peered at his report. "Yes. Armand. Italian no doubt."

"And his brother brought him in?"

"I suppose yes. I do not know."

"No police officers came with them?"

"I did not see any."

"Where is he now?"

"In surgery most certainly."

"How long ago did he go up?"

"Thirty minutes, more or less."

"Was he conscious? Did he say anything?"

"Oh yes, he was conscious. But he was cursing and crying. If not for his brother to assist us, we would have no information at all."

"Did his brother go upstairs with him?"

"I suppose yes. I do not know."

"All right, Doctor," Balzic said. "Thank you. I'd appreciate it if you'd have somebody type up a report as

6

soon as possible. Mrs. Havrilak knows about the forms and what to put on them. Thanks again."

"There is no need to thank me. It is my duty, is it not?"

"Yeah, but thanks anyway," Balzic said. He shook the doctor's hand, reminding himself not to squeeze.

As soon as the doctor left the office, Balzic picked up a phone on one of the desks and dialed Troop A Barracks of the Pennsylvania State Police.

"State police, Sergeant Rudawski."

"Rudi, this is Balzic. Who's in charge of CID now?"

"Johnson."

"He is? I thought he was going to be transferred out as soon as Minyon passed his physical."

"Well, put an extra quarter in the collection this Sunday, 'cause Minyon flunked his physical, and he is, as they say, being retired with honor." The ironic pleasure in Rudawski's voice was unmistakable.

"Oh beautiful," Balzic said, laughing. "Just beautiful. Well, let me talk to Johnson."

"Hold on." There was a click, then a dead sound, then another click.

"Criminal Investigation Division, Lieutenant Johnson."

"Hey, Walker, old buddy, congratulations. Rudi just told me Shitface flunked his physical and you're going to be with us for a while longer. That's the best news I heard today."

"Mario? Yeah. It looks that way. I almost feel bad for him though. That's a hell of a slice off his pension."

"Don't waste your sympathy. Even his mother had to know he was hopeless," Balzic said. "Listen, Walk, I got a problem. A guy was stabbed. His brother brought him to the hospital, and nobody reported it. I mean, the hospital people called me. And I know them, so it figures they wouldn't report it themselves. But I'm also taking a pretty good guess that it happened pretty close to home. What I'd like is for you to take your people over there and see if I'm right and see what you can come up with, okay?"

"No problem," Johnson said. "From the way you said it I take it he's not dead."

"Yeah, but he's still in surgery so I don't really know what kind of shape he's in. I'm on my way up there now. But listen, don't bother trying to ask any of the neighbors up there anything. They still haven't figured out this isn't Sicily. They see those uniforms, they'll forget how to speak English. Just do a job on the house, okay?"

"Okay, what's the address?"

"You remember where Norwood Hill is?"

"Yeah."

"Well, it's the last house on the right on Norwood Hill Road. Never mind about a number. It sort of sits off by itself. It used to be a half-decent house when their old man was alive, but there's just the two brothers living there now and they're both slobs."

"What's the name?"

"Manditti. Armand is the victim. He's a runner and gofer for Muscotti. His brother's name is Tullio. He runs Muscotti's dump. Couple of real beauties. They call the one Fat Manny and the other one Tullio the Tub. You'd need a truck scale to weigh them."

"Okay, Mario. I'll see what we can do, and I'll let you know."

"Really appreciate it, Walk. Just remember that I'm

8

guessing. It could've happened anywhere. Thanks, buddy."

Balzic hung up and then made his way to the main elevators and up to the seventh floor, where the operating and recovery rooms were, waiting in the corridor by the nurses' station. He looked around for Tullio Manditti but did not see him. Off to his left in an adjoining corridor he could hear a woman mumbling and giggling in that euphoria brought on by preoperative chemicals. Nurses in green surgical caps and gowns bustled about. A doctor in street clothes got off one of the elevators and hurried past Balzic, stripping off his tie as he disappeared through fire doors on the right.

Presently, a plump, middle-aged nurse in white appeared from yet a third corridor. She carried a cup of tea and smiled at Balzic. He held up his ID case, but she waved it away.

"I know who you are," she said. "And you want to know about Mr. Manditti, right?"

"You're a good thing," Balzic said. "What else you going to tell me so I don't have to ask?"

"Well, Dr. Ayoub did the work and he was assisted by Dr. Mitchell. They finished about five minutes ago. I'll go get Ayoub for you."

"Wait a second. Where's Manditti's brother?"

"Oh, God, he smelled up the place so bad I told him to leave. He wasn't supposed to be up here anyway. I told him to go home and change clothes. But the way he was carrying on, he probably didn't. He's probably downstairs in the lobby driving everybody crazy."

"He was still in his work clothes?"

"Well, I hope he doesn't sit around the house like that. Where's he work anyway?"

"Where could you work and smell like that? A dump. Excuse me. Sanitary landfills they call them now."

A doctor in surgical clothes appeared then, thin, short, very dark, his black hair glistening from perspiration. "You are from the police?"

Balzic nodded.

"I'm Dr. Ayoub."

"Where they getting all you Syrians and Lebanese?" Balzic said, laughing.

"From Syria and Lebanon, I suppose," the doctor said. His smile was forced.

"Well, uh, yeah. I guess they would," Balzic said and coughed.

The nurse busied herself with some charts.

"So what can you tell me, Doc?"

"He had nine wounds, all of them simple puncture wounds except for two. Those were made presumably by the blade being thrust in and then pulled down. Like so." The doctor demonstrated on Balzic's chest. "The instrument was not very large. None of the wounds was deeper than six inches. The procedure was simple."

"He's going to live?"

"Oh yes. Barring infection, which is unlikely, he will die of heart disease. But for the time being his obesity saved him. It required every nurse in all three rooms to lift him onto the table. And off again."

"How long will he be in the recovery room?"

"How long before you will be able to talk with him sensibly?"

"Yeah, I guess that's what I mean."

"The anesthesia was very mild. We were concerned

about his blood pressure. Forty-five minutes. Perhaps not even that long."

"Uh, Doc, would any of those wounds have been fatal to somebody built like me or you?"

"It's difficult to say. Most were in the area of the heart. Two were lower, near the stomach. To someone built like me, surely four or five would have been lethal, that is to say, each of four or five."

"So somebody wasn't just trying to cut him up. Somebody was trying to kill him."

"As I said, if the wounds had been inflicted on me I would be dead. Whether someone was trying to kill him is, I think, your department."

"Can you tell me anything about the kind of weapon?"

"Some kind of simple knife blade. No more than six inches. But I can say nothing more specific than that. I am a resident in general surgery, not in forensic pathology."

"Sure, I understand. Well, thank you very much."

"You're welcome. Good day," Dr. Ayoub said, turning at once and walking briskly away.

Balzic looked at the nurse, who was trying not to smile. "I guess I didn't score too many points with him."

"Oh, he's all right," the nurse said. "He's just all business."

Balzic thanked her and went with a wave over his shoulder to the elevators. In the lobby he looked around, trying to locate Tullio Manditti, but he didn't see him. Balzic approached one of the hospital security guards and held out his ID case. The guard nodded.

"You seen a short, fat guy, really fat, in dirty clothes?"

"In the coffee shop, feeding his face—as if he needs it. He chased everybody out."

"Coffee shop still in the same place? Every time I come up here they're moving things around, putting on all these additions and wings."

"Well, they haven't moved that yet. But give them time. They will."

"Yeah. So how's it going? They treating you all right?"

"No use complaining."

"Okay, pal, take it easy." Balzic oriented himself and then set off for the coffee shop. He found Tullio Manditti more than occupying a stool at the counter. Both waitresses were smoking in the farthest corner away from Tullio and whispering to each other, their eyes darting toward Tullio as he took a third of a glazed doughnut in one bite. One of the waitresses asked Balzic if she could help him.

"Just coffee. Black." He took a stool two away from Tullio. He wouldn't have sat closer to Tullio if he'd been able to.

"Tullio, why didn't you go home and take a bath and get cleaned up like the people asked you?"

Tullio stuffed the rest of the doughnut in his mouth in two bites and chewed rapidly. He turned to look at Balzic but spoke to the waitresses. "Give me two more. And another milk shake."

"We don't have any more doughnuts."

"You got any pie?"

"Just apple and cherry."

"I hate apple and cherry. Ain't you got no banana cream?"

"No."

"Then forget the pie. Give me a couple cheeseburgers with everything. Extra onions. And grill the onions." Tullio had been looking at Balzic while he spoke to the waitress. Now he turned back to the milk shake container in front of him. He looked inside, sloshed the last of the liquid around, and drank directly from it, letting out a thunderous belch when he finished.

"What did you say, Balzic?"

"You heard me."

"Why don't I go home and take a bath, huh? Is that what you said?"

"That's what I said."

"So tell the people to give their garbage a bath, don't tell me. Tell them to put deodorant on their garbage, then maybe I don't smell, how's that? Huh? What's the matter with you, Balzic? You stupid or something? My brother's up there dying and you want me to leave here and go home and get a bath, Cheesus."

"Well, I see it didn't interfere with your appetite."

"Eating, my brother understands. But going home and taking a bath, he wouldn't understand. He'd never forgive me."

"Come off it, Tullio. Your brother's not dying. Not yet anyway. He'll croak from a heart attack pretty soon, just like you. But he's not dying from those holes he got in him."

"That's what you say. Huh! What do you know? You some kind of doctor?"

"I just talked to the doctor. He'll live."

"When the doc tells me I'll believe it. What you tell me I stick up my gazoomey."

"Have it your way," Balzic said, shrugging. "So what happened?"

13

"What do I know what happened? I come home from work and there he was, bleeding all over the porch. Blood all over the living room, Cheesus."

"And you didn't talk to him about it?"

"What talk, you kiddin'? I'm trying to save him, I ain't worrying about no conversation."

"So how'd you get him here? He had to be conscious. You couldn't have brought him here if he's unconscious."

"So he was conscious a little bit."

"Conscious enough to walk, right?"

"Look, Balzic, I can see where you're going. If he's conscious enough to walk, he got to be conscious enough to talk. But I ain't asking him nothing. I'm just telling him to be cool, don't exert himself, we'll be there in a couple minutes."

"And naturally, that's what he did."

"That's exactly what he did."

"He didn't say one word about what happened or who or how or why?"

"He didn't say nothing."

"Okay. So he didn't say anything. So tell me what he's been doing lately."

"He ain't doing nothing. He's unemployed."

"What? He don't carry bags around for Dom Muscotti anymore?"

"What bags? Dom who?"

"Will you stop it. Who're you talking to? This is me, Tullio. And I know you and your brother since you were in Mother of Sorrows Elementary. You're not talking to some state horse or the FBI. I know how long you and your brother been working for Dom and I know what you do, so don't give my head a pain, all right?"

14

"I'm telling you my brother is unemployed."

"Wait a minute, what is this? You trying to tell me your brother doesn't pick up and deliver for Dom Muscotti anymore?"

"How many ways I got to say it? Cheesus."

"Tullio, you know just as soon as I leave here I'll go straight to Dom and ask him."

"I can't stop you from going nowhere."

"What happened with Dom and your brother?"

"What're you asking me for? What do I look like—the labor relations board? I don't know nothing about it."

"Tullio, that's two lies. You tell me one more I'm going to bust you as a material witness, and then I'll go to the DA and tell him you need to be locked up for your own safety. I can fix it so you stay in the slam for six months."

"You got to have a hearing before that, Balzic. Don't shit me."

"Hey, Tullio, you think I don't know the magistrates in this town? You think I can't have a hearing postponed as long as I want? You think about it, Tullio. And while you're at it, think about something else. Think about those twenty-two hundred calories you'll get every day down at the hotel . . . and lookee here. Here comes your milk shake."

Tullio sneered and swiveled around slightly on his stool, the plastic and metal creaking. He started to say something in Italian.

Balzic waved his index finger from side to side. "Easy, Tullio, easy. You don't want to say anything you're going to have to apologize for."

"What was I going to say? Was I going to say something, huh? Me? Nah. I was going to ask you to loan me a deuce, that's all. I'm a little short, and I didn't want to make no speech for the United Nations. So now you made me make one anyhow."

Balzic snorted and shook his head. He brought his money out, stripped off two bills, and pushed them toward Tullio. He stood and said, "Don't even thank me. Just go home and get cleaned up. Your brother'll understand. And everybody here'll love you."

Tullio drank his milk shake and seemed to be thinking, but he said nothing and did not look up as Balzic walked out.

Balzic debated with himself in the lobby whether to try to talk to Armand Manditti or to go straight to Dom Muscotti. An elevator opening in front of him made up his mind as much as anything else did. He rode up to the seventh floor, there holding the door open with one hand and calling out to the nurse he'd talked to earlier. "Is Manditti out of recovery yet?"

"He's on the third floor."

Balzic waved, stepped back inside the elevator, and pushed the button for three. Once there, he asked at the nurses' station for the room number. On his way, he chatted briefly with one of the charwomen, a friend of his mother's.

He found Armand Manditti in the first bed inside the door of a ward with four other beds, all empty. Balzic stopped in the doorway and laughed. The mound of white on the bed gave him the feeling that he was going to try to talk to a snow drift.

He stepped inside and saw Manny staring sleepily at the tube taped to the back of his hand. Manny blinked incredulously, the blinks coming very slowly. Every time his eyes opened, they would roll, and then Manny would shake his enormous head slowly from side to side, once each way.

"Manny? You hear me?"

"Huh? Am I dead?" The words came as ponderously as his blinks.

"You're not dead, Manny. At least you don't look it."

"Huh? Good . . . I'm glad . . . I thought I'm dead. . . ."

"Who stabbed you, Manny?"

Manny muttered something and closed his eyes and let out a long sigh. Balzic started to ask again, but Manny's sigh had turned into a snore and then another. Balzic took off his raincoat and threw it across the foot of the opposite bed. He looked around for an ashtray, found one, and then settled onto a straight-backed chair just inside the door. He smoked and hoped Manny wouldn't stay under the effect of the anesthetic too much longer.

He should have known better. An hour later, he was still waiting. He had talked to some nurses, then briefly to Dr. Ayoub, who had stopped on his way home. Manny continued to snore, the mattress, springs, and sheets groaning and rustling with each breath. Balzic inspected the bed and then the others in the room. Manny's bed was the same as the rest, and Balzic wondered how long it could take the strain.

Balzic could hear Tullio coming as soon as the elevator doors closed. With each heavy step came a breath as heavy. Tullio, freshly shaved and wearing clean coveralls, huffed into the room carrying a paper shopping bag. He stopped upon seeing Balzic and rolled his eyes toward the ceiling.

"Cheesus Christ, Balzic, state cops all over the house and you here. Whose idea was that—them state cops, huh? Yours? What's the big fuckin' idea? They come in there, they didn't have no search warrant or nothing."

"They don't need one."

"What do you mean, they don't need one? You cops can't just go busting into people's houses. Us people got some rights."

"Tullio, don't make my ass tired, okay? Don't say stupid things."

"Don't make my ass tired. Don't say stupid things." Tullio mimicked him, looking around for a place to put the shopping bag, deciding finally on the dining table at the foot of his brother's bed.

Out of it he took a loaf of Italian bread, two long pieces of pepperoni, a thick slab of provolone cheese, a jar of green olives stuffed with pearl onions, a can of black olives, a jar of banana peppers, and a transparent half-gallon bottle with no labels on it that obviously contained wine. Then he brought out a folded dish towel and opened it up. A small paring knife, a can opener, and a fork rolled out. Tullio took those and the towel and put them in the drawer in the stand beside his brother's bed. He looked around, as though thinking where to put the food.

"Tullio, why don't you just eat it yourself? Your brother's not going to be allowed to eat anything like that for a couple days."

"That's how much you know, Balzic. I know what you get in this place. I been here. You can die in here from the food. Half the cooks are niggers. When they find out the food's for a white person, they spit in it. You think I don't know that? They bring up a lunger, a real oyster, and they let you have it. My brother ain't eating in here, period."

"I don't know, Tullio," Balzic said, smiling. "I can

remember the time Manny scarfed up seven barbecued chickens in about an hour. That was at the Sons of Italy picnic a couple years ago. Looks like all you brought him was a snack."

"Don't sweat your head, Balzic. My brother'll do okay in here, I'll take care of that."

"Tullio, Tullio. . . ." Manny's eyes opened wide.

"I'm here, Manny. Right here. What do you need?"

"Oh, Tullio, I ain't dead . . . that prick . . . I thought I'm dead."

"What prick, Manny?" Balzic said, going immediately to Manny's side.

"Aw take a hike, Balzic, willya!" Tullio said. "Can't you see he don't know what he's saying? Everybody's delirious when they wake up for crissake, everybody knows that . . . listen, Manny, don't try to talk. You just get some rest, okay? I'm here now. I brought you something to eat when you wake up. But keep sleeping now. You need it. You look bad, Manny. You look all green and yellow. You got to sleep that crap out of your system —that crap they put you out with. Just keep sleeping."

"Okay, okay. Just give me some water, okay? My throat's dry."

"Sure. How 'bout some wine in it? It'll make you sleep better."

"Yeah, sure . . . wine too. . . ."

"You better ask a nurse before you give him any wine, Tullio. It might make him really sick if it doesn't mix right with the anesthetic."

"What do you know? Go on, Balzic, take a walk. You don't think I know my brother's system better than any nurse? Go on, hit the bricks. You're making him nervous. Me too." Tullio peeled the wrapper off a glass, filled it half with wine, and added a little water. He rooted through the drawer of the bedstand behind him until he found a flexible straw. "Here, Manny, here you go. Take a couple big sips. It'll do you good. Really make you sleep good."

Manny raised his head and grimaced. "Holy shit, it hurts. . . ."

"Don't raise up. This straw bends. You don't have to raise up. Just lay there. I'll put the straw in your mouth . . . there, like that. See? Listen to Tullio. He'll take care of it."

"You going to take care of who did it too?" Balzic said.

"Listen, Balzic, I told you to take a hike. He don't have to say nothing and neither do I."

Balzic laughed. "Tullio, you been in trouble so much in your life you don't understand. Your brother's the victim. Get it? He's the victim, and the victim don't need a lawyer. The victim isn't supposed to keep quiet. The victim doesn't get any guarantees. I can stay here forever if I feel like it and ask as many questions as I want."

"Yeah? And what's to stop us from staying here forever and not answering any of them, huh? Tell me that, wise guy."

"Not a thing, Tullio, not a thing," Balzic said, reaching for his raincoat. "But there's one guarantee I will give you. I guarantee I'm going to keep asking until somebody gives me some answers. Your brother gets cut up, something is bent out of shape, and six will get you five it had something to do with somebody else's money. And I'll tell you something else, Tullio, and you better pay attention. Somebody else winds up in this hospital with so much as a split lip, I'm going to collar both of you. There isn't going to be any bullshit like that, you hear me? There hasn't been as long as I've been the man here, and it isn't going to start now. And just to make sure, I'm going to give the same message right now to Dom Muscotti, you hear me?"

"I hear you, Cheese, I hear you. What am I? Deaf? But I don't know what you're talking about."

"Oh you know all right. You know." Balzic pulled on his raincoat and walked out.

Balzic eased his cruiser out of the hospital parking lot and drove just fast enough to keep up with traffic, all the while trying to comprehend what had happened and why. . . .

Armand Manditti had worked for years for Dom Muscotti as a runner. He picked up and delivered—money, betting slips, payoffs, layoffs, special case-lot orders of wine from state liquor stores for Dom, groceries and household necessities for Dom's mother—whatever Dom wanted or needed. Now, by Tullio's words, he was unemployed.

As for Tullio, he managed Muscotti's garbage dump. It was the third part of Muscotti's Rocksburg-bound empire. Since Muscotti's father before him, every piece of garbage collected in Rocksburg and in Bovard Township to the north, Westfield Township to the west, and Kennedy Township to the south and east—all public and private refuse—wound up on land owned by a Muscotti. It made no difference which collection outfit bid for the right to collect the stuff; they all paid Muscotti for the privilege of emptying their trucks. And long before anybody publicly talked about recycling waste, Dom's father and then Dom paid a squad of pickers, usually true wops —that is, Italians without papers—to swarm over each load as it was dumped and cull every tin, steel, or aluminum can they could find, then to separate, clean, and pulverize them into one-foot cubes to be sold wherever the market was best.

World War II guaranteed the family fortune in that third of Muscotti's empire; each load of garbage since only added to it, and the uproar over ecology did nothing in Rocksburg so much as show Muscotti the potential of paper and glass. Muscotti persuaded friends in Rocksburg's Sanitation Department who in turn prevailed upon Rocksburg's City Council to pass two ordinances: the first required that newspapers be bundled separately from other garbage; the second required that bottles and jars be placed in separate cans at each residence and business, public or private. While compliance with the two ordinances was far from total, it was sufficient to make life easier for Tullio's squad of pickers to turn garbage into money.

Garbage turned into money so fast that Muscotti had to start giving it away to keep from going into higher and higher tax brackets, and his philanthropy so charmed the Rocksburg Chamber of Commerce that in 1971 they named him Rocksburg's Man of the Year. It seemed not to matter to them that for fifteen years out of the last twenty Muscotti had been summoned to the Pittsburgh office of the Internal Revenue Service to explain his income, or that at least every other year for the past twenty-five Muscotti had been subpoenaed by county, state, and federal grand juries and assorted crime commissions to testify about the sources of his income. It also had not seemed to matter that Muscotti had been indicted six times, tried five times, and convicted three times since 1945 for operating lotteries and bookmaking establishments. What seemed to matter was his charity, though it had been rumored around town that the Chamber of Commerce was more concerned and greatly more relieved by the fact that there had been no violence even remotely attributable to Muscotti for sixteen years.

Bodies may have turned up in the trunks of cars in other parts of Conemaugh County, certain small newsstands and confectionaries in other towns may have suffered unexplained explosions, but nothing like that had happened in Rocksburg for sixteen years.

Balzic had to smile thinking about it. I been chief for sixteen years, he thought, and those Chamber guys never gave me a phone call. Maybe it was all just a coincidence. . . .

Balzic parked his cruiser beside Muscotti's side door on State Street, and the smile left him. He was back to Armand Manditti again, Fat Manny who was alive only because of his fat, and to Tullio Manditti, who was behaving as though his brother was anything but a victim.

Balzic paused outside Muscotti's door and told himself that he had to control the anger he felt rising in him. There was no reason to believe that Manny's unemployment—if that were true—had anything at all to do with his being stabbed. Still, Balzic was getting a bad taste from fuming over that possibility, and he didn't want to blow the opportunity of finding out by losing his temper.

It was nearly five o'clock when Balzic came down the back stairs into Muscotti's. The bar was lined elbow to elbow with the mill and construction workers who habitually stopped after work to drink and learn the day's winning numbers. Shortly, the office brigade from the courthouse would be coming in, as would the merchants who kept shops in the vicinity. Some students from the county community college sat drinking beer out of quart bottles at one of the tables. At another sat Tom Murray, managing editor of *The Rocksburg Gazette*, with two of his reporters—Dick Dietz, who covered the courthouse, and Bob Armour, who covered City Hall. Surrounding the end of the bar nearest the side door were three of Muscotti's closest friends, Dom Scalzo, Tony DiLisi, and Bruno Cercone.

At the other end of the bar nearest the front door, Vinnie the bartender was arguing fruitlessly with Iron City Steve.

"If the war's over," Iron City Steve was shouting, his elbows flapping and his head bobbing, "how come we got all this combat?"

"Enough already!" Vinnie shouted back. "Just sit down and shut up a while. I had you up to my eyeballs today."

Steve's shoulder jerked and twitched. His hand sawed under his nose and then he pinched the corners of his mouth to wipe away beads of saliva. "You had enough, but who do I get enough of? I don't even see anybody I want a little piece of. . . ."

Balzic walked to that end of the bar, exchanging greetings with everyone he knew—which was everyone except for the students—and wondering why Dom Muscotti wasn't in sight.

"Are we approaching or proceeding?" Steve said to Balzic.

"Can't say for me, Steve. How 'bout you?"

"As for me, I approach a little, then I proceed a little. It all comes out the same—I don't go backward."

"Go sit down," Vinnie said. "Sit down and shut up or else go upstairs and go to sleep."

"See there?" Steve said, his hands flailing in all directions. "For every doer there's a teller. Comes out even that way. Gives everybody something to do."

"Shut up, I'm telling you. Jesus Christ, you been going since nine o'clock this morning."

"If I could just believe that," Steve said, picking up his beer and his muscatel and shuffling to the table nearest the front door.

"What'll it be, Mario?"

"Beer. Where's Dom?"

"He had to go someplace," Vinnie said, drawing the beer and setting it in front of Balzic. "He should be back pretty soon. What's the matter? You don't look too good."

"I don't feel too good right now, to tell you the truth. You hear about Fat Manny?"

"No. What about him?"

"Somebody tried to kill him."

Vinnie stopped wiping the bar, his face expressing genuine disbelief and surprise. "No shit. Who? What the hell for?"

"Pretty good questions. I thought maybe you might know something."

Hey, Mario, honest to God, this is the first I heard about it. When'd it happen?"

"Sometime this afternoon. Tullio came home from the dump and found him on the porch. Somebody really carved him up. Whoever it was wasn't fucking around."

"No-o shit. Man, oh man. Mario, I—I don't know what to say."

"What's the meeting about down the other end?"

"You mean Soup, Digs, and Brownie?" The names he used were the nicknames of Muscotti's friends.

Balzic nodded.

"Nothing special. Usual stuff, you know."

"Yeah? Well, do me a favor. Go down there and tell them what I just told you. I want to see what happens."

"Hey, Mario," Vinnie said, leaning close over the bar, "don't even talk like that. That ain't right."

"Just go tell them, will you please?"

"Okay, I'll tell them, but I'm telling you right now, Mario, you're thinking wrong. Those guys don't have nothing to do with Manny. Or Tullio either. If they got some bitch with either one of those two, I'd know about it, believe me. And they don't."

"I believe you. Just go tell them."

"Hey, Vinnie," someone called out. "Couple more here."

"Take it easy, take it easy. I only got two legs."

"Yeah? Well how 'bout using them?"

Vinnie shrugged at Balzic. "See what I got to listen to every day? Comedians. This should be Hollywood, and I should be Cecil B. DeMille. I got a cast of thousands in here every goddamn day." He hurried away to fill that order and then went to the far end of the bar, where he talked briefly with Scalzo, DiLisi, and Cercone.

Balzic couldn't see DiLisi's face too clearly, but Cercone looked like he was going to choke on his drink and Scalzo's face went slack. Scalzo shot a glance toward Balzic, then said something to the other two. He bent his head forward to hear their replies, then picked up his

26

beer and came down the bar toward Balzic.

Scalzo, heavy-lidded, squatly built, indifferent about his appearance, and without pretensions about himself or his work, seemed more and more disturbed the nearer he came to Balzic. It figured, Balzic thought, that he would be the one to talk. He was much older than DiLisi or Cercone—he was sixty-four—and had been with Muscotti longer, since 1945, right after his discharge from the army. That had been his last legitimate employment and was the reason for his nickname. He had been a cook.

He set his beer on the bar and stood very close to Balzic. "What's this about Manny?"

"Well, it's this way, Soup. If it wasn't for all that grease on him, you'd be drinking to his memory."

"Now who the fuck'd want to do that? He's a pain in the ass, Mario. You know that better than I do. But you got to admit, he never hurt nobody. He's just a slob, that's all."

"Well, he must've hurt somebody."

"Nah, I don't believe it. Somebody must've went nuts. Why? Why him? What do you think? You think something else?"

"Right now I'm not sure what I think. All I know is the same thing you know. He's been Dom's gofer for a lot of years, but in the hospital Tullio tells me he's unemployed."

Scalzo laughed. "Come on, you kiddin'? When wasn't he unemployed?"

"You know what I mean. Tullio says he don't work for anybody, though I got to admit he didn't say he wasn't working for Dom anymore exactly, but that was the impression I got—"

"Ah, Tullio's pulling your chain. He don't know what he's talking about. That was nothing. Dom sets him down every once in a while. It's no big deal."

"Yeah, I know Dom's set him down occasionally before, and I got a pretty good idea why. But what was it for this time?"

Scalzo took a moment to reply. "Listen, Mario, I know you for a long time, right?"

Balzic nodded.

"Have I ever fucked around with the rules? Huh? Have I?"

"Not with me. No."

"Well, listen. Neither has Brownie and neither has Digs. I don't know what you're thinking, but I can see you're pissed off. But believe me, you got no right to even start thinking like, uh, well, you know, like sending Vinnie down there to tell us. Like you're going to watch us, you know? You shouldn't've done that, Mario. In fact, I'm a little surprised you did it."

"Well, maybe that was a little chicken-shit on my part, but it's been a long time since anything like this happened, and I'll be goddamned if it's going to get any bigger."

"Hey, I can see your point," Scalzo said. "I know what you mean. But me and Brownie and Digs got nothing to do with those two. They do whatever they do for Dom. We don't have nothing to do with them, believe me. I don't like Tullio. Never did. I used to go up their house when their old man was alive. I liked the old guy. We used to sit around and drink his wine and play *morra*. Even then I didn't like Tullio. He was always a smart-mouth. Even when he's three, four years old, he was a wise little prick. And all the trouble Manny got in, all the

28

trouble he ever got in, it was 'cause Tullio put him up to it. And Manny always got caught. See, Manny ain't too swift in the head, and the old man used to look out for him, and Tullio, he didn't like it. So he was always trying to get Manny in the heat with the old man. It's the same way now. They're the same way with Dom. Tullio tells him, 'Hey, don't turn all them numbers in. Who's going to know?' Shit like that. But Manny always fucks up somehow, you know."

"Is that what happened this time?" Balzic said.

Scalzo shrugged. "Hey, maybe I said too much already. I think maybe you better ask Dom. I'll tell you what. Ask Vinnie. He knows more about that than I do. Believe me." Scalzo picked up his beer and took a sip. "Mario, I been around a long time. Believe me, don't try to make nothing out of this. Somebody went nuts. Had to. Couldn't be nothing else."

Balzic shrugged. "Well, I'll tell you this, Soup. I'm going to keep asking until I find out you're right, how's that? And believe me, I hope you are right."

"I'm right. You'll see," Scalzo said, turning away and walking back down the bar to where Cercone and DiLisi were waiting for him.

Balzic stared moodily at his beer, then picked it up and drained the glass in four swallows, holding it up when he finished for Vinnie to refill it.

Vinnie refilled his glass and set it on the bar. He took some moments wiping the bar and the stem of the glass. "So what'd they say?"

"Soup says they don't know anything about Manny or Tullio."

"Ain't that what I said? Huh?"

Balzic nodded. "He also said to ask you. He said you

29

knew more about those two than he did. Or Digs or Brownie."

"I already told you, Mario. They couldn't have any bitch with those two fat-asses or I'd know about it. Ain't that what I said?"

"That's what you said, all right. So tell me. Is Manny still running for Dom? Tullio says he isn't."

"Listen, Mario, I could tell you, but I think it's better you hear it from Dom, you know?"

"So he isn't."

Vinnie nodded with his eyes downcast and then shrugged. "I don't think it's any different this time than it was all those other times, understand. But you talk to Dom. I got enough aggravation with him lately. He even thinks I'm putting any more of his business in the street, I won't be able to live with him—which ain't to say I been putting any of his business in the street. But he thinks I have."

"What's your aggravation with him?"

"Oh, Mario, honest to God, you don't know?"

"I don't know what you're talking about."

Vinnie nodded for them to move to the very end of the bar. He faced the window overlooking Main Street and spoke very softly. Balzic had to lean over the bar to hear him.

"How old is he?" Vinnie began. "Fifty-seven, right?"

Balzic nodded and shrugged.

"You know how long since he could get it up? Five years. All that Canadian Club. Why do you think I quit drinking? I take maybe two shots of brandy a day. One in my coffee, the other one around noon. He told me to quit. *He* told *me*, get it? So what do you think now?"

"Oh don't tell me."

"Yeah. Younger than his daughters for crissake."

"Hey, it happens, Vinnie. It happens. It's happened to better men than him."

"Hey, those better men ain't got his wife. She ever finds out for sure, I'm going to be the second one she buries."

"You mean she asked you?"

Vinnie shook his head and winced. "She called me at home last week. You know the last time she called me? When Dom's father died. Twenty-two fucking years ago, that's the last time she called me at home. You know what she asks me? She wants to know how's business. How's business! Are you kiddin'? You should've heard the lies I told her. Jesus Christ, I should get an Oscar for that performance."

"What's wrong? How's she know something's up?"

"The register's down a yard, a yard and a half every week for like two months now." Vinnie shook his head and sighed. "This fucking Tuscan, what is he? A medical miracle? He got to get a hard-on now? And me, I'm in the middle. I got to be nice to the broad, you know. Whatever she wants. Booze, bread, food—oh, Christ. I'll tell you, Mario, I wasn't this scared when Sammy Weisberg was still alive. Dom's old lady is something else. Ah, what am I telling you for?"

"Is he dipping into the other stuff or just the register for her?"

"What do you think? I'm telling you, I'm ready to go to California or some fucking place. This has got me nuts. And him, he's like in junior high school, the way he's acting. Twenty, thirty beans every day. Oh, brother.

You know what really scares me? Sometimes I think the bastard really wants to hear how big the bang's going to be."

"It'll make some noise all right."

"Hey, Vinnie, you working today or not?" someone called out down the bar.

"Keep your pants on, what is this?" Vinnie shouted back. He started to hustle away but came back. "You know what I did last Sunday? Go ahead, think about it."

"I can guess."

"Uh-huh. First time since I buried my mother. On my knees, with a candle, in front of Mary yet. Holy fucking Christ. . . ."

Balzic shook his head sympathetically and then resumed staring at his beer between sips. He drank that one and another before he heard the door open behind him and heard Dom Muscotti's voice speaking in Italian to someone still on the sidewalk.

The first person Muscotti saw after he closed the door was Balzic, and he smiled broadly and extended his hand, asking in Italian how Balzic was.

"I'll know better after we talk."

"In the back?"

"In the back."

Muscotti had held Balzic's hand until then. It was a strong grip but with no attempt to show strength, for Muscotti, in spite of his age and perpetual drinking, was somehow still a powerful man. Except that his once-red hair was now iron gray, the only obvious signs of aging about him were the deepening creases in his face and neck and the increasing paunch below his belt. He had given up driving an automobile years ago, and no matter what the temperature or the weather, he walked everywhere without an outer coat. He would ride in an automobile only when he had to leave Rocksburg, asking for a lift from whoever happened to be in his saloon and paying for it with drinks. His shoes were handmade in Philadelphia, and he joked that he would live only about a year longer than his shoemaker.

Speaking to everyone by name, Muscotti led Balzic to the second of two small rooms beyond the kitchen. He held the door for Balzic, flipped the switch for the light over the round table in the center of the room, then closed and locked the door behind them. There were ten chairs in the room, seven of them around the table, and two ancient, wooden filing cabinets in one corner. Muscotti went to the nearest of those and brought out a bottle of Valpolicella and two thick-stemmed glasses.

"Sit, Mario, sit," Muscotti said, screwing out the cork and pouring the wine to within a half-inch of the tops of the glasses.

Balzic picked up one of the glasses and toasted Muscotti's health while still standing. Muscotti returned the toast and then they both sat, pulling out the chairs and sitting obliquely facing each other.

"How's your mother, Mario?"

"Fine. How's yours?"

"Oh, couldn't be better. She's a little mad at me though."

"Why's that?"

"I made her put her money in the bank. She says to me, 'All of it?' And I said, 'Well, you can keep a little in the house.' So how much you think she wants to keep?"

"How much?"

"Five grand. 'Just in case,' she says. Can you beat that? I said to her, 'Hey, what kind of emergency you think you're going to have?' She just laughed. I laughed like hell myself." Muscotti drank the rest of his wine and said, "Drink up, Mario. Have some more."

"Thank you," Balzic said, drinking his and then watching the color of the wine as Muscotti refilled the glasses.

"How's Ruth? Emily, Marie—they okay?"

"They're fine," Balzic said. "Your family?"

"Oh, you know. What do they got to complain about? Hey, did I tell you what I got my daughters for last Christmas? I think I must've told everybody but you."

Balzic shook his head.

"Telephone credit cards. They're better than all the rest of those cards. You can get anything on those AT&T cards, d'you know that? I told them, I said, 'Hey, don't you do it. Just phone calls, that's all,'" Muscotti said, laughing. "Those credit cards, Christ, what a friggin' hustle. I wish I'd've thought of them. They're better than football. Better than boxing used to be."

Balzic coughed and crossed and uncrossed his legs.

Muscotti had been sitting back in his chair. Now he straightened up and put his hands on his knees, looking directly into Balzic's eyes. "Okay, Mario, I'm listening."

"You know about Fat Manny?"

Muscotti nodded. "I heard right before I came in. Young DeNezza told me out on the street."

"Well, what's going on?"

"I don't know," Muscotti said, shrugging.

"Is he still running for you?"

"No."

"Why not? What happened?"

"He did something he wasn't supposed to do."

34

"Hey, listen, Dom, maybe you don't see what I see—"

"Oh, Mario, wait a minute. I see plenty. I knew you were going to be here as soon as young DeNezza told me. I said to myself, I'll bet a hundred to one Mario's waiting for me when I get inside."

"Okay, so you won. So what's going on?"

"Mario, I'm telling you, I don't know."

"But for sure he's not working for you anymore."

"Oh, you know, it wasn't nothing permanent. I just had to sit him down a little while, that's all. He'd've got his job back."

Balzic sipped his wine and thought a moment. "Dom, sixteen years ago next month, we made some rules, remember?"

"I remember," Muscotti said, nodding vigorously.

"No whores, no dope, no muscle, right?"

"That's right."

"And it never cost you a penny tax, right?"

"Not to you, that's right."

"Or to any of my people either."

"I can't argue with that."

"So all of a sudden we get some muscle and you're telling me you don't know anything about it?"

"Mario, honest to God, I don't. It shocked me to hear it. I mean it. I don't know where it came from or why. On my father's grave it didn't come from me. What the hell do I want with muscle? What am I—one of those crazy New York guys? All muscle does is bring heat. Who the hell wants heat? Right now, look what's happening. Somebody goes Hollywood, and here you are, looking at me like I'm a crazy. Christ, Mario, how long's it been since we talked back here like this? You think I want this?" Muscotti threw up his hands. "Over Fat Manny?"

"Okay," Balzic said. "So why'd you sit him down? Was he booking on his own?"

"What do you think?"

"I'm asking. Was he?"

"Yeah, sure. What else? The sonofabitch, I should've had him out the dump. That was my mistake. Giving him something better because my mother likes him. I should've put him out there."

"Why didn't you?"

"I just told you. My mother likes him. He brings the groceries, they sit around and gossip. He knows just what to tell her. She feeds him, he eats like six plates of pasta, he tells her how she's the best cook in the world since his mother died, and she loves him. Then he tells her who he saw coming out of church, who was in the A&P, who was buying zucchini, who was buying egg-plant, and she wants to know all that stuff. I tried other guys. They don't know how to talk to her. She gets mad and I got to put him back on. She's really been hollering at me since I set him down this time."

"How long's it been this time?"

"A week."

"Okay, so he booked something and he got beat. You don't think there could be any other reason?"

"What else? He books a winner, he can't pay, the guy takes the heat. What the fuck—I'd do the same thing myself." Dom shook his head. "I told the goddamn dummy a hundred times. I said, 'Manny, you can't do this. One of these times you're going to get burned, and everybody's going to think I'm backing you. And I ain't. And you're going to have to take the weight, and where the fuck are you going to get the five-forty if you take a buck on a solid hit? You ain't getting it from me; not even at five percent a week, you ain't getting it.' I told him that so many times I can't count them. You think he listens? Huh? What am I talking for?

"What kills me, you know when he does it? Five minutes after he passes a bakery. He sees all those jelly doughnuts and cream puffs in the window and right away the eraser starts going. He got twenty, twenty-two bets, he turns in eighteen. And that friggin' Tullio, he tells Manny, 'Don't worry about it. Dom got so much paper the government's coming to him. What's a buck and a half to Dom?' And friggin' Manny listens to him and thinks it's all right. I'd like to kick Tullio's ass myself. Manny's too. But see, Manny ain't as smart as Tullio. So as mad as I get at him, I really can't get too mad, you know? 'Cause he's dumb . . . I should've kicked his ass the first time he did it. I knew this was going to happen. . . ."

"Well, you kick both their asses if you want to, but there's two things you better do first."

"Me? What do you want me to do?"

"First, tell Tullio not to get any ideas. 'Cause something happens, I'm going to come straight to you."

"Aw, Mario—"

"Aw Mario nothing. We made the rules. You and me. You get the action, you keep the odds right, you pay no taxes. Everybody who wins gets paid, and no more than five percent on the shylocking to the losers. Did I leave anything out?"

"No."

"Okay. Then convince Tullio."

"Or else?"

"Or else you all go to the slam, and I'll fix it so

everybody has to put up cash bonds. All the street people you got. It'll cost you a fortune."

"But, Mario, you know it's not me!"

"I know it's not. But I'm making it you. Because Tullio won't listen to me. He thinks I'm a jackoff. *Your* jackoff. But he does something, and everything stops. And it won't be me serving the warrants. It'll be U.S. marshalls."

"Aw, come on now, Mario. I been straight with you all these years and you're going to talk like this to me? Over something you know I didn't have nothing to do with?"

"All I'm telling you to do is tell Tullio. Because, Dom, this town is not going back to the way things were when Collela was chief and you and Sammy Weisberg were burning each other down. Collela worked both of you pretty good, and from what I heard he paid seventy-five thousand for that place in Florida. Which must've made you and Weisberg feel pretty smart." Balzic stabbed the air with his index finger. "Goddamnit, I don't have any retirement like that to look forward to, and you got a lot more money because I don't. So you tell Tullio."

"Okay, Mario, okay, take it easy," Muscotti said, shaking his head with his eyes downcast. "But I can't make any miracle for you. Some things you just can't control."

"Put somebody on him."

"Like who?"

"Cercone would make a good keeper. Tell him what's going to happen."

"Brownie? At the dump?"

"Hey, Dom, how you handle it is how you handle it. All I'll tell you is this: I'll do everything I can to find whoever it was as fast as I can. Which brings up the second thing you have to do. Tell Manny to quit listening to Tullio. As long as Tullio's got his ear, Manny's not going to tell me anything. But he opens up, it's simple. I go collar the guy and that's that. But if Manny keeps shut, then I got to find the guy myself, which is going to take time, which is going to give Tullio time, which means you got to keep somebody on him longer, which means you lose business somewhere else. And if Tullio shakes whoever you put on him and does something stupid, then I guarantee it'll cost you a fortune in bail."

Muscotti shook his head and rubbed his palms together. "That fat-ass. I should've got him on with the county. Dumb as he is, he ought to be working for the government."

Balzic drove immediately to his station after leaving Muscotti's. He was so preoccupied with what he'd said to Muscotti and the way he'd said it that he ran a red light two blocks from City Hall, spinning the wheel wildly to swerve between a pickup truck and a station wagon loaded with cub scouts. He didn't even slow down. He slouched against the seat, tucking his chin into the lapels of his raincoat, and hoped he hadn't been recognized.

Going up the steps, he said under his breath, "You dumb bastard, it's a good thing you got sense enough to have an unmarked car. . . ."

Inside the duty room he found Desk Sergeant Vic Stramsky talking on the phone, taking a description.

"Another runaway," Stramsky said after hanging up. "Cleaned out his old lady's purse and split. Thirteen years old. I wonder how far he thinks he's going to get on four bucks and change."

"Well, put it out to the troops," Balzic said. "Maybe we'll get lucky with this one. What's that, the third one this week?"

"Yeah," Stramsky said, nodding, "but we found the second one."

"Well, that makes it two to one, the kids are still leading." Balzic went to the coffee urn and poured himself a cup. He took a sip and scalded his lips, spitting the coffee on the floor. "What the hell's wrong with this machine? Everything comes out boiling."

Stramsky ignored him, rolling over to the radio console and putting out the name and description of the runaway. When he was finished, he said, "What're you screaming at the machine for? If you know everything's coming out boiling, why can't you wait?"

"Go ahead, give me a lecture about patience. My head's going six ways at once—all wrong—and I'm supposed to improve my character. I burn myself once more, that machine goes in the can, and nobody'll have to worry about my character." He went to the log on the table in front of the radio console and ran his finger down the list of calls. "Some day this is. Two bent fenders, a mattress fire, a runaway, and Fat Manny—and he doesn't even make the log."

"What're you mumbling about?" Stramsky said, rolling his chair over beside Balzic.

"Put down here that Armand Manditti was the victim of felonious assault, sometime between three-thirty and four-thirty. Assailant unknown. Give it the whole treatment."

"Did you say Fat Manny?"

"Yeah. Listen, I'm going up to Norwood."

"Why?"

"Because that's where Manny got it."

Stramsky started to smile, but caught himself and turned away.

"What's so funny?"

"You. You're really gunned up about something. If you were going up to Norwood, why'd you come back here? You could've told me that on the radio."

Balzic snorted. "You think that's pretty dumb, huh?"

"Well, you know. . . ."

"Yeah? Well, you should've seen me ducking after I almost took the front end off a station wagon full of kids. You'd've really got your jollies over that. . . . What the hell do I know what I came back for? Maybe to burn my mouth on the coffee, all the weight I tried to lay on Muscotti. I couldn't believe it was me talking."

Stramsky chortled. "What'd you say to him?"

Before Balzic could reply, the phone rang. Stramsky answered it and then held it out for Balzic. "It's Johnson from the state CID."

"Hello, Walk. What do you got?"

"Not much, buddy. But I'll tell you one thing. You weren't joking about those two being slobs. I never saw a house like that. God, newspapers up to the ceiling in, uh, I guess it was the living room; garbage in the kitchen you wouldn't believe; in the bathroom, so help me, there was a radiator and two batteries for a car. And stink! Jesus. You couldn't tell if there had been a struggle or not. My people kept looking at me and saying, 'How would we know?' "

"Yeah. So did you get anything?"

"We scraped up a lot of blood. There was no forcible

41

entry. We got a couple sets of prints, but that's really the best I can offer."

"How about somebody stepping in the blood—any chance?"

"No. There was a lot of stepping and stumbling going on, but not one damn thing clear."

"How about tire tracks?"

"All over the place, but we could only make out one matched set, and then when this Tullio showed up, it didn't take any expert to see they were all off his car." Johnson paused and chuckled. "That Tullio, is he something. He came in and started screaming where was our search warrant. I tried to tell him that his brother was the victim and that his residence was the scene of a crime, but I wasted my breath. He raised holy hell for about ten minutes, then all of a sudden he says, 'I got to take a bath. Don't bother me no more.' And off he goes and takes a bath."

"So, uh, you really didn't get anything, huh?"

"Sorry, Mario. I wish I could give you something more, but about the only thing I have are the prints. I sent our print man up to the hospital to get the victim's, and we got Tullio's. Once we get a comparison we might have something, but that's about it."

"Well, thanks, Walk, I appreciate it."

"Listen, you also weren't kidding about the neighbors. I didn't find one who could speak English."

"Oh, they can all right, don't kid yourself. But they won't. Not even to me." Balzic sighed. "Okay, Walk. So let me know how the prints turn out."

"Will do. Take it easy."

Balzic hung up and swore.

"I take it they didn't come up with anything," Stramsky said.

"You take it right, brother."

"So now tell me what you said to Muscotti."

"Huh? Oh. Nothing much. I just told him that if anything happens because of Manny getting chopped up, I was going to guarantee his whole operation was going to the slammer, that's all. Just the goddamnedest threat I ever made in my life. And then I sat there with all the face in the world and tried to make out like it's no threat. Like it's a sure pop. Christ, I must be watching too much television or something. But you know the real capper?"

Stramsky shook his head.

"I think he bought it, how's that grab you?" Balzic shook his head and snorted softly. "Now can you feature me walking into the U.S. Attorney's office in Pittsburgh, bigger than shit, and I'm trying to convince those guys that I let the second biggest banker and lay-offer in the county—I let him run for sixteen years, and not only did I never bust him or anybody connected with him, but I never took a penny from him. Now just what do you think they're going to say? They're not going to be able to say anything. They'll all be laughing so hard they'll have hernias."

"Don't you think Dom knows that? Or don't you think he's going to think of it?"

"I don't know. The look on his face, I couldn't believe it. But maybe all that Canadian Club finally got to his brain. Then again, maybe he got himself in too deep in something else."

"What's that?"

"Something Vinnie told me. Seems that old Tuscan

is going to do adolescence over again. He got Vinnie so shook up, Vinnie went to church last Sunday and put up a candle in front of Mary. Dom's wife finds out for sure what's going on, everybody'll be putting up candles in front of St. Jude."

"You mean Dom got himself a broad?" Stramsky threw back his head and roared with laughter.

"Yeah, it's funny now, but what do you think's going to happen when his old lady starts asking him how come the register's down a yard and a half every week? How many stories you think he can come up with?"

"Is that what he's throwing at the broad?"

"According to Vinnie. I'll tell you, I never saw Vinnie so rattled. Which, the more I think about it, the more I think is the reason Dom bought my bullshit." Balzic sighed heavily. "Which just gives me another thought. Holy Christ!"

"What's the matter?"

"The matter is, Dom's old lady blows the whistle on him, we're right back in the U.S. Attorney's office, are you kidding?"

"So? You're clean. The whole force is clean."

"Come on, Vic, you know better than that. There's two ways to be dirty. Everybody knows the first way. The second applies to us. We don't do what we get paid to do, we're dirty, brother, and that is all she wrote."

"Hey, Mario, don't you think you're getting a little carried away? Hell, Dom's wife never goes near his joint. And who's going to tell her?"

"Nobody has to, Vic. She's already wise. She called Vinnie at home last week and asked him how business was. She knows something's up. She goes through

Dom's pants every night as soon as he starts snoring. Hell, Dom'll tell you that himself. She just hasn't figured out how come he's been short—oh, Jesus Christ." Balzic clapped his hands and threw them upward and then held his head. "No wonder he bought it! He's looking at me and listening to me, but he's hearing his old lady."

"I don't get it," Stramsky said.

"Dom. I'm thinking he bought *my* bullshit. But that's exactly the same story his wife's going to give him. The only difference is I was bitching about Manny. But he's already been through this in his head with his wife. In his head, he knows that's what she's going to say. I could've been talking about the broad for all the difference it makes. He knew goddamn well I can't put him in the slammer without taking a lot of heat myself, but she can put him away forever just on the income taxes alone. Ho, boy, what an ego I got. I wish I had a brain to match." Balzic pounded his fist on a desk and then walked quickly toward the door.

"Hey, where you going now?"

"Someplace. Wherever I can find somebody smarter than me. Wherever the hell that is. Hell, right now that's practically anyplace."

Balzic took the alleys to avoid traffic, pulling in ten minutes later to the rear parking lot of Rocksburg Bowl. He hustled inside to the lounge and bar, looking around for Mo Valcanas. It had to be ladies' day at the bowling alleys because the only man Balzic saw was the bartender, an aging and overweight one-time pretty boy who brushed his hair with his hands and straightened his tie each time he filled an order. He seemed to have found paradise serving alcohol and stale jokes to leagues of women bowlers. Balzic surmised this in a minute, then started for the room behind the bar where the gin games were played daily.

He found only Mo Valcanas and Dick Gervasi, the owner of the alleys, playing cards. Gervasi was writing on a small pad, and Valcanas was shuffling the cards while trying to read the score upside down. Both looked up at the same time.

"Mario," Gervasi said. "Long time no see, buddy. Where you been keeping yourself?"

"It should be longer," Valcanas said. "He comes here, he's got something in mind for me."

"Gentlemen," Balzic said, drawing up a chair and straddling it. "I'll come right to the point."

"The day any cop comes right to the point will be a first in American history," Valcanas said. "And that includes you."

"Oh, you're so sweet. I could just give you a big kiss."

"You want something to drink, Mario?" Gervasi said, standing.

"No, thanks. What I really want is to talk to the Greek for a couple minutes. You mind?"

"What the hell are you asking him for? You want to talk to me, why don't you ask me if I mind?"

"Oh, you're so lovable. I'll bet your mother just beamed the whole nine months, just beamed and glowed waiting for you to pop your cute little bald head out."

"Hey, I'll be glad to let you two alone, Mario. This Greek's killing me today. I need a breather."

"I see you got a new bartender," Balzic said. "What happened to Jimmy?"

"He's in the hospital. He'll be back in a couple weeks.

You sure you don't want something to drink?" Gervasi went for the door.

"Nah. I had plenty already today."

Gervasi left then, closing the door firmly behind him.

"Okay, Mario," Valcanas said, "I hesitate to ask, but what is it this time?"

"Just a couple questions about the law, that's all."

"And naturally these couple answers I'm expected to give will be for free. You couldn't ask in my office, where I might feel justified in sending you a bill."

"Naturally. Besides, every time I walk into your office I start to feel like I'm really in trouble, like I really need a lawyer."

"Uh-huh," Valcanas grumbled. "I ought to set up an office in all the saloons I go into. I might start making some money."

"Boy, there's a contradiction for you. You set up offices in all the saloons you go into, you couldn't afford the light bills."

"Well, let's quit fucking around. It'll cost you two drinks. I got to get that much out of you."

"Fair enough. So here it is: now I know that a wife can't be forced to testify against her husband, but how about if she volunteers? What's she worth on the stand?"

"That depends. Give me a situation."

"Well, the woman, after a long and faithful marriage on her part, finds out that her old man's screwing around, which he's never done before. In the meantime, he's been involved for most of his adult life in illegal activities. She may not be an accomplice exactly, but she's the closest thing to it there is. She knows everything, in other words."

Valcanas grinned and then broke up laughing. "Christ, don't tell me you're getting worried about Dom too? Half the goddamn courthouse is walking around on eggs about that. That's all I've heard down there for the past two weeks."

"Well, I guess I must be the dumbest guy in town then."

"You said it, Mario, I didn't."

"Aw fuck you too. Well, what about it? How much damage can she do?"

"That would depend on a couple of things. First, it would depend on whether she has access to records or had been keeping records herself. I mean, her credibility goes down to practically zero if she just walks into the U.S. Attorney's office and says, 'I know my husband did this or that or whatever.' That's for openers. Then suppose she has records, enough to get the whole thing to trial. It would depend on the attorneys—how good the prosecutor was in leading her through her motivation for coming forward at this late date in her life—and on his lawyer—Dom's—for trying to wreck that motivation. But the big thing would be the jury. The prosecution would want as many old ladies in the jury box as they could get, preferably Italian Catholic, and the defense would want as many dirty old men as they could get. Whoever wins that battle wins the war, that's what it comes down to."

"So given the worst suppositions, Dom's wife could really raise some hell."

"If you have something to be concerned about, sure. Hell, Corcoran is so rattled that yesterday he called a recess in the middle of a drunk-driving trial. Two more minutes and it would've been over. But he called a recess. I thought his tipstaff was going to faint. But, hell,

Corcoran's got reason to be nervous. All the fines he's laid on Dom's people in the last eight years wouldn't add up to two thousand bucks. That time the state boy scouts caught Digs DiLisi with forty-two-thousand bucks and about ten pounds of numbers slips, Corcoran let him off with costs. Just what do you think that was worth?"

"I don't even want to guess," Balzic said.

"Well, you ever get curious, you go ask Digs how much was in the briefcase when he went to pick it up. He came bitching to me afterward, and I told him, I said, 'You dumb bastard, you ought to be glad you got that much back. Maybe now you'll think of something better to do with those slips than leave them laying around on your kitchen table.' "

"But I thought you beat that for him."

Valcanas smiled. "Come on. I filed a motion to suppress evidence on the grounds that the boy scouts' information was based on hearsay. The law's changed now, you know that. Now the so-called confidential informant has to appear himself in front of the magistrate. But then, Christ, a cop's hearsay was good enough.

"Anyway," Valcanas went on, "if I hadn't known that Corcoran was going to hear the damned thing, I wouldn't even have wasted my secretary's time typing up the motion to suppress. But I knew what he'd do. Exactly what he did, which was give Digs a speech about how the tentacles of gambling reach into all sorts of nasty nasties, and then fine him a hundred bucks and costs. But Digs, that egotistical ass, he can't get it through his head that you put forty-two big ones on the wheel of justice, somebody pushing is going to think lifting is easier. And to this day, he thinks that if it had come up in front of some of Dom's other friends, my motion to suppress—to put it mildly—would've been received with anything more than a smile. He thinks those other guys would've hit him with a fine and costs—and let him walk out with a full briefcase.

"Christ, sometimes these wops make me laugh. He gets half a briefcase back, and he gets pissed at me. He says—and I quote—'It would've been cheaper to go to jail.' I said, 'Why you stupid sonofabitch, you go to jail and you don't get anything back.' But do you know, to this day he's never paid my bill. Not only that, he refuses to speak to me. Christ. . . ."

Balzic chewed his thumbnail thoughtfully.

"Besides which," Valcanas said, shifting around on his chair, "this has got to be the biggest joke in this county since Froggy ran for judge."

"Why's that?"

"Dom's not screwing anybody for crissake. He can't. You can't drink as much as he drinks and still grind your organ. If anything, his genitourinary tract is in worse shape than mine—if that's possible."

"Well, I wouldn't pretend to know whether he's screwing anybody," Balzic said. "But a hell of a lot of people seem to think so. And his wife know's the register's short in his saloon. What difference does it make whether he is or isn't or can or can't—if she thinks he is, what's the difference?"

"None. If she acts on what she thinks. If that is what she thinks. Why don't you ask her and be a real cop—prevent a crime instead of waiting until it happens and then trying to prove that whoever you caught is the person who did it? Hell, what could be more salutary than that?"

"Oh, up yours. What do I say? 'Hey, Gina, there's

something I been meaning to ask you—is that how I start?"

"How you ask is your problem. I'm not interested in the answer myself. All I know is, the most Dom can do is rub bellies. And that would be pure nostalgia. I'll make you a bet though."

"What bet?"

"I'll lay twenty against one that all he's doing with that broad—whoever she is—is talking. And giving her money for being kind enough to listen. People are waiting in line to talk to the brain strainers, either because it's fashionable or because their families can't stand them anymore. But can you feature Dom going to a shrink? Hell, I can imagine him exposing himself to a little girl sooner than I can see him admitting that there was something going on in his head he couldn't handle.

"And what about a priest?" Valcanas went on. "You know what a priest is to Dom? He's a guy in funny clothes who read too many books when he was a kid because the nuns scared the shit out of him. And all he's good for is saying the words that make your wife feel all right about screwing you, or that make the family feel okay when somebody dies. But most of all, he's good for saying the right words in front of a jury when you get busted for running a book. And unless he's had some genuine change of mind, those are the reasons he takes up the collection every Sunday at twelve o'clock mass. Go ask Marrazo if I'm not right. Better yet, go ask him if Dom ever came to him with a problem—any problem."

"I don't have to ask," Balzic said. "Most of what you said I agree with, except for that part about paying the broad just to listen."

"Oh, come on, Mario. Hell, I had a client once who

51

used to pay a whore fifty bucks an hour once a week, sometimes twice, just so he could cuss her out and call her names. He never went within three feet of her. What do you think he was doing?"

"You tell me."

"He was telling her everything he didn't have the guts to tell his wife. The whore used to sit around doing her nails, listening to records, and all she was required to do was look up every ten minutes or so and say, 'What do you know about it, dummy?' Then he was off for another ten minutes. But do you think his wife believed that? Especially after she went to the trouble of hiring a private dick to find out where he was going? And you want to hear something really stupid? I actually arranged a meeting in my office."

"Oh, are you kiddin' me?" Balzic said, laughing. "With the wife and the whore?"

Valcanas scratched his throat slowly. "I was a lot younger then. A lot younger. God, when I think about it, I can't believe I was ever that young."

When Balzic finally quit laughing, he said, "I still can't get it through my head. I—"

"Look," Valcanas said, "I know you talk with Marrazo a lot. And I think I know you well enough to be reasonably sure that if something was really bothering you, you'd go to a shrink. But what do you think would happen in this town if word got around that the chief of police was seeing a shrink?"

"I wouldn't tell anybody about it."

"Then what's so hard to understand about paying a broad to listen to you?"

"I don't understand it because I can't see myself doing it, that's all."

"Well, Christ, you just said that if you had to go to a shrink you wouldn't tell anybody about it. Now you say you can't see yourself paying a broad for practically the same thing. You're as bad as the people you'd be scared of."

"That's not what I mean."

"Oh, hell, I'm starting to get thirsty. You owe me two drinks, don't forget."

"I didn't forget."

"Then let's go get them," Valcanas said, standing and going toward the door. He stopped short of it. "Think about this, Mario. You wouldn't tell anybody about going to a shrink; now just try to imagine what happens to the *padrone*. I mean, who's he have to talk to? Don't forget, you and I both know where Dom fits in the scheme of things in this part of the state, but most people around here have a vastly inflated notion of who he is and what he can do. And the ones who work for him? Christ, they think he's got a bulletproof soul, except for Vinnie. Vinnie knows that's a crock. He knows Dom better than anybody."

"Well, okay," Balzic said, "but just for the sake of argument, if he does need somebody to talk to, why wouldn't he go to his *padrone*?"

"How should I know? I don't know their rules. For all I know they may play as many silly word games as the Shriners. Maybe there are some things they just don't talk about. Hell, I don't know what's ailing Dom—if anything is. Maybe he suddenly found out he's mortal. Maybe he started paying attention in church. I don't know. Go talk to the broad, I'm telling you. Find out what she's like. See what her angle is. Or go talk to Marrazo. Maybe he knows something. But if you really want to know what's going on, talk to the broad. That's what I'd do . . . come on. You owe me two drinks."

They went out to the bar and Balzic ordered for Valcanas.

"Don't you want anything?" Valcanas asked.

"No. I'm trying to think where I should go, whether I should go talk to the broad or to Father Marrazo."

"You know, Mario," Valcanas said after his drink came, "I'm starting to wonder why you're so concerned about this in the first place."

Balzic shrugged. "Something happened today that is really giving off a bad odor. If I don't get it straightened out in a hurry, it might stink all the way to Pittsburgh. And believe me, the last thing I want is for that U.S. Attorney to get his nose open—no matter what causes it to get open . . . I'll see you, Mo. Try not to hurt anybody driving home."

"Aw go pound sand. Hey, what about the other drink?"

"I owe you one," Balzic said, laughing and clapping Valcanas lightly on the shoulder as he turned to leave. He heard Valcanas cursing in Greek as he left.

Balzic went in the back door of St. Malachy's rectory. He found the door to Father Marrazo's study slightly ajar and knocked gently. He heard some movement but no answer to his knock, so he pushed the door a bit more open.

The priest was sitting at his desk as though he had just put something on the floor, and when he saw that it was Balzic he reached down and brought up a jelly glass half full of wine and an unlabeled bottle which looked to be about two-thirds empty. He didn't bother to stand or speak, nor did he smile. He simply looked at Balzic and then nodded toward a chair for Balzic to sit. He opened a drawer in his desk and brought out another jelly glass, filling it and his own, again nodding to Balzic to have the wine.

"*Salud,*" the priest said, just above a whisper. He drank half his glass without waiting for Balzic to return the toast.

Balzic sipped the wine, just enough to taste it, then put the glass back on the desk and sat in the chair the priest had nodded to.

"Uh, Father, you sick?"

"Not physically, no."

"Well, uh, listen, if there's a better time for me to come back, you know, just say the word and I'll—"

"No, no. Don't leave. Let's just drink some wine and sit here a little while."

Balzic waited some moments, sipping the wine. Then he asked, "Is it that bad?"

"Mario, it's the worst thing—ah, listen to me. I almost said it's the worst thing that's happened to me since I've been in this parish, but that's how bad it is. It's got me thinking about myself instead of what's really involved, as though—ah, never mind . . . I'm really glad you came. There's nobody I know better able to understand this . . . but, please. Drink up."

Balzic took up his glass and drank. "Is this Mr. Ferrarra's wine?"

The priest nodded. "And when we finish this, I've got another bottle, and if we finish that—if you're still here

—I've got a half-gallon of California chablis." The priest spoke with his eyes closed, and his face was going through the very obvious contortions of a man trying to keep from crying.

Balzic lit a cigarette and sat on the edge of his chair, trying to decide whether to speak or keep silent. He couldn't recall ever seeing the priest so distraught.

Some minutes passed. They emptied their glasses, the priest refilled them, and they drank that. The bottle was almost empty. Father Marrazo looked at it, poured the last drops into Balzic's glass, and then left the room. He reappeared shortly, carrying another bottle of Mr. Ferrarra's homemade wine in one hand and the chablis in the other. He set both bottles on his desk and refilled their glasses from the Ferrarra. Then he sank slowly into his chair, picking up his glass and holding it up to the light. "What a color," he said. "Isn't it beautiful?"

"Lovely."

". . . he taught my introductory course in philosophy, can you imagine? Good Lord, how long ago was that?"

Balzic frowned quizzically but said nothing.

"What a roar he caused over at St. Vincent's," Father Marrazo said. "He was supposed to be giving us Aristotle and Augustine and Aquinas, and there he was, throwing Kierkegaard and Heidegger and Jaspers at us as well. My God, it's a wonder he was allowed to go on as long as he did. But, uh, he left eventually. In my junior year. He was made assistant here, and then when he got to be too much here, out he went to St. Jude's."

"Uh, Father, who're you talking about?"

"What? Oh, I'm sorry, Mario. I thought I said. Father Sabatine. From St. Jude's, out in Westfield Township."

"I think I might've met him," Balzic said, "but I don't know him."

"Oh, he raised some hell in this diocese, believe me. He had old ladies of both sexes running to the bishop every week about something he said the Sunday before. Once, long before the encyclical absolving the Jews of any responsibility for killing Christ—long before that— he said it straight out in a sermon. He said to blame the Jews for the death of Christ was absolute nonsense. Remember, this was twenty years ago at least, but years before that encyclical came out. He couldn't have shaken up this diocese more if he'd walked into Aldonari's office and called him a Fascist to his face—which Aldonari was."

"Bishop Aldonari?"

"Well, you know, Mario, I don't mean that literally. But there was no mistaking Aldonari's sympathy when it came to Mussolini. Anybody who could make the trains run on time in Italy and still let the Vatican alone—hell, according to Aldonari, that was practically the Second Coming. So when Sabatine said what he said about the Jews, Aldonari nearly had a stroke.

"And do you know what started all that?" the priest went on, suddenly quite animated. "It was all over Sam Weisberg. Yeah, can you believe it? The thing was, in those days Sabatine had a real passion for golf. The only two things that could keep him off the course were snow and lightning, otherwise he was out there, swinging away. And it must've been on some public course that he met Weisberg. Of course, Sabatine could play any time he wanted to at Westfield Golf Club.

"Apparently, what happened was that he became

friendly with Weisberg—how I can't even guess—but he did, and Weisberg probably mentioned something about playing at Westfield. So Sabatine took him—can you imagine?—two or three times from what I heard."

Balzic just shook his head.

"Well, then, apparently Weisberg started making noises about wanting to join Westfield. I don't need to tell you what that club was like right after the war. Every Italian beer distributor, saloon keeper, bartender, and cook in the county was a member. Half of them were members of this parish, and all of them were friends of Muscotti's. Some of them real friends. It's a small miracle that Weisberg wasn't killed the first time he set foot in the parking lot."

"And you mean to tell me that nobody told Sabatine who Weisberg was?" Balzic said.

"Maybe it was because Sabatine was a priest and wasn't supposed to know about such things," Father Marrazo said, shrugging. "Hell, I don't know why nobody told him, but it's obvious that nobody did. Anyway, he got tired of the polite runaround every time he brought the subject up, so he took it right to the membership committee—formally. They listened to him, thanked him for taking an interest in their club, drank some wine with him, all courteous as hell. Then they waited a couple days and sent him a nice, neat little note saying they were sorry but their membership was filled.

"Well, Sabatine didn't just jump to the wrong conclusion. He flew. And apparently, it never occurred to him that there might be some other reason besides Weisberg's ancestry. And I know damn well that it never entered his mind that any one of two or three guys on that membership committee would've considered it an

58

honor to kill Weisberg. And I'm equally certain that Sabatine never suspected for a second that Weisberg was anything but sincere. He'd've probably fainted if he'd heard that Weisberg was laughing himself silly every time he thought of the looks on those guys' faces when Sabatine was in there trying to talk them into letting him join their club.

"Looking back, it's easy to say that Sabatine was naive, or stubborn, or just plain stupid—and that's hard for me to say, especially now. But Sabatine apparently never said a word to anyone. He just had a fit, I mean, he just got righteous as hell, and the very next Sunday he really let those golfers have it, all the ones from the club at what we used to call golfers' mass. I think the last thing he said was something like, 'You insufferable bigots, don't you know or have you ever stopped to think that Jesus was Himself a Jew?' He was about as subtle as a kick in the balls. But even worse was what he did to his hair.

"In those days," Father Marrazo continued, "his hair was fiery red, and very curly, kinky, like Muscotti's used to be, and for some reason he combed it so that it looked like he had sprouted horns. The only possible reason I could give for that was that he had a small reproduction of Michelangelo's *Moses*—he'd had it for years, and he loved it and loved to tell the reason why Michelangelo gave Moses horns—or what he said was the reason—which was that somebody had made a mistake in translating the Hebrew word for light, that the Hebrew for beams of light radiating from Moses' head somehow came out 'horns' in Latin.

"I don't know if that was Sabatine's reason for combing his hair that way or not, but the effect on all those

59

golfers was, well, it just stunned them. They rang Aldonari's phone off the wall, and when Sabatine finished high mass Aldonari was waiting for him; he was right there at the side of the altar.

"He gave Sabatine twenty-four hours to pack and present himself to the cardinal in Philadelphia. I can't remember that cardinal's name, but anyway, he kept Sabatine there for almost six months to make sure he'd emptied his head of what was then flaming heresy. But the day Sabatine came back, he called me, and I'll never forget what he said. He said—without even bothering to identify himself—he said, 'Well, I ate them. I ate my words and I genuflected like a proper little altar boy, but I'll be damned if the Jews are responsible. Who the hell was responsible for all those Jews in Germany—the Lutherans and Communists I suppose?' And then he hung up, just like that. I remember holding my stomach I was laughing so hard. I was thinking, well, hang on to your crucifix, Sabatine's back." Father Marrazo sank back into his chair and shook his head. He seemed to grow smaller. "But now, oh, God. . . ."

"What's the matter now?"

"Well, part of it is that he's got cancer."

"Oh, that's rough," Balzic said. "That's really rough."

"Mario, my friend, that's not the half of it. Not even the half."

Balzic frowned. "I don't know what could be worse—"

"Ho, Lord, Lord, Mario, let me think how to tell you." The priest drank the rest of his wine and motioned for Balzic to do the same, then he stood and turned away from Balzic. When he turned back, his eyes were brimming with tears. He didn't bother to wipe them. He sniffed a couple of times and refilled their glasses, sitting again with a thump.

"Last week, Bishop Conroy called me and ordered me to form an *ad hoc* committee to oversee the auditing of the financial records of St. Jude's parish. He told me to call Kelly from St. Mary's and Marcellino from St. Francis' and to drop everything everybody was doing and meet with the diocesan auditor immediately. All Conroy said was that we were supposed to be there when the auditor went over Sabatine's books and that we were supposed to verify any irregularities. He said he'd gotten some, uh, disquieting information was the phrase he used—yeah, some disquieting information about the mortgage payments from the bank which holds the mortgage on St. Jude's. And that's all he would say.

"So I called Kelly and Marcellino and we met with Jack Raymond, the auditor, and about nine-thirty this morning the four of us went out to St. Jude's unannounced—as Conroy had specified. Well, as soon as I saw Sabatine I wanted to get back in the car. I hadn't seen him in six months or so, and he'd lost so much weight I almost didn't recognize him. And the pain in the man's face, oh, it was awful to look at. It was so obvious the man has only months to live. Maybe not even that long. Weeks perhaps. Shaking hands with him was like grabbing a handful of kitchen matches.

"Well, I stuttered and stammered all over the place, but I finally managed to say why we were there. He never took his eyes off me the whole time I was trying to tell him, and when I finished he took my hand in both of his and he said, 'Anthony, why did he send you? He had to know how much you'd take this to heart. But don't.' And then he just turned around and let us follow him into his office, and he pointed at the books. They were all laid out as though he'd been expecting us.

"And I asked him if he had been expecting us, and he said, 'No, not you necessarily, but somebody.' Then he said he was very tired and he had to lie down, but if we needed him all we had to do was knock on the wall and he'd come over.

"Now, remember, we still had no idea what we were supposed to be looking for. I suppose I shouldn't be speaking for the others, but I had not the slightest idea. So Jack Raymond went to work, and Kelly and Marcellino were right with him, but I didn't even want to look at the damn stuff. I just kept pacing around, looking at the books on his shelves. He has a fantastic library, the library you'd expect to belong to a man who loves ideas and words. Really great stuff. And I kept looking at his books and remembering what he'd been like in that philosophy class I mentioned earlier and about the hell he'd raised—not for the sake of raising hell. Not at all. He really loved the Church, and he always wanted Her to be better so the people could be better, more loving, more giving, more gracious. And there we were, picking over his books like he was some damn embezzler. It just didn't make sense.

"I mean, what the hell would a man, one of the most honest men I've ever known, certainly the least ambitious for church office—he didn't give a rat's can to be anything more than he was. He never disgraced the Church after he'd been dismissed from the faculty at St. Vincent's. I don't mean that he didn't fight like a tiger for the ideas he discussed with us, but when it was finally decided that he had to go, he went gracefully. The same that time he had to recant to the cardinal in Philly. He went. He ate his words. And he came back still believing that his idea was right—not that he was right but that his idea was—but there was never, never a word out of him about leaving the Church or, or about doing anything to disgrace the Church by disgracing himself. That just wasn't like him. So what the hell were we doing there?

"I mean, would this man who had never disgraced himself when he was young and healthy—what would he be doing now that he's dying of cancer? About his mortgage payments? It didn't make sense. And the longer I stayed there, the less sense it made and the worse I felt. . . ."

Father Marrazo paused to drink some wine. He had been speaking quickly and rather loudly. His face was flushed and there were traces of perspiration on his forehead and upper lip.

"And then I started to think about St. Jude's," Father Marrazo went on suddenly. "Do you know, Mario, what that parish was when he took it over? When he was practically exiled there?"

Balzic shook his head.

"Mass, Mario, he said mass in a garage! A three-bay garage owned by Melago's, that trucking outfit. And the parish was so small that if you put every member of every family in the parish in that garage for one mass, there would still have been room to park a truck in the third bay.

"His altar was a workbench. Think of it, Mario, a workbench! Tools, cans, tires, chains, dirty rags, oil and grease on the floor—the first collection went to buy tarpaulins to cover the floor so the people wouldn't get greasy when they kneeled.

63

"Hell, he didn't break ground on this building until 1954. He practically begged for the money. And there wasn't one person in the diocese, bishop on down, who didn't know what the man was doing or how hard he was working. He didn't have an assistant until a couple years ago when his health started to go. Now he's got two. But what work he did by himself . . . and there we were, going through his books like he was a thief. I thought I was going to be sick. The idea that he could, or would, do anything for his own gain was absolutely ludicrous.

"And I said so. I told Kelly, Marcellino, and Raymond that we had no right, no reason, no matter what Conroy had said. And I'd no sooner got the words out when Raymond looked up and said, 'We may not have the right, but we have a reason.'

"And do you know what Raymond showed us? He showed us that for the last five months the mortgage payments had increased by twelve hundred and ninety dollars a month. Since November, the payments increased each month by exactly that amount. And we all looked at the figures Raymond showed us and we could see it was true. But I said, 'Well, what the hell's wrong with that? That's great!' But Raymond said, 'There's no explanation for it. There's nothing here to show where the money's coming from.' And I said, 'So the hell with the figures. So it's irregular. So it's unusual. The man's doubled the mortgage payments on his church building, what the hell's wrong with that?' But Raymond kept insisting. 'You don't understand,' he said. 'There's no explanation where he's getting the money.' And I said, 'But why do we have to assume there's something suspicious about it?' And he said, 'Suspicious is your word, Father.

All I know is the bank is concerned and the bishop is disturbed.'

"And I just started to howl. It was ridiculous. We go out there looking for who knew what and we find out that Sabatine's doubled his mortgage payments and this damned auditor is talking as though he'd just got the evidence on the greatest swindler in history. And I'm laughing my head off. I'm looking at this pompous-assed auditor and I can't stop laughing, and Kelly and Marcellino are starting to laugh too, and then, uh, I feel someone touch my arm.

"It was Sabatine. I hadn't even heard him come into the room. And he looked awful. Just terrible. And everything got quiet, and I finally managed to stop laughing. And he—Sabatine—he looked at me with those eyes so full of pain that it hurt me to look at them, and he said, 'Anthony, the bank has every right to be concerned, and the bishop has every right to be disturbed because it's all a fraud. All that money, that twelve hundred and ninety dollars every month since November, all of it was obtained through a fraud I instigated.'

"Mario, I thought I was going to be sick. . . ." The priest leaned back in his chair and covered his face with his hands and began to sob very quietly. "Damn it!" he cried out, and his shoulders shook.

Balzic jumped up and hurried around the desk and behind the priest. He put his hands on the priest's shoulders. "Let it go, Anthony," he said. "Let it go."

They remained like that for some minutes, Father Marrazo sobbing in his chair and Balzic standing behind him and rubbing and kneading the muscles in the priest's neck and shoulders. Then Father Marrazo began to speak, his words coming in bursts between gasps. "It's so easy to say it's all pride . . . an old man getting old because he starts to think he's indispensable . . . so easy to say he fell for the duty . . . but only 'cause he found out he was dying . . . that's crap, Mario, real crap . . . that man is more than that . . . he just saw his work unfinished . . . he knew it would be done, he knew it . . . but he didn't lose hope . . . and he didn't get smug and arrogant . . . it's not the same, Mario, if you lose your patience, that's one thing . . . if you misplace it, it's not the same as thinking you can't be replaced—or that you won't be . . . my God, Sabatine was too smart for that . . . he hadn't succumbed, he'd surrendered . . . he hadn't given up, he gave himself up—Mario, for Christ's sake, there is a difference . . . he just lost his perspective . . . it wasn't even that he lost his patience . . . it was his perspective . . . he got out of joint with himself . . . he dislocated his spirit, Mario, that's all. . . ."

Father Marrazo broke down completely. He wept until his eyes were puffed and mucous and spittle dribbled over his fingers. He looked helplessly at Balzic several times, each time trying unsuccessfully to speak. Balzic kept kneading the priest's neck, stopping once to give him his hanky, and then continuing while the priest blew his nose and coughed up phlegm, all the while baffled about the sort of fraud Sabatine had committed which Marrazo was trying so desperately to explain away. Balzic debated with himself whether to ask questions in order that Father Marrazo could get everything out and be done with it or whether to keep silent and let the priest decide if there was more he wanted to say or felt he could say.

Soon, the priest waved his hand and leaned forward, signaling to Balzic that he was feeling better, and Balzic stopped rubbing and went around the desk and back to his chair.

"I'm sorry, Mario."

"For what?"

"For acting like a kid."

"Hey, that wasn't any act and you ain't no kid and don't ever apologize to me for crying over a friend."

"Thank you," the priest whispered.

"Aw come on, Father. I'm going to get embarrassed if you don't cut it out. Here, have a little wine. Make you feel better."

"I think I had too much already. You shouldn't drink when you're depressed. It just makes it worse."

"Yeah, but sometimes it also makes it better. Go ahead."

"Maybe you're right." The priest picked up his glass and sipped what was left in it. Balzic stood and filled both their glasses, still debating with himself whether to prod the priest to talk more about what Sabatine had done. When he sat down again, he had decided against it. If Father Marrazo wanted to say more, he would, and if he didn't, nothing Balzic could say would persuade him to say anything. The priest could be as close with his thoughts as any man Balzic had ever known. He might let his emotions go now and then, as he had just done, but he was very careful with his thoughts. Now that Balzic thought about it, he was sure this was the first time he had ever heard Father Marrazo reveal anything about another priest or about priests in general. Perhaps he had had too much wine.

"Mario, I think I've said enough for one night. I know I don't have to ask you not to repeat anything I've said. There is one thing though."

"Name it."

"There are bound to be rumors. His housekeeper, Sabatine's, was in and out all the while we were out there. We tried to shoo her away, but she's a, well, never mind what she is. You know her. Mrs. Tuzzi. Gatano's widow. So I'm sure there are going to be rumors. If you hear anything, just do your best—hell, you know what to do."

"Say no more, Father. Anything comes my way, I'll handle it."

"Thank you." The priest paused. "Mario, I really am sorry to put you through this—"

"Forget it, Anthony."

"No, let me finish. You came here obviously with something on your mind. You never just come to pass the time of day. You always have a reason. I'm sorry I couldn't listen to you. But I couldn't. Tomorrow I'll be able to, but tonight I just can't. This has, uh, this has really thrown me. I mean, I just can't imagine Sabatine doing this. And I've really got to sort things out. I have to be able to say something coherent to the bishop. I can't understand why he hasn't called me. . . ."

Balzic stood and drank the last of his wine. He felt suddenly quite drunk. He knew full well that nobody gets suddenly drunk, and the only explanation he could give himself was that he had managed somehow to ignore the gradual sensations of it because he'd been engrossed with what the priest had been saying and going through. He had to hold onto the back of the chair to keep from weaving. "Listen," he said slowly so as not to slur his words, "you don't have to say anything. I understand.

And listen, if there's anything else I can do, you know I will."

"I know."

"Well, good night, Father."

"Good night, Mario. And thank you."

Balzic pulled into the driveway of his house and sat in the cruiser for a minute or so after he'd turned off the ignition, trying to comprehend how he'd gotten as drunk as he was. Then he remembered the beer he'd drunk at the bar in Muscotti's, the wine he'd drunk with Dom Muscotti in the back room, and all that wine with Father Marrazo. "Hell," he said aloud, "it's a wonder I'm alive." He stumbled getting out of the car and tripped twice going up the steps to the porch. While he was fumbling for his house key, the door was jerked open by his daughter Marie, and she was smiling wryly.

"Oh, hell, Marie, don't do things like that."

"Hi, Daddy. What things?"

"Never mind. You going to let me in or do I have to stand out here till you tell me what you're going to tell me or whatever?"

"Daddy, are you drunk?"

"Can I come in first?"

"Sure." She backed out of the doorway, and Balzic slid by her, kissing her hair as he passed. Marie closed the door and began taking off his coat. Balzic resisted at first but then let her.

"Are you happy drunk or sleepy drunk?"

"I am definitely not happy drunk. Where's your

mother? Where's my mother? Where's your sister?"

"Mom and Grandma are in the kitchen talking. Emily's in bed watching a movie."

"Ho, boy, why don't I ever hear she's in bed reading a book? How come it's always she's in bed watching the tube? I ought to throw that thing—ah, never mind."

Marie stood behind him with his raincoat draped over her arms. "I don't know why she's always watching the tube, Daddy."

"Well what are you so full of? You look ready to bust with something."

"Can't I just meet you at the door and help you take your coat off?"

"Huh, the last time you met me at the door and helped me off with my coat, it cost me forty bucks. Not that I don't appreciate your help. It's your sincerity I can't stand."

"Ohhhh, Daddy."

"Oh Daddy my rump. Come on, what's it going to cost me this time? On second thought, don't tell me. Wait'll I get some coffee, okay?"

"I can wait."

"Okay? Some coffee first, okay?" Balzic slung his arm around her neck and headed wobbily toward the kitchen. "I'll even let you pour it for me. That way, you'll have two things going for you."

She wriggled free of his arm and hurried away, saying, "Wait'll I hang up your coat."

"Okay, so hang it up, hang it up." Balzic loosened his tie and unbuttoned his collar, sputtering out a long sigh.

Marie bounced back into the room, ducked under his arm, and started steering him toward the kitchen.

"Easy now, not so fast, somebody might've moved it.

We get going too fast in the wrong direction, it might wind up taking us twice as long to get there."

She giggled. "Daddy, sometimes you're really funny when you're drunk. Especially when you're trying to be serious."

"Ho-ho, backhanded compliments yet. Go 'head, keep working your hustle, daughter. It's a little crude, but it's not bad. Smoothe out the edges, you'll be pretty good in a couple years."

They bumped into the door frame going through the dining room and then came to a halt by bumping into the door frame leading into the kitchen.

"Hello, ladies," Balzic sang out to his mother and his wife. He hoped he didn't look or sound as drunk as he felt.

"Mario, are you all right?" Ruth said.

"Yeah, sure. Just had a little too much to drink, that's all. I'm okay."

"Hey, kiddo," his mother said, "you better sit down before you fall down."

"Hey, I'm not that drunk."

Ruth stood and took him by the arm and pulled him toward the chair she'd just left. "Sit down, Mario. Marie, turn the water on. Come on, Mario, sit down, sit down. My God, look at your eyes. There's no white left at all."

Balzic slumped into the chair Ruth held for him. He rubbed his eyes with his palms and yawned noisily. He shook himself and stretched and then twisted around to look at Marie who was waiting for water to boil so she could make instant coffee for him.

"So whatta you want, Marie? You meet me at the door —you hear that, Ruth? Ma? She meets me at the door, she helps me off with my coat, then she tells me she just

71

wants to meet me at the door and help me off with my coat. D'you believe that? So come on, Marie, let's have the words, I already got the music."

Marie was nearly finished preparing the cup of instant coffee. "It's just nineteen ninety-five, Daddy." she said.

"Ouuu, just nineteen ninety-five, Daddy, that's all. For what? For what am I gettin' grabbed this time?"

"A blazer."

"A which?"

"You know what a blazer is, Mar," Ruth said. "The girls' athletic teams don't get jackets the way the boys' teams do, so the girls decided to buy them for themselves."

"What jackets? What're you talking about?"

"Mar, you know how the school gives jackets with letters on them to the boys who play football and basketball. But the girls don't get anything except a letter. So they got together and decided they'd buy them to shame the school board into doing it from now on."

"Oh, wait a minute. This is goofy. Marie, you mean to tell me you got to have a jacket to remind you of all the time you spent in that swimming pool?"

"Daddy, that's not the point," Marie said, setting the coffee in front of her father.

"What's the point then? I don't need a jacket to remind me I'm a cop. If it was up to me, the only cops in uniform would be traffic duty. Everybody else would be in civvies."

"Daddy, we aren't cops. We're girls who compete for the school and all we get are letters. The boys get letters *and* jackets. We just think we ought to get the same as the boys."

"Ho boy, that's how it starts. Equal strokes for equal

folks. He got a pretty uniform, I got to have a pretty uniform . . . next thing you know it's everybody get in step and the next thing after that is you need a bulldozer to make the cemetery—"

"Mario!" Ruth said. "What're you talking about?"

"Nothing, everything. I was just thinking of all the cemeteries scattered all over the world, all of them full of guys who happened to get the privilege of wearing a uniform."

"Aw, Mar, now wait just a minute. This is a school jacket we're talking about, and that's all we're talking about."

"Sure. And all I'm talking about is that's how it all gets started." Balzic stifled a yawn. "School jackets, letters, aw, forget it."

"Mario, it's only right," his mother said. "If the school gives to boys, they should give to girls too."

"Yeah, Ma, I know, I know. But how come I got to be part of it? Marie wants the jacket, the blazer or whatever, why don't she do something? She thinks it's right, then she should do something."

"Like what, Daddy? Like what should we do?"

"What do those band kids do? They want to go march in the Miss America parade or down the Orange Bowl, what do they do—sell pizzas, hoagies, wash cars, stuff like that. Hold a raffle, raffle something off, a TV or something. But I don't like uniforms, and I think to want a uniform is wrong. But I'm not you. You want something to wear to make you special, go ahead, but don't ask me to get it for you—and it doesn't have anything to do with money."

There was silence, the women glancing uncomfortably at each other while Balzic stirred his coffee.

73

Finally Ruth said, "Maybe that's not a bad idea, Marie, holding a raffle I mean."

Marie frowned and scratched her ankle with her other foot.

"Hey, kiddo," Mrs. Balzic said brightly, "you talk about raffles, guess who won seven hundred dollars."

"Who won seven hundred? I don't know, Ma. Who?"

"Rose Abbatta. Nicolao's widow. You remember."

"Oh, yeah, yeah. I remember her. Good for her. She could use it. She had a lot of rough luck in her lifetime."

"Ho boy, Nicolao was sick so long with that black lung. And then Rosalie, all her life with that poor girl."

"What's wrong with her?" Marie asked. "I don't even know her."

"The people Ma's talking about are old friends of hers," Ruth said. "You've never met them. And the girl she's talking about, Rosalie, she's very retarded."

"Yeah. Is born with brain damage," Mrs. Balzic said. "Have to take care all the time. They got schools for them now, but then it was like a sin to have that happen for you. God was punish you for something. So they never can do nothing without the girl, never go nowhere, all the time have to watch for her. But they been let her go places by herself now. Rose told me Nicky bought her a bike even."

"How old is she?" Marie asked.

"Oh, yoy-yoy, she must be thirty-six, thirty-seven anyhow."

"At least that," Ruth said.

"Is she a mongoloid or something?" Marie asked.

"No," Ruth said. "You can't tell anything from looking at her, except she's sort of, you know, she doesn't have much of a shape. But she had to be watched all the time. A couple times she set fire to the house just playing with matches. And her mother, well, she just never could relax. Except when young Nick got old enough to help her."

"I was just going to say," Balzic said, "he really took care of them after old Nick died."

"Oh sure," Mrs. Balzic said. "He work very hard. Never marry. Always looking out for his mother and sister. He's a good boy."

"Is he still working for the paper, the *Gazette*?"

"He must be," Ruth said. "I don't know why he wouldn't be. He has a really good job there. He's a, oh, what do you call them?"

"Linotype operator," Balzic said, yawning.

"Yeah. That's right. He makes good money."

"Well, yoy-yoy, I tell you something," Mrs. Balzic said, "that's some kind of luck, huh? All those ladies win all that money."

"Huh? What ladies?"

"Well, first was Amelia Motti. You remember, Mario. She's Alfonso's widow. Then was Flora Ruffola, she was marry to Amadie—you know her, Mario?"

"No, Ma, I don't know her."

"Well, okay, then was Sophia Cafasso, she was marry to Domenico—you know her?"

"Uh-uh."

"Sure you do."

"Maybe I do, Ma. I just can't think too clear right now."

"Well, okay. So then was Olivia Tuzzi, Gatano's widow, and now is Rose Abbatta." Mrs. Balzic laughed

75

and slapped the table. "Son of a brick, how you like that? Alla win seven hundred bucks. Yoy-yoy, I like to win sometime, don't you think, kiddo?"

"That'd be nice, Ma."

"Hey, lady, you do all right at bingo," Ruth said.

"Yeah, sure. But seven hundred bucks? How nice!"

Balzic sipped his coffee and scratched the inside of his thigh. "Hey, Ma, d'you say Mrs. Tuzzi won seven hundred too?"

"Yeah. Why?"

"I don't know. I haven't heard her name in a long time, and I could swear I heard it before today someplace. I'll be damned. I can't remember where, but I thought—"

"Mar, I think you better go to sleep," Ruth said. "You look like you're getting ready to fall off the chair."

"Huh? Oh yeah. I better . . . listen, Marie, go tell your girl friends to wash some cars or something. And I'll tell you what. I'll make up the difference, whatever you're short. But if you want that blazer, if you really want it, then I think you ought to try to get it for yourself. Start it anyway. Okay?"

Marie came behind him and hugged him and kissed the top of his head.

Balzic patted her hands and then pulled them apart as he lurched to his feet. He reached out for Ruth's arm and let her direct him into the bedroom. He plopped on the bed and didn't argue when she pulled off his shoes and socks and undid his belt. She struggled to get his pants, coat, and shirt off, giving up finally when Balzic kept falling backward. She left his shirt on.

Balzic was asleep before she left the room, and his last

conscious thought was an effort to remember where he'd heard Mrs. Tuzzi's name before today. He couldn't. His mind was flooding with flags and crosses and Stars of David and school monograms and acres and acres of graves. . . .

Balzic awoke with an oppressive fog in his head and the feeling that he had tried to eat tissue paper sometime during the night and hadn't been able to swallow it. He hoisted his feet over the edge of the bed and tried to focus on the alarm clock. He looked at it between rubbing his eyes and yawning, each time disbelieving what he saw. It was twenty minutes after ten.

He could hear pans being washed and rinsed in the kitchen, the sound of soap pads against metal alternating with sudden rushes from the faucet.

He found fresh clothes and went out to the kitchen, hugging his mother as she bent over the sink, and then started up the stairs to the bathroom. He stopped on the third step and asked where Ruth was.

"She's get her hair fix. She just leave."

"How come you let me sleep so long?"

"We try to get you up, kiddo. Ruth try. Me too. But you just no want to get up, that's all."

"Oh." He turned and continued up the stairs, holding onto the wall. He brushed his teeth first to get rid of the tissue-paper taste and then stood in the shower for ten minutes, letting the hot water beat on the back of his neck. By the time he'd finished shaving, the fog in his head was starting to lift.

Downstairs, his mother had coffee and tomato juice waiting for him.

"You want eggs, Mario?"

"No, Ma. I couldn't eat anything. This is enough right here. Just the juice and coffee. Wow, I was really blown away last night. Hope I didn't say anything out of line."

"You?" His mother laughed. "Since when?"

"I don't know. When you get that drunk, you can get out of line anywhere. Even here."

"No, sonny. Not you. Not last night." She was smiling and chuckling as she wiped the pans and put them away.

Balzic drank the juice slowly, savoring it. He was half finished with the coffee when he remembered what he wanted to ask his mother. "Hey, Ma, last night you said something about Mrs. Tuzzi. Remember? When you were talking about somebody winning a raffle or a lottery or something?"

"Yeah, sure I remember. What about?"

"What was it again—four ladies—"

"Five."

"Okay, five. And Mrs. Tuzzi was one of them?"

"Yeah. That's right."

"Well, I was trying to think where I heard her name before."

"What you mean where you heard her name before —you know her all your life."

"Yeah, I know that, Ma. What I mean is, yesterday I heard her name mentioned before you said it, what you said about her. And I really can't think where."

"Well, what difference it makes, huh, kiddo? She no do nothing bad, that's for sure."

"It doesn't make any difference. I'm just trying to remember."

"Well next time, don't drink so much. Maybe your head work better."

"Ho boy, you're beautiful, you are." Balzic finished his coffee and stood. "Did anybody call me?"

"No. Only one call. I call Rose Abbatta, tell her how good I feel for her."

"How good you feel for her? What for? What happened to her?"

"Boy, kiddo, you really was drunk last night. You forget that too? She win seven hundred dollars, don't you remember?"

"Oh yeah. That. Yeah, sure. Well, she pretty happy, huh? So what's she going to do with it?"

"Oh, she very happy. But I don't ask what she's going to do with. She tells me, but I don't ask. She thinks maybe she buy a new icebox."

"A new icebox? Hell, that's no present. She ought to take a vacation. Ah, that's none of my business where she spends it. It's her money." Balzic started out of the kitchen but came back. "Hey, Ma, I don't know why this is bothering me, but it is. What's Mrs. Tuzzi do?"

"She keep house."

"Doesn't she have a job? I thought she had a job."

"Yeah. That's her job. She keep house."

"For who?"

"For Father Sabatine."

"Out at St. Jude's?"

"Yeah, yeah, that's right. Why?"

"Nothing. I just remembered where I heard her name before. Yesterday I mean. Father Marrazo mentioned her. Okay. That settles that."

79

"You happy now, you remember?"

Balzic kissed her on the cheek. "It doesn't make me happy or not happy. I just couldn't remember and it bothered me. You know how that bothers you when you can't remember something you know you know. Listen, I got to go now. I'll see you later, and if I'm going to be late, I'll call you."

"Okay, Mario. Be careful. And be nice. Give somebody a break."

"Give somebody a break? Why today?"

"Oh, I don't know. I just say that, that's all."

"Okay, Ma. I'll give somebody a break today. You and Ruth. I'll stay sober, how's that?"

Balzic learned upon arriving at the station that nothing was going on which couldn't be handled by Desk Sergeant Angelo Clemente. He also learned that Lieutenant Walker Johnson had called to report that a set of fingerprints belonging to someone other than Armand or Tullio Manditti had been found on the door frame of their house and that those prints were being forwarded to the FBI in Washington. That was all the information Johnson had. Balzic screwed up his face thinking about it.

He was just starting out the door when the phone rang. Clemente answered it and waved to Balzic to stop.

"It's Eddie Sitko," Clemente said.

"What's he want?"

"What do I know, he wants to talk to you."

Balzic picked up another phone. "Yeah, Eddie."

"Good morning, Mario."

"Ho boy. When you start in like that, that 'Good morning, Mario,' I can hear trouble coming. What do you want to do this time, Eddie? You want to burn down the hospital to see if your troops can put it out if they ever have to?"

"Be nice, Mario, be nice."

"Hey, Mr. Fire Chief, the last time you asked me to be nice, you told me you were going to hold a foam drill at two o'clock in the afternoon, remember? At the intersection of Main and Market. Remember?"

"I remember very well. That's what I want to talk to you about."

"Oh, Eddie, say not so. You're not going to do that to me again." Balzic closed his eyes and rubbed his temple.

"Mario, we made a mess last time. I mean a real mess—"

"I know, I know. I remember the mess. Traffic backed up six blocks in every direction, foam like meringue a foot deep, and the goddamn phones had smoke coming out of them. You know how long I heard about that?"

"Mario, I heard about it long after you did. But the complaints don't change anything. We got that foam equipment because as long as the goddamn state highway department won't come up with a bypass for Route 66, and as long as gas tankers are using 66, we're sitting on dynamite—"

"Eddie, what do you want me to do—write my state rep? I know what you're saying, and I agree with you one hundred percent. But why do you have to practice on Main and Market? I practice shooting three times a week, but not on Main Street."

"Mario, we've been through all this before—"

"A hundred times."

"But if nobody can move the state people off their asses, then I want my people ready."

Balzic sighed. "So you're really going to do it?"

"Certainly I'm going to do it. Only this time I'm not going to warn anybody except you. I'm not even going to tell my people. I'm just going to have my wife phone in the alarm, and that way, everybody'll think it's the real thing."

"Oh, Eddie, Eddie, Jesus Christ, don't do this to me."

"It's something that has to be done, Mario. But I want your word you won't tell your people."

"Eddie, for crissake, I'm in the middle of something. I can't fuckin' take time off to go direct the people who're supposed to be directing traffic."

"Mario, it has to be done."

"Look, Eddie, I give you a bad time sometimes, I know I do, but that's because I don't want you to start believing your press clippings. I respect you. I think you're one hell of a fireman. You got more balls than anybody I know. I've seen you do things they wouldn't put in the movies because nobody would believe them, but for crissake, will you do me this favor and hold off for a while? I mean it, Eddie. I'm in the middle of something and I don't even know how big it is yet."

There was momentary silence on the other end. "Is it that bad?"

"I don't really know. I just got a bad feeling. Please hold off for a while. Please? And I promise you, as soon as I get this straightened out, you can hold foam drills to your heart's fucking content—at four-thirty, at eight in the morning, at twelve o'clock Sunday in front of St.

82

Malachy's. You can hold disaster drills until your joint falls off. You can pour ketchup on my head and make me a victim, I won't care. But not now, okay?"

"Okay, Mario, okay. I'll hold off. But not forever."

"Eddie, what can I say? I hope you have to rescue a widow tonight, and she just can't stand it she wants to be so grateful." Balzic hung up and let out a long sigh. "Christ, I should be selling repossessed cars. What a bullshit artist I'm turning into."

"You talking to me?" Clemente said.

"Huh? No, I'm talking to myself. Hey, I'm going to Muscotti's. I got to do another bullshit job on somebody."

"Who?"

"I don't know."

"Then how you—"

"Angelo, when I know what I'm doing, I'll tell you, okay? In the meantime, try to make sure nobody robs the place, okay? We must have close to seven bucks back there in the coffee can."

"Ouuu, sorry I said anything."

"Angelo, what're you, getting old? I can remember when I used to get wise with you, you'd tell me to bug off. All of a sudden you're sorry? So you didn't retire, so what're you doing? Going senile on the job?"

"Okay, so shove it. You got problems, so do I."

"That's better. That's the Clemente we all know and love. See you later, Ang. Anything happens, I'm at Muscotti's."

It was five minutes to noon when Balzic, following a courthouse stenographer and two sheriff's deputies, entered Muscotti's. The bar was crowded with people eating or waiting to eat one of Vinnie's hot sausage sandwiches. The sausage itself was made by Vinnie's Uncle Lou. What Vinnie did was boil and brown the sausage, combine tomato sauce, tomatoes, sweet peppers, onions, thyme, and oregano into a sauce, and then, as he put it, "let the sausage fall in love with the sauce."

Because Vinnie's Uncle Lou kept no schedule about making the sausage, Vinnie had no schedule about preparing the sandwiches. But when he did, word spread quickly. Within a half-hour after he announced that the sausage was ready, that sausage and sauce had made love, it was gone—pounds of it in four-inch portions sliced lengthwise, dripping with sauce, and served on hard rolls.

The amount was never the same because Uncle Lou never delivered the same amount. One morning he might appear with eight pounds. He might not appear again for three days, and then, as likely as not, he would have ten pounds. A day later he might appear with four pounds. Sometimes two weeks would pass before he would appear at all, and he might come empty-handed and roaring drunk, bellowing popular songs from the 1920s in a quaking tenor until Vinnie called a cab for him and gently told him to go home.

Questioned about the erratic delivery of sausage, Vinnie's reply was usually something like, "Hey, my uncle don't only make sausage, he also makes wine. Sometimes he goes down the cellar to make the sausage, he starts tasting the wine, and he forgets what he went down the cellar for. He makes the sausage when he feels like.

The rest of the time he sits in the cellar and drinks and thinks about the old country. Hey, I hope when I'm fuckin' seventy-six, I still got enough stomach left to eat it and drink it the way he does, never mind make it. . . ."

Balzic had not come for the sausage. He had come to see if he could meet Dom Muscotti's supposed girl friend, and, if he talked right, to learn if she was—as Mo Valcanas had predicted—merely a sympathetic audience for Muscotti. Balzic didn't know how he was going to go about learning this. He had not even thought of a sensible opening line. But he knew that it was something he had to learn. The presence of Gina Muscotti loomed large in his mind, just as he knew she loomed large in her husband's mind.

Gina Muscotti was a grandmother, frail, fair-skinned, with snowy hair, who looked as though she should be making television commercials for floor wax or vegetable shortening, but she was Italian in her heart and Catholic in her soul. Only God would help her husband if she became convinced that he was treating another woman differently from any other female patron. Balzic shuddered to think that giving a woman booze and twenty dollars a day was hardly Muscotti's custom with female bar patrons.

The bar crackled with the cheer of people drinking and eating food they relished. Adding to that cheer was a truck driver for a beer distributor who had hit a number for fifty cents and was buying drinks all around.

Balzic found a place at the bar near the front door and stood alone for more than five minutes before Vinnie got a break to come and ask if there was something he wanted.

"As long as I'm here, let me have one of those sausages."

"Oh, Mario, honest to God, I just sold the last one to that kid over by the radiator. I didn't have much today. Only six pounds."

"Then give me a beer. Wait a minute, don't run off. Tell me if the Tuscan's girl friend is here."

"The who? Oh." Vinnie rolled his eyes. "Down the other end. You want the beer here?"

"Yeah, sure." Balzic pushed a quarter toward Vinnie and glanced down the length of the bar. He could see only one woman, thirty or so, with straight auburn hair and no makeup. She wore a faded denim jacket over a white tee-shirt. As Vinnie set the beer down and picked up the quarter, Balzic said, "That one standing by herself? At the end?"

"That's her," Vinnie said without moving his lips.

"Oh you're shittin' me. She used to be a caseworker down the Juvenile Home. She worked with Dom's daughter, Louise."

"You got it, pal."

"Christ, she's married. She got three kids."

"Wrong," Vinnie said. "She got two kids, but she ain't married no more. She also don't work down the Juvenile Home either."

"Why, hell, she used to come in here all the time with Dom's kid. Nobody paid any attention to her. Then I didn't see her for a long time. Come to think of it, I haven't seen her down Juvenile for a long time either."

"That's what I'm telling you."

"Oh, I don't believe it. She was Good Samaritan to the world. Used to take those kids home, all that crap. What's she trying to do—save the Tuscan's soul?"

"Mario, I don't know what she's trying to do. I only know what she does. She drinks bourbon and beers all day long and she walks out with at least a twenty. You want to know what she's trying to do, you got to ask her. As for me, I wish she'd get eyes for me or for you or for Iron City Steve, I don't care for who. But she keeps up with Dom, I'm going to get ulcers in my shit." Vinnie started to walk away, but turned abruptly and came back. "You know where she was all that time you didn't see her around?"

Balzic shook his head.

"Mamont. Uh-huh, that's right. The funny farm. She just got out about two months ago. Six months she was in there. I don't know what you can do with that, but I'm telling you 'cause sometimes she don't make too much sense—that's if you're really going to talk to her."

"I don't know where I'm going yet, Vinnie. But thanks for telling me." Balzic sipped his beer and mulled that one over. Mamont State Hospital. Six months on the farm and out to twenty a day and free boilermakers, compliments of the number-two numbers banker in the county who years ago announced his impotence. A hundred and twenty a week or more and all the booze she could handle—for what? For sympathy? Huh, Balzic said to himself, maybe she's a faith healer. Nah, no way. If she could cure that problem with faith, she'd be filling more stadiums than Billy Graham.

Balzic had not realized it but he'd been staring at her, and when his eyes refocused, he saw that she was returning his stare. There was no hostility in it, nor even discomfort. What he saw was bemused curiosity. He turned his face away and pretended that he'd found an itch on his neck. Then he turned his back and took a long drink of beer. He tried to think how to approach her and then found himself trapped in a debate whether he really had any business approaching her at all. This was personal, he said to himself, but then he said, it could become the worst that Muscotti feared. And if Muscotti feared it, there was good reason for lots of other people to start fearing it. Still, it was personal. And it was one thing to be summoned by neighbors to end a family argument before it turned into assault or worse, but it was something else again to invite yourself into the middle of a potential family argument—no matter that this potential family argument could wind up in the U.S. Attorney's office. Oh, hell, he groused to himself, nobody even knows what Gina Muscotti's thinking about. All she did was call Vinnie to find out how business was at the bar. Who am I kidding? Balzic thought. She calls Vinnie, that's got to be a first. She knows something's up. She knows. . . .

Balzic felt someone brush against his shoulder and then felt someone drawing a stool near to him.

"Hi, Chief," the voice said pleasantly.

Balzic turned around while in the midst of swallowing beer. He nearly choked. It was her. He gagged and coughed and felt his eyes bulging.

"Easy," she said, patting him on the back while he bent over the bar and coughed violently. "Don't hurt yourself," she said, laughing. "If I'd've known I'd cause all this, I wouldn't have come."

"It's all right," Balzic said after his coughing passed. "It just went down the wrong way. You didn't cause it."

"Chief, don't lie. I saw you staring at me."

"You did? Yeah. Well, I guess I was."

"Honestly, you too? Everybody's staring at me lately. I'm going to get crazy again if this keeps up."

"Crazy again?"

"Oh, Chief, come off it. I saw Vinnie telling you."

"You saw Vinnie telling me what?"

"That I just got out of the zoo a couple months ago."

"You could hear that from clear down where you were?"

"I didn't say I could hear it. I said I could see it."

"You could see it?"

She nodded.

"You must be some kind of lip reader."

"I don't mean that. I mean I could see the exchange between you two. I got the vibrations. I saw the auras."

"The what?"

"The auras. Don't you know that people give off electrical charges?"

"I know we got a lot of electricity in us. I don't really understand—"

"Well, it doesn't matter. But one of the definitions of aura is that it's a current of air caused by a discharge of electricity, and when people give off their electricity, they disturb the air around them and create color. Haven't you ever seen a painting of a saint?"

"Well, sure I have—"

"Well why do you think painters put them there? You think it was something the Church invented? To make people think saints were special? I mean, sure they're special now, but see, a long time ago, before painters began to work exclusively for the Church, they used to paint everybody like that, not just saints and martyrs, because, well, a long time ago people believed everybody had one."

"You might be right," Balzic said. "I don't know enough to argue."

"Oh, you can't argue at all. This is true. It's how I got my head together. I used to see auras all the time around people's heads, but then I found out that this was true historically, that people used to believe it, and if I hadn't found that out I'd still be in the zoo wiping old ladies' asses and mopping up their vomit."

"This got you out, got your head together?"

"Sure. Because once I found out it was true a long time ago, then I knew it was still true and I wasn't seeing things. I mean I was seeing things, but—"

"Well, you just lost me there, 'cause a long time ago people used to believe the world was flat, but just 'cause they believed it didn't make it true. I mean, we know it ain't flat."

"Sure, but the world's not flat. I mean, we know the world's not flat because of science. And science is the very thing that drove away the idea that people had auras. I mean, it wasn't scientific. Nobody could measure it, and if you can't measure something, then it's not scientific to talk about."

Balzic shrugged. "I guess so. In some respects."

"Of course," she said, laughing, and then she put her hand, her palm with her fingers together, on the middle of Balzic's back. She kept it there for two or three seconds, her eyes sparkling, her lips parted, her head canted. "Don't be afraid," she said after taking her hand away.

"I'm afraid?"

"Sure. You think I'm going to tell you something destructive. And I am—in a way. I mean, you can't ever tell anybody anything constructive without telling them something destructive. They go together like black and white. But everybody always gets scared at first until they know that."

"Okay, I'll play," Balzic said. "What do I think you're going to destroy that's going to shake me up so much?"

"What else? Your ideas."

"Like which ideas?"

"Well, like the one that I can know you were afraid while you were looking at me with this great stone face that says, 'Hey, I'm tough. I'm imperturbable.'"

"And you knew I was, uh, afraid because of my aura, is that it?"

"Well, I felt your fear in your spine."

"Oh."

"Just oh? Is that all? You don't have to be so damned reserved or polite. You can laugh or argue or do anything you want. Except don't be a goddamn American on me."

Balzic laughed. "That's pretty hard."

"Oh, you don't know how hard. For crissake, a third of the world is American. Everybody who believes that time is a line that goes from left to right and can be numbered from one to ten is American. And you believe that. It's practically in your genes. And you know who are the worst about that? Those goddamn psychiatrists. They're so goddamn wrapped up in their little left-to-right, one-to-ten world, they're convinced that anybody who doesn't believe in that is crazy. And they almost had me believing it! And when I tried to tell them about time being an orbit and a revolution, a circle with no beginning and no end, they put me in the rubber room and shot me full of dope."

"They shot you full of dope? The psychiatrists?"

"Sure. There's no difference between heroin and Thorazine. Only chemically. It's all dope. Anything that makes you not want to find out who you are is dope."

"Uh, what's booze then? I mean, what's in those glasses in front of you?"

"Oh, see what a bastard you are! You look for contradictions," she said, laughing impishly and touching Balzic's back again with her palm. "Just because I use dope in a glass doesn't mean I don't know I'm using it or don't understand why I'm using it."

"Why are you using it?"

"Oh, look how serious you say it! Everything coming off you looks like something Rembrandt painted, all dark brown. If he were here now, he'd probably want you to go home and pose for him."

"Yeah, well, so how come you use it? Come on, don't give me any more stuff about my auras or whatever the hell they are. How come you take dope in a glass?"

She took her hand away slowly and touched Balzic's cheek with the back of her index finger. "You promise not to arrest me?"

"Aw be serious, willya?" Balzic snorted a laugh.

"I won't be serious, but I will be sincere. You have to promise."

"That I won't arrest you?"

"Yes. Absolutely."

"Okay, I promise." Balzic smiled and then caught Vinnie's eye and motioned for him to refill their glasses.

She said nothing while Vinnie was doing this, and

Vinnie said nothing to either of them. He refilled their glasses, took Balzic's money, brought the change, and left quickly without a word.

"See how well Vinnie understands auras?" she said.

"Who? Vinnie?"

"Sure. See how he knew not to intrude?"

"Well, I don't know if it's because he understands auras. But I know he understands people pretty good."

"Oh, he won't admit it, but he understands," she said.

"So, uh, now that I promised not to bust you—what's your name by the way?"

"Oh, my name, my name. We were having such a good talk and now you want to spoil it with a fact." She grimaced. "Now I don't know whether I ought to tell you why I drink dope. Even though you promised." She pressed the heel of her hand against her forehead and hit herself gently twice, thinking for a long moment. "Okay. My name is Mila Sanders Rizzo. Feel better now? Is that enough, or do I have to go through the whole bit—name, age, marital status, social security number, phone number, address? Why does every conversation have to start out like an interrogation, like everything has to start according to the Geneva Convention . . . oh, wow, I hate that. Every time I talk to Dom, the first thing I have to say is where my children are, who's watching them, do I trust them, what time do I have to pick them up."

"Well what do I call you?"

"I don't care. Call me yoo-hoo, only when you say it, think of it as being spelled y-o-u-w-h-o. Think of it as a nickname for my full name, which is you-who-are."

"Does that have capital letters?"

"Oh, God," she said, groaning, "don't you Americans ever give up? Put capital letters on it if it makes you feel better, I don't care."

They were both laughing by the time she finished talking. She paused to sip her bourbon and followed that with a sip of beer.

"So come on," Balzic said, "I want to hear why you take your dope in a glass."

"Okay, but remember your promise."

"I remember."

"Well, I have certain hangups. One of them, the biggest I guess, is that my father owned a bar."

"So? Lots of people who own bars have children."

"Yes, but you see, I'm—I'm still trying to get my head together. And I keep trying to find out where I came from, what I was before I was. I'm trying to go back in order to get here. I think it's crucial to know what I was before so I can know what I am now."

Balzic rubbed his chin. "And you're finding that out in here? Taking dope in a glass?"

"This is the best place! I come in here, it's like a womb. And then it's like infancy. All these glasses need are rubber nipples on them. And then during the day when I talk to Dom I'm in puberty and adolescence. And then later on, when everybody goes home at night, when there's only Dom and me in here, then I'm almost me— where I am now. And then when I give him some head, it's everything all at once, it's—"

"When you give him what?"

"You heard me. Oh, come on, don't look so innocent. Don't tell me you don't know what I'm talking about."

"Oh, I know what you're talking about," Balzic said, feeling himself blush. "I just never heard anyone say it so matter of fact before, that's all. No, that's not it. You just surprised me."

"Well it's no big deal. I mean, everybody knows it, so what's to hide?"

"Uh, listen, uh, maybe you shouldn't be telling me these things. I mean, they're, uh, pretty personal, you know?"

"Well, Christ, everything's personal! There isn't anything you can say that isn't personal. Talking about the weather is personal. Somebody says, 'You think it's going to rain?'—what do you think they're saying? They're making noises that say, 'Hey, I'm harmless. Let's talk.' And if that's not personal, what is? Besides, you're lying when you say you don't want to hear this. 'Cause this is exactly what you do want to hear. You think I don't know that? I mean, why'd you come in here and talk to Vinnie about me if you didn't want to know what was going on?" She spoke quickly but softly and there was not even annoyance in her face or tone.

"Well, uh, I guess you got me," Balzic said.

"Of course I do. But I'm not trying to get you. I just want you to be as sincere and honest with me as I'm being with you. Is that so much to ask?"

"No."

"Well, then why don't you give yourself a break? I mean, if you want to know how to handle this, then you better know what there is to know, don't you think?"

"How do you know I want to handle it?"

"Oh, stop it, will you please? You're the chief of police. Dom's, well, you know what he is better than I do. Everybody knows his wife. And everybody, including you and Dom, is scared shitless that she's going to find out and want to get some kind of silly revenge or something just because I'm using him to grow up on. Everybody thinks he's using me to prove what a man he still is. But that's a load. I'm using him a hundred times more than he'll ever think of using me. Whose idea do you think it is that he gives me all the money? You think it's mine? He's showing off. And I let him because that's the only way he can make any sense of me. But I don't want his money. I haven't spent a penny of it. It's all in the bank. All he has to do is give me the slightest indication that he regrets giving it to me, and I'll tell him how soon he can have it back. There's no big deal."

"Uh, how about running that down again?" Balzic said. "I'm a little confused."

"Well how many ways do I have to say it? I'm into where my head is. Right now. I have to find out what I'm doing, and I'm using Dom to help me. Because my father owned a bar. Because—"

"What happened to your father?"

"Nothing happened to him. He's still alive and healthy as hell. He just can't help me, that's all. He's always making judgments about what I'm supposed to be. He won't ever just let me be who I am—if I could ever find out. But if I'm ever going to get myself together, then I have to have a substitute. It's called acting out. All those creepy psychiatrists know about it. They're the ones who told me about it. So just because I understand it—no. Just because I really do it, really do act it out, everybody gets excited. And it's really no big deal."

"Not even if Dom's wife decides it is? I mean, suppose she thinks it's the biggest deal there is. Like adultery."

"Oh, come on. Who knows better than her that he isn't capable of adultery? I just told you, giving him head is like sucking shots and beers with nipples on the glass. He never has an erection. He can't! Christ, afterward, he cries every time."

Balzic shook his head and sighed. "Wait a minute. Don't you understand that that might not make any difference to her?"

"Well that's her hangup, not mine. God, I've got enough of my own. I can't handle mine and hers too."

"Well okay then. Just who the hell is supposed to handle it? Me?"

"Isn't that what this whole conversation is about? Isn't that what you want to do? Handle this? Protect everybody? 'Cause if it isn't, then you're sure sending off some funny auras."

"Oh, Christ, we're back to them again," Balzic said. "Vinnie! Hey, Vinnie! Give us a couple more here."

Vinnie approached, grinning slyly. "So how we doin', Mario? Everything okay? How 'bout you, kid? You okay?"

"I'm okay," Mila said. "But I don't know about the chief here. He's confused. There's gray around his head a foot high."

Balzic started to say something but was stopped when he felt someone touch him on the left shoulder. He turned and was confronted by Brownie Cercone, somber and scowling.

"We got problems," Cercone said. "Come here."

Balzic followed him to the far end of the bar.

"Listen, Balzic, I didn't want any part of this, I want you to know that."

"Any part of what? What're you talking about?"

"What do you think I'm talking about? What did you talk about yesterday?"

"With Dom?"

"Sure with Dom. D'you think the fuckin' Pope?"

"So okay. What's the problem?"

"Dom did what you said. He stuck me on Tullio out the dump."

"And?"

"He split. I lost him."

"How the fuck could you lose him at the dump?"

"Not so loud for crissake. Just listen and I'll tell you." Brownie's eyes darted over Balzic's shoulders. "He told me he had to go take a crap. So I'm with him all day, right behind him from the time he wakes up this morning, but I ain't going in the can with him. I mean, Jesus Christ, I got stink all over me from that dump—"

"Forget that. What happened?"

"He goes in the can. I'm waiting and I'm waiting. Ten minutes goes by, and I holler in at him. I say, 'Hey, d'you have a fuckin' heart attack or you jackin' off or what're you doing?' Nothing. So I open up and he's gone. Turns out there's another door in the back so guys can get in from outside without going through the office. So I start running around looking for him, but one of the pickers tells me the fat-ass climbed on the back of a packer when it was pulling out."

"Whose truck?"

"Nobody knows," Cercone said. "What do you think I'm telling you we got problems for? Jesus, don't you think that's the first thing I'm going to ask? There was only one guy saw him going, and that guy's just off a boat last year. He can't read English. He don't know what that fuckin' print means on the truck. He also don't know one truck from another."

"Oh for crissake. Does Dom know yet?"

"No. I ain't been able to find him either."

"Well you're having some kind of day, Brownie, I'll tell you that."

"You can't tell me nothing. You think I don't know Dom's gonna shit hand grenades when I tell him?" Brownie winced and whistled softly. "You know, I thought this was a bunch of nothing yesterday. Real nothing. But being around that fat-ass all day, now maybe I think he's really gonna do something. But listen, Balzic, you got to know this is something those two whales did on their own. The rest of us didn't have anything to do with it."

"I know that."

"Well then what the fuck was all that noise you gave Dom yesterday? What the fuck was that about?"

Balzic turned away without giving Cercone a reply. He paused at the door, turned back to Mila Sanders Rizzo, and said, "I got to go. But I want to talk to you some more."

"I'm right here every day," she said, smiling. Then she put both her hands together over her head and made sweeping motions as though she were doing a breaststroke. Then she pointed at Balzic and laughed.

"Oh fuck," Balzic said under his breath and hurried out to his cruiser.

Balzic scrambled out of his cruiser at the station and trotted into the duty room, loosening his tie as he went. Sergeant Angelo Clemente looked up, startled, and swiveled around on his chair.

"What's up?"

"Get on the phone. Call every fourth guy and tell him to call the other three. Everybody doubles up until further notice; extra shift in plain clothes."

"What do I tell them?"

"Just tell them to get the fuck in here. And I don't mean two hours from now."

"Mario, I hope you know what you're doing. That's a lot of overtime. Council ain't going to go—"

"Do it, Angelo! You let me worry about City Council."

Clemente shrugged and shook his head several times, his eyes half closed, his lips pursed. He muttered something else, but he rolled his chair over to one of the phones and started dialing.

Meanwhile, Balzic went to the radio console and opened the switch to all channels.

"All units, all personnel," he began. "Priority, priority. Apprehend and arrest one Tullio Manditti, male, Caucasian, age approximately thirty-five, height approximately five feet seven inches, weight approximately two hundred and eighty, ninety pounds, build extremely obese, usually wears and was last seen wearing coveralls. Street charge is material witness. Bring him to the station. Repeat, bring him to the station. Do not, repeat, do not remand him to a magistrate. Manditti may be armed. Do not let his build fool you. He is agile and extremely strong. Do not attempt to apprehend him by yourself. Call for backup. Repeat, call for backup . . . and for the

100

rookies and all you other dumb fuckers out there, that means I want Tullio Manditti in here but you ain't supposed to try to make the collar by yourself. One on one, he'll get you off your feet and sit on you. Then you're his. If you do get stuck, mace him, but whatever you do, don't get close enough to use a baton. Guaranteed, you'll lose. . . ."

Balzic repeated the call and asked for and got confirmation of reception from all beat patrolmen and mobile units. Then he stood and went over beside Clemente. "How we doing?"

"I got two more to go. No problems so far. Lot of bitching, but no problems."

"Good. Stay with it. I want them all here."

Balzic went to another phone and dialed Muscotti's. Vinnie answered.

"This is Balzic. Are Soup, Digs, and Brownie there?"

"Just Brownie."

"How about Dom?"

"He won't get here for another fifteen or twenty minutes. Why?"

"If Tullio Manditti should happen to roll in there—which I doubt—you tell him to stay there and then you call me, got it?"

"Yeah, sure, Mario."

"Okay, let me talk to Brownie."

There was a whooshing sound, as though Balzic had had a clam shell shoved against his ear, and then a thump. Then Vinnie's voice called out to Brownie Cercone. More whooshing and scraping followed.

"Yeah?" Brownie said.

"Balzic. You get Soup and Digs and get on the street. Talk to all your people. I want Tullio, you understand?"

"Hey, now wait a minute, Balzic. I ain't no fuckin' beagle."

"Wait my ass. You turn beagle. You get on the street and start looking and talking. And when you find him, you stay with him until you call me, you hear?"

"Oh for crissake—"

Balzic hung up without letting him finish. Then he waited.

An hour later his entire force, except for the men already on duty, was assembled in the duty room. Few of them looked Balzic in the eye. There was much grumbling and subdued cursing until Balzic reminded them of the overtime pay. Then they grew quiet and attentive and some of them even looked eager. Balzic worried about the eager ones but tried to put them out of mind while he told them who he wanted and why.

Two hours later, after calling Walker Johnson of the state police and District Attorney Milt Weigh and asking for whatever assistance they could give, Balzic was still pacing around the duty room. He'd allowed Angelo Clemente to go home because Clemente's feet made it impossible for him to walk more than three or four blocks without having to rest for ten minutes and because his wife was using the family car to take her mother shopping.

Sergeant Vic Stramsky had taken over the desk, and he was being quietly proficient, handling all the nuisance calls without bothering Balzic.

By five o'clock it appeared to Balzic, who had quit pacing and was now sitting at one of the front desks with his feet up, that Tullio Manditti may as well have been in Florida. Balzic scowled up at the clock above the radio console and drummed his fingers on his stomach.

"Hey, Vic, see if my arithmetic's right."

"Huh?"

"Just add something. Right there, on the blotter." Balzic paused and pinched the bridge of his nose. "Me and you and Angelo. That leaves thirty-three of our people. Okay, so then we got Soup, Digs, and Brownie. How many people you figure they got?"

"All over Rocksburg and Southwest Rocksburg, and Westfield Township? Hell, they got to have ten or twelve apiece. More than that."

"I figure it's more like twenty apiece."

Stramsky shrugged. "Maybe so."

"Okay, so if only half of them are out looking and listening, that's thirty, thirty-five more, right?"

"Yeah, that would be about right."

"Okay, so then we got two mobile units from the state, one from Westfield in Westfield, and then we got three undercover narcs plus Carraza and Dillman from Weigh's office."

"Let me add it up here." Stramsky scratched the hair above his ear and started figuring on the blotter. After a moment he said, "I get between seventy and seventy-five, depending on how many of Dom's street people are cooperating."

"Yeah. That's what I came up with," Balzic said. He leaned back in his chair and kneaded his hands. "Just think, Vic. I mean, imagine it. Seventy, seventy-five people looking for one guy, a fuckin' dirigible on feet, in a town this size for—what is it now—three hours?"

"At least that long."

"And nobody sees him. Now what do you figure the odds got to be on that? Hell, I didn't even include the security people at the hospital." Balzic shook his head. "That's three, four more, right?"

"No. There's just two guys up there now. The other two won't come on until the nurses start changing shifts. That's at eleven."

"Even so, Christ, the sun is shining, everybody knows what he looks like. I mean, who could miss a walking mountain, even if it is short?"

Stramsky shrugged and was about to say something when the phone stuttered on the switchboard. He plugged in the line and listened for a short time. Then he said, "Mario, I think somebody seen him."

"Huh?" Balzic lurched forward on his chair and grabbed the phone. "This is Balzic. Go ahead."

"This is Mrs. Kwalick in Emergency."

"Yes, ma'am, how are you?"

"I'm fine, thanks. But I think you better come up here. We just had an admission, a man in his early forties named Francis Dulia, and he's in very bad shape. He has at least a dozen fractures, probably more, but no lacerations or abrasions. The man who brought him in says that he was beaten up."

"I'm on my way," Balzic said, dropping the receiver on the hook and scurrying toward the door. "That fat bastard did it. That sonofabitching lard-ass got him. All these people looking, and he got to him anyway. . . ."

"I did not make a thorough examination," the doctor said. He was Indian, tall, slim, with long, slender hands. His accent was British. He gestured apologetically. "I made really just a cursory examination and then I alerted radiology and the resident surgeons. I then requested that a neurosurgeon be summoned."

"Uh-huh. Well what did it look like to you?"

"There had been severe concussion, and quite possibly fractures of both the left parietal and temporal bones—"

"The skull?"

"Yes. Here." The doctor pointed to two places on his own head, just above the left ear and then slightly above and behind the ear. "His eyes responded very poorly, and there was extensive bleeding from the left ear. From the swelling and from the position of his teeth and chin, it was clear his mandible was fractured—his jaw. Excuse me, I will speak in layman's terms. His left collarbone was obviously fractured. That was visible. I did not even have to touch it."

"What else?"

"The upper left arm was fractured in at least two places, as was the forearm and quite possibly the wrist. Again, that was clear to the eye from the position of the left arm. His left knee was extremely swollen, indicating fractures there. There were other swellings up and down the length of his left leg, from the hip to the foot. But there was something very curious."

"What's that?"

"There were not even abrasions of the skin. I admit that I am relatively inexperienced, but I have never seen anything like these injuries. I do not see how it is possible to have that many fractures without laceration—in fact, very little evidence of trauma except for the contusions. I don't understand it."

"Well, unfortunately I do," Balzic said.

"Then perhaps you can explain it to me."

"Listen, do you know the county coroner?"

"Dr. Grimes?"

"Yeah. You get him to explain it to you. He knows all about it. He's the one who explained it to me. Okay, Doc, thanks. Oh, what about the guy's wife?"

"Understandably, she was quite hysterical. I prescribed Nembutal for her."

"Can I talk to her?"

"Not for three or four hours at least. She was much too active physically and vocally. My first prescription only slowed her somewhat."

"What about the guy who brought him in? Where's he?"

"Oh, I don't know that. You should ask Mrs. Kwalick."

Balzic nodded and patted the doctor on the arm. He headed out of the office to find Mrs. Kwalick, stopping at each of the treatment rooms and leaning in to ask if she was there.

At the last treatment room, he was hailed before he leaned in by a grizzled, powerfully built, elderly man wearing a tee-shirt and green trousers. His soiled green cap was dotted with outdated United Mine Workers union buttons. He had no teeth, and he was rolling a cud of tobacco from cheek to cheek.

"Ain't you the chief of police?"

"Yes. What can I do for you?"

"I brung him in. Him and his missus. The fella that had the hell beat out of him."

"Ah, you're the man I'm looking for," Balzic said, putting his hand on the man's shoulder and steering him gently toward the office where moments ago he'd spoken with the Indian doctor.

"Have a seat, Mr., uh—"

"Harsha. Andrew T. That's for Theodore. Just call me Andy."

"Well, Andy, are you a neighbor?"

"I live next door to them if that's what you mean, but I ain't their neighbor."

"How close is next door?"

"It's twenty-one feet from my house to my property line. It's forty feet from the property line to their house. They say it's fifty feet. *He* says. She never said nothing about it. That's why I ain't their neighbor. I got a lawyer working on it right now. I don't know what the hell he wants with that other ten feet, but he ain't gonna get it, and right now, it looks like he ain't gonna be able to use it even if he does get it, which he ain't, and—"

"Uh, Andy," Balzic interrupted him, "I'm sure your lawyer'll take care of your property rights, uh, so just tell me what happened—if you know."

"Huh? Oh, I know what happened all right. I seen the whole thing."

"Okay. Exactly what did you see?"

"Well, I come home from work, and I was standing in my kitchen just ready to pour myself a shot and a beer, to cut the dust, you know, and then I was going to go out and clean up the mess them goddamn raccoons made. They—"

"Go on," Balzic prodded him.

"Well, Dulia come out the back door of his house, and I thought he was gonna come over and start breaking my hump about the goddamn property line again. So

I was getting ready for him. I had a few things I was gonna let him have, but as soon as I could see his face close up, I could see he looked real confused and kinda scared, sorta all flustered like he didn't know where he was. I seen guys coming up out of the shafts like that after old Mother Earth shakes her ass a little bit. You know, they made it out okay, but they're still pretty shook up.

"So, anyway, he starts to look around like he's trying to find something. Then he looks up at the woods behind us. Then he sneaks over to the far corner of his house and peeks around the corner. He pulls back real quick. Then he runs, sorta tippy-toe, over to the other corner, the one closest to me, and he peeks around that.

"So now I'm thinking this is pretty comical, so I'm really watching him. I got a shot in my hand and I didn't even drink it until it was all over. Anyway, all of a sudden he starts to run up toward the woods, and he gets only, oh, maybe four or five steps when this thing come flying from down around the front of his house, I guess, and smacks him right square in the back and down he goes. And, oh, you can see he's hurting. His face is all twisted up, and he's having a hard time catching his breath."

"What was this thing that hit him?"

"Well, I couldn't tell right then. Not until the fat guy picks it up."

"Then what?"

"Well, then I could see it was a bat, you know, a baseball bat, except it had something white wrapped all around the end. Looked like a towel but I couldn't be sure."

"Go on."

"Well, next thing I know this real fat guy, I mean really fat, he comes up and grabs the bat and he whacks

108

Dulia across the leg with it. He don't say nothing. He just whacks him. Then he leans down close to Dulia and says something to him, but I can't hear it. But I heard Dulia say, 'Oh, Christ, don't hit me again,' something like that. But that guy whacked him anyway. Right here." Harsha pointed to his left forearm.

"You heard them through the window?"

"No. I had the window open a couple inches. I just painted my kitchen the last couple days. Just did the last coat on the woodwork yesterday. That's how come I had the window open."

"Okay. Go on."

"Well, the fat guy whacks him again. Right across the side of the knee. Right here." Harsha stood and pointed to the outside of his left knee. "He was laying on his side like this." Harsha got on the floor on his right side and propped himself on his right forearm and held up his left arm as though to cover his face. Then he scrambled up and demonstrated as though chopping wood with an imaginary ax. "The fat guy was whacking him like this, see?"

"I see," Balzic said.

"Then he leans down and says something else to Dulia. But I can't hear that either. All I can hear is Dulia begging him not to hit him again. But the fat guy don't pay no attention. He straightens up and whacks him again. Right here." Harsha pointed to the outside of his left wrist. "And Dulia is screaming like hell and then he starts to bawl."

"And you were just watching all this?"

"Sure I was watching it. What do you think I'm telling you? Oh. You mean how could I just stand there and watch it? Oh, hell, I seen fellas pinned under tons of shale, man. Just their head sticking out. I seen guys with half their face blowed away, their guts hanging out, their legs and arms maybe four, five feet away from them—over in Italy during the war. It don't bother me."

"I understand. Well, go on. What happened then?"

"Well, this fat guy leans over again and says something else. I can't hear him. But this time, Dulia, he starts hollering something which I couldn't make no sense out of. He starts hollering, he says over and over, 'It couldn't lose. It wasn't supposed to lose.' "

" 'It couldn't lose? It wasn't supposed to lose?' He said exactly that?"

"Yup. I heard it clear as a bell. He must've said it, oh, four, five times," Harsha said. "And this fat guy, he whacks him two more times. Right here on the hip. Oh, he's really bringing it to him. And Dulia's screaming. Then it's the same thing all over again. 'Bout five more times. He'd lean down and say something to him, then he'd up and whack him, all up and down his left side."

"How long did all this take?"

"Huh? Oh, not more than a couple minutes. Everything I told you so far. Maybe not even that long. No time at all."

"Okay. Go on."

"Well, by this time Dulia's all cried out. I mean, his face still looks like he's crying, see, but there ain't no noise. So then this fat guy, he puts the bat down, you know, leans it against his leg, and he takes out a hanky and wipes his face and neck. He's really got a sweat going. Then he leans down real quick, and Dulia says something I can't hear. He talks for a real long time, oh, maybe five minutes, and the fat guy's leaning over and listening real intent and wiping his face. Then, all of a sudden, he shoves the hanky back in his pocket and he hollers, 'You motherfucker, I'm gonna beat your fuckin' brains out. I wasn't, but I'm going to now.' "

"He said exactly that?" Balzic said.

"Just what I said. It was only the second time he said anything I could hear. And he kept saying it. And he starts in whacking him again, and he steps over him and whacks him four or five times real fast. Once here"— Harsha indicated where by drawing his thumb downward over his left collarbone—"and at least three times on the head. I couldn't tell where exactly, 'cause by this time the fat guy is between me and Dulia, but I knew where when I went over to Dulia after."

"Then what happened?"

"Well, then the fat guy, he just turned around cool as you please and walked off toward the front of the house. Then I heard a car start up and drive off. That's when I went over to see how Dulia was. Soon as I got close, I could see the blood coming out of his ear, and I knew I had to get him in here real fast. I couldn't wait for no ambulance. So I backed my truck up the lawn and I went and got some blankets and I laid him in the back as easy as I could and I brung him in. Then I went and got his missus from where she works."

"And that's it?"

"That's it. That's everything. I didn't leave nothing out."

"Okay. Now, is there any doubt that you'd recognize this fat guy again if you saw him, I mean positively recognize him?"

"Shoot, you couldn't mistake him. Not that lard-ass."

"Did he ever see you?"

"He never even looked in my direction. Not once."

"How far away were you?"

"I told you before. My house is twenty-one feet from the—"

"Yes, I know. But where were they? How far from Dulia's house?"

"Oh, they was maybe ten yards from the back corner of his place and, lemme see, maybe five yards over toward my place."

"And you had a clear, unobstructed view?"

"Sure. There's nothing but the fence I put up 'bout two months ago."

"What kind of fence? How high?"

"Regular chain-link fence. You can see through it. I bought it out at Sears and put it in myself. Three feet above ground and a foot below ground. I was looking over it at the fat guy, but I had to look through it to see Dulia."

"But there was nothing else between you and them, no trees or hedges or anything like that?"

"Not a damn thing 'cept the fence."

"Okay, Andy, that's enough about that. Now what can you tell me about Dulia?"

"Aw, he was okay until he hurt his back. Then he couldn't work no more, and he started to get moody as all hell."

"When did he hurt his back?"

"Oh, must be over a year now. He was in the hospital a long time. Five or six weeks. Oh, he was a mess. They took a piece of bone out of his hip and put it in his back, and then he got an infection or something. He looked like hell when he finally come home. And then it wasn't too long before he had to go back in. But I never had no trouble with him before that. They been living there for ten years, and he never said a goddamn word about the property line till after he come out of the hospital the second time. Then that's all he talked about. One time I said to him, 'What the hell you think's under there, oil or something?' "

"How about the people on the other side of him? Did he have any trouble with them?"

"I don't know nothing about that. There's just an old lady living there, and she ought to be in the county home. But I don't think Dulia could've given her a bad time 'cause his missus used to look out for her, that old lady I mean. I seen her taking food over lots of times and I think she used to wash her clothes."

"Uh-huh. Well, what else do you know about him? How were they living if he wasn't working? Was he on workmen's compensation?"

"Yeah. Then his wife works at that supermarket. She's a checkout. They was getting by, I guess. Not like when he was working, naturally. He was a bricklayer. You know how much those guys make an hour. So it was a comedown, but hell, they didn't have no kids."

"Did you ever hear him talk about gambling, betting on anything?"

"If he did I never paid no attention to it. Course, he might be like a lot of fellas. Play the numbers just like they was breathing, but they never say nothing about it until they hit or until they miss by one number and then you hear 'em bitching."

Balzic nodded. "You ever see the fat guy before?"

"Never."

"Ever see anybody who looked like him, built the same way, only a little taller and a couple years older?"

"Nope."

"Well, is there anything else you can remember about Dulia, anything at all?"

Harsha shook his head. "No. I didn't have much to do with him. I keep pretty much to myself. Ever since my missus died, I don't feel like socializing too much, if you know what I mean. No, until he starts getting this screwy idea that his property goes ten feet more than it does, we never did nothing but pass the time of day. I never even drunk a beer with him."

"Was he a drinker?"

"Well, till he hurt his back, all I ever seen him drink was a couple beers after work when it was hot. But now he drinks a lot. Sweet wine. Buys it by the gallon, least twice a week. I heard him say once it was the only thing made his back quit hurting. Sounded to me like he was trying to kid somebody. But maybe it did. I been pretty lucky. I never had no back trouble, but I seen a lot of guys with it and they ain't worth a fart for working, so it must hurt. But that's all I know about him drinking."

"What about his family, his relatives?"

"Well, I think I already told you they didn't have no kids. Only relatives I ever seen visiting them was an old lady and her son and daughter. The daughter looked a mess. The only reason I even knew they was relatives at all was his missus told me, 'cause she felt sorry for the old lady on account of the daughter. But I don't even know their name. All I know was they was on his side of the family. But how they was related, hell, I don't even know that."

"The daughter was a mess? How do you mean?"

"Oh, I don't know, she just looked all lumpy, like a pile of putty. And Dulia, he used to look out for her. Every time they come, he used to follow her around their backyard like he was trying to make sure she didn't mess around with nothing, or maybe he was trying to make sure she didn't hurt herself. That's the way it looked to me."

Balzic thought a moment. Something struck him, some connection. He didn't know what it was, but he knew he knew what it was without being able to think of it clearly.

Balzic took out his notebook and asked for Harsha's address and phone number. Harsha gave his address but said, "I don't have no phone. I had them take it out after my missus died . . . hey, I been meaning to ask you. I mean, I guess you know what you're doing, but how's come this is the first thing you wrote down? All them detective shows I see on TV, them cops are always writing things down, making notes and all, when they're getting stories from witnesses, I mean."

Balzic smiled. "Andy, I was just about to tell you to come down the station so a stenographer could take your story in shorthand. She wouldn't miss a word, and if I was writing things down I wouldn't be able to read it tomorrow. Anyway, we have to notarize your statement and then we have to take it to a magistrate to file an information against this fat guy; otherwise you'd have to appear before a magistrate yourself, and there's no point in you doing that."

"Oh. I don't know what all that means, but I guess you know what you're doing."

"Well, don't worry about it. The thing is, I won't be able to get a stenographer until late tomorrow afternoon. Can you come in around four?"

"I could get there by about ten after, how's that?"

"That's fine. In the meantime, don't die on me—"

"Oh, hell, I'm healthy as a horse."

Balzic laughed. "I can see that. What's really important is that you don't forget anything you saw."

"Oh, shoot, I couldn't forget none of this, no sirree."

"Good. Then go on home and have a couple cold ones. And listen, if I'm not there tomorrow, just tell the desk sergeant what you're there for and he'll take care of you, okay?"

Harsha nodded and left with a shrug and a wave.

Balzic then called Stramsky at the station and told him to put out the word that Manditti was now wanted for attempted murder. "There's no question the dummy did it, Vic. He just beat the hell out of a guy named Francis Dulia with a baseball bat. Call Muscotti and tell him he better tell his people to get off their asses. Tell everybody to get off their asses. Something tells me Tullio ain't finished yet. I don't know why I got that feeling, but I do. In the meantime, I'm going to stay here and try to talk to Dulia's wife and Fat Manny."

Dulia's wife was still deep under the influence of the Nembutal, so Balzic went up to the third floor to see Fat Manny. He found him flat on his back gnawing on a stick of pepperoni, licking his fingers between bites.

"Hello, Manny. How you feeling?"

"I'm going to live. You feeling okay, Balzic? You going to live?"

"For a while I think."

"Good. We wouldn't know how to act around Rocksburg if you wasn't the chief of police. You keep the streets safe and everything. Us citizens are really grate-ful."

Balzic saw that the other beds were still empty. He turned around and closed the door quietly. "Okay, Manny, let's cut the happy horseshit."

"What happy stuff? Am I giving you happy stuff? I thought we was just being nice."

"So okay, so keep on being nice and tell me why you screwed Francis Dulia."

"Huh? Who? Who was that again?"

"You never heard of him, huh?"

"Never heard of him," Manny said ponderously.

"Then why do you suppose your brother would want to put a job on him with a Louisville Slugger?"

"What're you talking about? What job? What slug-ger? My brother? You must be eating wrong, Balzic. You must be eating too much American bread or something. That stuff messes up your system. My brother would not even hurt a stray cat."

"Manny, I got everybody looking for him. Everybody on my force, plus all of Dom's people, plus state people, plus county people. Your brother's up for attempted murder. And even if Dulia doesn't die, which is unlikely considering that his skull is fractured in two places, not to mention a dozen other fractures—even if Dulia doesn't die, your brother's going away on every assault rap the state ever wrote. And as pissed off as Dom is at you, you have to know that Tullio's going to go it alone. He won't get any of the fringe benefits, not so much as an extra pack of cigarettes a week."

Manny took another bite of pepperoni and chewed it slowly, thoughtfully, but he said nothing.

"I mean, think of it, Manny. When we get him there

isn't going to be anybody standing up for him. He's going to go up in front of the man all by himself, and then he's going to do all that time by himself. And he won't do it at the hotel down the road, Manny. He'll be doing it in Pittsburgh, in The Wall, where they keep the bad guys, the crazies. And not a friend, inside or out. So why don't you give your brother a break and tell me where he's going? He turns himself in and maybe he won't have to go to Pittsburgh. Maybe he'll find out he has some friends."

"That don't make no sense, Balzic. I mean, even if I knew what you were talking about, and even if I knew where he was going—hell, who says he's going anywhere? He's probably home. Besides, how could he turn himself in if you had to go get him? And what's he going to turn himself in for anyway? He ain't done nothing."

"You just tell me where he is, Manny, I'll call him on the phone. You let me talk to him for five minutes, I guarantee he'll be begging me to let him turn it over. You know there's about ninety percent spades down there? Do I have to tell you how your brother likes spades?"

"Balzic, you're trying to pump carbon monoxide up somebody's ass, that's what you're trying to do. I don't know what you're talking about."

"You don't know any Francis Dulia?"

"How many times I got to tell you?"

"And you never booked a winner for him and then told him to take a walk?"

"I don't know where you're getting this stuff. I don't book nothing. I'm a chauffeur, everybody knows that."

"Who're you trying to shit? You haven't driven anything anywhere for anybody for over a week. How'd you get those holes in you?"

Manny thought for a moment. "It happened like this. I was carrying a bunch of quart pop bottles in a bag. I was gonna take them back for the deposit. The bag broke and one of them fell out the bottom and I tripped on it. Then I fell down on top of the rest of them. They broke. I mean, I'm pretty heavy, you know?"

"Oh, Jesus, Manny, that's enough. I'm going to ask you just once more not to be dumb. What do you say?"

Manny rolled over on his side, grimacing and wheezing, the bed creaking ominously. He laid the stick of pepperoni on his nightstand. "Hey, Balzic, there's some olives and bread underneath there. You wanna hand it to me, huh?"

"You tell me where Tullio is, I'll go get you a banquet."

"Aw fuck you. I'll call a nurse. Who needs you?"

"I think you and your brother are both going to need me pretty bad before this is over. But with all the static you're giving me, maybe I won't be around."

"Hey, Balzic, all of a sudden I'm tired. I don't want no more conversation. I think I need my rest."

Balzic snorted. "I wish you'd give me a rest. Right now I'm wondering how Tullio's going to take it when I tell him what kind of diet you're trying to put him on. After all the food he brought you in here? And you're not going to be able to take him a pepperoni."

"See you around, Balzic. I'm asleep."

"Have it your way, fatso. You just better start praying that Dulia doesn't die."

"Everybody dies, Balzic. And don't call me fatso. Fat

Manny, that's okay. But I don't go for that fatso stuff."

"Just what're you going to do about it, fatso?" Balzic snarled. "Laying there with your lard full of holes, just what do you think you can do about it? Go call your fatso brother and tell him to put a job on me with his bat? I wish you would. And I wish he would. 'Cause I'm so pissed at you two fat-asses, I'd like nothing better than to have him coming at me with a bat. I keep a three-foot baton in my car, fatso. Your fatso brother ever comes at me with a bat, I'll show him some moves with that baton he won't believe. You hear me, fatso?"

"Blow it out your ass, Balzic. You're giving me a headache."

Balzic turned and left, muttering and cursing under his breath. Once out in the hall, he stopped and faced the wall, making his hands into fists, chewing his lips, and fighting the urge to knock holes in the plaster. The way I'm going, he thought, it'd be my luck to hit a stud. That's all I'd need. My hand in a cast. . . .

He shoved his hands into his pockets and went to the elevators, taking one to ground level, then walking quickly to the Emergency Unit. He found Mrs. Kwalick and had her direct him to the room where Mrs. Dulia was. It was a waste of time; Mrs. Dulia woke in wild-eyes starts only to doze off in midreply to one of his questions. Nothing she managed to blurt out was of any use to him.

Balzic paced around the room for some minutes trying to think if there was something he should be doing that he had forgotten or overlooked, but the more he paced and looked at his watch, the more he knew that the only thing he could do was wait and hope for some good luck. Maybe I ought to get somebody praying, he thought, and went out to the pay phone in the lobby. He dialed St. Malachy's rectory.

Father Marrazo answered gruffly.

"This is Mario, Father. How you doing?"

"The same," the priest said in Italian.

"You having any luck with your problem?"

"You mean about Father Sabatine?"

"Yeah."

"It's going to take more than luck, Mario."

Balzic waited for him to go on, but the priest said nothing. "Well, uh, how 'bout praying? Isn't that helping?"

"Mario, I hope you never hear me say anything like this again, but I'm nearly prayed out. The bishop is so angry he can't talk, and Sabatine is so depressed he won't talk. And I'm getting ready to dump the whole thing on Kelly and Marcellino."

"Oh." Balzic didn't know what else to say.

"Was there something you wanted, Mario?"

"Huh? Oh, no. No, I just wanted to see how you were making out with your problem, that's all."

"Well, what can I tell you?"

"Nothing—I guess. Sorry to bother you. I hope you, uh, I hope it works out." Balzic hung up without saying good-by. Well, he thought, no help there. Not even a little shot of consolation. But there's no use getting worked up about it. He has his own problems. I can't expect him to do my work. Probably wouldn't have done any good anyway to have him praying, but it sure would have made things feel better. "My ass," Balzic said aloud, as he turned away from the phone and looked around. "My ass. . . ."

"Such language," said an old woman with hair so gray it was turning yellow. She was sitting on an imitation leather couch beside the phone. In front of her was a four-legged aluminum walker. She clucked her tongue at Balzic. "What would your mother say?" she said sharply.

Balzic stared down at the woman, but he could not bring himself to tell her that if his mother had been there she would have told the old woman to mind her own business and stay out of other people's conversations.

"Young man," the woman snapped, "if you don't leave me alone, I'm going to call the police." Her eyes were as hard as the set of her mouth.

"Old woman," Balzic said, "I am the police. And right now there's nothing I'd rather do than leave you alone. Good afternoon."

The old woman's face softened suddenly in a crooked smile. "It was so nice of you to bring me here," she cooed. "The people are all so wonderful. Have you met my son?"

"No, ma'am," Balzic said, recognizing at last the woman's senility. "No, ma'am, I haven't."

Her face pinched as she squinted meanly at Balzic. "You should," she hissed. "He's a bastard just like you."

Balzic shook his head and walked away from her. He stopped in the center of the lobby and looked around. Every seat was occupied. He turned slowly and looked at each of the faces, seeing on one confusion, on another irritation, on still another impatience, on still another grim-lipped pain. There was a woman, enormously pregnant, with her ankles and feet so swollen that she had taken off her slippers and stockings and was staring glumly at her feet. There was a teenaged boy with a blood-soaked hanky wrapped around his hand. There

122

was an old man, his nostrils half destroyed by cancer, who was staring blankly at his hands. A black woman, her face stony, was trying half-heartedly to soothe a young girl who would not stop crying though outwardly nothing appeared to be wrong with her. There was another old man, breathing in phlegmatic bursts, who was turning an unlit cigarette over and over in his fingers. There was a young woman with long, frizzy red hair and very fair skin who sat with her chin in her hand. She seemed to be talking to herself, and when Balzic looked at her, she jumped up suddenly and hurried past him toward the exit, saying to herself, "Fuck this place. I mean, this place can just go fuck." And then she was gone.

Balzic could not look at the rest of the faces. He felt suddenly that if he didn't get out of there, if he didn't get outside into the crisp March air, he was going to choke on the confusion and irritation and impatience and pain. He stood transfixed for a moment and then wheeled about and nearly ran out of the lobby.

Outside, he gulped air and loosened his tie and wanted to untie his shoes and undo his belt. He tried to remember when he had felt such an overpowering sense of oppression. Then he asked himself what the point was of trying to remember that. A comparison was senseless. Besides, he thought, what the hell do you expect to see in an emergency waiting room? That's the way it looks every day of the week. And on the holidays? When the solid citizens are out having fun? Hell, man, today that place was practically healthy.

It was eleven-thirty-two in the evening when Balzic got the phone call from the hospital. He had never met the doctor and had to ask him twice to repeat his name. Even then he wasn't sure he could pronounce it. The doctor was another Lebanese.

"Not that it matters all that much," Balzic said, "but when did he die?"

"Eleven-twenty," the doctor said. "I just completed the death certificate."

"Did he ever regain consciousness?"

"No."

"What did you put down as the cause of death?"

"Massive brain damage as a direct result of multiple fractures of the left parietal and left temporal bones."

"Is Dr. Grimes there?"

"Not now, no. He had the body removed immediately to the morgue. I am sure he will have a full report for you in the morning."

"How's Dulia's wife taking it?"

"I'm told she is quite incoherent."

"Well that's natural, I guess. Thank you." Balzic hung up and stared at the phone. He scratched the back of his left hand and thought for a long moment, his eyes wide and unblinking.

"Hey, Vic," he said, looking up to see Stramsky looking back at him expectantly.

"It's murder now, right?" Stramsky said.

Balzic nodded. "Poor sonofabitch never woke up . . . it was probably better." Balzic stood and went to the window overlooking Main Street. He jingled coins and keys in his pockets and listened vaguely to Stramsky calling all units and personnel to change the charge on Tullio Manditti to a general charge of murder. Stramsky then called the state police and told them that the investigation was now officially theirs.

There were only a few cars moving on Main Street and no pedestrians that Balzic could see. The temperature had dropped fifteen degrees since the afternoon, and Balzic fully expected to see snow. Wind lifted bits of paper from the gutters and off the sidewalks and swirled them about, but there was no snow. He watched the paper being blown this way and that, and he found himself thinking that his mind was working the same way: bits of information were coming and going with little apparent sense.

It should have been a simple matter. Manny had booked a winner on his own for Francis Dulia, and when Manny couldn't come up with the money Dulia went berserk. That was logical enough. One guy with an appetite bigger than his brain hustles a guy with a bad back, an unemployed guy who lately was given to moods of surly indignation. Nothing to it. Enter the brother with his bat, exit one guy who thought the world was out to screw him and found out that he was right. What could be more logical than that?

But what was Dulia telling Tullio during that couple of minutes before Tullio straightened up and said he was going to beat his brains out? Tullio didn't go there to kill him. You don't put a towel around the bat if you're looking to kill him. The towel's there to keep from killing him. And Tullio never hit him in the head until after Dulia quit making his speech—whatever it was.

Then there was that thing Dulia said. "It couldn't lose. It wasn't supposed to lose." That's what Harsha said he said, and Harsha had absolutely no doubt about it. "It wasn't supposed to lose." . . . Ah, that's crap.

There isn't a bettor in the world who thinks he's booking a loser. Still, this wasn't the ordinary bettor. This guy was ballsy enough to try to collect his winnings with a knife.

So what the hell did he bet on? It had to be a number. That's the only bets Manny ever carried. But how does this guy think a number couldn't lose? Old stock, new stock, New York race, Brooklyn race—that's all the numbers there are. The stocks come out of *The Wall Street Journal* and the races come out of the *The New York Daily News* . . . every guy who ever tried to fix one of those numbers got dead in a real hurry. And this Dulia, this square from Westfield Township? Who the hell could he know to even begin to fix anything?

So why am I thinking fix? Good question. Why am I? Because it doesn't make sense for a guy who's about to lose his life to say something like that? Okay. So what would he be saying? Oh, shit, I don't know what all he said to Tullio. Just that.

No, goddamn it. He said that because he was sure, that's why. Because he was right. That was a guy looking for what was his, what belonged to him, what was owed. Maybe they weren't much—what the hell is ten feet of property more or less? But if you've hurt your back and you can't work and you feel like the world has just given you the shaft, you start making sure you get what you think is really yours. That was a guy with a grudge against the world, and he was looking for sure things. A guy getting ready to die who cares more that what he bet on wasn't supposed to lose—he cares more about that than he does about living or dying. That guy had to know something. He knew a fix was in. Some kind of fix. Had to be. . . .

Balzic reached for a phone and dialed.

"Yes?" Dom Muscotti answered curtly.

"This is Mario. Dulia died."

Muscotti made growling noises. "That's—that's a shame. A friggin' shame. I'm sorry, Mario, I really am."

"Are you sure you didn't know him, Dom?"

"Sure I'm sure. I told you before when you called. I thought then that I maybe heard the name someplace, but now I'm sure I didn't." Dom paused. "That friggin' Tullio, wait'll I . . ." His voice trailed off.

"Wait'll what?"

"Nothing, Mario. Did I say something?"

"Skip it," Balzic said, sighing impatiently. "You sure this guy didn't book with one of your people?"

"Mario, I asked everybody, honest. Listen, what would I be lying for now?"

"Keep your shirt on. I didn't say you were lying."

"Well, nobody knows him, I'm telling you."

"D'you talk to Manny yet?"

"Not yet. I'm going up the hospital as soon as I close up. I don't know what the occasion is, but I got a bunch of college hot dogs in here and they're celebrating something. I'd've closed up an hour ago if it wasn't for them, but I need the paper."

"You need the paper?" Balzic laughed.

"What're you laughing for? You think I don't take a beating every once in a while? I'll write you a letter. There's some guy killing me. I think he must have something on a couple jockeys or something. Christ, I can't handle him no more this week. I laid him off yesterday to Pittsburgh and today to Buffalo. What do you think that's gonna cost me?"

"I don't want to know," Balzic said. "Well, tell your people it's murder now. And when you talk to Manny, tell him I'm making him an accessory before and after. Conspiracy, the whole bit."

"I'll tell him," Muscotti said. "Don't worry about nothing. I'm gonna talk to him like a father."

Balzic hung up and thought it over. If Muscotti did know Dulia, why would he say he didn't? To protect Manny? Not likely. Muscotti was sore enough a week ago at Manny to give him a vacation despite his own mother's fondness for Manny's company and conversation, and there was no one alive Muscotti tried to please as much as his mother.

What's more, it had been sixteen years since Muscotti had used muscle for anything. Since Sam Weisberg retired to Florida, there had been no reason to use muscle. Muscotti was solid with the old men in Pittsburgh, and nobody would dare provoke him without provoking them.

Balzic could only conclude that Muscotti was telling the truth: neither he nor any of his people knew Dulia, professionally or otherwise.

So what the hell did Dulia fix? Balzic drummed his fingers on the desk and began to think that there was a good chance he was complicating a simple thing.

He shook his head. There was still Dulia's life-and-death insistence that what he had bet on couldn't lose, and try as he might, Balzic could not put that thought out of his mind. He kept rattling it around, thinking that there was something right in front of him that he was overlooking, something everybody took for granted which he just couldn't connect to Dulia. He was sure it had to be something local. Dulia couldn't be anything but a local square who tried to make a local score.

At five to twelve Sergeant Joe Royer came in and took

over the desk from Stramsky. The rest of the shift changed, and everybody brought in the same word: no Tullio.

By one that morning, Balzic had decided that Dulia had been a square, a dumb square who had stumbled onto something.

By one-thirty, Balzic had decided that Dulia had been the most cunning man in the county.

By two o'clock, Balzic admitted that he didn't know a damned thing about Francis Dulia.

He called Romeo's Diner and ordered a cheeseburger. When it was delivered, he took two bites out of it and wrapped the rest of it up and put it in his desk. His tongue was biting from all the cigarettes, his throat and chest were burning, and his stomach was growling from all the coffee.

He drew oblong boxes on a note pad, filling them in until they were solidly black, then drew some more and filled those in. Dozens of questions about Dulia rumbled through his mind, and he fumed that he couldn't get answers to any of them until the workmen's compensation bureau opened in the morning. He'd have to work backward from there, and with any luck, he might know something about Dulia by noon. Until then, all he knew was that he was trying to grab a handful of smoke by even thinking about Dulia until he had some pertinent details about the man's life.

At two-twenty-five the phone rang, and Balzic lurched to answer it.

"Hey, kiddo," his mother said, her voice hoarse, "how come you no come home?"

"Huh? Ma? What're you doing still up?"

"Aw, my ankles hurt. They wake me up. But never mind. How come you no come home, no call or nothing? Ruth li'l bit worried, kiddo. She li'l bit mad too. You should call at least."

"I know, Ma, I know. I'm sorry."

"Better make up with Ruth tomorrow. Not me. Tell her you sorry."

"Okay, Ma, I will. Now go back to bed, okay? Try to get some sleep."

"Oh, Mario, sometime I don't mind I can't sleep. Sometime I just like sit here by myself. I take some wine, and I think about long time ago."

"Well, don't think too much. You can't get it back, that's what you're always telling me."

"Sure, I know that. But I don't feel sad about the long time ago. I just like to think about, that's all."

"Okay. Well, good night, Ma. I don't want to talk much right now, okay?"

"Hey, wait, kiddo. Is you—you stay late because of Frankie Dulia?"

Balzic frowned at the receiver as though it were responsible for what he'd just heard. "Yeah, Ma. But how'd you know about that?"

"Oh, I talk with Rose today. She feel very bad."

"Rose who?"

"Oh, Mario, what's wrong with your memory all of a sudden? Rose Abbatta, that's Rose who."

"Mrs. Abbatta told you about him?"

"Yeah, sure. Didn't I just say?"

"Yeah, but how'd she know about him?"

"Mario, he's her nephew."

Balzic straightened his back. "Say that again, Ma?"

"What'sa matter with you, you drunk? Frankie Dulia is Rose Abbatta's nephew."

"No I'm not drunk. Just tell me how Mrs. Abbatta found out what happened."

"Well, Nicky, he buys Rosalie a bicycle couple days ago, last week sometime, and right away she want to take over to show Frankie. But Rose don't let her until today. So Rosalie go over, but nobody's home. So the neighbor man, he tell Rosalie Frankie's in the hospital, got all beat up. And Rosalie come home all crying and wet her pants and, oh, was just carry on terrible. Rose said it took her half-hour to get Rosalie calm down so she can say what's happen. Rosalie really love Frankie a lot. Ever since they was kids, he look out for her, and—"

"Ma, I should've known. I should've known," Balzic said, shaking his head and thumping the desk with the side of his fist.

"You shoulda know what?"

"I should've known to call you in the first place."

"Hey, I call you, kiddo, you forget?"

"It doesn't make any difference, Ma. I got to hang up now. Don't worry. Go to sleep. And thanks."

"For what?"

"I got to go, Ma, honest. I can't talk anymore now. Wait a minute. What's Mrs. Abbatta's address?"

"Huh? What you want that for?"

"Please, Ma, just give it to me, okay?"

"Okay, okay. She live on Pinewood Drive. In West-field Township. I don't remember number. But she's live in third house on right-hand side."

"From which end?"

"From this end. From when you go out from town."

"Oh thank you, Mother. You're beautiful. G'night."

"Hey—"

Balzic cut her off, held his finger on the receiver button, and waved to Royer to come over. He lifted his finger and dialed the operator and then scribbled a note for Royer. Royer looked at it, puzzled, and held up his hands questioningly.

"Tell somebody to get down there and pick him up," Balzic said.

"What charge?"

"Make one up. But tell them to move it. Operator? Operator, this is the Rocksburg police. This is an emergency. I want you to get the residence of a Mrs. Rose Abbatta on Pinewood Drive in Westfield Township. The number may be listed under her son's name. Nicholas or Nicolao. And keep ringing until somebody answers."

The operator said she would and clicked off. There was a long pause. Then the operator came back on. "Sir, that line is busy. If this is an emergency, do you authorize me to interrupt that call?"

"Hell yes. Cut in on it!"

Balzic looked up at the clock above the radio console. "I hope you worked overtime tonight, buddy," he said aloud. "Of all nights, I hope you got some time and again tonight. . . ."

The shriek ripped into Balzic's ear and set his flesh tingling. He thrust the phone outward and then brought it slowly closer to his ear until he could hear without

132

being hurt by the pitiful but piercing cries of Mrs. Abbatta.

"Please send ambulance! Please, God, my Nicky is hurt! Please, please send ambulance quick!"

Balzic shouted to Royer, "Forget that last thing I told you. Get Mutual Aid and send them over to Pinewood Drive in Westfield Township—hold it till I get the address.

"Mrs. Abbatta, this is Mario Balzic. Listen to me. What's your house number? Mrs. Abbatta, do you hear me?"

She would not stop. She kept calling, pleading, for somebody to help her help her son.

"Mrs. Abbatta, goddamnit, I am trying to help you. This is Mario Balzic. Stop yelling a minute and tell me your house number!"

She sucked in her breath and then coughed violently. It took her nearly a minute to stop and control her voice. "God forgive me," she said. "Mario, I know your mother all my life . . . God forgive me."

"Mrs. Abbatta, never mind about God right now, okay? Just tell me your house number."

"It's all my fault, oh, God," she whispered. Then she sobbed and fought the sob so that she sounded as though she were being strangled. Finally she blurted out, "Number fifteen. Fifteen, you hear?"

"I hear. Fifteen." Balzic called it out loud enough for Royer to hear. And then he repeated the address so there could be no mistake. "Okay, Mrs. Abbatta, you go be with Nick now. There's an ambulance on the way right now. You hear me? Mrs. Abbatta, you hear me?"

"Yes, yes, I hear."

"I'm going to hang up now, Mrs. Abbatta. You just

133

go stay with your son. People will be there to help him in just a few minutes, you hear?"

"Yes, I hear. Thanks God. Oh, thanks God. . . ."

"Good. Just go be with him." Balzic depressed the receiver button, lifted it, and dialed Troop A barracks of the state police, asking for the duty officer.

"Lieutenant Poli," a voice said after a moment.

"This is Balzic in Rocksburg, Poli. I need a couple mobiles real quick."

"No kidding. Do you now?"

"Cut the crap, Poli. We got one murder tonight and we may have another possible. Same suspect, and he's got to be in the area. I need—"

"Balzic, I can't help what you need. I got three people down with the flu. I was told to assign you one unit, and that's the one you got cruising Norwood Hill. In the morning you're supposed to get another one. I couldn't give you another one if I wanted to because I don't have one to give."

"Okay, Poli, thanks anyway." Balzic hung up and pushed the cuticle back on his thumb, calling out to Royer, "Tell all the mobiles to concentrate on the area between Westfield Township and Norwood. I'm betting a thousand to one that fat-ass is just going to go on home and make out like nothing's happening. That would be his style."

Royer sent out the message and then said, "She was calling Mutual Aid when you cut in."

"Huh? Who?"

"That woman, Abbatta. She was trying to call them herself. The Mutual Aid dispatcher said to thank you. He couldn't get her house number out of her until you cut in."

"Oh. Big fuckin' deal. I did something right."

"Hey, uh, Mario, what's going on? I mean, how'd you know to call that place? And what did you want this Nick Abbatta picked up for down at the paper?"

"Oh, Joe, Jesus Christ, it's a long story. A long, messy story. But to make it quick, it has to do with a lottery. You know the kind I'm talking about. Everybody with a building fund or a mortgage or some fuckin' charity for some guy who broke his leg playing softball runs them. The American Legion, the VFW, the Moose, the Sons of Italy, the Polish Falcons, the Kosciusko Club, the Russian Club, the churches, all those phony athletic clubs, the Amvets, Christ, you name 'em, they've all run them at one time or another. Most of them run off the stock numbers, but lately a lot them are picking the winner from the last three digits of the U.S. Treasury balance . . . hell, I got two in my wallet right now. One from the VFW and another one from the Polish Falcons Stramsky sold me."

"Yeah, okay," Royer said. "I got one from Stramsky myself. But I still don't get it. How'd you know to call that house? I mean, I can't figure what the hell happened up there."

"Tullio got to him, that's what happened," Balzic said, standing and stretching and letting out a long, disgusted sigh that sounded more like a snarl. "What a fuckin' stupid I am. Right under my face. I knew there was a fix, I just fuckin' knew it! But you think I could put it together? Goddamn! . . . I also knew it was a pile of crud, but I never thought it was going to be this big a pile

. . . oh, Jesus, Mary, and Joseph, wait'll the newspapers and TV guys get hold of this—well, at least there's going to be one newspaper that ain't going to be playing it on the front page."

"Mario, I must've left my head out in the car," Royer said, "but I still don't know what you're talking about."

Balzic walked toward the door. He was in no hurry. He knew it was only a matter of time before they got Tullio, and he knew Tullio was finished. Right now he was probably burying his bat or sawing it in little pieces and burning it. "You just think about it some more, Joe. I'm sure you'll put it together. In the meantime, stay on the horn. I want everybody awake out there. That fat-ass can't have gone too far. I'm going up the hospital, see if there's anything I can do for Mrs. Abbatta."

Balzic didn't use his light or his siren to get to the hospital. Because he passed only three other cars, he didn't have to use them. But he wouldn't have used them anyway, not even if he had been in five o'clock traffic. He was feeling so stupid he didn't want anybody to know he was a cop. They'd all bust a gut, he thought. If they knew how much I didn't know, they'd all crawl into caves and get themselves some rocks . . . aw fuck this. What the hell am I thinking about? Christ, if you don't know the relations, you don't know anything. You got to know who relates to who, 'cause until you do, you're as dumb as the day you were born. You got to know who knows who, who has what, who wants what, who can do which for how much—you got to know that or you can sit around all day long picking fuzz out of your bellybutton. . . .

The Emergency Unit waiting room was improbably quiet when Balzic walked in. He had thought an ambulance would have had sufficient time to bring Nick Abbatta in, but he saw in a glance that there was only one person in the room. A middle-aged black man, thin as sticks, sat slumped in the corner of the couch nearest the fire doors leading into the treatment rooms. There was a large swelling above his left eye, his right eye was puffed nearly closed, and his lower lip was split so badly that it looked like beef liver. He was trying to smoke a cigarette, but the paper kept sticking to his lip and he was cursing under his breath about it.

Balzic walked directly to the admissions desk but found no one there. In an adjoining office to the rear he could hear someone talking on a phone. He started to go into the treatment rooms, but stopped when he felt the presence of someone close behind him. It was the black man.

"Ain't you the chief of police?"

"That's right. Something I can do for you?"

"I think maybe you better arrest me or somethin'."

"Oh yeah? Why should I do that?"

" 'Cause I just beat the motherfuck outta my woman."

Balzic sighed, wanting to say, not right now, don't bother me, some other time maybe, right now I got enough people getting worked over, but he didn't. He said, "Is she here? Is she trying to file a complaint against you?"

"Naw, she ain't here. She at her place," the black man said. "And I don't know if she goin' file no complaint. All I know is I come on over her place and she don't say two words, she jus' start into bangin' on me with a skillet. She like to tore my head off."

"And then you beat her up, right?"

"Not jus' then. I wait till she asleep. Then I beat the motherfuck outta her."

"Oh, Christ," Balzic said. "How do you know you didn't kill her?"

"Oh I ain't killed her. She was still runnin' her motor mouth when I walked out the house."

"So you think that means she's still alive, huh?"

"Well I ain't never heard no dead person talk, has you?"

"Why the hell did you have to pick tonight?" Balzic said. He was sorry immediately after he'd said it.

"Hey, man, all I'm doin' is tellin' you. You don't wanna do nothin' 'bout it, that's cool with me. That's jus' fine with me. I'll jus' go on back over there and sit down and wait some more till they gets ready to stitch up my lip."

"You know what? That's a good idea. If she files a complaint against you, then I'll be happy to arrest you, how's that?"

"That's fine with me," the black man said, turning away to take a seat again. He took a couple of steps and then turned back. "Say, man, you wouldn't happen to have no cigarette with a cork filter on it. This paper keep messin' over my lip."

"There's a cigarette machine around the corner down that hall," Balzic said, pointing to the hall behind the man's back, but he recognized from the man's expression that he had no money. Balzic rooted in his pockets and found enough change for the man to buy a pack. The man took the money with his eyes downcast.

"I'll pay you this back in the mornin'," he said.

"Forget it. Pay me back by not beating your wife anymore."

"Oh, she ain't my wife. I learned long time 'go, you don't marry no woman. You marry a woman, you wrong with the law right from the go. She can put you out, put you in jail, put you in a mental institution, take your money, take your clothes, your car—she can jus' get over you somethin' terrible. And there ain't a motherfuck you can do 'bout it." The man set off toward the cigarette machine, shaking his head, and saying repeatedly, "She ain't my wife. Ain't no woman my wife. My momma didn't raise no fool. . . ."

Balzic heard the commotion outside then but didn't even bother going to the door because he knew that the ambulance crew knew its business and that the best thing he could do was stand clear.

The attendants, hunched over and scurrying the stretcher along, bumped through the outer swinging doors and past Balzic and then through the fire doors, entering the treatment rooms.

One quick look at Nick Abbatta's face was enough for Balzic. If Abbatta was alive at all, it was only because the paramedics in the ambulance crew had found some dim signal of life and were hurrying more out of duty and hope than sense.

Balzic felt himself going queazy in the stomach and cold across the chest. Then he saw Mrs. Abbatta herding her daughter Rosalie through the outer doors. Rosalie was mumbling something inaudible over her shoulder to her mother, but Mrs. Abbatta paid no attention; instead she put both hands in the middle of Rosalie's back and shoved her forward. Rosalie stopped short at the sight of

Balzic, and her mother cried out, "Go on, move, you, you stupid!"

Balzic walked quickly toward them and held out his arms to embrace Mrs. Abbatta. She fell into his arms and sobbed against his chest. Rosalie scooted clumsily out of the way and dropped onto a couch, bumping her legs against it. She put all four fingers of her right hand into her mouth and began to whimper.

"Shut up, you," Mrs. Abbatta snapped at her. "This my fault, God forgive me, but you—you stupid!"

"Easy, Mrs. Abbatta," Balzic said. "Easy."

"Oh, no," she said. "I can no be easy with her this time. All her life I be easy with her. But no, not this time. This time she should be in there. Not Nicky. Not my Nicky."

Balzic had no doubt that if he hadn't been holding her around the shoulders, she would have attacked her daughter. Rosalie sucked backward against the couch, one foot on top of the other, and she tried to get all the fingers of both hands into her mouth. Tears streamed down her plump cheeks and mucous bubbled from her nostrils.

Balzic tried to steer Mrs. Abbatta toward a chair, but she resisted him. "I want be with Nicky," she cried. She repeated it over and over, and Balzic had all he could do to keep her from tearing loose and rushing into the treatment rooms to find her son.

"Please sit down, Mrs. Abbatta. Please."

"What goods to sit? I got to do something."

"Mrs. Abbatta, believe me, you'll only be in the way in there. These people know what they're doing. They'll take care of Nicky." It was a kind lie to tell, but a lie nonetheless, and from the way Mrs. Abbatta looked at

140

him, he could see that she knew he was just telling one of those kind lies. She glared at him fiercely for it, but then she seemed to droop. She covered her face with her hands and let Balzic ease her into an overstuffed chair.

She began to speak in Italian, but talking so low and quickly that Balzic could not follow her accurately. She sounded as though she was saying something about her daughter, about what a burden God had given her in this life, about how she had been able to stand it until now, but that this was too much. This was the last weight she could—or would—carry. From now on she was no longer going to take the responsibility for her daughter. It was her fault, God knew, but it was Rosalie's just as much.

Balzic wasn't positive about the first part of what she'd said, but he felt sure he'd understood her when she'd said that she was not going to be responsible for her daughter anymore and that it was Rosalie's fault as much as hers.

"Mrs. Abbatta, you can't mean what you're saying."

"About what?" she demanded suddenly in English. Her eyes flashed toward her daughter, still sucking her fingers and whimpering on the couch. "About her? God-damn right I mean. As God my witness. If God forgive me for Nicky, then God forgive me for her too."

"Hey, what's goin' on? I was 'posed to be next." It was the black man back from the cigarette machine and looking outraged.

"You'll get your turn," Balzic said to him, at the same time putting his hand on Mrs. Abbatta's shoulder.

"Ain't this a bitch," the black man said. "This stuff always goin' on. Let a white man get in here and—"

"Sit down and shut up," Balzic said. "You don't have

half an idea what's going on. Just find yourself a seat."

"Don't tell me find no seat! I can stand if I want. You can put me in the back the line, but I can damn sure stand if I wants. Huh!"

"I don't care if you hang from the ceiling," Balzic said, moving toward the man. "Just turn it off."

The black man grunted, turned and looked at Rosalie, and said to her matter of factly, "See how they do, girl? Onliest way it ever been. Black men and ugly women always gets in last."

Balzic wanted to knock him down, but in glancing at Rosalie, he saw that what the man had said had had a curiously calming effect on her. She took her fingers out of her mouth and wiped them on her robe. She sniffed and looked up at the black man as though wanting him to say more and as though it didn't matter much what he said.

The black man walked over and stood in front of Rosalie. "You better blow your nose, girl. We both know you a mess, but ain't no use you makin' a bigger mess." He walked off suddenly, disappearing behind the admissions desk, his head bobbing as he looked for something, and then returned carrying a box of tissues. He held them out to Rosalie and said, "Here, girl, clean up your face. You lookin' sorry as a Salvation Army suit."

Rosalie did not hesitate. She took the box of tissues, said "Thank you very much," and wiped her face and blew her nose. When she finished, she giggled up at the black man, her lumpy torso shaking with relief and gratitude.

Balzic turned back to Mrs. Abbatta, whose lips were stretched like wire across her teeth. "She how she does?" she whispered hoarsely. "Anybody treats her li'l bit nice, see how she does?" In Italian, she hissed the word for nigger. Then, still speaking Italian, she said, "Frankie was a nigger too."

Balzic went quickly to her side and sat on the arm of the chair. "What did you say?"

Again in Italian she said, "Frankie was the same. A nigger."

"Mrs. Abbatta, what're you talking about?"

"I'm the worst of everybody," she said, still speaking in Italian, but slowly and distinctly enough for Balzic to understand her clearly. "Nobody is worse than me. I made it come to this. If I had not agreed, it would never have come to this. So who am I to call names, to blame her or Frankie? Who am I to do this? I'm the real nigger in this."

Before Balzic could reply the ambulance crew came back out, and one of them motioned to Balzic that he wanted to talk to him. Balzic hurried to the man's side and listened with his head canted close to the man's mouth.

"I think somebody better get him a priest," the attendant whispered. "His heart's just fluttering."

Balzic cursed to himself as he went through his pockets looking for a dime. All he found were some pennies and one quarter. He went to the admissions desk, stepped behind it, and hit buttons on the phone there until he got a dial tone. Then he dialed St. Malachy's rectory.

Father Marrazo answered on the second ring, sounding as though he had been using wine to get to sleep and had succeeded only in getting a little drunk.

"This is Mario, Father. I'm at the hospital. They just brought in Nick Abbatta, and he needs you fast."

"Give me five minutes," the priest said. "Uh, Mario —never mind. I'll talk to you when I get there."

Balzic hung up, then ducked inside the treatment room doors and asked one of the nurses if the paramedic with the ambulance crew had been exaggerating. He got a somber, negative shrug in reply. He didn't know why he'd bothered to ask; he'd sensed as much when he'd seen Abbatta's face earlier.

He turned away slowly and walked as slowly back toward the doors leading to the waiting room, wanting to kick holes in the walls as he went. He came suddenly alert when he heard the scuffling in the waiting room.

He rushed out to find the black man hanging onto Mrs. Abbatta's left arm and trying to pull her away from her daughter. Mrs. Abbatta, old and portly though she was, kept leaning away from him, staying close enough to slap with her right hand at Rosalie's face but not getting close enough to connect. Rosalie had drawn herself into a corner of the couch and was shrieking wildly, begging her mother to stop.

Balzic darted around the black man and bear-hugged Mrs. Abbatta from behind, pinning her arms to her sides.

"For God's sake, Mrs. Abbatta, leave her alone. She's not responsible for this. Come on, leave her alone. Calm down."

"You think so, huh?" Mrs. Abbatta twisted herself, not to get free from Balzic but to look into his eyes. "Who you think tell Frankie? Her, that's who! This stupid!"

She sagged backward against Balzic and began to rock with sobs. "My God, my God . . . what did I do? . . ."

Balzic eased her across the width of the waiting room and gently pushed her down onto another couch. "Why don't you lay down for a while, Mrs. Abbatta? Really, try to lay down a little while."

She shook her head violently, then closed her eyes and pressed the heels of her palms against them. She began to speak very quietly between sobs. It took Balzic some moments to understand her Italian.

". . . I promise thee, O blessed Jude, to be ever mindful of this great favor, and I will never cease to honor thee as my special and powerful patron and to do all in my power to encourage devotion to thee. Amen. . . ." Then she began to say Hail Mary, finishing in a whisper.

Balzic had been squatting in front of her, holding her shoulders, but he had to straighten up to shake the cramps out of his thighs.

Mrs. Abbatta began to pray again, this time in a voice almost less than a whisper, her hands still pressed tightly against her eyes. She finished just as Father Marrazo hurried into the waiting room, but she didn't look up to see who had come in.

The priest merely nodded at Balzic on his way through the lobby. In five minutes he was back out, shaking his head. His eyes were as near desperation as Balzic could ever recall seeing them.

Mrs. Abbatta took her hands away from her eyes, and instantly upon seeing the priest, she began to wail.

"Do you hear his confession?" she shrieked.

The priest nodded, but when Mrs. Abbatta cast her eyes downward in momentary relief, he shook his head no to Balzic.

"What can we do for her?" the priest asked after Mrs.

Abbatta had cried and shouted for her son until she seemed unable to take another breath without collapsing.

"We can take them to my house," Balzic said. "My mother's really good at this." Balzic glanced over at Rosalie, who was still cringing on the couch. The black man was standing beside her, patting her on the head as he would have petted a puppy.

"The thing is," Balzic went on, taking the priest a few steps away, "she's really got the heat for her daughter. I can't take them alone, and neither can you, so she's going to have to sit up front with me and Rosalie can sit in the back with you; otherwise we're going to have one bitch of a time. We got to keep them apart until my mother can talk some sense into her—if that's possible."

"Well, let's do it," Father Marrazo said.

"Yeah, but I got to do something first." Balzic walked over to the black man and took his arm. The man cursed and tried to pull away, but Balzic wouldn't let go.

They went into the treatment rooms, where Balzic stopped the first nurse they came upon. "Will you see to it that this man is treated? He's been waiting a long time, and he's been damn good about it. And if he doesn't have any insurance, send the bill to the Rocksburg Police Department, you understand?"

Puzzled, the nurse nodded after a moment, then pointed to a room one door away and walked toward it, motioning for the black man to follow her. The black man scratched his head and then shook it, looking as though he couldn't think of anything to say and knowing that he would later regret that he hadn't been able to think of anything.

Balzic left him without another word, going back out

to the lobby quickly. It took some persuading, both by him and by the priest, to convince Mrs. Abbatta that the best place for her to be now was with one of her best friends. She kept saying she wanted to be with Nicky, and then she tried to insist that she ought to be home. Together, Balzic and the priest got them into the cruiser, and Balzic drove to his house as fast as he thought he could without alarming either mother or daughter.

He didn't have to wake his mother; she had been sitting in the kitchen since she'd phoned him earlier. And when Balzic led them all into the kitchen she seemed instantly to sense what was wrong. She began immediately to soothe Mrs. Abbatta, asking nothing of anyone but reading all their faces.

Balzic relaxed then, knowing there was no one more capable of talking some sense into Mrs. Abbatta about Rosalie as soon as Mrs. Abbatta emptied herself of her next rush of grief. He also knew that before he closed the front door Ruth and the girls would be out to help. He and the priest got as far as the dining room when Ruth appeared.

"Mario, what the hell is going on?"

"In the kitchen. Mrs. Abbatta and Rosalie. Nick's dead."

"Oh my God, how?"

"I'll tell you later. Go help Ma, will you? I got to go."

"Oh for Christ's sake," she said and hurried into the kitchen without another word to her husband.

Balzic was checking the lock on his front door to make sure it would lock behind him when he heard his call signal crackling over the cruiser radio. He ducked around Father Marrazo and bounced down the steps two at a time.

"Balzic here. What's up, Joe?"

"Tullio's in his house, Mario," Desk Sergeant Joe Royer said.

"He's in his house? How the hell'd he get past those people up there? Never mind. I don't want to know. Is anybody talking to him?"

"Stramsky."

"Well tell him to tell everybody to sit on it. I'm on my way."

Balzic dropped the speaker on the seat, turned the ignition, and put the cruiser in gear. He looked out his window and saw the priest still standing on the steps. "What're you going to do, Anthony? Where you going? Your car's up the hospital. You can't do anything here. Come on, get in."

The priest shook his head thoughtfully, then trotted down the steps and around the front of the cruiser and got in. He had barely closed the door when Balzic stomped on the accelerator, throwing him against the dashboard.

"Easy, Mario, easy. I don't think he's going anywhere."

"Probably not. But I'm not hurrying because he might try to take off. I want to get there before one of my people decides to play the Lone Ranger."

Balzic made it to Norwood Hill, a distance of four miles, in less than three minutes. Father Marrazo was crossing himself when they got out.

All four of Balzic's mobile units were there with their spotlights trained on Manditti's house, as were one mobile from the state police and one from the county detectives, all of whom trailed after him as Balzic approached.

"What's the story, Vic?"

"Well, we got two in the back and two on each side, and the rest of us girls are where you see us."

"How long's he been in there?"

"The state guy signaled Fischetti about twenty minutes ago and he called me. After that it's all confusion. There's something wrong with the fuckin' radios again. Sometimes we can send and we can't receive, and then sometimes it's the other way around. My car radio's all fucked up too. Mario, you got to get some money from Council. We can't keep operating like this. Christ, somebody's—"

Balzic held up his hands. "I know all about the radios, Vic, but first things first, okay? Now, how'd he get in there?"

"He didn't drive in, that's for sure. He must've walked up over the back of the hill. It's a wonder he didn't have a heart attack."

"Who's been talking to him?"

"Just me. I don't know what the state horse said. I don't think anything."

"He said anything back?"

"Just once. He said for us to leave him alone before he got mad."

"Before he got mad, huh?"

Stramsky shrugged. "That's what he said, Mario."

"Okay, give me the horn."

Stramsky handed over the amplified bullhorn, and Balzic walked with it to the end of Manditti's front walk.

149

"Tullio? You hear me?"

No answer.

"Tullio, it's late, everybody's tired, we got half the hill up already, and the more noise I make on this thing, the more people we're going to wake up. There's lots of old people and babies up here need their sleep, so don't put any frost on my tomatoes, huh? Just get your butt out here. Now!" He turned to Stramsky and handed him the keys to his cruiser. "Go get the gas out of my trunk. I'm not gonna fuck around with this clown, not even for one minute."

A window squeaked open to the left of the front door.

"What're you, kiddin' me, Balzic?" came Tullio's voice from behind the window. "Whatta you want? What're you doing, screaming about old people and babies? What're you doing out there making all that racket and with them lights? You don't hear me making no noise. I ain't the one waking people up. So why don't you take them boy scouts and the rest of them fruitcakes and go on home? Cheesus."

"Tullio, for sure you're putting a frost on my tomatoes. I'm gonna tell you once more. If you're not out here in five seconds, you're gonna think you're in a gas factory."

Tullio let out a long groan and slammed the window shut. In four seconds he was standing in the doorway, shielding his eyes from the lights with his forearms.

"Turn them lights off, for crissake. What is this, Balzic? What're you doing this to me for? What'd I ever do to you, huh?"

"Just shut up and turn around and put your hands against the side of the house."

"Put my hands on the house, Cheesus. Turn them

lights out so I can see what I'm doing."

"Go 'cuff him, Vic," Balzic said, "before I go up there and break his head."

Stramsky and the state trooper darted forward and handcuffed and searched Tullio after they'd made him lean his forehead against the side of the house.

"Hurry up, willya?" Tullio kept shouting. "This hurts my head. I got a little weight here to hold up, you know."

"He's clean," Stramsky called back to Balzic, who was leaning against the fender of one of the cruisers. Father Marrazo stood next to him and started to pat his pockets, looking for cigarettes.

"There's some in my glove compartment, Father." Balzic faced the porch again. "Tell him his rights, Vic, and say 'em loud enough for the man from the state to hear."

Father Marrazo got the cigarettes from Balzic's car and began opening the pack in the spotlight from the cruiser Balzic was leaning against. Just then, Stramsky and the state trooper, each holding Tullio by an arm, led him down the walk and stopped in front of Balzic.

Tullio had come peacefully, if not quietly—he had never stopped complaining about the lights—but he took one look at Father Marrazo and went wild, screaming, cursing, kicking, lifting both Stramsky and the state trooper off the ground as he jerked his massive shoulders from side to side, all in a frenzied effort to get at the priest.

"You fuckin' priests! What're you doin' here? You fuckin' goddamn thieves! You're the biggest thieves! You got all them collection boxes, you ain't happy . . . you got to fix things, you motherfuckers!"

"Tap him!" Balzic called out to one of his own patrolmen who had just come from around the side of the house.

The patrolman drew his baton, scurried around the front of the frantic group, and when he'd taken aim, tapped Tullio on the forehead just hard enough to stun him and make him stop thrashing.

"Move again, Tullio," Balzic said, "and I'm going to take that baton and split your goddamn head open, you hear me?"

"I hear you, I hear you, Cheesus. What're you guys getting so rough for? I wasn't doing nothing."

"I'd hate to see you when you're doing something," Stramsky said, breathing heavily.

"I'm just looking out for my rights, that's all. That's all I'm doin' . . . us citizens got some rights, ain't that right, Balzic? . . . What's the priest doing here? Somebody getting married or something?" Tullio rattled on and on, but his jokes were only words.

There was no doubt now in Balzic's mind about who Tullio had really wanted to work over with his bat. Until this moment, until he had heard and seen Tullio's reaction to Father Marrazo's presence, Balzic had not been certain, but now he was absolutely sure. All he had to do was watch Tullio's eyes while he kept trying to make jokes. Tullio's gaze worked the priest over from head to foot and back up again.

It must have been a real struggle for him, Balzic thought, though it was hard to imagine Tullio ever struggling over a matter of conscience. Still, the situation had been the kind that would force even a Tullio into a struggle. Maybe for the first time in his life Tullio had had a real war in himself about who to get after he'd gotten

Frank Dulia, and Balzic wondered how much had been added to that struggle by the thought of all those women . . . ah, it's all a lot of wasted wondering, Balzic concluded. I could ask him about it from now until I retire and he wouldn't tell me a thing.

"I want to see a lawyer, Balzic," Tullio said, his gaze still fixed on the priest.

"You'll get to see lots of them."

"You know what I mean," Tullio grumbled. "My own."

"Don't worry about it, Tullio. I'm sure Muscotti'll make sure you get the best lawyer he can get for you."

"Oh yeah," Tullio said disgustedly. "Write me a letter."

Balzic turned away and started for his own cruiser. "Book him, Vic. And no mistakes. I don't want to lose this clown over some bad bookkeeping."

Stramsky nodded, and he and the state trooper led Tullio off to the state mobile unit.

"Somebody put some locks on the house," Balzic called out to no one in particular. "I don't want to give these good people up here a chance to go bad on me . . . okay, let's go home. Let's everybody go home and think about what we're going to do with all that overtime, all that time and again. . . ."

In the cruiser, driving back to the hospital so Father Marrazo could get his car, Balzic said, "Okay, Father, are you going to tell me, or am I going to tell you?"

"Mario, if we both know, then what's the point? Any explaining either one of us has to do has to be to somebody else anyway."

"I don't know, Father. Maybe we ought to just clear the air with each other, you know?"

The priest shook his head slowly. "This is a real mess, Mario. No matter how much we talk about it, we still won't be able to change that."

"I know it's a mess. But what I can't get through my head is why Sabatine would go for something like this. I mean, sweet Jesus, rigging the Treasury balance—wow. I mean, I remember what you told me before about him. I didn't even know what you were talking about. I mean, I'm not sure I'd understand you now if you told me the same things all over again, but hell, Father, he had to be smarter than this."

"What can I tell you?" the priest said disconsolately. "He did. For all I know it might have been his idea. I don't really know whose idea it was. Something tells me it was Mrs. Tuzzi's. But that's just a feeling. I can't get her to say anything about it, nothing at all. But no matter who approached who in the beginning, Sabatine could have stopped it any time he wanted, and he wouldn't have had to say a word."

"Well why the hell didn't he?" Balzic said, slapping the steering wheel repeatedly.

"You got a cigarette?"

"I thought you got the ones out of the glove compartment. Never mind. Here, take these," Balzic said, handing over a nearly crushed pack he had jammed behind the sun visor.

"There's only one left, Mario. I don't want to take your last one."

"I can get more in the hospital."

"So you want to give me this one?"

"What is this, Anthony? You got the ones from the glove compartment. What'd you do, lose 'em?" Balzic shot a quick glance at the priest. "Oh. Don't tell me. I can feel a homily coming on." Balzic waited, but the priest seemed content to smoke and stare out the window.

"Okay, Anthony, you got me hooked. What's the message?"

"It wasn't any big deal," the priest said. "You had something I seemed to need. We're friends. You gave it to me."

"You trying to tell me that's why Sabatine went for this?" Balzic screwed up his face and sighed. "Come on, Anthony. I don't know, but when I saw you a couple nights ago, before I knew any of this was connected, before I even had the first idea—damn, man, you made it sound a lot more complicated than that. A lot more complicated."

"It is a lot more complicated. But maybe when you cut all the details, maybe it was as simple as one person having something another person needed. You know, of all those women, only two of them had any kind of half-decent income? . . . You know where Mrs. Cafasso's son is? Domenico's widow—you know they only had one son —you know he's in the alcoholic ward in the Vets Hospital in Pittsburgh?"

"No, I didn't know that."

"He is. You know why? Because he was with Graves Registration at Normandy. He—"

"I know what they do, Anthony. They pick up the pieces and try to pair up the dog tags."

"That's not what I was going to say. I know you know

155

what Graves Registration means. What I was going to say was that he hasn't been sober two days in a row since he was discharged. He got something like ninety percent disability, but he spent the whole check every month on booze. She never got a dime from him. And Domenico died of black lung before anybody thought of giving pensions for that . . . God, Mario, she was eating dog food. Imagine it! Dog food!

"And Mrs. Ruffola's story isn't much different," Father Marrazo continued. "Her husband went the same way, same disease. Their only son was killed at Salerno, about three miles from where both of them were born, her and Amadie. You know that Amadie refused to accept the insurance check from the government? He threw the guy who tried to deliver it, threw him bodily off his porch."

"Yeah," Balzic said. "My mother told me about that."

"Did she tell you that he never went out of the house after that? Never worked another day? And that he died less than a year later? Did she tell you that?"

"No, she didn't. But I heard it around."

"Well, do you know what Mrs. Ruffola's social security check was worth? Seventy-two dollars a month. A month, Mario! Imagine trying to live on that."

"Yeah, but—but, goddamn, Anthony, there had to be a better way."

"Sure. The Pope should auction off the Sistine Chapel. He could feed a lot of people with what he got for that."

"Aw come on, Anthony. I didn't say anything to deserve that."

"It wasn't what you said. It was your tone . . . okay, so maybe I shouldn't have made that crack. I apologize.

I was out of line. But for a second there, you started to sound a little Presbyterian on me."

Balzic wheeled the cruiser over to the curb and jammed on the brakes. He twisted around to face the priest.

"What the hell is this, Anthony? We going to go through a whole thing about who's supposed to take care of the poor people, the old ladies with all their sad stories? Jesus Christ, there's a thousand stories like that around here, probably more. Anywhere there's a mine or a mill, anywhere there's widows old enough with husbands who never got in on those pension plans or got screwed out of them by some goddamn bookkeeper or lawyer—what do you got? But, goddamn it, you said there were only two women with any kind of half-decent income. Who was the other one? Sabatine's housekeeper, Mrs. Tuzzi? Well what's she going to do now? Who do you think's going to hire her again? After this gets out, who's going to give her a job? The bishop maybe?

"And what's the other one going to do, the one we took to my house a little while ago, what's she gonna do? In a couple days you're going to say the words over her income. I'm sure Abbatta had a damn good insurance policy. That printers' union took care of its own for a long time now. But tell me something, Anthony. You think she's really going to have the heart to spend any of that insurance? After what she set up with him? After tonight?"

"Mario, please don't shout, will you?" The priest opened the window and flipped out his cigarette butt. "I was just trying to suggest some of the motivation, that's all. I don't like it any better than you do. Sabatine was as far out of line as any priest can get. All I'm saying is that if you give him the benefit of some doubt, you have to recognize that he saw a chance to help some people, some old women, who really needed help, and—"

"He also saw a pretty good chance to pay off the mortgage on his church, don't forget that."

"Mario, I'm not forgetting anything," the priest said sharply. "But that man was running out of time, and who knows what was going through his head? All I'm sure about is that never, never did he think anything like this was going to happen."

"Anthony, what're you telling me, huh? For everything there's a price. You pay in money or time or sweat or blood, but you pay, and—"

"I know that, Mario," the priest said, holding up his hands as though to ward off the words.

"Let me finish," Balzic said. "When you get into a fix, when you start trying to make funny things happen, you open the door for somebody else to get in there. And, goddamn it, you know that as well as I do. The pros know it. But they know it before they start. Before they do anything, they add up the taxes they're going to pay, and they're almost a hundred percent sure who they're going to pay them to.

"But what's this amateur doing? Where'd he come from? Why the hell didn't he run a bingo game and give all those ladies a percentage? What—he was too good for bingo? He never had a game in his church as long as I can remember. If he did my mother would've been there, and so would a couple hundred other women. Bingo he can't handle. But he goes for a fix like this? With his eyes open and he doesn't even think to look? You knew who blew it for him? That poor slob Rosalie. She's the one

who told Frank Dulia. She figured it. And she isn't supposed to have the brains of a cow!"

"Mario, you're shouting again."

"Anthony, two guys are—aw, fuck it. I'm sorry. I'm
sorry for everybody."

"You're sorry," the priest said, laughing feebly. It
was a bitter and rueful sound. "What do I tell the bishop?
Never mind the bishop. What do I tell Sabatine? He
doesn't know anything about this yet."

"I don't know," Balzic said, pinching the bridge of his
nose as he drove away from the curb. "But maybe we
ought to stop talking for a while. We're both getting a
little salty."

"I'll agree with that," the priest said. "But just tell me
one more thing and then I'll drop it. How did you know
what Sabatine was doing?"

"Huh? Until Tullio started screaming at you, I didn't
know. But that's when it all went together. My mother
was the one who told me about those women winning
seven hundred apiece. And something kept bugging me
about that, about the amount, but I didn't even know
how to think about what was bugging me until I remembered what you told me about Sabatine's mortgage payments. And even then I didn't figure it went together.
But then my mother told me, tonight as a matter of fact,
that Frank Dulia was Mrs. Abbatta's nephew. 'Cause at
that time, right before she told me that, I was still trying
to understand what Dulia said to Tullio."

"What was that?"

"He said that whatever he bet on wasn't supposed to
lose. That's when I started thinking fix. But it was all a
mess in my head until just a little while ago. Then when
Tullio starts on you, I thought, hey, what do we got here?

We got a priest, five old ladies, a linotype operator at the only newspaper in town, the paper that puts out the Treasury statement every day, and one thousand tickets at two bucks a pop. So what's the payoff on those tickets —fifteen hundred? Fourteen hundred if whoever is hustling them is greedy. You know the attraction better than I do. They pay seven hundred to one, maybe seven-fifty, which is a hell of a lot better than the five-forty a number pays.

"So if the ladies get seven hundred apiece, that leaves thirteen bills. Subtract ten bucks for printing, and that leaves twelve-ninety, which is what you said Sabatine's mortgage payments went up.

"It would've been a sweet thing," Balzic went on. "It was, until Rosalie told Dulia. And how smart could he have been? He bets with Manny. On a Treasury number! Nobody, but nobody in the world would've taken that bet except Manny. I don't know a bookmaker who would've touched it. They just don't fuck around with those things."

Balzic stretched and yawned at a stop light. "Well, I got Tullio. That's the only part of it I want. The rest is all yours. And believe me, Anthony, I don't envy you."

"Uh, Mario," the priest said hesitantly, "do I understand you? Are you saying you're not going to do anything about Sabatine?"

Balzic looked at the priest. "Anthony, you really surprise me. What do you want, huh? What am I supposed to do, huh? I mean, I know what I'd like to do. I'd like to go kick Sabatine in the ass even if he does have the big casino. But you didn't really think I was going to bust him? The women too? Ho, man, for what? Fraud? Who made the complaint? Uh-uh, Anthony, they're all yours. And if I'm you, I'd just hand it over to the bishop. I'd just dump it on his desk; let him figure it out. That's all you're supposed to do, right? Isn't that all he wants from you? A report?"

"Yeah. A report," the priest said. "It'll be the hardest thing I ever did."

Balzic drove away from the intersection slowly and pulled into the hospital parking lot. "Well, Father, you got two masses to say in the next couple days. I don't think either one of them's going to be what I'd call easy."

"No, they won't. But Sabatine's still alive." The priest got out and started for his car, but stopped after a few steps and came back.

"What's the matter?" Balzic said.

"Your cigarettes. Here." The priest handed them in.

"You want a couple to hold you?"

"Just one. I'll stop someplace and get some. Muscotti's will still be open. I could use a little wine. Maybe even a little competition with the cards."

"Yeah. Well. Maybe I'll stop down myself."

Balzic didn't stop at Muscotti's. He didn't go home either. He didn't want to discuss Father Sabatine with Father Marrazo anymore, and he knew that if he went to Muscotti's they would inevitably begin to fret and fume over the whole sorry business again. And if he went home he would have Mrs. Abbatta and Rosalie to contend with, and he didn't want any part of that either. He didn't even want to know whether his mother and Ruth were handling that well or whether they had had to be reinforced by his daughters.

He drove aimlessly around town for more than an hour, then finally turned the cruiser in the direction of his station, knowing that he was copping out on his family, but he didn't care because he made himself not want to care. He had had enough. All he wanted now was a cot in one of his lockups and a little bourbon out of the pint he kept in his desk for just such times as these, times, as he usually thought of them, when he wanted to become a bug.

Inside the duty room he asked Royer if the booking and arraignment of Tullio Manditti had gone smoothly and correctly.

"Here's copies if you want to read them," Royer replied.

"Did you read them?"

Royer nodded.

"Any mistakes?"

"I couldn't see any."

"Is he down at Southern Regional?"

"Yeah, county guys took him."

"What was the bond?"

"Hundred thousand."

"Well, then he stays until the trial. Nobody he knows is gonna put up ten percent of that. Good. That settles it. We got the bum, we got the motive, we got the witness, and we got the bond."

"We got a witness? Who? I didn't know we had a witness."

"I didn't tell you that? Sure. Hell yes. A guy named Harsha. Lives right next door to Dulia. Saw the whole thing from less than twenty-five, thirty feet, unobstructed. What could be better than that?"

Balzic scratched his chest, pulled his underwear loose from his crotch, and went back to his office, returning in moments with the pint of bourbon. He went toward the door leading to the stairs down to the lockups. "There's nobody down there, right?"

"Not yet," Royer said.

"Well, I'm going to sleep down there. So don't let anybody bring anybody in. Tell 'em to give 'em a lecture and send 'em home. And if anybody calls, unless it's a nuclear attack, I ain't here."

"Okay, Mario. I don't know how you can sleep on those things."

"Hey, Joe, you're not insinuating that we don't provide adequate facilities for our, uh, wayward citizens, are you?"

"Who? Me?"

"Listen, if it's good enough for the rabble, it's good enough for the rousters . . . you know, sometimes I think it ought to be part of the training for the rousters to spend a couple nights in the slammer, and, oh, would it ever be good for the DAs and the judges, and man, oh, man, wouldn't it be terrific for all them fuckin' politicians? Huh? Think of it, Joe. As a requirement for public office, the first thing you had to do after you got elected was spend a weekend in the slam. Man, oh, man, wouldn't those fuckers think a little bit about some of the laws they write? Huh? Wouldn't they now? . . ."

"I don't know if I'd go that far," Royer said.

"Yeah? Well, once I read about a Jap. He built himself a coffin, and every once in a while he used to sleep in it, you know, just to get used to the notion. I think

163

that's a hell of an idea. And that's why I sleep downstairs sometimes. You know, to get used to the notion."

"Well, it's your back," Royer said. "Sleep easy." He turned back to his desk and picked up the newspaper. "I didn't know we had a witness," he said, speaking more to himself than to Balzic.

"Well we do," Balzic said, starting down the steps. "And it's a damn good thing, 'cause if we didn't—well, I don't even want to think about that."

Balzic slept well indeed. And he hadn't needed more than two swallows of bourbon to get him started. When he woke, he accidentally kicked over the paper cup out of which he'd been drinking, and he saw with some surprise how little he had drunk.

He went to the end of the corridor to the shower room, undressed, relieved himself, and showered and shaved. He almost didn't mind putting on the same clothes, he felt so rested and refreshed. When he came up the stairs and walked into the duty room, he was humming.

"Mornin', Angelo," he said to Desk Sergeant Angelo Clemente. "What're you looking so sour about? Christ, man, look outside. It looks like spring for sure. Look at it."

"Yeah," Clemente said. "It might look good to you and me, but it ain't going to look too good to some people."

"Why? What happened? Something happen?"

"Four guys in a wildcat mine out in Westfield Township. Two guys got out, but two of them didn't."

"When'd this happen?"

"Well, the story I get from Eddie Sitko is they were just going to work. They just started in the shaft when the roof let go. They weren't fifty, sixty feet in."

Balzic shook his head and looked at his shoes for a long time, struggling not to remember what had happened to his own father. He could have walked on the ceiling more easily. "Well, that happens, Angelo," he said finally. "That happens a lot with those small outfits. Sometimes they just try to cut the costs too much. They from here?"

"Nah. Both fatals were from Westfield Township. All four of them were. I never heard the names though. Couple of good hunkies. One of them had a wife and five kids. Smolensky. George John, forty-six. The other one didn't have no family. And it might've been time for him. He was sixty-four. Harsha."

Balzic had started to walk back to his office, shaking his head in that immediate gut commiseration he felt for anyone who died as his father had. He stopped as though stung when he heard the name Clemente had said.

"What was that other one's name?"

Clemente read it off the log to make sure. "Uh, Harsha. Andrew Theodore."

"You sure?"

"Well, that's the name I got from Eddie Sitko."

"Andrew Theodore Harsha, sixty-four, from Westfield Township?"

"Yeah. I'm telling you. What's the matter?"

Balzic let out a long groan and then kicked a metal desk and then kicked it twice more until he had put three dents in it. "Jesus fuck!" he roared.

"What's the matter? Hey, Mario, Mario, what's the matter?"

"He was our witness! I'm sorry he died. I'm sorry anybody dies that way, but Jesus fucking Christ, he was our witness!"

"What witness? What're you talking about? How come nobody tells me nothing?"

"He lived next door to Dulia. He saw Tullio kill him. You know what kind of case we got against Tullio without a witness? Without Muscotti, understand, without Muscotti's help—'cause Muscotti ain't about to help him —Tullio got cousins scattered all over western Pennsylvania, and those cousins got friends. He can come up with twenty guys who'll say he was playing cards with them or whatever they have to say for him. For crissake, I'm the only person who heard Harsha's story. He was supposed to come in today at four o'clock to make a statement, that's how sure I was—sure, my ass. That's how sloppy I was. Jesus Christ," Balzic said, holding his head, "no worse testimony in the world than second-hand testimony from a cop who got it from a guy who's dead. Agghhh, bullshit! . . ."

Balzic sat sulking at the end of the bar by the kitchen in Muscotti's. He had been drinking for nearly two hours, starting with a double whiskey and then changing to wine, chasing both with large glasses of ice water. He kept telling himself not to get drunk, at the same time telling himself there wasn't anything he'd rather do.

Muscotti's was quiet. It was midafternoon. The lunch

crowd had long gone, but it was still a couple of hours before the afterwork crowd would come in. Solitary customers, the retirees, the lonely, the lushes, had drifted in and out. Now there was no one except for Balzic and Vinnie.

"Mario, you better take it easy," Vinnie said, as he poured still another double wine and refilled the other, taller glass with ice and water. "It don't look good, you know what I mean?"

"What're you worrying about, huh?"

"Hey, you know, take it easy. This ain't like you. You don't look good."

"Which is it now: *it* don't look good, or *I* don't look good?"

"Ah, you know what I mean."

"Well, what are you worried about? How I look to the public? Or how I'm gonna look to the rest of your customers? They're all fuckin' squares anyway, so what's the worry?"

Vinnie sighed and shrugged. "Well, you know."

"Yeah, sure. Well, up the squares, how's that?"

"Look, why don't you stay with the ice water for a while?" Vinnie said. "Dom'll be in in a couple minutes. You can talk it over with him. Maybe he can come up with something. But don't make a mess of yourself. That's not right."

Balzic sipped the wine, then looked at Vinnie and drank it down in four swallows. He knocked over the glass setting it on the bar. "Vinnie, we been friends too long for you to start making like a teacher with me, huh?"

Vinnie threw out his hands and let them fall against his legs. "Okay, Mario. I don't say nothing. No more."

"Then put some more in there."

"You got it, buddy. You can drink 'em all day, I can damn sure pour 'em all day."

Balzic stifled a yawn and rubbed his palms together. He spun around slowly on the stool and looked at the opposite wall, then spun back and read the community college basketball schedule for the fifth or sixth time. He took a sip of the chablis Vinnie brought him and then a sip of the ice water. A motorcycle roared by on State Street, its engine noise piercing, causing Balzic to close his eyes and cover his ears.

He felt someone tap him on the shoulder. When he opened his eyes and took his hands away from his ears, he saw Dom Muscotti and heard him saying something about ". . . arresting those friggin' nuts."

"What nuts?"

"Those motorcycle nuts. They make me crazy with all that noise. There got to be something stupid about people who like noise. Ain't there an ordinance about how much noise you can make?"

"Sure," Balzic said. "Three of them."

"Well why don't you tell your guys to enforce them?" Dom screwed up his face and walked around behind the bar. "You know what noise does to you, Mario? I been reading about it. It can send your blood pressure up twenty, thirty points, a real sudden noise, d'you know that?"

Balzic scratched his scalp, rubbed his lips, and took another sip of wine.

"Did you know that, Mario?"

"Yeah I know that. But do you know what I'd have to do to enforce any ordinance about noise? I'd have to have ten more cars and twenty more people. For crissake, I'm supposed to have two lieutenants, one for juveniles and one for administration, and I been waiting three years for Council to approve the money for them. Do I have to say any more?"

"Okay, Mario, okay. Take it easy. I was just making conversation anyway." Muscotti turned away and went through the letters and bills Vinnie had handed him. He said nothing, put the envelopes and bills in a nook beside the coffee machine, then coughed and leaned under the bar to spit in an empty beer case.

"What're you drinking for now?" Muscotti said when he straightened up. "You know, you look a little drunk."

"Your bartender been giving it to me for twenty minutes, now you're going to start. Maybe you ought to start selling candy."

"Hey, I'm sorry I asked. Just pretend I didn't say nothing, okay?"

"No, I won't," Balzic said. "You want to know what I'm drinking for, I'm going to tell you. You're just the guy who ought to hear it anyway. It was one of your *paisans*—no, not one. Three of them. First it was Manny. Then Tullio. Then Brownie for letting Tullio get away from him. And those three assholes got me in a real bind."

"Let's go in the back, huh, Mario? If you're going to drink wine, you might as well drink good stuff."

"Okay. Fine. That's fine with me. 'Cause I got plenty to say."

"Okay, okay, take it easy. Come on back and say it."

Balzic left his wine and water on the bar and followed Muscotti to the room where they'd talked before when he'd made his senseless threat to shut down Muscotti's operation. He let Muscotti go in first and then dropped woozily on a chair, running his fingers through his hair and then rubbing the back of his neck.

"Hey, Dom," he said, "no more wine for me. I had more than enough about an hour ago."

"Whatever you say," Muscotti said, sitting opposite Balzic. "So, uh, what's the problem?"

"I told you, I'm in a real bind. The worst one I ever been in."

"So tell me."

"I had a witness. He saw Tullio put the job on Dulia, watched—"

"You 'had' a witness?"

Balzic nodded and rubbed his temples. "He got killed this morning. A fuckin' mine roof caved in on him. But without him, the only case I got against Tullio is circumstantial. It's a hell of a case. Any third-rate assistant DA could nail Tullio easy."

"So what're you worrying about?"

"In order to do it that way, I got to open up a real can of worms. I'd have to bust six people, including a priest and five old ladies, for operating a lottery, for fraud, for conspiracy, that whole number. Then I'd have to get the DA, Weigh, to go along with immunity for them so they could testify about the circumstances. And, uh, in any other case, that's no big deal. But this time it might not be so easy. I don't have to tell you Weigh ain't Catholic, and he just might get a hair up his ass because this is all Catholic and it all smells.

"But forget that," Balzic went on. "I mean, even if Weigh played it straight, even if he went along with the immunity, once these people testify, they're finished. The papers, the television, the radio—they'd eat 'em alive. No matter that nobody prosecutes them, they testify and they may as well crawl in their coffins."

"Wait a minute," Muscotti said. "You lost me. What priest? What old ladies?"

"Sabatine—"

"What?" Muscotti's eyes went wide and his head jerked forward. You mean the Sabatine from out St. Jude's? The one who tried to get Weisberg in Westfield Golf Club?"

"Yeah, yeah—"

"Why, Christ, I heard he got the big casino."

"Yeah, yeah, that's him. But wait'll you hear who the ladies are. You're gonna shit. Listen to this lineup: Mrs. Motti, Mrs. Ruffola, Mrs. Cafasso, Mrs. Tuzzi, and Mrs. Abbatta. You know what they did?"

"Hey, Mario," Muscotti said, standing suddenly and folding his arms and taking a step backward. "I'm not so sure I want to know. And I don't know if you ought to be telling me."

"Yeah? Well, sit down, 'cause you're going to hear it. 'Cause your fat gofer jumped right in the middle of it. And his brother finished it last night. He killed Nick Abbatta last night—"

"What?" Muscotti had to support himself on the back of the chair he'd been sitting on.

"You heard me. So sit down and—"

"Holy shit," Muscotti said. "And this was because of what the priest done?"

"That's right. They started it, and Dulia heard about it—"

"Yeah. But, Mario, you're still talking, you're still gonna tell me about a priest, and when you start talking about a priest, there's some things you just ain't supposed to say, I don't care what he done."

"My ass. Sit down and listen. Because this priest is

171

going to get a lot more grief if I don't come up with something, you understand?"

Muscotti scowled and chewed his lower lip and paced around the tiny room for nearly a minute. At last he sat and nodded. "All right. I'm listening."

"Okay, so here it is. Now I don't know whose idea it was in the beginning. I don't care. It doesn't matter anyway. But Sabatine went for a lottery. You know the kind, off the Treasury balance at two bucks a throw on a thousand tickets. Then somebody convinces Nick Abbatta to rig the numbers to match up with one of the ones those old ladies had. The women got seven bills apiece when it was their turn to win—or maybe they split it every month, I don't know—but the rest of it went on St. Jude's mortgage. Anyway, Abbatta's sister, the retarded one? Rosalie?"

Dom nodded vigorously. "I know her."

"Well, somehow she put it together. With her brains, I can't see how, but she did. What I figure is everybody was doing a lot of talking about it in front of her, figuring, you know, what does she know? But it turns out she worshipped Dulia, and she spilled it to him, or maybe just told him enough so he could figure the rest out for himself. But he couldn't have been too smart because you know who he booked it with."

Muscotti held up his right hand. "Say no more, Mario. I got it figured from there . . . boy, I see what you mean. This could really stink. And that friggin' Weigh, he collects taxes from me like two sponges. He charges me twice as much as Froggy used to. It took him two years to get around to it. Christ, I have to laugh now. I remember thinking, son of a gunsky, hey, maybe this

Weigh is really an honest square. But, boy, when he got around to it, he really put it to me. And I can't get a goddamn thing on him. I been trying ever since I started to pay, but he's smart, that bastard. Someday, remind me to tell you the ways I got to wash the money before he touches it . . . but never mind that. The important thing, Mario, is you're right. There's no doubt, he's a friggin' Mason all right. He'd love this. He'd prosecute it all by himself. He wouldn't let no assistant get the glory. That fucker'd have it both ways. He'd have my money and he'd be laughing at all us Micks."

Dom paused and shook his head harder and harder as though trying to resolve something very difficult. "That fat-ass. What's my mother got to like him for, can you tell me that? He got more fat between his ears than he got anyplace else. But she likes him. She really does. She calls him twice a day in the hospital. She must've sent him three baskets of fruit already . . . I'm stuck, Mario. I can't do nothing to him. You got to understand that. She'd never forgive me. And I couldn't handle that."

"Okay. So we got your mother and Manny on one side. But what do we got on the other side? Huh? Six widows and a priest with cancer."

"Six? I thought five."

"What's Dulia's wife? Don't she qualify?"

"Okay, okay." Muscotti held up his hands. He stuck his lower lip out and rubbed it thoughtfully with his index finger. "Okay," he said slowly, "okay. I can handle it. I paid enough taxes down that friggin' courthouse. But, Mario, you got to understand, I can't let Manny take too much weight. He can't do no more than three months. My mother can handle that. I'll talk to her. She'll understand that much. But, uh, one thing. Whoever I get, you got to school him. You can't let nobody else do it. It got to be right."

"Don't worry," Balzic said. "I'll make him a genius."

Tullio Manditti was brought into courtroom number four of the Conemaugh County courthouse five weeks to the day after Nicolao Abbatta Jr. was buried, five weeks and a day after Francis Dulia was buried.

There were few spectators in the room and no reporters. Tullio's trial had been docketed for the fall session of criminal court, but for reasons Clerk of Courts Louis Cepola wouldn't have explained to Jesus if He'd come back, the trial was suddenly called for the last day of the spring session. In fact, only Cepola, presiding Judge J. Harold Corcoran, Assistant District Attorney Ralph Manganero, Defense Attorney Louis Harmonich, the witnesses, the prospective jurors, the bailiffs and other court officers, and two spectators knew it was to be a trial. Tullio kept leaning over to his lawyer during jury selection and whispering hoarsely, "How come they're picking a jury? I thought this was supposed to be the preliminary hearing."

"I already told you," Louis Harmonich said back each time, "you already had one of those."

"So how come I wasn't here?" Tullio snapped during the last of these exchanges.

"You didn't have to be here. I was here, Mr. Mandizzi. That was enough."

"How many times I got to tell you? My name ain't

174

Mandizzi! It's Manditti. Ditti. Like ditto, only with an 'i' on the end."

Harmonich shrugged sheepishly.

Balzic, sitting in the first row between Father Marrazo and Dom Muscotti, leaned over to Muscotti and whispered, "Who found that guy?"

"Corcoran," Muscotti whispered back. "D'you think the Pope?"

"He must've had help."

"What help? That guy was sitting in the public defender's office like an apple waiting to fall off a tree."

"Oh yeah?"

"Certainly. Been in court about three times, all for drunk driving. Flunked the bar exam twice. Finished fifth from last in his class."

"And Corcoran found him all by himself, huh?"

"So? He was looking. What can I tell you?"

Balzic shook his head.

"What's the matter? Even Tullio's entitled to a lawyer. So what's a judge supposed to do if all the other lawyers are busy? He got to appoint one. So he appointed one."

Jury selection took three hours, two before lunch and one after. Court reconvened at exactly one-fifteen—when Judge Corcoran said it would—and the bailiffs and court stenographer were so surprised by Corcoran's attack of punctuality they had to be phoned twice in the basement coffee shop by Corcoran's tipstaff before they believed it. At one-nineteen, when they hurried in, Corcoran had been on the bench turning his gavel end over end for four minutes.

At two-nineteen, the last alternate juror was picked, the jury was sworn, and then Corcoran began to explain their duties and responsibilities. He was just at the point where he usually became loquacious, the point where he usually told juries how the whole system of American justice was based on the common wisdom of twelve ordinary citizens reasoning together, when he and everyone else in the room heard the insistent rapping of metal on wood coming from the first row of the spectators' section to Balzic's immediate left.

Balzic glanced over in time to see Muscotti putting a quarter in his pocket.

Corcoran coughed, drank some water, apologized for the laryngitis he felt coming on, and said, "Just pay attention to the evidence you hear. That's all that counts. The evidence. I'll tell you what you're supposed to do later on. Mr. Manganero, Mr. Harmonich, are you ready?"

Both attorneys stood and said they were, and then both waived making an opening statement.

Manganero began the case for the Commonwealth of Pennsylvania by calling Dr. Aram Sharma, the Indian Balzic remembered as the doctor who had been on duty when Frank Dulia was brought into the Emergency Unit of Conemaugh General Hospital. Dr. Sharma referred constantly to a small note pad, describing vividly in precise English in both medical and layman's language Dulia's condition when he had examined him.

Louis Harmonich said he had no questions.

Manganero next called the Lebanese doctor, who told of witnessing Dulia's death and filling out the death certificate.

Louis Harmonich said again that he had no questions.

Manganero next called Coroner Wallace Grimes and led him through a series of questions designed to illuminate Grimes' qualifications in forensic pathology. Louis Harmonich interrupted him to say that that wasn't necessary. "Everybody knows Dr. Grimes' reputation."

"All right, Dr. Grimes," Manganero said. "Did you perform an autopsy on one Francis Dulia sometime during the early morning hours of March 24?"

"I did."

"And would you tell us the cause of Mr. Dulia's death?"

"Massive brain damage as a direct result of multiple fractures of the left parietal and left temporal bones." Grimes did not have to refer to his own report, which lay in his lap, nor did he have to be instructed to indicate on his own head for the jury's benefit exactly what he was talking about.

"Where there other bruises or fractures or marks on the deceased's body, Doctor?"

"There were. Many of them." Grimes went on to enumerate the fractures. "There were no abrasions or lacerations. Just contusions. No cuts or burns. Just swellings."

"What would cause that, Doctor? In your expert opinion, what would cause the sort of injury to a human body such as you've described?"

"Well, the body is struck with some instrument which has been padded, something like a baseball bat that's been wrapped with a towel. The body receives the blow without suffering laceration or abrasion, but if the blow is powerful enough, something has to give somewhere, and what usually happens is that a bone fractures."

Manganero then repeated all the fractures that Grimes had enumerated previously, asking after each one if Grimes would say that that particular fracture was caused in the manner he'd just described. Grimes agreed after each one that it had.

Louis Harmonich said he had no questions.

Manganero called Balzic next. Right after he asked Balzic to identify himself, Louis Harmonich stood and said that there was no need to elaborate on Balzic's background or on his integrity. "Everybody knows who he is."

Balzic had to look at his shoes to keep his nervous smile from being seen by the jury.

Manganero led Balzic through a series of questions which focused on and skirted the periphery of the fact that Francis Dulia had been transported to the hospital in a pickup truck owned and driven by one Andrew T. Harsha, since deceased, who had witnessed something in the backyard of his neighbor's—Mr. Dulia's—house on the afternoon of March 23.

Manganero began to ask Balzic what it was that Mr. Harsha had witnessed, but Louis Harmonich objected, saying that though Balzic's testimony was obviously the best evidence since Mr. Harsha was dead, it was still second-hand evidence and he wanted the court to instruct the jury in that regard. Judge Corcoran looked sternly at Harmonich and was about to reply to his objection when Manganero said, "It's all right, your honor. We have another witness. I have no more questions for this witness."

Louis Harmonich said he too had no questions for this witness.

"Step down, Chief," Judge Corcoran said.

"Call Mr. Domenic Scalzo," Manganero said.

Dom "Soup" Scalzo passed Balzic on his way to the witness chair as though he had never seen him before in his life. He said, "I do," before the clerk finished reading the oath and took the witness chair with his eyes fixed on Manganero. He looked at no one else while he spoke.

"Mr. Scalzo," Manganero began, "would you state your full name and address and give your occupation?"

"Domenic G. Scalzo. I live at 531 Theobald Avenue, Rocksburg. I'm self-employed."

"At, uh, what are you self-employed, Mr. Scalzo?"

"I'm a business consultant."

"Could you be more precise than that?"

"I advise people about investments and what their chances are of making a profit."

Judge Corcoran had a coughing fit, interrupting Scalzo's testimony for almost a minute.

"Uh, Mr. Scalzo," Manganero said after Corcoran managed to get control of himself, "did you happen to be in the residence of one Andrew T. Harsha, now deceased, on the afternoon of March 23?"

"I was."

"What were you doing there?"

"I was advising Mr. Harsha on an investment he wanted to make. If he'd've listened to me, he'd still be alive today."

"And what was that?"

"I told him to get out of that mine he was in. I told him he was getting too old for that kind of work. It was all right to own a part of it, but he shouldn't be working in it."

"Yes. Well, unfortunately, Mr. Harsha did not take your advice. We all know that he died in that very mine

179

one day later. Well, Mr. Scalzo, will you please tell us if you saw anything unusual that day while you were visiting and advising Mr. Harsha?"

"Yes. I did. I mean, I will. We were in the kitchen having a drink. He just came home from the mine, and he said he wanted to cut the dust a little. . . . "

Balzic could stand to listen to no more. He bumped Muscotti's knee with his own and waved his hand feebly from side to side to show that he was leaving. He had to step in front of Father Marrazo to get to the aisle. The priest looked up at him, and his eyes were disturbingly hard and disbelieving. Balzic rushed from the courtroom, looking at the carpet, avoiding everyone's eyes.

Outside in the corridor, Balzic went to the marble balustrade overlooking the circular stairwell which was directly under the dome of the courthouse. He looked up at the dome and fumbled to loosen his tie and unbutton his collar. He felt himself breathing rapidly and tried to take long, slow breaths. He licked his upper lip and tasted perspiration. He looked at his palms, and they glistened wet in the light of the great globe suspended from the center of the dome.

Someone touched his arm, and Balzic swung his head around so quickly that he nearly became dizzy. It was Father Marrazo.

"Mario," the priest began and then stopped as though he had no idea what he was going to say, but his gaze was so intense that Balzic had to turn away. "Mario, what's—what the hell is going on?"

Balzic leaned his backside against the balustrade to support himself and jerked at his tie and collar. "You know what's going on, so what're you asking for?"

"I don't know," the priest said. "I sat in there and I

listened and I couldn't believe what I was listening to. And then you jumped up and your face was white. Mario, I want you to tell me what's going on.''

Balzic started to walk away from the priest, but Father Marrazo caught him by the sleeve. "Mario, I've never interfered with you before, and I may not know everything you know, and I may be way out of line, but I know when something is wrong, and there is something really wrong going on in there.'' The priest was trying to whisper, but his words sounded to Balzic as though he were shouting.

"Aaagh,'' Balzic growled. "What the hell did you want to go on, huh?''

"The right thing.''

"I did the right thing. What do you think I did?''

"Mario, you may think you did the right thing, but it's coming out all wrong. The way you're doing it is all wrong.''

"And how 'bout if I did it the right way, huh? I could've done it that way, sure. But do you know Weigh's a Mason? Huh? Do you know—''

"I don't care what he is. That doesn't change anything.''

"I don't believe this,'' Balzic said. "I don't believe this is you talking. After all you know?''

"You don't believe it? Huh? You don't believe it's me? Then what're you doing out here with sweat all over your face? Look at me. You can't even look at me. And you talk about after all I know? That's right, that's right. I hear Mrs. Abbatta's confession every day. The others, two, three times a week. And I heard Sabatine's. He asked for me. He could've asked for the bishop. I wish he had. But I was with him right up to the end and I heard him. Which means I heard everything. But what I haven't heard is what Soup is doing on that witness chair." The priest's face was flushed, and the veins stood out on his forehead and throat from trying to whisper while talking so forcefully.

Balzic took a long time before he answered. As many ways as he thought to say it, he knew finally that it didn't matter how he said it. He could give only one answer. "I know where the confessional is."

"Okay," Father Marrazo said. "Okay . . . okay. . . . " He repeated that word several more times as though trying to find satisfaction in its mere repetition. He cleared his throat and tugged at his own collar. Then he looked at his shoes. "You, uh, you want to go, uh, get some wine? Huh?"

Balzic nodded slowly. "Right now I could drink just about all the wine there is in the world."

They walked in silence to Muscotti's and did not speak to each other until they began to quibble over who was going to pay for the drinks. What little conversation there was took place between Balzic and Vinnie who kept demanding to be brought up to date on the trial. He couldn't understand why they'd both left if it had not yet gone to the jury. Neither Balzic nor Father Marrazo would answer that.

Their drinking was joyless, mechanical, a seeking after the alcohol rather than the wine. It took nearly an hour before they started to feel the wine flowing in them, and by that time they were threatening to drink all the chablis and chianti Vinnie had on the shelves. Balzic even started making noises about going to the backroom to help himself to Muscotti's private stock of Valpolicella.

Mila Sanders Rizzo, sighing giddily, came in then and plopped down on the stool next to Balzic. She leaned close to him and whispered, "I understand you solved your problem."

"Well, that depends," Balzic said, glancing uncomfortably at Father Marrazo. "In a way I did, and then again I didn't. How you coming with yours?"

"Well, I guess that depends too. Dom wants me to manage a store for him."

Balzic started to smile. "What kind of store?"

"Oh, this woman's husband died, and she's sick and she wants to get rid of it. Dom says there's a real market for what they sell." She was smiling impishly, sardonically. She leaned close to him again and whispered, "Religious supplies. Bibles and crucifixes and plaster saints and rosaries and medals and bumper stickers that say all kinds of goopy stuff like, 'God's only dead if you're Red,' and crap like that. Dom says with all the halos I see on people I'd make a million dollars in ten years. I told him I'd do it if he let me put up a big yellow neon cross with a sign on it that said, 'Two million rosaries sold.' You know, like hamburgers. Boy, did he get mad."

Balzic nodded as though it was all the most reasonable thing he'd heard in weeks. "What's his wife say?"

"Oh, you don't think he talked to her about it, do you?" she said, pulling back and laughing loud.

Before Balzic could reply Dom Scalzo barged through the front door, scowling and cursing under his breath until he drew even with Balzic's back. Then he tapped Balzic on the back and started to speak but he was too furious. For some moments all he could do was curse.

"What's the matter with you?" Balzic said. "You just did the good deed of your life and you look like you just got robbed."

"I'll tell you what's the matter," Scalzo said. "You wanna hear what's the matter? I'm gonna tell you what's the matter. Jimmie Salio, that bastard—Corcoran's bailiff?"

"I know who he is. Who doesn't?"

"Yeah, well, he thinks it's a big joke. I come down off the stand and I start to walk out. I'm done, what am I gonna stick around for? He's standing back there at the back door and he's looking at his watch. I'm almost past him, and he grabs me and he whispers—you know how he whispers? Like normal people talk that's how he whispers—he whispers, 'You stopped testifying at exactly four-twenty-eight.' And then he hands me six bucks and he whispers again, 'A buck around. Four-twenty-eight. On the new stock.' So I'm going, no, no, you know. I'm shaking my head and I'm not taking the money. So the cocksucker—excuse my language, Father—so the dumb bastard shoves the money in my coat pocket. So whatta you think? Don't you know there's a state cop sitting right there, right in the last row, and he hears everything. And he follows me outside, and Jimmie's following me and I'm trying to give the money back to Jimmie and that goddamn state cop arrests me! Right there in the hall! Jesus Christ, I wanna throw both them bastards right over the balcony.

"I go in there to do something good for once in my life, for justice—for justice, you goddamn Mario, ain't that what you told me? For justice I go in there and tell the biggest lie I ever told in my life and now I'm under arrest for bookin'. Stick your justice up your ass."

Balzic turned to Father Marrazo and both of them looked at Vinnie and then all three roared with laughter until tears were streaming down their cheeks.

"Oh, God, God," Balzic said at last, his eyes, mouth, and stomach aching from laughter. "Vinnie, give him a drink. Give everybody a drink. And keep them coming. I got everybody's."

And Vinnie did. He said later on when he told the story that he'd never poured so many drinks or laughed so hard in an hour's time in his life, and no one who had been there that day ever doubted him. Just as no one ever doubted him when he said that the next day he laughed even harder when Dom Muscotti told Soup Scalzo that he had put Jimmie Salio up to it, had told him to have someone else tip off a state cop and make sure he was there in the last row, and that it was he himself who had given Salio the six dollars Salio kept trying to force on Soup.

"You should've seen Soup's face," Vinnie would tell the story time and again. "Oh Christ, I thought he was gonna choke. All he could say was, 'Why? What'd you want to go and do that to me for?' And Dom looked at him and said, 'Soup, I knew how you were gonna think when you came down out of the chair. Like you did something really good. And you did. But I didn't want you to start thinking you were too good. You start thinking you're too good, you're gonna forget who you are.' "

And no one laughs harder at that story than Balzic.

K.C. CONSTANTINE

UPON SOME MIDNIGHT CLEAR

It's Christmas time in Rocksburg, Pennsylvania, but the goodwill spirit does not affect everyone. Police chief Mario Balzic finds himself investigating a nasty mugging and an alleged theft . . . presents he and the town can do without.

'Bristles with the stuff of life, the dialogue spurts like Old Faithful'

The Observer

'Great dialogue and an atmosphere you could cut with a coal shovel . . . an ear for dialogue that matches George V. Higgins'

Times Literary Supplement

'The sum of the parts crackles with veracity, subtlety, wit and life'

The Times

'One of the best things going on in current American mystery fiction'

Washington Post

Post·A·Book

A Royal Mail service in association with the Book Marketing Council & The Booksellers Association.
Post-A-Book is a Post Office trademark.

FAYE KELLERMAN

THE RITUAL BATH

When the call came in, Detective Peter Decker could hardly believe it.

A rape at the *yeshiva* up in the canyon and hill country behind Los Angeles! True, there'd been some recent anti-Semitic vandalism but never ever any violence.

Not only that, but this was a strict Orthodox Jewish community, self-enclosed and suspicious of outsiders. Not much chance they'd co-operate with the police.

And he was right. Rina Lazarus, the young widow who'd found the victim and rung the police, tried to explain the religious practices that stopped them helping. An insight into a fascinating world coming from a frustratingly fascinating woman.

But, outsider though he might be, as a policeman he felt in his bones that the cost to the community of their determined privacy could turn out to be murderously high.

'Irresistibly plotted and the two main characters are convincingly human and appealing'
Financial Times

'Classy debut . . . Tension is craftily maintained'
The Guardian

'Top marks all round for writing, narrative and background'
Time Out

HODDER AND STOUGHTON PAPERBACKS

JEREMIAH HEALY

BLUNT DARTS

A kid had gone missing.

Run off? Maybe. Kidnapped? Possible. Still some-where local or out of state? No telling – not when the trail is two weeks' cold and there's no hard evidence of anything.

Not when his father, the Judge, doesn't even want an investigation. When there's no mother to worry since she'd died mysteriously a while back. And when the local police make it clear that private investigator John Cuddy is the sort of stranger they don't want in town.

Only the kid's grandmother and the kid's school teacher seemed to care – along with John Cuddy. Who was being well paid and who had already caught a whiff of a very nasty small-town scandal . . .

'The plotting is impeccable, and everything comes to-gether to make BLUNT DARTS one of the outstanding first mysteries of the year'

The New York Times

'A splendid debut performance'

Financial Times

HODDER AND STOUGHTON PAPERBACKS

JEREMIAH HEALY

THE TETHERED GOAT

Al Sachs hadn't just been killed.

He'd been tortured and mutilated. The Boston police had decided early. Put it down as another ritualistic gay murder.

Only John Francis Cuddy thought different.

They'd been old buddies back in the Army. Come civilian life and they'd drifted apart. Until an early morning phone call from Al, in town from Pittsburgh. An oddly nervous Al, fixing a motel meeting and making a cryptic reference to their time together.

An appointment he never kept and a reference that started Cuddy on an avenging trail that led deep into the inner circles of the Pentagon and back into their Vietnam-scarred past.

HODDER AND STOUGHTON PAPERBACKS

IAN RANKIN

KNOTS AND CROSSES

It's frightening . . . And in Edinburgh of all places, I mean, you never think of that sort of thing happening in Edinburgh, do you?

Already two young girls have been abducted and killed. Now a third is missing. Nothing in common between them: different areas, different circumstances. A random killer.

Polite, self-regarding Edinburgh is in a state of shock. All police leave is cancelled; the reporters gather like vultures.

Meanwhile Detective Sergeant John Rebus, smoking and drinking too much, his wife gone taking their young daughter, has another, more personal puzzle on his hands. Someone is sending him taunting, anonymous letters with little pieces of knotted string and matchstick crosses.

Annoying but hardly very important. Not when a cold, methodical killer is stalking the frightened streets . . .

'Quite brilliant and enormously compelling'
Martyn Goff

'Highly recommended'

Literary Review

HODDER AND STOUGHTON PAPERBACKS

MORE TITLES AVAILABLE FROM
CORONET CRIME

K.C. CONSTANTINE

☐ 43052 4   Upon Some Midnight Clear   £2.50

FAYE KELLERMAN

☐ 48767 4   The Ritual Bath   £2.99

JEREMIAH HEALY

☐ 43073 7   Blunt Darts   £2.50
☐ 49127 2   The Tethered Goat   £2.50

IAN RANKIN

☐ 48766 6   Knots And Crosses   £2.50

All these books are available at your local bookshop or newsagent, or can be ordered direct from the publisher. Just tick the titles you want and fill in the form below.

Prices and availability subject to change without notice.

Hodder & Stoughton Paperbacks, P.O. Box 11, Falmouth, Cornwall.

Please send cheque or postal order, and allow the following for postage and packing:

U.K. – 55p for one book, plus 22p for the second book, and 14p for each additional book ordered up to a £1.75 maximum.

B.F.P.O. and EIRE – 55p for the first book, plus 22p for the second book, and 14p per copy for the next 7 books, 8p per book thereafter.

OTHER OVERSEAS CUSTOMERS – £1.00 for the first book, plus 25p per copy for each additional book.

Name ....

Address ....

....